**"I WARNED YOU,"
HE MANAGED TO SAY.
"BACK OFF, JULIANA,
BEFORE IT'S TOO LATE . . ."**

For answer she stepped closer and threw her arms around his neck. The wind caught her hair, sending it dancing like a golden halo about her head. Cole captured it in his fingers, crushed the fine, velvet-soft curls.

"Or what?" Her voice was a purely feminine invitation. Cole felt his control slipping dangerously.

He kissed her hard. It was a fierce, powerful kiss. He didn't need her, damn it, he didn't need anyone, but he sure as hell felt like he did. It wasn't fair, Cole thought desperately, what she'd been doing to him since the first moment they met, dogging his thoughts, distracting him, making him want her. His mind reeled, he knew only driving need and a deeper emotion, something tangled and confused, but strong as whiskey, and he swept her off her feet, into his arms . . .

CHERISHED

· Jill Gregory ·

A DELL BOOK

To Rachel, who dares to dream and to dance—with all my love forever

Published by
Dell Publishing
a division of
Bantam Doubleday Dell Publishing Group, Inc.
666 Fifth Avenue
New York, New York 10103

ISBN: 0-440-20620-0

Printed in the United States of America

Published simultaneously in Canada

March 1992

10 9 8 7 6 5 4 3 2 1

OPM

PROLOGUE

New Mexico Territory,
March 1873

Reese Kincaid was a liar, a coward, and a murdering thief who had never earned an honest dollar in his life, but there was one thing he was damned good at, and that was laying an ambush. And as he laid out the ambush for Cole Rawdon, the bounty hunter who had been making his life a living hell for the past weeks, a demon light of joy sprang into his coal-black eyes. Kincaid gazed around at the hard, grizzled faces of his gang in triumph.

"There ain't no way in hell Rawdon's going to ride out of this place alive," he crowed.

His four companions and the redheaded whore, Garnet, squirming on his lap, all chuckled happily.

The hideout cabin where they waited was a squalid pesthole of a place, square-walled and dank. Filthy with spittle and discarded coffee grounds and dead flies, it was furnished with little more than a half-dozen roughly carved chairs circling a scarred pine table. It reeked of

sweat and tobacco and whiskey—but no more so than did
its six inhabitants. Everything in the cabin, from the torn
and grimy bedding scattered about the dirt floor to the
piles of unwashed dishes heaped on the table, all en-
crusted with remnants of food and crawling with ants,
looked as foul and disreputable as the five men and one
woman who waited with such malicious glee for Cole
Rawdon. Reese Kincaid felt even more feverish anticipation than the others. He wanted Rawdon bad.

Rawdon had been pursuing Kincaid for weeks now
with the cold-blooded relentlessness and uncanny tracking skills that had earned him a reputation among the
bandits and desperadoes of New Mexico, Texas, and Arizona. Kincaid was desperate and wily, a man much experienced at evading the law, but even he recognized it was
only sheer luck that had kept him one step ahead of Cole
Rawdon for this long. Now, though, things were going to
be different. The hunter was about to become the prey.
Kincaid had Rawdon right where he wanted him—or he
would, soon as the bounty hunter rode that paint horse of
his into the canyon. Rawdon knew about this cabin at the
bottom of Stone Canyon—Garnet had seen to that. Her
girl friends in the saloon in Black Creek by now had told
him all about the snug little hideout seventy miles from
the town, and he was so eager for that reward money
waiting back in Tucson, and so damned sure of himself,
that he'd be after Kincaid like a thunderbolt.

Cole Rawdon was as fearless as he was determined,
and Kincaid knew it. That was the most frightening thing
about him. That and the fact that he was good with his
gun. Too damn good. Even though he was barely twenty-
eight years old, his reputation throughout the southwest
territories was practically a legend already. The hombre
never missed. It was enough to make anyone sweat bullets just to hear about it. But, Kincaid reflected as he
stroked Garnet's lithe body with a filthy, callused hand

and ordered Ed to bring him more whiskey, he had the advantage now. Brains and cunning would win out over guts and skill. There was no way he could lose. Rawdon didn't know that the rest of the gang was here in the canyon, too, that they'd slipped in one by one over the past few nights, after splitting up following the Tucson stagecoach job last month. Now they were all back together again, just in time to prepare a neat little welcome for Cole Rawdon. *Hell,* Kincaid thought, his florid, heavy face flushed with pleasure as he nuzzled the whore's neck and then paused to inhale a deep swig of whiskey, *I think I'll kill him slow, one bullet at a time, each fired about an hour apart and in a different place. And the last one,* he decided with a grin, *will go right between his eyes.*

The sun was just coming up outside the cabin window, touching the sage-colored hills with a faint yellow-gray light. Kincaid shoved Garnet away and pushed back his chair. Time to get ready. He didn't want any mistakes or any surprises. He stood up, his blood heating with anticipation of the ambush ahead. Barking out his orders, he sent each member of his gang stomping off to take his assigned place.

Kincaid peered past the grime-streaked curtain at the distant empty mesa overlooking the canyon. In stark contrast to the squalid cabin, the mesa was quiet. Peaceful. Almost eerily calm in the growing light of the new dawn. Up above, the sky was turning blue as a mountain lake. Not a cloud to be seen. Birds sang in the juniper tree outside the window. *Yep,* Reese Kincaid thought, grinning out from beneath the dingy mane of brown hair that hung over his face. It was going to be a real fine day for a killing.

Cole Rawdon worked his way to the lip of Stone Canyon with the stealth of an Indian. He had learned much from Sun Eagle during the time he had spent with the Cheyenne, and it had served him well in his present occupation. Though he was a tall young man, with broad shoulders, and a well-muscled, powerful frame, he had the ability to step as lightly as a feather when he wished to remain undetected. He wished that now.

Cole spotted the lookout man first, crouched in a high crevice of rock north of the canyon's entrance, a rifle in his hands. The rough, handsome planes of the bounty hunter's face showed no emotion, but a grim smile just touched the edges of his lips. It never reached his eyes. Since he could move about more silently on foot, he had left his horse, Arrow, tied in a grassy dell well out of sight and hearing. Now he slowly crept upward and across the ledge of rock, toward the lookout. His movements were lithe and graceful; he was more like a shadow slipping among the rocks than a man. His hard young features were set with single-minded purpose, and his remarkable vivid eyes shone with cold blue fire as he made his way toward the man watching the canyon entrance from high above.

Cole came upon him from behind, and quick as a flash had one powerful arm around the man's neck. The lookout never stood a chance against his larger, stronger unseen foe. When his victim had slumped into unconsciousness, Cole trussed him efficiently and then moved on, with no wasted time or movement. Always he was listening, watching. It was these incredible abilities at keen perception combined with razor-sharp reaction that had kept him alive all these years in the wildest, most savage regions of the frontier. Only once had he been caught unawares, a long time ago. But he'd been little more than a kid then, seventeen years old, green and foolish. He'd been lonely and stupid enough to trust another human being—a mistake he would never make again. That one time had taught him well—never to trust any man, or any woman. Ever.

Of course, Jess Burrows and Liza White were both dead now. But the lessons of greed and betrayal they had taught Cole would be with him forever. He'd never forget the way a beautiful woman could lie and deceive, smiling all the while, or the way a man who said he was a friend could shoot you in the back and leave you for dead in the scorched heart of the desert, without blinking an eye. He ought to thank them. They had tried to kill him, but they had only made him stronger. They had taught him to stand alone, to steer clear of all entanglements with others of his species. They had taught him what it took to survive.

And now they were the ones dead and buried, Cole reflected, scanning the desolate cliffs and boulders with a practiced eye. And he was still here, too ornery to bid the world *adiós* until he'd sent a few more no-good hombres to hell first.

By the time the sun had come full up in the sapphire sky, he had found and knocked cold two more of Kincaid's men.

There were no more to be found, none that he could see anywhere around the steep walls of the canyon. That meant the fourth member of the gang, Ed Weeks, was holed up in the cabin with Kincaid, probably posted near a window. Rawdon got his horse, and headed for the entrance without wasting further time. Two against one, considering the circumstances, were fair odds.

Ed Weeks grinned when he saw the lean, sun-bronzed bounty hunter ride toward the clearing. Murphy, Burr, and Slade would be right behind him, hemming Rawdon in. He cocked his Remington revolver and stuck it out the window. Ed had an impulsive, fun-loving nature. He always liked to be the one to get things rolling, but he knew Kincaid would be mad as fire if he jumped the gun.

Squinting against the glare of the rising sun, he waited and watched as the bounty hunter took cover behind a boulder. *Won't do you no good, Rawdon,* Ed chuckled to himself. Then he waited for the fun to start.

Crouched behind the boulder, with just the tip of his Stetson showing, Cole scanned the cabin and its surroundings with a keen, sweeping glance. When he was satisfied with his assessment of the layout, he moved on to the next step of the hunt. It was a well-worn, all too familiar process. He'd give Kincaid a chance to turn himself in alive. He doubted if the outlaw would take advantage of it. It didn't matter to Cole, though, either way. The reward would be turned over to him whether the fugitive was brought back dead or alive.

"Kincaid!" he roared.

An instant later the cabin door opened and Reese Kincaid stepped outside into the light.

"Howdy, Rawdon."

The outlaw was one of those big, clumsy men who swagger when they walk, and he swaggered now across the patchy grass of the clearing. His gut stuck out beneath his plaid shirt, and his gunbelt, slung tight across heavy hips, emphasized his huge girth. Even from this distance, Cole could smell the foul stench of his greasy, sweat-soaked clothes, though the girl who slithered out of the cabin after him, clad only in a dirty chemise, appeared not to notice or care. She was watching Kincaid with proud, possessive eyes, and she giggled when he yelled for the bounty hunter to show himself.

But when Cole stood up and strode forward, Garnet gasped. She hadn't expected anyone as handsome, nonchalant, and yet deadly-looking as the black-haired bounty hunter who came forward with easy strides and perfect composure. His thick midnight hair just reached his shirt collar, glinting like coal in the bright light of midday. Beneath his hat, she saw eyes the color of sapphires, but so cold, so merciless, they filled her with sudden terror. He had wide shoulders and a broad, muscular chest beneath his shirt and leather vest. His stomach was flat and lean. Tight-fitting trousers encased powerful thighs and legs, and were tucked into calf-leather boots. A gunbelt with a polished silver and turquoise buckle that was the only adornment he wore completed his attire —except for the big pair of silver-handled .44 Colts he wore with the ease of a man wholly comfortable with killing. Garnet had seen a great many rough men in her day—gamblers, outlaws, drifters, and cowhands—but there was something about this one that made her shiver and hug her bare arms about herself. Handsome devil, that's what he was. And both words equally fit: Cole Rawdon was undeniably, stunningly, irresistibly handsome. And yet there was a look about him, something in the hard, cold planes of his bronzed face, that told her he was as tough and mean as the devil himself. *Handsome devil,* Garnet whispered to herself, and fought the urge to dart back into the cabin and run for cover.

What had Kincaid been thinking of, letting this man catch up with him at all? There was something so implacable and dangerous about the bounty hunter that it made her forget all about the brilliance of the ambush Kincaid had devised. Cole Rawdon wouldn't be a man to go down easy. For the first time since she'd met and fallen in love with Reese Kincaid, she began to fear and doubt.

"Took you long enough to track me, Rawdon," Kincaid taunted as the other man came slowly forward, pausing at a distance of ten feet away. Kincaid was intimidated by no man, though he felt a surge of annoyance at Rawdon's coolness. Kincaid couldn't wait for him to realize he was trapped. He wanted to wipe that damned self-confidence right off the son of a bitch bounty hunter's face. "You must be losing your touch," he added. "Right, Garnet?"

The girl made no answer. She was uneasily studying the canyon entrance, looking for some sign of the other three men. It seemed to Garnet that they should have been here by now.

But Kincaid was too preoccupied with baiting the bounty hunter to notice the delay. "You started out real good from Tucson, but you kept lagging behind, boy. I tried to let you catch up a couple of times, just to get killing you over with, but you were too pokey for me. Garnet was waiting for me, and I was real eager to get here. You don't blame me, do you, Rawdon? I bet you'd ride like hell for a woman like Garnet, too, if one would be dumb enough to have you."

"I wonder if the lady would let you touch her if she knew what you did to those women on the stagecoach before you killed them," Cole commented in his quiet voice, dagger-edged with ice. "You're real good with a knife on innocent women, but how are you with a gun against a man?" He heard the redhead's sharp intake of breath that told him she didn't know anything about the passengers' murders, but he didn't take his eyes off Kincaid long enough to spare her a glance. "Guess you didn't tell your ladyfriend about that."

"Those folks got what was coming to 'em. They tried to get away. And you're going to get what's coming to you, Rawdon. Real soon."

Rawdon's eyes narrowed. "The only thing I'm going to get is the reward for your worthless hide, Kincaid."

"Hey, Weeks—ya hear that?" The outlaw raised his voice to a shout. "This here boy thinks he's going to get a reward! Haw! Haw!"

"Throw down your guns, Rawdon—we got you covered!" Weeks called from inside the cabin.

"I'm giving *you* a chance to throw down your gun,

Kincaid. You, too, Weeks. It's the only chance either of you will get."

From the cabin came the hearty cackle of Ed Weeks's laughter. It was echoed by the jeering chuckles of Kincaid. Through it all, Cole stood perfectly still, at ease yet prepared. His muscles were ready, his brain was prepared for what would happen soon. Very soon. Deep within his heart was an iciness more solid and cold than the snow that never melts at the very peaks of the Rockies.

"You're downright stupid, boy!" Kincaid was shouting at him now, his face flushed and sweating with excitement, split by a huge, evil grin. "You're about to meet your Maker, and you don't even know it. You've been out-thunk, outsmarted, and out-tricked, plain and simple. You'll never see the sun set on this day."

"Sounds to me like you're stalling, Kincaid. You expecting someone?"

The bounty hunter's unperturbed countenance made Kincaid's face darken to purple rage. Where the hell were Slade and Burr and Murphy? They should've been here by now. He wanted to see the bounty hunter *sweat,* gawddammit. Hell, he wanted to see him bleed. He'd make him beg for death before he was done with him. What were those idiots waiting for?

"Slade! Come on down! Burr! Murphy! Get your butts down here. We got 'em!" he called. There was no answer.

Only the cry of an eagle circling far, far above.

"Murphy! Slade!"

Rawdon watched as Kincaid's face underwent a dramatic transformation. Red-hot fury and smug triumph faded away and with them went all the color in the fleshy cheeks. Kincaid was left staring at the empty walls of the canyon towering above them, peering in disbelief at the canyon entrance where nothing moved, no one came. He was ash-gray now, and shaking. But not only with fear. A new, animalistic rage swept over him, a rage born of the urge to survive, to kill, to conquer and smash to bits any enemy.

"Murphy! Slade! Burr!" he called once more, desperately. Then he brought his gaze swiveling to Cole Rawdon. The black depths of his eyes shone with virulent hatred. "You gawddamned son of a bitch," he rasped. "What the hell did you do to them?"

"Nothing near as bad as what I'm going to do to you, Kincaid." The cool glint of the bounty hunter's eyes filled the outlaw with stark terror.

"Weeks! Now!" Kincaid bellowed, and went for his gun.

Cole Rawdon moved faster. Like lightning he had a Colt in each hand, and like lightning he fired them each in a different direction. One bullet ripped through Kincaid's heart; the other slammed through the cabin window and plunged into Ed Weeks's brain. The roar of the two guns thundered through the sunlit canyon, echoing from rock to rock. Then came silence, but for the high, keening screams of the woman.

Garnet, filthy and half naked, threw herself down beside Kincaid's body, shrieking at the top of her lungs. When Rawdon approached, her grief turned to terror for herself, and she gasped and stared up at the man looming over her, consumed by hysterical, helpless fright. But he only walked past her into the cabin. It took less than a second to see that Weeks was as dead as a man could get. By the time Rawdon came out again into the light, the woman was quieter, huddling over Kincaid's bloodied body, sobbing on her knees in the dust.

Rawdon glanced at her, then away. He felt no pity for her. He had stopped up all his emotions a long time ago. He would not harm her, but he would do or say nothing to comfort her. Her grief, her loss, were none of his concern.

Kincaid was dead, and Ed Weeks with him. The rest of

the gang had been captured, and it shouldn't prove too difficult forcing them to reveal where the stagecoach loot was hidden. All in all, Cole Rawdon thought as he looked at Kincaid's blood seeping into the dirt floor of the canyon, it had been a good morning's work.

But as always, he took no pleasure in the killing, and his face was grim and worn when at last he had buried the dead, and left that desolate place behind. The woman stayed of her own accord, but Cole left her Kincaid's horse before riding out to gather up his prisoners.

The Kincaid gang had proved no more difficult than most of the others to track and bring down. As Rawdon rode the narrow track that led up and out of the canyon, he realized that, even with the reward money from bringing in the Kincaid gang, he was still damned short of having enough to buy back Fire Mesa—if he really wanted it back. Did he? Or was it just that he didn't want the home robbed from him in his childhood to be sold to that greedy bastard Line McCray? It would serve his father right if Fire Mesa was lost forever because of his drunken gambling. But his father was long dead, buried with his shame, as was Grandfather, he who had once ruled Fire Mesa with such pride and iron strength. Perhaps it was better to let the land go, to forget the glorious wild hills and buttes of his childhood, to remain a wanderer, belonging to no one and no place. And yet, when he thought of Line McCray building a railroad through his grandfather's land, his jaw clenched with fury.

He'd need a pile of money to outbid McCray. And he'd need it soon.

Fire Mesa . . .

With sheer effort of will, Cole pushed all thoughts of the beautiful, vast Arizona spread from his mind, and forced himself to think instead about dealing with his prisoners. He was here, today, in this godforsaken New

Mexico Territory beneath a hell-blazing sun, with three hombres to transport and the Apache up in arms over treaty violations. Reality was here, now, harsh and full of danger. Fire Mesa was the past, a memory, distant and unreal, part of his life that had brutally ended twenty years ago on a day of death and destruction.

Fire Mesa was a dream. Or was it, Cole wondered, his eyes dark with memory, a nightmare?

· 1 ·

Colorado,
April 1873

The dusty Kansas Pacific railroad car chugged across the Colorado plains with the steadfast determination of an ant crawling across a vast park lawn. Juliana Montgomery, fetchingly attired in plumed hat, a turquoise taffeta traveling dress, silk gloves, and dainty half-boots, sat with clasped hands and rapt, glowing face, watching the scenery glide past her window. Absorbed as she was by the newness and beauty of her surroundings, Juliana had no way of knowing that every mile crossed brought her nearer and nearer to the giant trap that had been carefully laid out for her. She had no inkling of the fate her aunt and uncle had decreed for her, not a single premonition or qualm of unease. Her heart was light and happy, filled with hope, as she took in the endless, rolling plains and crystal skies of Colorado, drinking in the wild splendor of land, sun, and sky unbroken by human habitation.

Magnificent, she thought on a little breath of wonder

as she gazed out at the spring-bright plains. She had
never seen such a boundless expanse of land: the prairie
seemed to roll on and on forever, the buffalo and grama
grass adorned here and there with beautiful wildflowers
and shrubs. Beneath a lemon-drop sun, lovely sand lilies
and coral-colored wild geraniums burst forth in riotous
profusion. Scotch thistle appeared in scattered clumps,
festooned with their gay purple tassels, and she was fasci-
nated by the variety of cacti that rolled past: the conduc-
tor had pointed out to her the creosote bush and the
yucca with its blaze of creamy flowers blossoming forth
from bladelike leaves, and the deep red of an occasional
prairie cactus shimmered against the pale green of the
plains grasses. There were graceful cottonwoods and in
the river bottoms, alongside the shallow green waters of
the South Platte, she had spotted wild iris and cattails
waving in the wind. *Lovely.* Compared to the tame, carefully cultivated gardens she had known these past nine
years in St. Louis, the colorful blaze of wildflowers and
cacti set against that rough prairie were a delight for the
eye and the soul.

"Isn't it breathtaking?" she murmured, her heart lifting at the wild beauty of the scene. Her cousin Victoria,
dozing beside her, merely grimaced.

"You keep saying that," she complained.

Juliana's gaze never left the window. "Look, the
mountains in the distance—they must be the Rockies.
Oh, surely, Denver cannot be far!"

In the seat across the aisle from them, Katharine Tobias, Juliana's aunt, worked her painted silk fan frantically against the stifling heat. She was a handsome,
imposing woman with upswept dark hair, piercing mahogany-colored eyes, and wide shoulders. She was tall,
with regal bearing and a proud carriage—and absolutely
no sense of humor. "Well, at least the scenery here is far
more interesting than those dreadful boring plains in

Kansas. I do admit fearing I would never again see anything but green grass and dull yellow sunflowers."

Uncle Edward set aside his sheaf of papers and removed his spectacles. He rubbed the red spot on the
bridge of his nose and shifted uncomfortably in his seat.
"We'll be in Denver by suppertime," he prophesied with
relief. A man behind him blew his nose loudly into a big
square handkerchief. Edward ignored the interruption.
"You girls had best catch a few winks now if you want to
be rested up for tonight. I don't want you feeling peaked
when we attend Mr. Breen's party."

"Yes, Papa." Obediently, Victoria leaned her head
back and closed her eyes once more, all too eager to blot
out the blinding sun, the jerking motion of the coach, and
the heat and dust of the day. But Juliana was still staring
out the window, transfixed, a dreamy smile playing about
the edges of her pretty mouth.

Well, Edward reflected as he set his spectacles back in
place, *let her soak up the western scene if she has a mind
to. If everything goes as planned, this untamed, uncivilized
land she's so enamored of will shortly be her new home.*

With his spectacles on he could see her more clearly,
and he was not displeased with her appearance. Far from
looking the least bit peaked, his golden-haired niece was
the picture of glowing feminine health. Even in her wilted
traveling dress of stiff taffeta buttoned up to her throat,
and with damp tendrils of hair clinging to her temples,
Juliana looked as lovely as any of those wildflowers that
charmed her so. The train was unbearably hot and dusty,
and everywhere one looked women were fanning themselves, men perspiring and licking dry lips, and the odor
of sweat positively clung to the air. Yet Juliana still
glowed, her skin as fresh and lovely as a summer peach,
her pale hair shimmering in the sunlight. Edward's smile
deepened as he studied her. The girl could dazzle, no
doubt about that. With her lush cloud of sun-drenched

hair, her winged brows and slender, enchantingly curvacious figure she looked like a fairy-tale princess. Even the pale dusting of freckles across her small, straight nose, and the full mouth just a shade too wide for fashion only added to her loveliness, for they saved her from cold, classic perfection, and imbued Juliana's elegant, chiseled features with a warmth and unconscious sensuality that added immensely to her appeal. Her laugh was low, husky, her smile as bright and captivating as a summer's day. A beauty, everyone said, and they were right, but unfortunately his niece was a headstrong, troublesome beauty, flawed by her own willful spirit as well as her family's questionable background. Though she was the toast of St. Louis society, ardently courted by scores of smitten beaux, it was common knowledge that no young man of breeding and wealth would marry her. ·

But I'll show them all, Edward thought gleefully as he rubbed his sweating palms on his pants. *I'll marry her off to the richest businessman in the western United States, and ride his coattails to the top.* There would be no more small-time profits for Edward Tobias, no sir. From now on, words like *comfortably established, prominent,* and *well-to-do* would no longer suffice to describe him. He would be a millionaire, a tycoon, a magnate, just like John Breen himself—all within a year, if the marriage went ahead as planned. And why shouldn't it? John Breen, after meeting Juliana only that once, had made up his mind to have her, and Edward would see to it that the girl accepted his offer. She had better not get it into her head to be difficult about it either, for Edward would have none of that. John Breen had invested in the Tobias factories a year ago in a small way, his capital helping to spur them on to previously unthought of success, but once he married Juliana, he had promised to open doors for Edward that would guarantee him wealth beyond most men's wildest imaginations.

And the marriage would do wonders for his daughter, Victoria, Edward reflected, glancing over at the dark-haired girl snoring lightly against the upholstered seat. She hadn't withstood the journey near as well as Juliana. Only passably pretty at her best, Victoria looked much the worse for wear after their long, weary days of travel. Her olive skin shone with oily perspiration and her hair hung limply against her neck. Still, though her lips were straight and thin, her chin a shade pointed, and her voice a trifle shrill, she had a neat figure and well-bred manners, not to mention her pleasing ability on the pianoforte and with an embroidery needle. All attributes that would someday be valued by the right man, Edward was certain, if only Juliana was not there to dazzle and distract him. No, Victoria would never again be a wallflower once she was free from comparison with her spectacular cousin. And with Juliana married and settled in Denver with John Breen, Edward knew it could not be long before his Victoria would find herself the object of some appropriate suitor's attention.

He settled back beside his wife and her fluttering fan, content with himself and his expert arrangements for the future, dreaming of the mines and lumber mills and railroad shares he would soon own, possibly as many as John Breen himself.

The saloon in Denver, Juliana decided, *will be the perfect place to begin my inquiries.* The only trouble was, how would she manage to elude Aunt Katharine and Uncle Edward long enough to manage it? If she was caught . . . A knot tightened inside her stomach at the thought of what would happen if she was discovered going into the saloon. She had already been forced to promise Uncle Edward she wouldn't try to find Wade and Tommy, and if she was discovered doing anything as scandalous as entering a saloon to ask about them she would have to endure the most horrible censure. But it was worth the risk, Juliana told herself, as she unbuttoned the top button of her dress trying to alleviate the effects of the heat. She had to find Wade and Tommy—and this visit to Denver might be her only chance.

"Juliana, fasten that button!" Aunt Katharine's furious whisper made the girl jump and hastily obey. Her aunt was glaring at her, her face puffed out with disapproval.

"I'm sorry, Aunt Katharine. But it's so dreadfully stuffy."

"Try to remember that you are a lady and behave like one! You don't see Victoria undressing herself in public, do you?"

Victoria is half dead—and too frightened of you to wiggle her toes without permission, Juliana thought, with a pitying glance at her slumbering cousin. "No, ma'am," she said.

Life would be easier, she acknowledged, if she were more like Victoria—biddable, cowed by authority, terrified of breaking any of society's conventions. The only problem was, much as Juliana tried, she couldn't get the knack of decorous behavior. She laughed out loud when the Reverend Davis sneezed at the high point of his Sunday sermon, rushed to help when the serving maid spilled soup on the dining room floor, and carried on elaborate conversations with Aunt Katharine's lapdog, Charlotte, conversations so outrageous and nonsensical that the Tobias family could only stare at her as if she had gone mad.

"It's that mother of hers," Aunt Katharine frequently remarked in an undertone to Victoria, unaware that Juliana overheard several times. "She was a wild, disgraceful young thing, and you mark my words, some of that has rubbed off on poor Juliana, despite our best efforts. Why, just look what's become of her brothers—you can't tell me there isn't a bad taint in her blood!"

When she heard things like that, it was all Juliana

could do not to explode with anger. Usually she stopped whatever she was doing and left the room without a word, retreating to her own pretty bedroom on the second floor of the Tobias home. She would sink onto the bed and try to conjure up memories of her home back in Independence before Mama and Papa had died, and especially of her mother, whose past as a dance-hall girl before she married Papa had always been the subject of so much whispered gossip and contempt. It had been nine years since her parents' deaths, and during that time, since Uncle Edward had come to fetch her east, the life she had led in Independence during the wagon train days, with Mama and Papa and Wade and Tommy all living together above the busy general store, had mostly faded into fuzzy memories. She could still, when she closed her eyes tight and concentrated hard, see Mama's sad, pretty face with her yellow hair and pale lime-green eyes as she worked so busily packing supplies for the families and traders setting out for the West. And she could see Papa outside helping to load the wagons and horses with the gear, or sitting down to supper with them when the store was finally closed for the day, and the curtains were drawn against the setting sun. He would wink across the table at Juliana and say, "Peanut, eat every crumb now, you're far too thin. You want to grow up to be a beauty like your mama, don't you?"

And then there were Wade and Tommy, several years older than she, both boys handsome and energetic and filled with mischief. They had helped Papa vigorously in the store, but they had never liked the monotony of town work. "We want to be scouts," they used to say, listening in rapture to the tales of buffalo herds and river crossings, Indian raids and fierce desperadoes, related by travelers returning from the West, who stopped in Independence and were all too happy to share their adventuresome tales with any who would listen. "We want to cross the Cimar-

ron River and sleep beneath a Texas sky." The bustle and
commotion of thriving Independence held no allure for
Wade and Tommy. Horses and cattle, wide-open spaces,
gunfights, and buffalo hunts had captured their young
fancies.

But nine years had passed since Juliana had seen her
brothers. Mama and Papa had been killed, shot by
drunken outlaws trying to rob the store, and Uncle Edward had come to Independence to take charge of the
orphans. He'd wanted to fetch all three of the Montgomery children back to St. Louis with him, but Wade, aged
fifteen, and Tommy, two years younger, had refused to
go. They'd quarreled horribly with Uncle Edward about
it. When Juliana begged to be allowed to stay in Independence with them, Uncle Edward had steadfastly refused,
and even Wade and Tommy had insisted that their ten-
year-old sister go to St. Louis and be raised "like a lady."
She would live with Aunt Katharine, they told her,
Papa's own sister, in a fine house, with pretty clothes, and
a governess to teach her, and her cousin Victoria for a
playmate. It wouldn't be right for them to raise her. They
were going to leave Independence and head for Texas.
They wanted to catch wild horses, start a ranch. Someday, they told her, they'd have the grandest horse ranch
in Texas and build her a fine house. Then she'd come and
live with them.

Only ten, and heartbroken by the death of her parents,
Juliana had agreed to be separated from her big brothers,
thinking with childish optimism that they would soon
come east to visit her, and could perhaps be convinced to
stay. But it hadn't worked out that way. Wade and
Tommy had not kept in touch. At first there had been
letters posted from various towns south of the Arkansas,
but then the letters had become few and far between. The
last one had come from someplace called Payville, Texas,

when Juliana was twelve. Then all correspondence had abruptly stopped.

Several years passed during which time she hadn't known where Wade and Tommy were or what they were doing. But slowly, slowly, the life she had led in Independence with all of them together had grown distant and blurred. One day, when she was fourteen, Uncle Edward informed her in disgust that she was never to mention those "no-good" brothers of hers again. They had become desperadoes, he said, savage, roaming criminals who robbed stagecoaches for a living. She hadn't believed him, not one word, until he had shown her the newspaper account detailing one of the robberies. "The Montgomery gang" was known throughout the Southwest, Aunt Katharine had lamented in horror. If anyone were to find out about them, well, coupled with Juliana's mother's past, the results, she told her sobbing young niece, would be disastrous.

Juliana was forbidden ever to speak her brothers' names again.

They think I've forgotten all about Wade and Tommy, Juliana reflected as the train sped across the plains toward the looming peaks of the Rockies. But how could she? She could still picture Wade, so smart and tough, the one who had taught her how to defend herself against the blacksmith's bullying son, the one who had given her piggyback rides to and from school each day. And Tommy, with his golden hair the exact same shade as Juliana's, and mischievous eyes of bold, sparkling blue like Papa's. He had had a favorite shirt of blue and yellow plaid, she remembered, which he'd worn nearly every day, except when Mama managed to get it away long enough to wash it. Tommy had taught her how to ride anything on four legs, shoot a row of tin cans off a fence, and cheat at cards without anyone guessing. Full of tricks had been Tommy, as quick-witted and lighthearted as

Wade had been ingenious and determined. They had been
happy-go-lucky boys back then, full of high spirits and
with minds of their own, but Papa had always been able
to keep them firmly in hand. To think that they were
outlaws now . . . Juliana swallowed past a lump in her
throat. When she found them, things would be different.
And she *would* find them. Even if she had to sneak circles
around Aunt Katharine and Uncle Edward to do it.

As if reading her thoughts, Aunt Katharine suddenly
glanced over at her niece. "Juliana," she said in a low
tone. "I want you to renew your promise."

Juliana forced herself to meet the piercing gaze that
stabbed at her across the aisle.

"Ma'am?"

"Promise me that you won't attempt to locate those
scoundrel brothers of yours while we're in Denver."

Uncle Edward started, and turned his protuberant blue
eyes upon her as well. Shorter than Aunt Kate by a good
four inches, he was a fat, paunchy man with a face as
round as a melon's and a thatch of wiry graying hair he
kept carefully combed back from his brow. He was not a
particularly intelligent man, but he was a shrewd one,
possessing a keen instinct for business, a fondness for
good sherry, and a habit of studying his thumbs. Punishment from him had always been swift and firm when
Juliana had misbehaved as a child: hours spent alone in
her room without any supper—or a favorite toy or possession taken from her and never returned. But Aunt
Kate's retribution had been worse than anything Uncle
Edward had ever done, for Aunt Kate did not forgive.
She had a way of staring at you until you felt as big as a
pin, and she would do it for weeks and weeks after the
slightest infraction, treating you with withering contempt
and ice-cold disdain until life in the Tobias house became
totally unbearable. Those were the times when Juliana
daydreamed about running off with Wade and Tommy,

far, far from the great formal house in St. Louis, with its
rules and orderliness, its somber-faced servants, its elaborate, silent meals, and most of all its austere mistress's
frosty displeasure.

"Promise me, Juliana," Aunt Kate insisted, exactly as
if her niece were still a recalcitrant ten-year-old. "We
must have your word."

"But . . ." Juliana began, squirming uncomfortably in
her seat.

"No buts." Uncle Edward pointed a finger at her.
"Give us your word."

Outside, the Colorado prairie raced by. Inside the
coach, her aunt and uncle both stared at her, Uncle Edward frowning, Aunt Kate glaring with that haughty,
expectant look she wore whenever Maura was late bringing in tea.

Juliana took a deep breath. "I promise."

They exchanged satisfied nods. Then they smiled at
her.

"That's a good girl," Aunt Kate approved. Uncle Edward went back to his sheaf of papers.

What they didn't know was that beneath the folds of
her taffeta skirt, two fingers had been crossed when she
issued her promise. *It didn't count,* she told herself, untying the ribbons of her hat, and smoothing her hair. She
was free to do as she pleased. And she would be pleased
to make inquiries about the notorious Montgomery gang
as soon as she arrived in Denver.

She didn't dare think what she would do if no one in
Denver had heard of the Montgomery brothers and had
no idea where they might be. Someone had to know
something, and she would simply continue asking until
she found the answers she sought.

At just past six o'clock that evening the Kansas Pacific
chugged into the Denver station and discharged its carloads of weary passengers. Juliana, stepping out into

fresh, mountain-cooled air, took a deep breath, reveling in the pungent scent of pine. She hurried across the platform for a better view of the town. She saw wide, dusty streets lined with wood-fronted and adobe buildings, many of them saloons. Garishly painted signs proclaimed names like the LUCKY DOG, GOLD DUST, and STAR DIAMOND SALOON, the latter boasting of dancing girls and faro. Denver was larger than she'd expected; rougher, too. Not at all like staid, pretty, proper St. Louis. The streets were teeming with wagons, horses, pigs, and people going about their business, and the faint odor of manure in the air mingled strangely with the clear pine scent drifting down from the mountains rising beyond the town. Brown-faced, sunbonneted women in gingham dresses and men wearing guns and Stetsons filled the streets. Tumbleweed blew down the alleys, children skirmished in front of Dade's General Store. She heard the neigh of horses, the clomp of a hundred pairs of boots on boardwalk, and the blare of tinny piano music and drunken shouts emanating from the Gold Dust Saloon, directly across from the depot.

"What an ugly, squalid, *dreadful* place." Katharine Tobias shuddered. "Edward, I thought you said Denver was a civilized town."

"It is, my dear, compared to most on the frontier." Uncle Edward mopped his brow with a handkerchief, and peered up and down the street. "It seems Breen's man is late coming to meet us. Well, let's gather up the baggage and hope he arrives by the time we've assembled it all."

Juliana held back as her aunt and cousin followed him into the baggage room. It would take some time to sort through the piles of trunks, crates, and boxes being unloaded from the train, and all she needed was a moment or two.

Quick as a wink, she slipped past a knot of travelers about to descend the platform steps, hurried down to the street, and then dashed toward the Gold Dust Saloon. It was the nearest one and the largest, from what she had seen. Her heart was pounding, for she couldn't help feeling the very real possibility that she might encounter her brothers within those swinging doors. Of course, that was highly unlikely, but now that she was out West, it *could* happen. . . .

She was just about to enter the saloon when suddenly gunshots roared from inside. The sound burst through Juliana's ears, stunning her. Someone screamed, windowpanes rattled, and on the street all about her, people ducked for cover. Juliana, one hand upon the door, froze with terror.

For a moment, time seemed to stand still. She was trembling all over, yet she was dimly aware of the rough town behind her. She was aware of the April wind caressing her cheek, aware of the unnatural silence that had followed those first thundering shots. She was torn between an urge to flee, and an almost overwhelming desire to burst inside and see what had happened. But her legs wouldn't move.

Then, before she could do anything, the saloon doors swung wide and a man charged out, colliding full force with Juliana. She was knocked sideways into the wall by the most stunningly handsome man she'd ever seen.

He was young, seemed to be in his late twenties, and very tall. Ink-black hair touched his shirt collar; steel-blue eyes stared out from a rough, sun-bronzed face. He looked as strong as Goliath, Juliana thought in a daze. She caught a fascinating glimpse of curly black chest hair beneath the collar of his shirt and something in the pit of her stomach squeezed tight. The snug black trousers he wore tucked into his boots emphasized rather than disguised a body that was lean and superbly fit, splendid with muscles. His physique bespoke power, but his expression bespoke danger. Dragging her gaze from that dark mat of chest hair to his face, Juliana nearly gasped. She had never seen anyone as handsome, and at the same time deadly-looking, in her life.

Danger emanated from him like heat from a stove. Beneath the black Stetson he wore the look of a man who had never once been tethered by the softening influence of love. This man had never been tethered by anything, Juliana realized. And those keen, intense blue eyes were like none other she had ever seen.

He was like none she had ever seen. As she steadied herself against the wall, recovering from being knocked aside, his gaze bored straight into her without a flicker of emotion.

"Beg your pardon, ma'am."

He didn't sound a bit sorry.

His cold glance swept past, scanning either side of the road. He spoke again, his voice soft and even as he appraised the empty street.

"If I were you, ma'am, I'd step back a pace or this hombre will bleed all over that pretty dress of yours," the stranger drawled without sparing her a second glance.

It was then that Juliana had the wit to tear her gaze from that magnetic face. Looking down, she saw with a quiver of horror that he was casually dragging behind him a man's blue-and-yellow-shirted, blood-spattered body.

Juliana had never fainted before in her life, but she'd never seen a dead body before either. She took one look at the blood and guts spilling from the dead man and felt a great dry coldness sweep over her. The man was wearing a blue and yellow shirt—oddly familiar. He had golden blond hair, thick and silky, falling over his face.

The shirt, the hair . . . it came to her with a jolt, it looked just like . . .

"Tommy!" she whispered with a breath of horror, and then she pitched forward like a rag doll straight into the stranger's arms.

· 2 ·

The stranger caught her just before she hit the ground. Cursing, he was forced to release his hold on the dead man's shirt and to sweep an arm about the swooning girl before she crashed onto the boardwalk. *Just what I need,* Cole Rawdon thought in disgust. *A fool woman to slow me down.*

"Damn it all to hell," he muttered under his breath as her hat fell off and a tumble of gold curls cascaded down, nearly touching the ground.

A crowd was gathering. Rawdon hated crowds.

"What are you staring at?" He glared at the sea of faces, and the onlookers scattered. With a grimace he turned back to the woman, really seeing her for the first time. She was a slip of a thing, no more. And pretty as pie. Pretty? No, Cole decided. Pretty didn't quite describe her. She was beautiful. For a moment he forgot about the dead man and the crowd, and found himself studying the girl.

Cole didn't remember ever seeing skin so creamy and smooth, or hair quite so pure and dazzling a gold. Or

features so elegant—as though they'd been cut from fine
crystal. Breakable, that's how she looked. Like she belonged on a china shop shelf, not the streets of Denver.
For a moment he just stared at her, mesmerized. Then he
came to his senses with a start. Hell, it was damned in-
convenient to be stuck holding on to this female in the
middle of Denver when he had to get Gus Borden's
corpse to Sugar Creek pronto. A two-hundred-dollar reward was waiting at the end of that four-hour ride—and
Cole meant to claim it, and get rid of Gus, before the
outlaw's body started to rot. For a moment longer he let
his eyes slide over the girl's willowy form, admiring the
soft curves beneath her fancy dress, the way her breasts
strained against the tight fabric. *Damn, she is something.
Too bad I'm in a hurry,* he thought, his eyes narrowing
with regret. *If I had more time, I'd wait around to see if
she knows how to show a man proper gratitude.* He
doubted it. Any girl who fainted at the sight of a little
blood was sure to be too weak-spined and silly to be any
fun at all. Besides, Ina Day was dancing in the Red
Feather Saloon in Sugar Creek tonight and she always
knew how to show him a good time.

Cole tore his gaze from the delicate planes of the girl's
face with an effort. A thin man with dark whiskers was
watching him warily from ten paces down the boardwalk.
"Hey, you, come here," he ordered. "Grab ahold of this
woman and . . . do something with her."

As the man nervously approached, Cole saw the girl's
eyelashes flutter. About time. Suddenly she opened her
eyes and gazed up at him in a dazed fashion. He felt his
insides tighten. She had the most exquisite eyes he'd ever
seen—huge, expressive, green as a Montana valley, and
filled just now with a touching uncertainty that, if he'd
been any other man, would have tugged at his heart. But
Cole had been delayed long enough, and life's hard blows
had toughened whatever he'd once had of a heart.

"Been a pleasure getting acquainted with you, ma'am, but I'm afraid I've got to be going now," he drawled, and dumped her without ceremony into the bewhiskered man's arms. Without another glance at the girl who had interfered with the orderly execution of his business, he seized Gus Borden's shirt collar and dragged him over to the sorrel horse tethered in front of the saloon. Flinging the body over the saddle and tying it securely in place, Cole forced himself to avoid looking at the little knot of bonneted women, curious children, and silent men who had gathered around the girl. He mounted Arrow and spurred the horse forward, directing the sorrel through the town. Denver, pretty much inured to violence in the streets and saloons, was already getting back to normal.

So much for Denver, and fainting women. As he left the town behind for the solitude of sagebrush and plains, Cole tried not to think about the girl with the golden cloud of hair. *Tommy,* she had said, just before she fainted. She'd been looking at Borden when she said it. Strange. Equally strange was the fact that the girl had been about to enter the saloon. She didn't look like any fallen dove he'd ever seen; she looked damned respectable – aristocratic, even – but then, Cole thought, spurring Arrow on across the foothills, what did he know about women? Only what he'd learned from Liza, and that was all bad. Ina Day and the other dance-hall girls and whores he frequented now and then were fine and dandy conveniences for fulfilling the needs of a man's body, but he didn't know a damned thing about any one of them, and he didn't care to, either. Women were tricky, cunning, and treacherous creatures, that's all he knew or needed to know. The prettier they were, the more dangerous they could be. According to this way of figuring things, that gold-haired beauty back there could be downright fatal.

Cole knew one thing. The sooner he forgot about her,

the better off he'd be. He turned his mind to Borden, and
the reward, and how he'd celebrate finishing the job by
looking up Ina and letting her entertain him for the
night. That kind of company he could handle. Short,
sweet, and uncomplicated, a night with Ina would make
him forget all about the girl who'd fainted, a girl Cole
was certain he'd never see again.

The foothills rose about him as he rode away from
Denver, soothing him with their wildness, their solitude,
their lonely embrace. Cole settled down for the ride and
fixed his sights on Ina Day, a feather bed, and a bottle of
the Red Feather's finest.

Juliana, meanwhile, came dazedly awake to find herself
in the arms of a thin, frightened-looking man with black
whiskers and a bulbous nose. *Ugh. No. That wasn't the
face at all.* Dizzy, she shut her eyes again, and a soft
moan escaped her lips. She tried to summon up the image
of a handsome young face, rugged and strong and hard.
Hadn't she just seen that face? Where had it gone?

Her uncle's voice rang with cold fury through the air,
shattering her dreamy haze. "Juliana, what is the meaning of this? What are you doing down here in the street?"

Her eyes blinked open. She found herself in the center
of a little crowd of people, all eyeing her curiously. Aunt
Katharine, Uncle Edward, and Victoria were glaring at
her as if she had just marched naked through a garden
party. Why? Frantically, she tried to clear her foggy
brain.

"Is she yours, mister?" The bewhiskered man peered
hopefully at Uncle Edward. His cheeks were red with
embarrassment. "Not that I mind helping a lady in trouble," he went on hurriedly, and then glanced up and
down the street with a distracted air. "But, you see, my
missus'll be along any time now and she might not 'xactly
understand why I've got a pretty gal in my arms. You
know how women can be."

Several people chuckled, another man slapped him on the back in sympathy, and Juliana's memory came flooding back with shocking force. Gasping, she jolted upright onto her own two feet, ignoring the light-headed sensation that washed over her. "Tommy!" she cried, and turned to Uncle Edward with terrified eyes. "That man—the dead man—it was Tommy—Uncle Edward, I saw his shirt, he—"

"Pshaw, girl, I don't know who you thought that feller was, but I kin tell you for right certain it was Gus Borden, the lowest kind of rustler and killer you ever met." An old-timer with bushy white hair and a bent back peered at her from under swooping eyebrows almost bigger than his leathered face.

"Are you sure?" Juliana put a hand to her heart as its pounding gradually slowed. "Oh, mister, are you sure?"

"Sure as shootin', missy. There was a price on Borden's head. Feller that shot him was a bounty hunter, name of Cole Rawdon. I saw the whole thing, and a damned fine bit of shooting it was."

"That bounty hunter shore was in a big hurry," the bewhiskered man put in. He had taken out a handkerchief and begun mopping his perspiring brow, obviously relieved that the lovely young woman was no longer reclining in his arms. "When he told me to grab ahold of you, you could have knocked me down with a feather. But damned if I knew what else to do. He looked mighty fierce, and I didn't want to do nothing to aggravate him —I've heard of Cole Rawdon . . ."

Cole Rawdon. Juliana, filled with relief that the dead man had not been Tommy after all, leaned against the wall for support. Her mind was spinning. As she tried to steady the jumbled whirl of emotions and events, her thoughts turned back to the lean, handsome gunman, the one who had done the killing and then had so calmly, coldly suggested that she step back apace.

"There he goes, riding out of town." Victoria pointed at a rising cloud of dust to the west. "I declare, what a monstrous, uncivilized place this is. A person shot and killed the very moment we arrive in town! When I saw that man—that bounty hunter—and the way he was holding you, and the way he was looking at you, Juliana, why, my blood ran cold. . . ."

"What I want to know," Aunt Katharine interrupted, turning toward her niece with a penetrating glance, "is what you were doing in front of the saloon. Why on earth didn't you come into the baggage room with us?"

Juliana forced herself to meet that suspicious stare. "I was about to, Aunt Katharine," she said in a small voice, "but . . . my handkerchief blew away and I was merely trying to retrieve it."

Katharine Tobias's gaze remained fixed upon her face. "And did you?"

"N-no . . . in all the excitement, I forgot."

Victoria clutched her father's sleeve. "After all that's happened, I think we should get on the next eastbound train and go home. I don't *like* this place, Papa."

"Now, now, my dear, don't be so quick to retreat." Uncle Edward patted his daughter on the shoulder, then straightened his lapels with a businesslike air. "I'm certain our stay will proceed more normally from this point on. As soon as Mr. Breen's man arrives for us, that is."

"Well, if it's Bart Mueller from the Breen ranch you're waiting for, he's coming this way now," the old-timer put in.

A thick-necked, beefy man in a black vest and hat was driving a buckboard up the street toward them. "Thank you, sir," Uncle Edward nodded as the old man shuffled off, and the bewhiskered man, still mopping his brow, went on his way as well. "Now things will settle down, my dear," he told his wife.

The driver of the buckboard pulled the team to a halt

and gave the family of easterners on the boardwalk an apologetic smile.

"Mr. Tobias? I'm Bart Mueller, foreman of Twin Oaks. Mr. Breen sent me."

"Well, it's about time."

"Sorry, sir, but we had a little problem at the ranch, and I got here as soon as I could. Mr. Breen sends his regrets for any inconvenience, but you'll still have plenty of time to freshen up before the festivities tonight." He studied the easterners with shrewd eyes, one after the other, his attention caught by the beautiful but deathly pale girl leaning against the wall.

"Something wrong with the little lady?"

"Nothing serious," Uncle Edward assured him quickly. "My niece had a bit of a fright, but she'll be fine when she's had a chance to rest up."

Suddenly, Katharine Tobias turned toward her husband, her full skirts rustling about her. It wouldn't do to have this man report back to Breen that Juliana was sickly, or fainthearted. The man might change his mind about everything. Best to divert attention from the girl as quickly as possible. She took charge with alacrity, and perfect ease. "Edward, why don't you and Mr. Mueller see to the luggage? Juliana, Victoria, and I shall wait here until all is ready."

"Yes, my dear, we won't be but a moment."

As the men departed for the depot, a great weariness overtook Juliana. She wished she could find a quiet place where she could rest and recover her composure. Her aunt's anger, and Uncle Edward's exasperation, not to mention Victoria's peevish expression, were not helping to soothe her troubled nerves. She was ashamed at her own weakness in having fainted. How silly to have jumped to the conclusion that the dead man was Tommy, all because of the color of his hair and shirt. It was humiliating to have fainted like a ninny within five minutes

of her arrival in Denver. She tried to tell herself it was the
fatigue of the journey, lack of food for several hours, and
the effects of heat and thirst that had contributed to her
extreme reaction, but she knew there was something
more. It hadn't been only the thought that it was Tommy
that had made her faint. It had been because of the dead
man himself, the blood, the sight of it. It was the same
ailment that had plagued her since her childhood—a
heart-palpitating horror of bloodshed. Ever since her parents' violent murder by bandits in their store, Juliana had
been possessed with a foolish weakness at the sight of
even a drop of blood. Once, when Victoria had pricked
her finger while stitching a sampler, Juliana, only fourteen, had gone into a fit of shaking that had forced Uncle
Edward to give her a strong dose of brandy to restore her
to a semblance of calm. When one of Uncle Edward's
grooms had endured a kick from a frightened horse in the
stables one day, Juliana, witness to the accident and the
bloody wound that resulted, had scarcely had the
strength to run and fetch help before her legs had given
way beneath her. Now, thinking of the hard-eyed young
gunman she'd just seen, she realized that he had killed
someone only a moment before running into her, yet he
had looked as calm and cool as a gentleman taking a
stroll in the park. She had heard stories about the savage-
ness of the frontier, the gunfights and hangings and Indian raids, but it had not seemed real. It was real though.
Real and brutal and bloody. Juliana shuddered. Suddenly
this town, and the men wearing guns, and the smell of
gunpowder in the air, all reminded her of Independence,
of that dreadful, unforgettable day when she and Wade
and Tommy had returned from school to learn of their
parents' deaths.

    She fought the nausea and the fear that rose unbidden
within her. She had to overcome these feelings if she was
going to make the most of her time in Denver, to try to

find Wade and Tommy. If she wanted a life out west with them, she would have to learn to be stronger, tougher. She wished desperately that she could sit down for a moment, only a moment, to gather her strength, and give her knees a chance to recover from their trembling. She was about to suggest to Aunt Katharine that they wait for the men in the buckboard, when her aunt spoke first, grasping her arm urgently.

"Juliana, listen to me—before your uncle and Mr. Mueller return. I must remind you—and Victoria, of course—to be particularly pleasant to Mr. Breen. It is most important that these business negotiations progress well. Do you understand?"

"Yes, Aunt Katharine, but—"

"Certainly refrain from complaining about any inconveniences you might encounter in Denver, or at Mr. Breen's ranch. You know, they may not have all the little niceties and refinements we have back home, but it would not do to insult our host in any way."

"Of course not. I wouldn't do such a thing." *But Victoria might,* Juliana thought, with a quick glance at her sullen-faced cousin. She couldn't help wondering why Aunt Katharine was staring at her so fixedly as she spoke, and seeming to direct all her instructions to Juliana—when it was Victoria who was prone to complaints and unfavorable comparisons between East and West. "I shall do everything to make you proud," Juliana added, but was baffled inwardly as to why her behavior was being called into question. Surely Aunt Katharine didn't really fear that she would do anything deliberately to offend John Breen.

Juliana had met John Breen on only one occasion, at the Governor's Ball some months ago. The man whose name appeared almost daily in every newspaper in the land had not exchanged more than a dozen words with her, and had left the party soon after supper—to catch a

train, Uncle Edward said. In the moment or two that
Juliana had spent with him, she had had an impression of
whipcord strength, iron will, and tremendous energy and
drive, all masked beneath a lean face, very large, deep-set
topaz-colored eyes, and a flashing, delightful smile. At
thirty, he had been younger than she had expected from
his reputation and all the wealth he had accumulated,
and far more handsome, with a slim build, glistening fair
hair, and rugged features. Juliana couldn't understand
why Aunt Katharine could possibly think she would af-
front him.

*She must think little enough of my character if she
expects me to complain about his hospitality, or make myself disagreeable to him and ruin all of Uncle Edward's
plans,* she thought. *Perhaps she only fears that my being
in Denver will bring out the tainted side of my nature, and
banish all the good breeding she has pounded into my
head these past nine years.*

At this, an irrepressible glimmer of amusement ran
through her, and she was able to shake off a little bit of
the weariness that had overtaken her after her faint.

"See that you do make us proud," Aunt Katharine
commanded in an undertone, as Uncle Edward and Bart
Mueller appeared at the buckboard carrying a hefty assortment of luggage. "Conduct yourself as a lady, and be
utterly charming—under all circumstances."

By the time she was seated beside Victoria in the buckboard and on her way to the Breen ranch, Juliana had
put aside her aunt's odd remonstrations. She was once
more thinking of her plans to locate her brothers, and
devising ways she might begin some careful inquiries,
perhaps even tonight. She ignored Victoria's groans,
which sounded every time they rode over a rut in the
trail, or swerved suddenly and were thrown sideways in
the seat. As the wagon made its way across the rose-hued
foothills, she thought of the future and the promise it

might hold. A cozy home, with just herself and Wade and Tommy. A new life, for all of them, together.

The killing she had seen today made it all the more imperative to find her brothers—to rescue them from the dangerous path they had chosen. It was a path that made them targets of men like the one she had encountered today, Cole Rawdon. Cole Rawdon, a bounty hunter, would have shot Tommy—or Wade—if he had found them. He hunted human beings for a living, tracked them down like animals, for a monetary reward. She shivered as his image swam into her mind's eye.

She quickly banished it. She didn't want to think about him, she didn't want to remember. He had killed a man and shown no remorse. He had frightened her, made her faint, and then ridden off without a backward glance to see how she fared.

Juliana clenched her hands together, realizing with a cold, hard knot of fear that the man who had run into her today was no better than the men who had killed her parents in their store. He represented violence, death—and ruthlessness. He was a loathsome animal who would hunt down Wade and Tommy without a moment's hesitation if he only knew where to look.

She prayed to heaven he never would. For something told her that Cole Rawdon got what he went after. She prayed he would never set his sights on Wade and Tommy, and that no other bloodthirsty bounty hunter or posse would either. With urgent desperation pounding in her heart, Juliana knew she had to get to them first.

For the remainder of the drive she struggled to put all thoughts of the bounty hunter and the ugly scene in town out of her mind, and to think of how she could most effectively search for her brothers. Her determination mounted as each mile passed. No longer did she want merely to find her brothers, but to save them. To save them from their own perilous course in life, and from the brutality of men like Cole Rawdon.

Just as the pale blue mist of dusk began its descent over the mountains, she saw, up ahead, the enormous lantern-lit yard and corrals of the Twin Oaks ranch.

Suddenly, a chill touched her. The skin at the back of her neck prickled. She didn't know why. The two-story stone ranch house and surrounding buildings looked beautiful silhouetted against the twilit mountains that rose against a purpling sky. Rolling and majestic beneath the looming shadow of the Rockies, the Twin Oaks ranch and environs were an impressive sight, one that should have filled her with delight and relief. The long journey was over. Refreshment and hospitality and festivity awaited. But she had to fight the sudden urge to beg Uncle Edward to have Mueller turn the buckboard around and head back toward town.

Why?

Nerves, Juliana told herself, irritated. Stupid, foolish jitters, like the ones that had made her faint. Nonsense feelings, to be subdued and controlled.

Cole Rawdon would have called it something else. *Instinct.* The kind of instinct he used every day to stay alive.

He would have been right.

· 3 ·

Tucked away in the foothills of the Rockies, John Breen's Twin Oaks ranch was a magnificent monument to the man who had built it and the center from which he ran his empire. Stretching over more than 250,000 acres, Twin Oaks was well stocked with horses, cattle, men, guns, and enough food and provisions to supply an army outpost for months. The sheds, barns, corrals, cookhouse, bunkhouse, and other buildings were immaculately maintained and run with hard-nosed efficiency, like all the rest of John Breen's business endeavors, from his mines and lumber mills to his railroad holdings. But it was the sprawling ranch house, with its gardens and white-columned verandah, sparkling like a jewel beneath the jagged hills and purple-shrouded mesas, that was his special pride and joy. The house was the showpiece of Denver—as luxurious and grand within as any New York mansion—complete with paintings, books, flocked wallpaper, Turkish carpets, and mahogany furniture. The only thing lacking, John Breen felt—had felt for quite some time—was a mistress to preside over Twin

Oaks. A woman, the perfect woman—the one he chose to
be his wife—would complement and adorn the house
more than any accessory or painting he could purchase
from anywhere in the world. He had searched for her,
methodically, patiently, critically, refusing to settle for
anything less than perfection, and at last, at the Governor's Ball in St. Louis not many months before, he had
found her.

Now, Breen thought, watching from the window in his
study as the buckboard drew up before the front steps
and the Tobias family alighted, she was here at last.

His waiting was over.

She's a jewel, a rare and spectacular jewel, Breen reflected as he surveyed Juliana's small, piquant countenance, softly illuminated by the night's first stars. He enjoyed the fact that she had journeyed all this way without
the faintest idea of his plans for her. As a matter of fact,
he had enjoyed everything about Juliana Montgomery
from the moment he had first met her at the Governor's
Ball. Her beauty, her gracefulness, her enchanting, tin-
kling laugh. He had known as soon as he set eyes on her
that she was everything he could ever want in a woman,
that she possessed the qualities he had long been searching for in a wife. She was lovely, sophisticated and re-
fined, yet spirited enough to make him proud when he
walked into a room with her on his arm. None of these
mealymouthed, insipid little debutantes would do for
John Breen, nor would a homespun Colorado girl suffice.
In marriage, as in everything else he put his hand to, he
had to have the best, a woman all other men would envy
him for possessing. As soon as Breen had glimpsed Edward Tobias's niece, decked out in pink tulle and lace,
waltzing round and round the ballroom with a score of
foolish boys panting after her like pups chasing a bone,
he had known that Juliana Montgomery was the perfect
bride for him.

It was time for him to marry, time to think about begetting himself a son to whom he could pass on the empire he had built and which he was constantly expanding. But his wife, and the mother of his son, had to be special, someone as remarkable in her way as he was himself. Juliana was that. Every inch a lady, yet not shy, not prim and boring. There was a natural grace and poise about her, a subtle, tantalizing sensuality that had struck him immediately. She looked soft as a kitten, yet when they had met there had been laughter and confidence in her eyes, a directness that he admired. He couldn't wait to get her in his bed. Breen had a sixth sense about such things. He'd have bet a fortune that beneath Juliana's golden innocence lurked a passionate woman, a woman just waiting to be driven wild by a man's caresses. He would be the one to oblige her, too. No one else. He'd kill any other man who touched her. Breen vowed that to himself as he let his gaze travel over the elegant features and feminine enchantments of the girl walking toward his door. He smoothed the tip of his mustache before turning from the window. Yes, he thought with satisfaction, he would have her, and before the month was out.

Walking up the lane to the ranch, Juliana breathed in the icy sweetness of mountain pine. She glanced toward the peaks of the Rockies, instinctively drawn by the vista of looming mountains, and was so transfixed, she did not notice the rest of the family lingering behind. As she trod up the steps of the porch, still gazing at the lavender sky and great dusk-shadowed peaks, the front door was suddenly thrown open. A tall man in elegant gray shirt and breeches strode across the porch and smiled directly down at her.

"Welcome, Miss Montgomery. Welcome to Twin Oaks." Taking her arm, John Breen guided her up the final step and drew her onto the porch.

Juliana murmured a greeting in response, and thought

he would turn to Uncle Edward and Aunt Katharine and usher them all into the house. But to her surprise he ignored the others, and drew her along the porch to a window where light streamed out. Still holding Juliana's arm, he stared down at her, studying her face and hair, illuminated by the glowing light. His smile deepened at her surprised expression. Behind his gaze was a keen, richly amused glint that she found somewhat unnerving.

He cut a splendid figure. Tall and slim, he had a rugged countenance browned by sun and wind and distinguished by a light, well-trimmed mustache and a pair of shrewdly intelligent topaz eyes. She remembered those eyes. His hair, a darker gold than Juliana's, was brushed smoothly back, each strand perfectly in place. His jaw was strong, with a cleft in his chin. His grooming was immaculate; he looked like a man whose suits would always be flawlessly pressed, whose boots were at all times magnificently polished. Even his teeth shone as he smiled down at her, but something about that smile, and the anticipatory expression in his eyes, made Juliana uneasy. His look was bold, victorious almost.

Like a mouse caught between a cat's paws, she suddenly wanted to squeak and run.

Silly, she admonished herself. *You're imagining things.*

But Juliana had not been the belle of St. Louis society for two seasons without having learned to recognize when a man was attracted to her. She felt a tiny shock race down her spine as she continued to meet the intent stare of John Breen.

He had shown no sign of being attracted to her that one time they'd met—had he? Thinking back quickly, Juliana realized she had been so busy with her swarm of overeager suitors that evening, she had barely paused for breath when Uncle Edward had introduced her to John Breen. Now, searching her mind with great rapidity, she did remember that he had held her hand an inordinate amount of time, and complimented her on her beauty before she had been swept off by her current dancing partner. But she had taken both the compliment and the warm look he bestowed on her as civilities, nothing more. She hadn't given John Breen another thought until Uncle Edward had told her of this business trip to Denver. Even then, she had thought of him merely as her uncle's associate, a mogul famous for his vast self-made wealth— never as a suitor with a romantic interest in her. Yet, as she stood before him now on the porch, she could not deny that he was regarding her with the glance of a man who has much more on his mind than business.

"Are you cold, Miss Montgomery? You're shivering. Come into the house and get warm." He glanced over at the rest of the Tobias family, who had come onto the porch and were standing silently by, waiting to be greeted.

"Edward! Here, at last," Breen threw over his shoulder. "Come in, everyone. You'll want to rest before the party gets under way."

To Juliana, as he led her into the house, he said, "I hope the journey wasn't too tiring for you."

"No, Mr. Breen. Not at all."

"You're a bit pale. Every bit as beautiful as I remember, of course, but . . ."

"Juliana fainted when we got to town," Victoria blurted out.

Juliana gritted her teeth and managed to restrain herself from glaring at her cousin, though at that moment she would have dearly loved to box Victoria's ears.

"Fainted?" Swift concern flashed across Breen's features. He swung Juliana around to face him. "Are you ill? Shall I send for a doctor?"

"Oh, no, please. It was nothing. Victoria shouldn't have mentioned it."

Victoria, having no idea of John Breen's marital intentions toward her cousin, had been feeling peeved at being so pointedly ignored. It was bad enough that Juliana commanded the attention of the handsomest young men back home, but to see John Breen positively doting on her the moment they arrived without scarcely a glance at anyone else was too much to bear. She knew Juliana hated any reference to her weakness regarding bloodshed, and it gave her a surge of pleasure to confide something to John Breen that would discomfit her cousin: this one missish quality, the only frailty she seemed to possess, embarrassed Juliana, and perhaps, Victoria thought with a flash of inspiration, it would even diminish their host's obvious admiration for her—for surely western men preferred women of a hardier constitution. But Victoria's satisfaction was short-lived. John Breen appeared only more intently interested in Juliana, and both her parents instantly shot her such a furious glance that she quailed inwardly and clamped her mouth shut.

It was Edward who cleared his throat and said: "You see, there was a bit of trouble in town, John, and Juliana became upset. A man was shot and she happened to run into the fellow who did it—"

"What? Who was it? Did he touch you? Hurt you in any way?" Breen questioned the girl swiftly, a hard look entering his eyes.

"No, no, it wasn't anything like that." Juliana could have happily strangled Victoria at that moment. "He was a bounty hunter," she started to explain, "and it wasn't really his fault at all—" but Uncle Edward cut her off.

"Cole Rawdon was the fellow's name. He gave the poor girl a nasty shock. You certainly can't blame her for fainting. Any girl of sensibility would have done the same."

"Rawdon." Breen frowned as he turned the name over in his mind. "I've heard of the man, but never met him. What happened?"

"Nothing, really." Juliana insisted, with a shake of her head. She was startled by the overly solicitous manner in which John Breen was behaving toward her, almost as if he was responsible for her safety and welfare. She was uncomfortable with the fuss being made over the entire subject. "I am feeling perfectly fine now—only a little tired—and I'd rather not discuss it," she said with what she hoped was a cool smile and her most dismissive tone.

But Aunt Katharine was not to be silenced until *she* had explained the matter to her own satisfaction. "Juliana was naturally distressed," she told Breen, stroking her niece's arm in a fond way. "She is such a sweet, sensitive girl, and cannot abide violence of any sort, and here she stumbles upon a brutal killing the moment she arrives in town—why, she actually saw the dead man. . . ."

"Damned unlucky." John Breen shook his head. The look he gave Juliana was regretful. "I'm sorry your visit got off to such a rough start. You've been gently raised— it's only natural such an event would shock you. Eventually, if you spend some time in these parts, you'll toughen up. But not too much, I hope." He grinned down at her. "You see, I like softness in a woman."

Juliana stiffened. How could her uncle stand by and let such a forward remark pass unanswered? But Uncle Edward was staring at his thumbs, and Aunt Katharine's gaze was fixed steadfastly upon the pattern in the Turkish carpet.

It was ludicrous. If any of the beaux who came to call in St. Louis had ever treated her to such intimate glances and bold words upon such a short acquaintance, she would have been forbidden any contact with them. John Breen was behaving as if . . . as if he were her husband!

She remembered what Aunt Katharine had said about not insulting their host, and she wondered with a little stab of anger just how far her aunt and uncle would go to

avoid giving offense. She swallowed back her anger, and
the setdown that sprang so readily to her lips. It would
not do to put him in his place, she realized reluctantly.
She had, after all, given her word to try to be charming to
the man. But not too charming, she told herself. In fact,
I'd do well to steer clear of John Breen before he seeks
favors I am not inclined to grant. It wouldn't surprise
me, she thought with what she imagined to be great so-
phistication, if at some point during our visit he even
tried to steal a kiss!

"Might we have a cup of tea, Mr. Breen?" was all she
said to change the subject, speaking in the chilly, even
tone she reserved for suitors not in her favor. "I am certain my aunt and Victoria are as in need of refreshment
as I am."

"Of course." Breen eyed her in amusement, sensing
that her hackles were up, though she did nothing overt to
snub him. He led the way toward the parlour with lanky
strides. "My apologies, ladies. Hearing about the incident
in town made me forget all my manners. You see, I have
no wife to act as hostess and remind me of the niceties
when guests arrive. You must forgive me. The party
won't begin for a few hours, so you'll have plenty of time
to rest and get ready. Miss Montgomery, right this way."

As Juliana followed him through the wide front hall,
she felt herself nearly swallowed up by the massive lines
of the house that surrounded her. The ranch house
seemed almost as big as the land encompassing it. The
dark-paneled walls gleamed in the bright lantern light;
beyond the hardwood floor of the hall she saw a huge oak
staircase leading to the second-story landing, and there
was a whole series of huge, sprawling rooms branching
off the main hall. The first of these was an enormous
parlour, big as a ballroom, and furnished with crimson
damask sofas and overstuffed blue velvet chairs, carved
mahogany tables, and a sideboard heaped with decanters

of whiskey and brandy and wine. A stone fireplace alive
with a crackling fire added its cheery glow to the crim-
son-draperied room. There was a Turkish carpet on the
floor and several fine watercolors gracing the parlour
walls, but despite the grand beauty of her surroundings,
Juliana was uncomfortable. Even as he poured a brandy
for Uncle Edward and watched the ladies sip their tea,
something calculating and expectant in John Breen's expression every time it rested upon her made her feel as if
she were a tasty morsel about to be consumed whole by a
hungry man.

Even later, bathing in the rose-scented bathwater
Breen's Mexican housekeeper prepared for her in her
room and patting herself dry with a luxuriously thick
towel embroidered in French lace, Juliana could not forget the gleam in John Breen's eyes whenever he was beside her, or the possessive touch of his hand upon her
arm. She shivered. Well, she would be polite to him, but
that was all. Surely Aunt Katharine and Uncle Edward
would not expect her to actively encourage his attentions
only to further Uncle Edward's business dealings! That
would be too much. John Breen disturbed her somehow;
despite his handsomeness, his charm and air of solicita-
tion, she sensed something cold, frightening about the
man. She didn't trust him. And she didn't want to get
into a situation where she would be alone with him.

But that was exactly what happened later that evening,
during a lull in the dancing. Juliana was aware that Aunt
Katharine and Uncle Edward had watched in cold disapproval as one dancing partner after another had spun her
about the room. They seemed shocked by the custom of
young men coming up and introducing themselves to a
lady in the most informal way and inviting her to dance.

"That isn't the way things are done back east," Victoria had sniffed to her mother at one point.

But we're not back east anymore, Juliana exulted as a

grinning young cowpoke whirled her about in a Virginia reel. Her heart lifted as she skimmed about in perfect time to the music, surrounded by a dozen other gaily spinning couples.

The blue and crimson parlour at Twin Oaks was ablaze with candles, and the air was warm. The heavy furniture had been pushed back to make room for the dancing, and against the walls long tables draped with checkered cloths had been set with platters of beef, venison, and gravy-smothered potatoes. Tempting homemade breads and pies added their fragrant aroma to the heady atmosphere of the room. Juliana guessed that at least one hundred guests, townspeople and neighbors, had come tonight to pay their respects to John Breen, Denver's most prominent citizen. From what she had seen as she danced, Breen had introduced her uncle to nearly all of them, but she'd had little opportunity to meet anyone but the cowboys who lined up, one after the other, to whirl about the floor with her.

When the Virginia reel ended, Juliana found herself breathless. Before she could even thank her partner, she was confronted by a lanky young cowboy with red hair and twinkling blue eyes that shone at her from beneath a dark gray Stetson. "Ma'am," he said, elbowing aside the cowboy she'd been dancing with, "would you do me the honor of accepting this glass of lemonade? You've been dancing so hard all night, I reckon you must be plumb tuckered out, not to mention thirstier than a hoss in the desert."

Juliana laughed. "How could I resist such a pretty offer?" she gasped, putting a hand to her thudding heart. "I accept the lemonade, if you'll join me, Mister . . ."

"Keedy, ma'am, Gil Keedy." Taking a sip from his own glass, he studied her over the rim, while all about them in the parlour, ranchers, cowhands, women in all manner of gingham and calico and townsmen in stiff collars and dark suits chattered and drank and jostled about the festively lit room.

Juliana, a vision in her lavender silk gown, liked Gil Keedy immediately. Her smile grew when he said: "Miss Montgomery, ma'am, I've been workin' for Mr. Breen here at Twin Oaks nearly a year now, and I've got to say, gals pretty as you out in these parts are rarer than gold in a snake pit. This sure is my lucky day."

His low-key, comical Texas drawl made her eyes dance. "Your lucky day? Really? Now why is that Mr. Keedy?"

"Gil, ma'am, I have to insist on Gil," he said gravely. He set his glass down on a table and took her hand in his, holding it with a light touch. "A hunch told me to come to this dance and darned if now I don't know why. Meetin' you, that's why. You're my destiny, ma'am. There ain't no doubt about it." He loosened the bright plaid neckerchief knotted about his neck and grinned at her in sheer boyish appreciation. "Tell me all about your-self, Miss Montgomery, quick—before some bowlegged, ugly old cowpoke comes along to steal you away."

"Oh, I'd much rather hear about you," she said teasingly. "Do you enjoy working at Twin Oaks?"

For a moment there was a tightening of his amiable freckled face, then it disappeared as quickly as it had come. "Why, shore, it has its moments. But never you mind about me. My story's a dull one. I'm just a kid from Waco who likes to punch cows and tell tall tales—and who spends a hell of a lot of nights—beg pardon, ma'am —dreamin' about a purty gal with spun gold hair and green eyes who'll hold the hand of a pore redhaided cow-poke and mebbe fall in love with him."

"Gil," she admonished, her face filled with laughter, "if I didn't know better, I'd think you were flirting with me."

"Wal, ma'am, I can't deny I'm sorely tempted." He

inched closer and regarded her with open admiration.
"Tell me why a beautiful young lady like yourself ain't
been hitched already to some lucky hombre and got herself a passel of kids? Those fellows back in Missouri must
be plumb loco to have let you git away."

"Gil, are you trying to tell me I'm on the shelf?" Juliana exclaimed with mock indignation.

"You're sure no old maid or nothin', but if you'd
growed up in these parts, you'd have been standin' before
the preacher the day you turned sixteen—and half the
men in the county would've been shootin' each other for
the honor of standin' beside you."

"Did they teach you how to flirt in Waco, Mr. Keedy,
or do you just come by it naturally?"

"Naturally, I reckon—when I'm with a sweet and
purty little gal."

She couldn't help but smile, yet when she had set her
glass down on a small table nearby she turned back to
him with a more pensive glance. Maybe she could trust
this likable cowboy to help her begin her search. She had
wanted to start her inquiries about Wade and Tommy
immediately, so why not begin with Gil Keedy? Something told her he would do his best to help her.

"Gil," she said slowly, "I need some information. It's
important. Did you ever hear of two men named Wade
and Tommy Montgomery?"

"No, ma'am, can't say as I have. Are they kin of
yours?"

"The very closest of kin. They're my brothers."

Briefly, while the other guests danced and stomped
their feet and clapped their hands to the fiddler's tune all
across the parlour, Juliana explained in low tones. She
expected him to frown when she told him that her brothers were desperadoes, and to warn her that she'd do best
to steer clear of them, but instead he merely stared at her
calmly and said:

"Ahuh."

Warmth flooded through her at this ready acceptance. Her delicate face flushed as she leaned impulsively toward him, hopeful at last of having an ally. "And I . . . I haven't the vaguest notion how to find them," she rushed on, "but I'm convinced they'd want to see me if they knew I was here in Colorado. What do you suggest I do?"

He met her eager gaze soberly. "Let me ask around. Some of the boys in the bunkhouse or someone in town will know something. You can be sure of that."

"Oh, thank you, Gil! I've been wondering how I should manage to make inquiries without Aunt Katharine and Uncle Edward finding out. . . ."

"Here you are, Juliana." Her aunt's voice boomed directly behind her, making Juliana jump. "Tiresome girl, I've been looking for you for quite some time." Buxom and formidable in her gown of rippling green silk, Aunt Katharine bestowed upon her niece a look of extreme annoyance from those great mahogany-colored eyes.

"Speak of the devil?" Gil muttered in Juliana's ear.

Aunt Katharine swung toward him. "I beg your pardon, young man?"

He gave her his lopsided grin. "No need to do that, ma'am. I was jest saying to Miss Montgomery here that speaking of dancing, I'd be honored if she'd step out with me for this here jig . . ."

"My niece is otherwise engaged."

Juliana knew that tone. Aunt Katharine was in no mood to brook an argument. She spoke up quickly, flashing the red-haired cowboy a swift smile. "Thank you, Gil, for the lemonade—and everything."

"It was shore my pleasure, ma'am. I reckon I'll see you again before too long."

"Why, yes, I hope so."

When he was gone, slipping into the throng of plaid-shirted men and gingham-clad women, Aunt Katharine fixed her with an exasperated glare. "Juliana, instead of parading around here like a common hussy with a bunch of cowboys, you could be dancing with Mr. Breen! He's been asking for you, and I'm certain he would like to engage you for a dance tonight, if you can find room for him with all of these scruffy cowboys sniffing around you."

"Aunt Katharine, I don't wish to dance with Mr. Breen."

Her aunt stared at her as if she'd gone mad. "Why in the world would you say a thing like that?"

Juliana tore her gaze from the circle of whirling dancers to meet her aunt's frowning countenance. "Because it's true," she said simply. "Aunt Katharine, Mr. Breen makes me most uncomfortable. His demeanor . . . it's all wrong. He seems to have feelings which I can't return . . . and he is so possessive, so overly concerned about me. I feel smothered—and I barely know the man. Something isn't right."

"Mr. Breen is merely being kind, Juliana. He is treating you with ordinary civility. Really, you are most ungrateful. And conceited. Merely because a man is solicitous of you does not mean he is smitten with you, young lady. And if he were, I can hardly think of a more desirable match—"

"Aunt Katharine," Juliana interrupted, placing one hand on her aunt's arm. "I truly wish to honor my promise to you not to offend Mr. Breen. The best way to do that is to avoid encouraging his attentions so that I am not in the position of rebuffing him!"

"Nonsense. There he is now." She smiled broadly across the room to the parlour entrance as their host paused on the threshold and surveyed the packed room. "Oh, Mr. Bree-en." Aunt Katharine raised her voice ever so slightly, and waggled two fingers in a delicate wave. To Juliana's dismay, John Breen turned toward them and made his way through the crowd, chatting easily with various guests as he crossed the room. She saw him pause by Bart Mueller's side and converse for a moment, before his gaze swung sharply toward Gil Keedy.

"Now, be amiable," Aunt Katharine whispered as he moved toward them once more, "and remember how important this business proposition is to your uncle!"

John Breen looked more handsome than ever against the festive background of the party. Head and shoulders taller than most of the other men, he paused before Juliana with a flashing smile. "Evening, ladies. Hope you're enjoying the party."

"It's delightful, Mr. Breen, simply delightful." Katharine Tobias's usually haughty tone was sugary now, making Juliana wince. "You westerners certainly know how to enjoy yourselves."

"Yes, we like to kick up our heels now and then. It takes our minds off our troubles."

"What troubles could you possibly have, Mr. Breen?" Juliana couldn't resist asking. "You have a lovely ranch and a successful business empire, and from the number of people here in your home tonight, I'd guess you have many friends and well-wishers. Surely you must be a happy man."

He stroked his mustache in a smooth, automatic gesture that she was coming to recognize as a habit with him. "Happy, Miss Montgomery? Mostly. Trouble-free? No, ma'am." His glance swept the room, missing nothing. "Every man has his enemies, Miss Montgomery. I have mine. Sometimes they try to get in the way of what I want. That makes me mighty unhappy—until I've rid myself of them. Then," he continued, smiling down at her, "I can be happy again."

"What sort of enemies?"

"There are those who resent when someone else has more wealth than they do—when he is more successful, more intelligent, more powerful. Men like that are troublemakers, and they become the natural adversaries of those who succeed in this world. They're pests, I'm afraid, every bit as loathsome as locusts and gnats and grasshoppers, and they must be stamped out the same way. But there's a worse enemy, Miss Montgomery," he added, "something more painful and awful and irksome than any other."

He was watching her with a keen, speculative glance, the glinting topaz eyes gazing directly down into her face. *Very well, Mr. Breen, I'll bite,* Juliana thought.

"And what might that be?" she inquired, suddenly aware that Aunt Katharine was melting away into the crowded room without a word to either of them. Juliana was alone in her corner with John Breen.

"Lonesomeness," he answered promptly, and slipped a hand under her elbow. Before Juliana could protest, he was guiding her toward the western windows of the parlour, where French doors opened onto the verandah. "In these parts, Miss Montgomery, life is hard and rough on a man. It can take its toll. A man gets lonely up here near the mountains, all by himself. He finds he has the need for a woman, someone who'll stand by him, be a helpmate to him. Someone he can love and cherish."

They were on the verandah now, isolated from the lights and the crowd, from the noisy company of voices and laughter. Juliana stepped away from him and gripped the smooth porch rail, very aware of John Breen's tall form following her in the darkness. "If lonesomeness is your enemy, Mr. Breen, I am sure that in your case it is easily vanquished." She shot him a steady look. "No doubt there are dozens of women in Denver who would be more than happy to give you their company."

"True enough, I could have my pick of women—but as you yourself observed, I hold a somewhat special place in this community. A man of my position and standing cannot ally himself with just any woman. I must choose a woman—for my wife, you understand—who will be an asset to me in every way, someone of style, wit, and intelligence—and, of course, beauty."

He was staring down at her intently, and as the moonlight touched his lean face, Juliana saw a flush of excitement darken his cheeks. "You know, Juliana"—and the way he said her given name for the first time was almost a physical caress—"there ought to be a law against women being quite as beautiful as you."

"You're very kind, Mr. Breen . . ."

"Kind?" He chuckled as she edged farther away from him, and he advanced upon her with deliberate slowness. "I'm not being kind, Juliana. I'm being honest. Surely you know just how ravishing you are." He grinned down at her and reaching out, clasped both her slender wrists in his hands. His strength was surprising. He stepped so close, she could smell both the pomade on his smoothly brushed fair hair, and the pungent tobacco scent of the cigar bulging from his shirt pocket. Queasiness washed over her. "After all, I saw all those boys pursuing you in St. Louis that night, making damned fools out of themselves. You can't bamboozle me into thinking you're unaware of your charms."

"You obviously are not unaware of them, Mr. Breen," she said breathlessly as she tried unsuccessfully to extricate herself from his grasp. "And I must tell you that I'm not accustomed to such advances from a man I scarcely know. So I insist that you let me go at once. If my uncle only knew . . ."

"He would do what? Challenge me to a showdown at high noon? Horsewhip me? Pack his bags and head east without signing the contracts he came here for?" Breen

threw back his head and laughed. "Your innocence is as
delightful as your beauty. Ah, Juliana, I see I've frightened you. Now come on, honey, don't be scared." To her
relief, he released her suddenly and stepped back with a
gallant bow. "I'm sorry if I stepped over the line—but
you're so darned pretty—and I like seeing that angry
sparkle that comes into your eyes whenever you think
I'm getting presumptuous. Now I promise to take things
nice and slow. But just the same, you and I are going to
get acquainted during this little visit."

"I suppose we shall," she retorted, dodging past him
and starting back toward the house. "As well acquainted
as anyone can become in two weeks. My uncle's stay here
will not be lengthy—which in my opinion is a very good
thing. Good evening, Mr. Breen!"

She plunged through the doors into the brightness of
the parlour like a fleeing deer, certain he would try to
seize her and draw her back. But Breen merely watched
her go, delighted with her display of spirit. Leisurely, as
the doors slammed shut behind her, he reached into his
pocket and removed his cigar.

"Your uncle will stay put right here in Denver until I
say otherwise, honey," he mused as he lit up, inhaling
with great satisfaction.

Juliana Montgomery didn't understand that yet. She
didn't recognize one tenth of the power he wielded. But
she would, Breen knew, and very soon. She'd take a bit of
taming, but there was nothing he liked better than to
exercise the power of his own will. He had no doubt of
the outcome. His reward would be the loveliest woman
this side of the ocean, presiding over his home, raising his
son, reaping the benefits of his empire. Not bad for a man
who started out fifteen years ago with little more than a
horse and saddle to his name. He'd had a fancy education
and a bushel of charm, but his purse back then had been

as empty as his soul. Now he could have anything he wanted—including Juliana Montgomery.

Especially Juliana Montgomery. The more he saw of her, the more Breen knew that she must be his next acquisition. Nothing and no one—including that greedy uncle of hers or that upstart cowhand Gil Keedy—had better get in his way.

Breen blew a smoke ring and watched it sail upward into the night. He smiled to himself in the dark.

Juliana, meanwhile, holding her skirts in one hand, dashed through the parlour without pausing and hurried straight upstairs to her room. She was mentally reviewing the entire conversation with John Breen while a dreadful icy fear slid over her.

How could Breen act so smug, so sure of himself, and behave with such odious presumption? It was as if he had no fear whatsoever of censure, as if Uncle Edward had given him carte blanche to do as he wished. . . .

But that was impossible. Wasn't it?

In an agony of uncertainty she kicked off her satin dancing slippers and threw herself down in the chair before the dressing table. Her fingers plucked ten gold hairpins from her hair and a riot of curls cascaded down, but Juliana ignored the fetchingly tousled image in the mirror, biting her lip instead as she concentrated on the situation facing her.

She knew Uncle Edward wanted these business contracts very badly. But would he actually make a bargain like the one she was envisioning? John Breen had practically told her he was in the market for a wife—and he had hinted that she was the most eligible candidate—but surely Uncle Edward wouldn't have arranged a marriage for her to a man she didn't even know—a man like John Breen.

Yet, as Juliana sat there facing her reflection, she realized with a creeping horror that Uncle Edward would not share in her opinion of John Breen. To him, Breen represented the perfect husband for his vexatious niece, the perfect solution to a thorny problem. He could secure his business relationship with one of the richest men in the country, and at the same time rid himself of the girl he'd been forced by duty to raise since childhood.

It wasn't as if she had any prospects for marriage awaiting her in St. Louis, Juliana reflected tremblingly. Mama's past as a dance-hall girl had somehow leaked out into polite society—and that, combined with Juliana's own feisty spirit and sometimes unorthodox ways, had branded her as ineligible marriage material—perfectly acceptable at parties, of course, thanks to Aunt Katharine and Uncle Edward's sponsorship—but certainly not as a prospective wife for any young man of good background. If word got out about Wade and Tommy's infamous exploits, Juliana knew, even social engagements might become scarce. . . .

She had realized this for some time, and lived with the hurt of it. But Juliana would rather die than let anyone see her rage over the way she was deemed "inferior stock." Pride got her through those parties and teas and balls, pride kept her head high and her smile brilliant while she endured the compliments and attentions of smitten young men too weak-spined to defy their parents by courting her seriously, yet too enamored of her charms to leave her alone. Even though the sting of over-heard words and superior glances bit through her tender heart, she never let a trace of pain reveal itself in her face or manner. So far, she hadn't met a young man she truly cared for, so she hadn't yet had to suffer because of the stigma attached to her, but she knew that if some day she did meet someone who mattered to her, he had better not come from the ranks of St. Louis society, or she would be doomed to unhappiness.

It was possible, she reflected with a wrenching of the

heart, that Uncle Edward, casting about for a solution to the problem of his unmarriageable niece, might indeed have jumped at John Breen's offer—if an offer had been made. Sitting before the mirror, with the fiddler's music just reaching her ears, she began to shiver uncontrollably. Dear Lord, had she been sold to that man down there? Bartered and sold to that tall, handsome John Breen with his strange eyes and a touch that inexplicably made her skin crawl? A wild throbbing born of panic began in her chest and spiraled upward to her temples until she thought her head would burst.

She jumped up from the chair and paced the room. There was a way out of this, there had to be a way out. She wouldn't sit idly by and let herself be sold on the marriage block like a piece of livestock. If Uncle Edward had made any deals behind her back, he could just cancel them. She would rather set out into the world on her own and work her fingers to the bone than marry a man she did not love.

Love. What did she know of love? Not one single thing, Juliana had to admit as she paused before the window and stared out in agitation at the shadowed mountains. Maybe it didn't exist, except in books and fairy tales. Maybe it didn't come to girls who laughed at the wrong times or who danced for the sheer pleasure of it or who unbuttoned their blouses on hot, stuffy trains—Aunt Katharine said wickedness was never rewarded. But wicked or not, Juliana knew without a single doubt that she would not find love with John Breen.

She had better find a way out.

· 4 ·

During the next few days Juliana found herself
thwarted in every attempt to speak privately with her
uncle. He was either closeted with John Breen discussing
"business," or they were all together: Breen, Aunt Katharine, and Victoria, and it was impossible for her to broach
either her fears, or her objections to the situation she
suspected was brewing. No matter how many times she
tried to waylay her uncle, she never was able to speak to
him alone. But she did manage to avoid being alone with
John Breen, which was something to be thankful for, and
to escape from the ranch every afternoon on horseback.
She and Victoria set about exploring the countryside, but
her cousin, not nearly as adept a rider as Juliana, after a
few days pronounced herself too sore to venture out
again. On Friday, Juliana led Columbine, the mare that
had been assigned for her use, from the corral and prepared to set out alone.

She needed a diversion from the confines of the ranch
house, which she found oppressive for all its grandness
and comfort. And she needed a release for the tension

that had been building inside her ever since she had arrived at Twin Oaks. She couldn't wait to race freely
through the wild grasses. Only when she was alone and
far from John Breen's watchful eye did she feel she could
breathe easily, and convince herself that she would not be
snared into a marriage she didn't want.

The cowhands were all out riding the range, but as she
stepped from the corral, admiring the cloudless sapphire
sky that stretched above, she heard angry voices coming
from behind the barn, disturbing the peace of the beautiful spring afternoon. The voices slashed through the
lovely crystal air like the scrape of knives against each
other, jarring her nerves.

"Don't ever show your face in this county again, boy.
No cattleman will give you work after this."

She recognized Bart Mueller's voice, even though she
had never heard that harsh note in it before. Juliana held
perfectly still, listening, as beside her the mare pawed the
dust.

"You're a liar, Mueller—and Breen, damned if you
don't know it." There was no mistaking Gil Keedy's
Texas drawl, agitated as it was. "I don't know what kind
of a game the two of you are playing but you know like
hell that Mueller's the one sent me down to the south
pasture to check on those calves. He never said a word
about riding the north range. Why would I have been
busting my back these past few days down by Flat Peak if
he hadn't told me to do it?"

"I don't begin to understand why a lazy, good-for-
nothing hombre like you does anything, Keedy, but you
can get the hell off my ranch."

John Breen. The icy-smooth, even tones reached Juliana's ears with unmistakable clarity. Juliana edged
closer, moving at an angle where she could glimpse behind the barn as the men continued talking.

"The boys on the north range were shorthanded because of you and I can't afford to have my ranch suffer because you can't follow orders," Breen continued. "Pick up your wages from Dusty and get out."

"Sure thing, Mr. Breen," Gil shot back hotly. "I reckon Twin Oaks has gotten a mite odorous for my taste. Matter of fact, the place stinks like a pig's innards." With that he turned on his heel and marched off, and immediately spotted Juliana. He motioned her out of sight in front of the barn, then joined her with quick strides, saying tersely, "Can't talk now, but I've got something to tell you. Meet me over by Durham's Creek. Know where that is?"

She shook her head, holding tight to Columbine's bridle.

His face was still flushed with anger; his usually merry eyes unnaturally bright and hard in the dazzling sunshine. "Half a mile west of here—there's a trail leading straight to the creek bank. You'll find it easy, there's a stand of willow, and some rocks piled up beside a yucca." He helped her to mount, glancing quickly over his shoulder. John Breen and Mueller were walking in the opposite direction toward the cookhouse and hadn't noticed them. "Mount up now and git," Gil whispered. "I'll be there directly." She had no time to ask him any questions even though she was bursting with them. But his grave expression was enough to quell her curiosity for the moment, until she could be sure no one was about.

"You won't be long?" was all she said as she gathered up the reins.

"Quicker'n a snake's bite," he replied with a swift smile. He slapped the mare's rump, and Columbine took off with Juliana leaning low in the saddle. She didn't look back, didn't see Gil heading toward his horse in the corral—and didn't see John Breen and Bart Mueller turn in time to notice her riding away.

It was hot in the sun when she reached the creek. The

water gurgled quietly beside the softly waving grasses of pale green and yellow. High red rocks piled up beside a yucca told her she was in the right place. The mountains rose beyond, towering granite walls that shimmered in amethyst splendor beneath the sun. Juliana dismounted and breathed a sigh of pleasure in the solitude of this lonely, beauteous spot.

From above came the sweet chirping of birds, but otherwise it was quiet, save for the murmuring water and the rustling of cottonwood leaves. The sky was so bright a blue, it hurt her eyes to look at it, and she immediately unbuttoned the bright red jacket of her riding habit and slipped it off, loosening the gray silk neckerchief about her throat as well. Her white linen blouse stuck damply to her skin, making her glance longingly at the creek, but she had no time to splash water on her face, or even to cup her hands and take a drink, for no sooner had she tethered Columbine to a nearby cottonwood than a horse and rider charged into the clearing. She hurried forward as Gil swung down from his saddle.

"Breen's fired me," he said without preamble. "You heard that?"

"Yes, I heard, but what I don't understand, Gil, is why? If there was some kind of mix-up . . ."

"There was no mix-up. He set it up deliberately so I'd get the wrong orders from Mueller, and not show up where I was needed. For some reason, he wants me off the ranch."

Gil was looking at her oddly, squinting beneath his hat, and Juliana suddenly remembered the night at the party when Mueller had said something to John Breen and Breen had immediately glanced over at Gil—that had happened right after she and Gil had had a long conversation. The horrible thought that Gil had been fired because of her made her blood turn cold.

"Something strange has been going on with Breen,"

Gil went on with a shake of his head. "I've heard a lot of rumors about him maybe . . . gettin' married. And all of the cowhands have been ordered to stay away from the ranch house—and the visitors."

Juliana felt the color draining from her face. "So it's true," she whispered. "He's made some arrangement with my uncle—and he doesn't want me to hear of it yet —and Gil . . ." She felt anger welling up within her. "You were fired merely because we struck up a friendship that night!"

He took a few turns about the clearing, his head bent in thought. "Maybe—maybe not. There's a few other reasons he might want to get rid of me, Juliana. I know some things about his way of operating, things that stick in my craw. You could say Mr. Breen and me have differin' philosophies."

Juliana paid no attention to the squirrel that darted through the brush beside her, startling the horses. She was watching Gil's troubled face. "What do you mean?"

"Oh, I reckon we don't agree on the right way to go about acquiring other people's land—and businesses. Mr. Breen has his own method of getting people to sell out to him. He plays rough, Juliana. And he always manages to get a real low price for what he wants. By the time he's through, folks are ready and eager to sell to him and glad to still be alive."

Stunned, she stared at him in growing horror. "He coerces them. Isn't that what you mean? Then you're saying he's dishonest," she cried, her eyes widening as she stared up at the red-haired cowhand.

"I ain't got proof of anything—but I will tell you that Breen's a dangerous man—ruthless as any I've seen. If he's built his whole empire using the kinds of tactics he's employed right here in Colorado, then he's not a man to tangle with lightly." He grimaced, and the toe of his boot scuffed at the dust. "I've been askin' a few questions about him . . . and I reckon he heard about it and didn't take too kindly to my curiosity. It all boils down to the fact that he's ordered me off the ranch." He regarded her searchingly. "That doesn't matter much, but I'm worried about you." He reached out suddenly and gripped her hands. "Is it true that you're going to marry him? Mueller let something slip to Shorty McMillen and the story's spread through the bunkhouse like wildfire."

"I am not going to marry him," Juliana flashed, her jaw tightening. "Though my uncle might think otherwise."

Quickly she told Gil about her own suspicions of the arranged marriage, ending with "I will have to make it clear to my uncle that I absolutely won't go along with his plans. He may try to force me, though. He is my legal guardian."

"He'd do somethin' like that?" Gil asked as she turned away and walked to the edge of the creek. Shaking his head, he followed her.

"Oh, yes." There was a bitter look in her eyes. "He'll no doubt tell me that I owe it to him to do as he wishes, since he has supported me all of my life. He may even threaten to cast me out if I don't marry John Breen. And in a way he's right." Her voice dipped lower. "I do owe Aunt Katharine and Uncle Edward a great deal—they have cared for me since I was a child. But," Juliana said, turning and gazing back at Gil with a forlorn expression, "I can't repay them by marrying a man I don't even like —much less trust. If necessary"—she swallowed, realizing the impact her rebellion could have upon her life from this moment on—"I'll leave my uncle's house and his protection and . . . set out on my own. But I can't agree to be tied to a man I find repugnant."

Gil's heart nearly burst with pity for this lovely, delicate girl who looked so unhappy. Juliana Montgomery deserved to be loved, protected, not thrown out to that snake, Breen, by her greedy, bootlicking uncle. He cast about for something to say that would ease the pain reflected in her face, then remembered what he'd been aiming to tell her all along. Grinning, tilting her face up to his, he cocked an eyebrow at her. "Maybe it'd cheer you to know that I got a handle on those brothers of yours."

Her emerald eyes lit with dazzling hope. "Oh, tell me Wade and Tommy are in Colorado," she begged fervently, clutching his hand.

Gil was almost too distracted by her touch and closeness to recollect what they'd been talking about, but her radiant face recalled him to the subject at hand. Her brothers. Dang it. He'd give a whole hell of a lot to have her be that interested in his whereabouts and doings. "Easy now," he drawled after a moment of gazing into those luminous eyes. "I don't know precisely where they are, but I can tell you this—they're alive, knee-deep in trouble, and were last seen somewheres in the Arizona Territory."

"Where in the Arizona Territory? When? Who saw them?" She fired the questions at him in rapid succession, her eyes wide and searching.

"Whoa, there." The lopsided grin split his freckled features. "For a little lady, you've sure got a pile of questions. Problem is, Juliana, I've only got a few answers. A gambler in Miss Hetty's Saloon told me he'd run across the Montgomery gang in Tombstone 'bout two months back. Played poker with 'em. All of a sudden the boys lit out—it seems there was a posse after 'em. A little matter of a payroll holdup."

A payroll holdup. Juliana bit her lip. She moved away from Gil, farther along the edge of the creek, and stared down into the tumbling water. She had read the newspaper reports, heard Uncle Edward's condemnations, even told Gil herself that Wade and Tommy were desperadoes, but it hadn't seemed as real as it did now, with Gil talk-

ing to her about a payroll robbery and a posse. Dear
heaven, what had happened to them that they had become hardened outlaws, wanted men? She fought down
the impulse to cry in despair. If the law and the posses
and the bounty hunters like Cole Rawdon couldn't find
them, what chance did she have?

*But I must find them. I shall. It's more important to
me than to anyone else and I'm going to do it.*

"Juliana." Gil came up behind her and laid a hand
tentatively upon her shoulder. "I'm sorry. I didn't mean
to upset you . . ."

"You didn't."

He turned her to face him, placing both of his hands
upon her shoulders. "I reckon I did."

Fighting back her emotions, she shook her head. "It's
not your fault, it's just that . . . Oh, Gil, I'm
scared . . ."

Suddenly, John Breen's voice boomed down from an
outcrop of rock behind them. "Why the hell are you still
on my property, Keedy?"

Juliana whirled about, so startled, she nearly fell into
the creek. Gil's hand steadied her and then he, too, swiveled about to glare at the intruder.

Silhouetted against the sun, John Breen looked like a
tall, fierce Viking. A Viking in black shirt, vest, and
pants, sporting cowboy boots, with a .45 strapped to his
gunbelt, Juliana thought. It was difficult to see his face
beneath the wide-brimmed Stetson, but from his voice
and the tense way his fists were clenched at his side, she
knew he was in no mood for cordiality. Fear trickled into
her heart, not for herself but for Gil, who stood very
straight and tall beside her.

"I stopped to talk to Miss Montgomery." She was
amazed at how calm he sounded. Her heart was still
thumping wildly. Breen had startled her out of her wits.
"Only you're not my boss anymore, are you, Mister

Breen?" Gil went on in his lazy way. "So I reckon it's no concern of yours what I do."

"You're on my land. That's my concern. You were warned to leave."

"It's my fault," Juliana spoke up, raising her voice as she addressed the fair-haired man staring down at them. "I waylaid Gil at the ranch and asked him to meet me here."

For a moment Breen frowned but said nothing. Abruptly, he climbed down into the clearing, jumping the last few feet with lithe grace. His face had an angry flush to it; the deep-set eyes were hard and narrow.

"Why?" he demanded, his gaze scorching her.

"I overheard you fire him and I . . . wanted to talk to him about his plans for the future." *As if it's any of your business whom I talk to or why.* But she didn't want to antagonize Breen further at this moment when he was staring at Gil as if he could shoot him on the spot.

"You shouldn't be out here alone with varmints like this one." His tone was curt, but whatever anger he felt toward Juliana he was suppressing for the time being. He swung toward Gil, a muscle throbbing in his neck. "Keedy, get out. Now, before I change my mind."

"Sure," Gil drawled, with mocking slowness. "But first I'll see Miss Montgomery back to the house. I don't cotton to leaving a lady alone when there's snakes and coyotes about." Gil directed an unmistakably meaningful stare at his former employer, a stare Breen had no trouble interpreting as the insult it was.

"Why, you damned insolent whelp," Breen swore softly. His face changed, hardening into an ugly mask of wrath. Before Juliana even realized what was happening, Breen's fist shot out and connected with a sickening blow to Gil's nose. The force of it sent the cowboy reeling backward against a tree, blood spouting down the front of his blue shirt. John Breen sprang toward him and hit him again, a cruel blow to the stomach. When Gil doubled over, Breen kicked him in the face, then shoved him sideways to the ground.

Screaming, Juliana flung herself down beside him, but Gil pushed her aside. He stumbled to his feet, dazed and bleeding, but furious enough to keep fighting. John Breen laughed.

"Too stupid to quit, eh, Keedy?"

"Stop it, you'll kill him," Juliana cried, trying to get between the two men. "Don't you dare strike him again . . ."

Gil stumbled around her and started toward Breen with deadly rage in his eyes, but a gunshot thundered out, echoing sharp and clear among the towering rocks above. Gil froze where he stood, inches from John Breen.

"Don't touch him, kid," Bart Mueller called down from the rocks above. His rifle was pointed straight at the red-haired cowboy's head.

Beside Mueller stood two other men, guns drawn and at the ready.

Juliana, pale as ice, sucked in her breath.

"Last chance, Keedy." John Breen's chillingly pleasant tone made Juliana's flesh crawl. "Clear out now or the boys'll have to shoot you for trespassing."

Gil was gasping for breath. Blood streamed down his face and neck. He wiped at it with his sleeve. "I'm not . . . leaving her here alone . . . with you," he rasped out.

"I'm all right, Gil. Please, don't worry about me." Juliana ran to him and gingerly touched his arm, gazing in sickened horror at his bloody, pain-racked face. She was shaking all over, but she managed to keep her voice steady as she swallowed and said in a low tone, "Please, just go—you should see a doctor."

He was coughing now, spitting up blood. Juliana was terrified for him—and fearful that if Gil didn't leave without more trouble, Mueller or one of the others would shoot him. Her glance flew upward to the armed men on the rocks above, then to John Breen's taut face, and she knew she had to get Gil away quickly. "Please, I'll be fine," she rushed on, her fingers gripping his imploringly. "If you stay . . . there will just be more trouble and I couldn't bear that! He won't hurt me. Please, just go!"

"If I were you, I'd listen to the lady," Breen recommended with a cold smile.

Gil glanced from him to Mueller and his companions, then drew in a painful breath. "You're sure?" he managed in a low voice to Juliana.

"Yes, yes. Don't worry about me. I'm so sorry for all this."

"Ain't no need to be sorry." Gil tried to grin. "Breen got in a lucky punch," he grunted. "Surprised me, that's all."

Men and their ridiculous, overbloated sense of pride! Juliana nearly stamped her foot in frustration, but she managed to stay perfectly still as Gil walked slowly to his horse. It hurt her to see him injured and bleeding, and she wanted to strike out at John Breen. But she didn't move, determined not to do or say anything until Gil was safely away. How he managed to mount she didn't know, but at last, with a small salute to her, he rode out of the clearing. He didn't bother to glance at John Breen, waiting patiently with his thumbs hooked in his pockets. When Gil's slumped figure disappeared down the craggy slope, she let out a long breath.

Sunshine poured down. The day was still, beautiful, filled with fragile beauty. And ripe with danger. Juliana felt it all around her, throbbing beneath the surface. She faced John Breen in the clearing with no trace of the apprehension she was feeling showing on her face.

"Do you still need those men for protection?" she inquired softly, but there were daggers in her eyes. She

smoothed a wayward curl from her face and met his stare
with icy hauteur. "I've no gun, Mr. Breen, and I'm sure if
we came to blows, you could defeat me."

His jaw clenched. Dark rage suffused his face, and for
a moment she feared he would indeed strike her, but then
the blackness faded from his expression as quickly as it
had come, and instead he waved an arm and ordered
Mueller and his companions to leave.

"You sure are something," he said when they were
completely alone in the clearing. The gurgling of the
creek sounded loud to Juliana's ears. "You've got more
spunk than ten other women put together. When I saw
you with Keedy, I wanted to blow that boy's head off."

"Mr. Breen, let me make one thing clear."

"No." He grasped her by the arms and jerked her forward so suddenly that her hat fell off. "Let me make
something clear, Juliana. It's John—not Mr. Breen. It's
going to sound mighty silly for a married woman to call
her husband mister."

A hawk wheeled overhead, its shrill cry piercing the
air in a forlorn call. Juliana envied that hawk its freedom.
It could soar away, far, far into the distant treetops on
the farthest peaks. She stared at John Breen, wishing at
that moment that she was a hawk, or even an ordinary
wren or a sparrow. Anything that could spread wings
and leave this man and this isolated place behind.

She chose her words carefully, wary of the intensity
she saw glinting in his eyes. Her hair tumbled loose about
her small face, and she saw his gaze upon it. His glance
shifted to her mouth, staring at its softness. She made her
voice as hard and crisp as she could. "If this is a proposal, Mr. Breen, I thank you. However, I must decline
your most flattering offer—and request that you escort
me back to the ranch house at once."

"Decline? Oh, no. You're speaking out of haste, honey,
and that's not good for either of us. You're a bit more

skittish than I expected, Juliana," he went on, with a short laugh. "I'm not doing this the way I planned—but seeing you with that no-good cowboy made me lose my head. I can't bear it for another man to look at you, talk to you. This was going to be a slow courtship, but I'm not as good at waiting for things as I used to be. I've gotten used to getting what I want—and there's no doubt about it, honey, I want you."

His fingers tightened around her arms. He drew her closer, and smiled down into her outraged face. "Maybe you're a mite stubborn, Juliana, but I'm willing to overlook it. You're beautiful, and feisty as hell, and I'm going to have the time of my life taming you." As she started to struggle frantically against his restraining embrace, Breen pinned her arms behind her, grinning. "I know females. You like to put on airs, and act as if you couldn't care less about a man, but what you really want is to be chased, caught, and conquered. Well, I've caught you—now comes the conquering part. You know as well as I do that deep down, this is what you've been wanting me to do," he murmured, and brought his lips down on hers in a bruising, greedy kiss that forced her head back and robbed her of all her breath.

Juliana tried to twist her head away, but he held her fast, and his mouth covered hers. Sickening revulsion filled her. She strained to break free but he suppressed her every movement and the kiss seemed to go on forever. His mouth was wet. His mustache scratched her face. The smell of his hair pomade sickened her as she struggled against his restraining arms. When he at last lifted his head, licking his lips at the taste of her, Juliana thought she would go mad with the urge to strike him.

"Animal! Let me go!" she cried, trembling with rage and frustration, but he appeared not to hear her.

"I've been wanting to do that since the first time I saw you."

"If you don't let me go, I'll . . ."

"You'll what?" he mocked, tightening his grip on her to make clear her helplessness. "Honey, I admire your spirit, but you can't win in a battle against me. You might as well just give in and enjoy it. As soon as you stop indulging these innocent airs of yours, you're going to make me a damned fine wife. I'll be the envy of every man this side of the Panhandle."

"For the last time, I will not marry you!"

He kissed the tip of her nose. "You'll do as your uncle tells you, Juliana, and he'll do as I tell him. It's all settled and agreed upon. Now if you don't hanker to living out West all the time, that's no problem. I conduct a great deal of business in the East—we can travel to New York, Chicago, Philadelphia, and a number of other cities a good many months of the year. Europe, too. My holdings are expanding all the time. You're not exactly going to be stuck in Denver for the rest of your life, so don't trouble your head over that. But Twin Oaks is special to me and that's where I'll expect you to raise our son."

"You're loco, Mr. Breen—as they say in these parts," she spit out, and tried to kick his ankles.

But to her chagrin he seemed unperturbed by her vehemence and immune to her booted feet. "Loco about you, honey," he said warmly. He was going to kiss her again. She read it in his eyes.

"I've decided the wedding will be Saturday." Breen shifted his grasp on her, so that with one hand he could stroke the tangled softness of her hair. He lowered his handsome, smugly smiling face toward hers with exquisite slowness. "No need to let any grass grow under our feet. Soon as the ceremony's done, we can send those relatives of yours packing and get down to the business of a honeymoon."

His lips were inches from hers. She felt the tension in his body and sensed the desire consuming him. Something told her he wouldn't stop with a kiss this time. Sure enough, even as he planted his mouth to hers, his hand groped at her breast. Desperate Juliana pushed against his chest with all her might.

Even as she did so, she remembered something—something Wade had taught her when she was seven years old. A technique she'd needed when the bullying nine-year-old son of an Independence blacksmith had made her life miserable. A technique that had sent the blacksmith's boy crashing to the dirt, whimpering like a beaten puppy. A technique so successful, she wondered how she could have forgotten it. It involved a swift, hard lunge of the knee against a particular part of the male body, and she executed it now against John Breen with every ounce of her strength, bringing her knee up with such a vengeance that he yelled in agony. She felt his body quiver with pain and a surge of triumph ran through her.

Then, gloriously, he released her, and sank down upon the grass. Juliana leapt free and bolted toward her horse.

Breen was still moaning on the ground when she wheeled Columbine about in the clearing, but she didn't even spare him a second glance. As she spurred the mare to a gallop and headed away from the creek as fast as Columbine could carry her, she had a momentary feeling of euphoria, but as the scrub brush and wildflowers flashed past, the feeling faded, replaced by somber dread. Everything was happening too swiftly for her. Things were out of control. She had to reason with Uncle Edward quickly, and get them all away from Twin Oaks as soon as possible. When her uncle heard how despicably John Breen had behaved, what he had done to Gil Keedy, and how obsessed he was with marrying her— even against her wishes—surely he would think twice about the arrangements he had made. Juliana trembled as she rode. She knew John Breen wanted her, but it certainly wasn't because he loved her. The man didn't even *know* her. No, John Breen loved the image of her—he wanted her because she was young and pretty and elegant, he wanted her because she was something he would like to possess, to pet and play with, a prize to flaunt before the world.

Back in St. Louis young men had been charmed by her, captivated, but her background had disqualified her as a possible bride. Here in Denver, John Breen thought her a treasure above all others and no doubt wouldn't give a hoot about her mother's past or her brothers' exploits. He wanted someone with society manners whom he could show off to his friends—and a beautiful ornament he could toy with in his bed.

Juliana vowed that he would have neither. At least, not from her. Not as long as she had a single breath left in her body.

She dug her heels into Columbine's flanks and rode for the ranch.

Uncle Edward faced her alone in Breen's library. His skin was ashen, but his face was set and calm as he stood before the massive shelves of leather-bound books. "It's quite true, Juliana," he informed her, his round eyes nearly expressionless. "The matter is settled. John Breen has offered to make you his wife."

Between clenched teeth, she managed to lash out a response. "I decline!"

He sent her a reproving look and smoothed the lapel of his coat. He blocked her view of the diamond-blue afternoon sky as he turned and paced to the window, staring out at the rough landscape. "Too late, Juliana. I have already accepted on your behalf."

Pain throbbed in her temples. She clutched the back of a chair for support. "You had no right, Uncle Edward!"

"On the contrary, as your legal guardian, I have every right." He turned and smiled bleakly at her. "And I know that once you have had a chance to get accustomed to the idea, you will see that it is a splendid opportunity for you."

"An opportunity for *you*—isn't that what you really mean, Uncle Edward?" she cried scornfully.

He had the grace to flush. His gaze dropped. Through the pain in her chest, Juliana managed to speak in a flat, even tone.

"I won't marry him. You can't force me."

He pushed his spectacles higher on his nose and squared his shoulders. "You're wrong, Juliana. Until you are twenty-one, I am your legal guardian and my actions are quite proper and legal. I am taking sensible steps to insure your future. Of course, your aunt and Victoria and I will miss you a great deal, but we would never stand in the way of what is best. And John has assured me that he will bring you to St. Louis for a visit within the year."

"I will not marry John Breen!" she shouted.

A sound at the door made her wheel about.

John Breen stood there, fingering his mustache.

"Your spirit does you proud, Juliana, but it's beginning to grate on my nerves." He came forward into the room, ignoring Uncle Edward, keeping his gaze riveted on the furious girl before him. Sunlight streamed in the window, glinting upon his fair hair and handsome features. "It's time to stop fighting your uncle and me," he said curtly. "Pretty soon you'll come to realize we know what's best for you."

She stared at him as the throbbing in her temples grew unbearable. "Why would you want a woman who doesn't want *you*?" she whispered.

He smiled at her as if she were an adorable though wayward child. "You do want me, honey. You just don't know it yet."

She ran past him and pounded up the stairs to her room. She slammed the door and threw herself facedown on the pillow, shaking with helpless rage. She had never felt so trapped, so frightened.

Even when she was a child and her parents had been killed, she had always known that there was someone to take care of her—Wade and Tommy, or Uncle Edward and Aunt Katharine. Now she had no one. No one cared. No one would do a thing to prevent her from being condemned to this marriage. No one would lift a finger to save her from being tied for the rest of her life to John Breen.

No one except herself.

Still trembling, Juliana sat up and dashed the tears from her eyes. She began desperately to plan.

· 5 ·

Juliana was watched closely the next days. She was not permitted to ride—all the horses were needed by the hands, John Breen told her. She was kept from going to town—the buggy was in need of repair, according to her fiancé. And she was not allowed to spend time alone —Aunt Katharine or Victoria continually followed her about and remained glued to her side for hours, chattering about the wedding plans as if nothing were amiss, as if she were the happiest, most eager bride-to-be in the world.

Juliana could scarcely bear to look at them. Aunt Katharine blithely ignored Juliana's grim silence, and rattled on about how fortunate her niece was to be marrying a man as handsome and wealthy as John Breen. Victoria pouted that she hoped everyone would make this much of a fuss when *she* decided to marry—quite ignoring the fact that Juliana had decided nothing whatever for herself. And John Breen set in motion a series of plans for the wedding and honeymoon, complete with extravagant festivities, oblivious of his intended's stony lack of interest in all that went on about her. To Juliana's relief, he made no more effort to be alone with her, apparently deciding it best not to pressure her further before the wedding. Juliana guessed he expected that by the time the vows were said and the wedding ring placed upon her finger she would face up to the reality of the situation and accept her position as his wife.

Well, we'll just see about that, Juliana thought the evening before the wedding as she stood at her window gazing out at the gold and lavender sunset spreading delicately across the sky.

The mountaintops glowed a soft, misty purple beneath the shimmering light. She stared at the distant peaks with a mingling of yearning and trepidation. Tomorrow this time she would be traveling by stagecoach somewhere in those mountains. Whatever dangers might await her, they would have to be faced and conquered, for they would be preferable, far preferable, to the certainty of the fate awaiting her here. Somehow she would get to Tombstone and try to track down where Wade and Tommy had gone. John Breen would set out after her, she knew, but if she could get away quickly, he would give up before long, and she would be free to search for her brothers, to start a new life with them.

If only Gil were still here, Juliana reflected as she turned away from the window and began to pace the room, scowling when her eye fell upon the ivory brocade wedding gown draped across the bed, a dreamy vision whipped up by Denver's best seamstress for tomorrow's occasion. Gil might have been able to help her, she thought wistfully, but he had left Twin Oaks the day Breen had driven him off, and there had been no sign of him since. She hoped he was all right. At least he was free of Twin Oaks, she thought with a sigh. She only hoped she would be so lucky.

Somehow she would have to pull off this plan of hers by herself.

She took a deep breath, trying to calm the fears somersaulting inside her stomach. There was a quick knock on the door of her room, and before Juliana could speak, Victoria stepped inside.

"Mama asked me to tell you that supper is being served and everyone is waiting for you downstairs," Victoria blurted out, frowning at her cousin's state of deshabille. Juliana's slender figure was enticingly draped in a pink satin dressing gown; her small, pretty feet were bare. She appeared ready for bed, not for supper.

"You'd best hurry," Victoria snapped. "Mr. Breen is eager to see you, and he looks especially handsome tonight."

"Well, I have a headache and won't be coming down to supper." Juliana went to her dressing table, and, sitting down, began with quick strokes to brush her hair. "You may give my regrets to Mr. Breen, Tory. He'll simply have to wait until the wedding ceremony in the morning to drool over me."

Instead of flouncing out in a huff to carry the message as Juliana expected her to do, Victoria came into the room. She was studying her cousin's set, pale face reflected in the oval dressing table mirror, and she gave her dark head a tiny shake.

"I don't understand you, Juliana."

"I know you don't."

"One would think you were the first girl in the world whose family arranged a marriage for her. Why, Dorinda St. Clair's parents did the same thing last summer and even though she didn't care two figs for Harold Lovelace, she welcomed the match. And their wedding was splendid. I never saw anything like it. But even Harold Lovelace can't compare to Mr. Breen. Mr. Breen has more money than half of the best families in St. Louis combined! And," she added, wagging a finger at her cousin, "he doesn't mind a bit about your brothers' exploits, Juliana. He did a complete investigation of your background even before we arrived here, Papa learned, and merely laughed when he was told of the scandal. 'Everyone has skeletons in their closets,' he told Papa. 'So long as your niece conducts herself as a lady and presents only clean linen to the world, I don't give a damn about those brothers of hers.' So you see, you ought to be grateful for this match. No man in St. Louis would be as broad-minded as that!"

"How admirable," Juliana bit out between clenched teeth. She threw the brush down and jumped up to face her cousin. "Did it never occur to you, Victoria, that I might wish to choose my own husband—if I want a husband at all! Marriage need not be the sole goal of womankind. And marriage to a man one doesn't like . . . or trust . . ." She broke off at her cousin's sneering expression. "Never mind. I can see that you will never understand," she cried.

Victoria grabbed her wrist. "I understand that you are being most selfish. Papa tried to do what is best for you—and he feels quite sad that you aren't happy about it. Can't you—for his sake—even *try* to put on a smiling countenance? This should be a happy time for him. His business dealings with Mr. Breen will make him a *very* rich man, and at the same time, he is discharging his responsibility to you in a most beneficial way—why, you'll want for nothing! You'll be the envy of everyone back home! But you," she said scathingly, her skin shining dully in the fading pool of light, "you fail to show him any gratitude for it! Or for the years that he and Mama have given to raising, clothing, and feeding you! I think you're hideous, Juliana! You don't deserve John Breen, you don't deserve this beautiful dress, and you don't deserve one whit of pity. I'm glad that we shall be rid of you after tomorrow—and I know that Mama and Papa will be glad too."

Juliana's eyes stung with tears. "You're right about one thing, Tory. You will be rid of me after tomorrow."

"It can't come soon enough for me," her cousin shot back, ignoring the pain in the other girl's face. Victoria turned on her heel and walked to the door. "I'll give Mr. Breen your message," she flung over her shoulder. "No doubt he will be most displeased."

Not as displeased as he's going to be, Juliana cried silently as the door slammed behind Victoria. She covered her face as hot tears flowed down her cheeks. Victoria's words had hurt more than she thought possible. So did the knowledge that her escape would enrage Uncle Edward and spoil his dreams of uncountable wealth. Was she so selfish that she would deny her uncle the vast success this alliance with John Breen would produce? What was wrong with her that she couldn't accept her lot in life and do as she was bidden? Maybe, she thought, on a gulp of misery, she should stay and make the best of this stupid marriage.

But at the thought of it a sick shaking overtook her. No. John Breen was an unsavory man, despite his smooth good looks, his impeccable fancy clothes, his wealth. And if the suspicions Gil had voiced about him were true, he was ruthless and crooked as well. She wasn't prepared to sacrifice herself to a man like that just to please her relations. Uncle Edward and Aunt Katharine had always had quite enough money to live in an elegant fashion, and they would simply have to continue in that mode, making do without the boundless grandeur they envisioned.

She strode to the bed and flung the exquisite ivory gown onto the floor. She was leaving. Tonight. And no one had better try to stop her.

* * *

She went at midnight. The ranch house was silent but
for the creaking of the floorboards and the moaning
whisper of wind against the windowpanes. Juliana tiptoed down the long flight of steps, carpetbag in hand, and
slipped through the darkened hall to the kitchen. The
kitchen door squeaked as she pulled it open, and Juliana's breath caught in her throat. Bright moonlight illuminated her path to the barn, filling her with apprehension that she would be outlined clearly to anyone
glancing outside, as she made her way around the vegetable gardens and past the stone well.

Several horses whinnied when she slid loose the bolt on
the barn door and ducked inside. It took a few moments
for her eyes to adjust to the darkness, but she dared not
use a lantern. She counted the stalls until she came to
Columbine's, then calmed the horse with a lump of sugar
and a few loving pats before hoisting the heavy saddle
into place. It took only a few moments to strap the gray
carpetbag to the saddle and lead the mare from the barn,
but every second seemed a lifetime of suspense.

She used a fence post to mount and swung into the
saddle, scarcely able to breathe. At any moment she expected to hear a shout, to find herself confronted by Bart
Mueller or John Breen himself. But when at last she sat
atop the mare and stared out at the moon-frosted land
before her, every nerve in her body started to tingle. She
urged Columbine to a gallop, leaning low over her mane,
and rode like fire across the plain, never looking back.

It wasn't Denver she headed for. That was the first
place Breen and Uncle Edward would look. Juliana's destination was Amber Falls, a little town seventeen miles
west. She was gambling that it was on the stagecoach
line, and that from there she could cross the Rockies to
the Arizona border. In her reticule was the handful of
gold she had sneaked from Uncle Edward's money pouch
under his mattress while everyone was downstairs at sup-

per. She had left in its place the pearl earbobs Aunt Katharine and Uncle Edward had given her on her nineteenth birthday. No doubt they would still call her a thief when they found out—a thief like her brothers—but Juliana was beyond caring what anyone thought. She gripped the reins more tightly and leaned forward with a little cry of exultation, reveling in the slap of the wind against her cheeks. The mare's legs tore at the earth, faster and faster, while the moon sailed overhead. And Juliana's heart swelled with the elation of a trapped creature set free.

But there was fear in her as well, a fear she had to fight to control. She would have only one chance for freedom. She couldn't slow down, couldn't hesitate, couldn't make a single mistake. Every second counted.

By dawn the search would begin.

·6·

Deathly silence surrounded Twin Oaks as John Breen confronted his foreman in the privacy of his library. Ice-cold calm gripped the tall man with the deep-set topaz eyes. Outside there was an unnatural peace: the hands had all ridden out on the range, glad to put distance between themselves and the uproar that had ensued only an hour earlier. No sounds came from the barns or the sheds or the cookhouse, not even a horse whinnied in the corral. Inside the walnut-paneled library, there was no such illusion of peace. Unspoken rage flickered through the room like the crack of a bullwhip. Breen's eyes glittered with a menace that went far beyond what Gil Keedy had experienced by the banks of Durham's Creek.

"Find her."

Bart Mueller nodded. "Yes, sir."

"Be discreet—but *find her*. And fast." Breen shot the words out like rapid-fire bullets. "There's a five-hundred-dollar bonus for you when she's delivered to my door."

Mueller nodded, eagerly turning his hat in his hand.

The muscles of his thick neck tightened in excitement as he anticipated the spending of that reward. He watched his boss with expectant eyes all the while, knowing how dangerous, how cruelly clever Breen was when he was in this mood. The expression on his face was as ruthless, as icily furious as Mueller had ever seen it.

"What do you want me to do, boss?"

Breen stalked up and down the hardwood floor, his thumbs hooked in the pockets of his vest. Despite the rage storming through him like a winter squall, his brain clicked along with relentless precision. He had already sent that idiot Tobias and his sniveling wife and daughter packing, the business contracts ripped to hell. Tobias was lucky he hadn't been shot instead of just run off. But deep down, even through his fury, Breen knew it wasn't Tobias's fault. It was the girl, that damned stuck-up little girl who had run off and made a fool out of him in front of the whole damned town.

Well, she would pay. Breen's mouth watered at the thought. When he dragged her back into this house, he'd make her pay. There'd be no marriage this time around. It would be all fun and games. His fun, his games. Then he'd turn her over to the sheriff on charges of horse theft.

A tight little smile twisted the corners of his lips. Who was to say she hadn't also stolen money from his safe, as well as the damned horse? Five thousand dollars ought to do it. The boys could plant it on her when they found her, and she could serve a nice long jail sentence—after he finished with her, of course.

Breen felt no qualms about framing the girl he'd only yesterday planned on making his wife. That little bitch deserved whatever she got. If she wanted to act like a no-good back-stabbing whore, he'd treat her like one. It wouldn't be the first time he'd been forced to get rough with a woman. He remembered another time, another woman who'd gone loco on him and tried to blow a hole

in his chest. But he'd taken care of her. Just like he'd
taken care of the kid. . . .

Breen's gaze clouded over for a moment, then he
jerked himself out of his reverie. That was all a long time
ago. He'd come a long way since those grub-grabbing,
desperate days.

But his craving for revenge against those who had
wronged him was still as vital as it had ever been. Now
every ounce of that potent deadly hate was turned against
the golden-haired bitch who'd sneaked out on him on
their wedding day.

"Mueller, you nose around in town and see if there's
any sign of her. Put out the word that I called off the
wedding yesterday, that I found out in time she was a
fortune-hunting little slut. Say that she ran off this morning with the mare and five thousand dollars in cash. And
send some boys over to Mottsville and Amber Falls," he
ordered, mentally reviewing all the places Juliana Montgomery might have gone. His shoulders were hunched
with tension, despite the evenness of his voice. "She can't
get far, not if we're quick and thorough about it. But if
for some reason you don't find her . . ." His voice
trailed off. A fearsome silence hovered in the air. Breen's
lips clamped together in an expression of grim determination. An odd little glow that Mueller recognized entered
his eyes.

"Yes, sir?" Mueller shifted from one foot to the other.
"If we don't find her, what should we do next?"

"Go to Judge Mason and tell him I want a bounty put
out on Miss Juliana Montgomery." Breen was smiling
now, a harsh, humorless smile that Mueller nevertheless
found contagious. "Offer a two-thousand-dollar reward
for her return to Denver. Make sure the posters specify
that I want her alive."

Mueller whistled. "Two thousand dollars. Bounty

hunters from here to California will be murdering each other to get their hands on her."

Breen nodded. *Precisely.* He turned away from Mueller, and his glance swept across the large, princely room, from the floor-to-ceiling shelves of handsome leather books, to the rich walnut paneling and imported Chinese carpet on his perfectly polished floor. Everything was in place, everything was magnificent, from the mahogany grandfather clock in the corner to the gleaming bronze chandelier overhead. Everything looked as expensive and immaculate as he'd always dreamed. He'd gone through a lot to get himself all of this. He deserved it, every damned bit of it. And no highfalutin eastern snip of a girl was going to get the better of him. No one—man or woman—was going to make him feel like a loser ever again.

He was the greatest success story this territory, hell, this *country,* had ever known.

"That's what I want, Mueller," Breen said, fingering the gold signet ring on his perfectly manicured hand. "I want them itching to get their paws on her and frankly, I don't care what they do to her when they get her. So long as they bring her back still breathing. I want Juliana Montgomery to know and understand just what it means to cross me."

"She will, boss, I guarantee you that."

Mueller left. John Breen stood a moment longer, gazing around in cold satisfaction at the elegant possessions, drawing energy from their beauty.

A sense of power filled him, swelling through his arms, his chest, his bones, his very soul. No one could save Juliana Montgomery from him now. She was his, as surely as if she had spoken her marriage vows this morning. They would be bound together by something more than a mere wedding. They would be bound by revenge, by hate, by the sheer volume of his power. Those things would bind them for as long as he wanted her around. He would teach her about all of them before he was through. He would make her sorry she had ever set foot on man's green earth.

· 7 ·

The sun blazed like a torch above the ramshackle town of Cedar Gulch, deep within the territory of Arizona. Looming mountains slumbered in the hazy June heat. No wind stirred the dust in the narrow, dung-filled street, no color brightened the flat grayness of the dozen decrepit buildings along either side of a crumbling wooden boardwalk. Even the Red Snake Saloon was quiet, the gold-vested piano player passed out over his tinny keyboard. The town was smack-dab in the middle of nowhere, huddled beneath the lip of a towering granite mountain under the Mogollon Rim. Few lived in this godforsaken region of Arizona beneath the sheer towering red cliffs and pine forests of the Mogollon except a small collection of hardy souls eking out an existence along the stagecoach line. Juliana, sitting with her fellow passengers inside the dining room of the Tin Horn Hotel, could see why. The town was a forsaken, squalid pesthole, dwarfed by the wild, awesome landscape that surrounded it. Who could survive long here, amid the filth and isolation? The only people she had seen since they'd

arrived, other than the hotel proprietor—a thin, sullen
fellow who had served them greasy fried prairie chicken
and hardtack biscuits—were a trio of savage-looking men
who had ridden in like a swarm of hornets a few moments ago and headed straight for the saloon. Watching
them through the dining room window, Juliana had
shuddered. The men had looked filthy—and mean. They
were caked with dust, and she had a feeling they smelled
as bad as they looked. She wasn't exactly at her Sunday
best either, she reflected wryly, smoothing a hand over
her soiled, wrinkled muslin skirt, the delicate rose color
faded from repeated washings during the journey. She
knew she must look a sight. Though her face had been
scrubbed clean that morning, by now it felt gritty with
dust. How she longed for a basin of clean, cool water. At
least her hair was neatly combed and fastened in a
topknot, so as to keep her neck cool during the long and
arduous journey across this treacherous land. Reaching
up to secure a hairpin, she realized that several gold tendrils had escaped and were wisping about her face in a
disheveled fashion. So much for looking presentable. But
then, crossing the plateaus and canyons of Arizona was
not exactly a civilized venture. Grueling, dangerous, and
exhausting perhaps, but not very civilized.

Two months had passed since her escape from Denver.
During that time she had sold Columbine in Amber Falls
and traveled by stagecoach through the Colorado Rockies and down into the wild hills and canyons of Arizona,
passing through dozens of dirty towns like this one along
the way, each one miles from any other glimpse of civilization. During all this time Juliana had kept mostly to
herself, conversing little with the other passengers on the
journey. At first she had been in constant fear that John
Breen would come galloping up to overtake the stagecoach, that he would throw open the door and demand
that she get out and go back with him to Denver. Thank-

fully, nothing of the sort had come to pass, and by the time she neared the Arizona border, she had begun to feel safe. John Breen may have had his men search for her for a time, but he must have given up before long, she had reasoned. By the time she reached the border, she felt convinced she was well beyond his reach. No doubt he had forgotten all about her, and as for Aunt Katharine and Uncle Edward, well, they would have gone back to St. Louis empty-handed—and, she thought morosely, furious.

Well, there was no help for it now. She had severed every tie with those who had raised her and with the only home she had known. Her stomach felt queasy every time she reflected on the enormity of what she'd done, and guilt plagued her when she thought of Uncle Edward's disappointment. But every time she thought of John Breen, his perfect smile, his grating air of patronizing warmth, and, most chillingly of all, his viciousness to Gil Keedy, she was thankful she had had the courage to act —and thankful she had escaped. Now, Juliana told herself as she took a final sip of coffee, every time her limbs ached after a torturous day in the stagecoach, every time her parched throat cried out for water when there was no water to be had, and every time she despaired of ever finding Wade and Tommy, she had to keep looking ahead. She had to think about Wade and Tommy, about settling down with them in a little house on a ranch somewhere, far away from John Breen, Uncle Edward, and everyone else. She had to think about cool starry nights on the prairie, and meadows of flowers, and a house of her own with lace curtains at the windows. And she had to think about her beloved older brothers coming home to that little house each day with fresh game for supper, complimenting her on her rhubarb pie, and playing checkers before a fire in the evening. Such dreamy thoughts had sustained her during the many long hours of grueling travel, and they would have to sustain her for as long as it took to find Wade and Tommy.

Starting out, the journey by stagecoach hadn't been as difficult as she had expected—they had met no Indians, or desperadoes, or trouble of any sort during the first leg of the trip—the twisting mountain trails and long hours in the cramped and stuffy coach had provided their share of discomfort, but her sore muscles and fatigue would be worth it, she had reminded herself many times, once she was reunited with her brothers.

In a grimy border settlement ten miles east of where Colorado met the Arizona territory, during a midday break in the journey, disaster had struck. When the passengers alighted to stretch their legs and drink a cup of coffee, a pickpocket had stolen Juliana's purse. By the time she realized what had happened, the culprit could not be found. Juliana, to her shock, was left penniless on the boardwalk, with nothing left of value except a few small pieces of jewelry, including the small locket that was the only memento of her mother, and a hair comb of ivory and pearls that she had worn to her first coming-out party. But the gold was gone, and with it her means of supporting herself until she reached Tombstone. Despair had almost overcome her. To have eluded John Breen and his search party, to have come all this way, and then to find herself stranded without money at the Arizona border, made her want to weep. But she hadn't wept, Juliana reminded herself as she shooed a fly from her hardtack biscuit and gazed out at the desolation of Cedar Gulch. She had continued on by stagecoach to the next large town, and there had found herself a job in a flea-bitten hotel. She had swept floors, laundered bed linens, and helped in the kitchen, saving up her weekly wages with excruciating care. After just a little more than a month she had enough to continue on her journey, and the money would get her all the way to Tombstone, if she was careful.

She would be careful, she promised herself as she set down her empty iron cup. No more delays, no more letting down her guard. Not when she was getting so close to the last place Wade and Tommy had been seen.

The stagecoach driver stuck his head into the dining room just as she folded her napkin and set it down beside her plate. "Horses ready," he bellowed. "C'mon, folks."

A number of passengers groaned at the prospect of continuing their torturous journey, and they slowly pushed back their chairs and headed out of the hotel. Juliana, though eager to leave Cedar Gulch, hung back a moment. In every town she had passed through for the past hundred miles she had made inquiries about Wade and Tommy, so far without luck. But her hopes kept rising as she journeyed deeper into Arizona, for surely the closer she got to Tombstone, the more chance there would be that someone would have seen or heard of them. Unfortunately, the sour demeanor of this hotel's proprietor didn't hold out much hope of helpfulness from him, but she couldn't afford to let an opportunity pass. She straightened her shoulders and approached him as he came shuffling through the kitchen door.

"Excuse, me, sir, may I have a moment of your time?" He froze, his brown hound dog eyes scanning her up and down with glaring hostility. Juliana flushed at his ill-mannered scrutiny but forced herself to offer a dazzling smile, hoping to soften him up a bit. "I'm looking for two men. My brothers. It's urgent that I find them. Their name is Montgomery, Wade and Tommy Montgomery. Have you heard of them?"

Something flickered behind his eyes. Maybe recognition, maybe just greed. He scratched his ear. "Could be I have," he said indifferently. "What's it worth to ya?"

Juliana started. She felt a small flame of hope, but

managed to keep it in check. Quickly, she opened her reticule and removed a gold piece, which she held up between her fingers. "Have they been here? In Cedar Gulch? Can you tell me when?"

He was silent a moment, studying the slender, beautiful young woman before him with suspicion. His glance darted back and forth between her and the gold piece. "What you want them for, girl?"

"I told you—they're my brothers," she said impatiently. "If you know anything about them, please tell me quickly. The stagecoach will be leaving any moment."

He jerked his thumb in the direction of the saloon. "Try Kelly in the Red Snake." He regarded her with a leering smile. "I reckon he knows 'em better than I do."

Juliana dropped the coin into his palm and spun about toward the door, pausing outside only long enough to request that the driver wait a few moments for her. She hurried across the street to the saloon, trying to subdue the excitement within her. She knew her fellow passengers, watching from the stagecoach window, would be scandalized to see her enter the saloon, but there was no help for it. If only she had inquired a few moments earlier! But she had not truly expected to meet with success. Now she had to find this "Kelly"—probably the bartender, Juliana decided—and convince him quickly to tell her all he could about the Montgomerys.

She pushed through the double doors of the saloon and found herself in a dimly lit, seedy chamber containing a dozen small tables flanked by broken-down chairs. The stench of liquor and tobacco and men's stale sweat overpowered her. Spittoons lined the walls beneath boarded-up windows. A piano stood against one wall beneath a lurid painting of a naked woman, and slumped over the grimy keys, asleep, was a thin-shouldered wisp of a man in a gaudy gold vest. Opposite the piano, along the near wall, stood a rectangular wooden bar littered with half-filled glasses and empty bottles. Behind it loomed the hugest man she had ever seen. He was a bear of a figure, well over six feet tall, and nearly as broad, with coarse red hair and bushy eyebrows and big, puffy cheeks. His bulbous nose was bright red in the dingy light, his chin full and wide. Powerful forearms encased in a sweat-soaked green flannel shirt bulged with muscles; his denim overalls were worn and stained and barely seemed to contain his enormous girth. The giant had a rusty beard that reached his shoulders, and his hands were the size of rocks.

For a moment, Juliana paused in trepidation at his intimidating form, but she quickly regained her composure and hurried toward him.

"Kelly?" she inquired, putting a hand to the bar, which felt sticky to the touch. She dropped her hand back to her side.

The bartender swiped at the perspiration dripping down his forehead with a damp sleeve and peered at her from beneath his brows. "At your service, me dear. What can I do for the likes of you?" he responded genially, his friendly tone a welcome contrast to his ferocious appearance.

Juliana, grateful for this amiable greeting and the kind way he regarded her, began quickly to question him.

Eager to learn something of her brothers, and pressured for time, she was totally oblivious of the effect she was having on the other occupants of the saloon. There weren't more than a handful, but among them, gaping in openmouthed admiration from a table several feet away, were the three disreputable-looking men she had seen ride into town.

Cash Hogan licked his lips and shivered all over as he feasted his eyes on the prime little filly who had just waltzed in the door. Seeing a woman like that in the Red Snake was a shock, for the girl looked like she belonged in some highfalutin parlour back east, eating cake and drinking tea out of a fancy china cup. She looked as delicate as a china cup, too, like she'd bust if you squeezed her too hard.

I'll have to remember that, Cash thought, his gaze traveling over the soft curves of her figure with hungry delight. *It'd be a shame to bust anything so downright purty.*

His partners, Bo and Luke Curry, had their own thoughts about the woman, and were about to call out to her to get her attention when the name *Montgomery* reached them. All three men started, glancing at one another. Cash set down his glass. Luke, his long, stringy brown hair parted in the middle, grinned broadly at his brother. In answer, Bo put a nail-bitten finger across his lips, signaling the other two for quiet.

The bartender, Kelly, regarded Juliana in amazement. "So those trouble-hunting rascals are your brothers, eh, me girl? Well, a rowdy pair they are, and that's for sure. They were here, with some of their boys, about a month ago and broke up me place."

"Broke it up?" Juliana demanded, puzzled.

Kelly indicated the boarded-up windows. "Did a good bit of damage they did. Fighting, you see. Over a woman. Never saw so many broken bones in one place, except when I was in the hospital during the war."

"Were they hurt?" Juliana had visions of Wade and Tommy lying in pain on this very floor, soaked in their own blood. But Kelly's next words allayed the fear that had seized her heart.

"Those two? Not more'n a scratch between 'em. They've got the devil's own luck, they do. Rode out of here right as rain and bless their scoundrel hearts, paid me right generous for the damages."

Excitement flooded through her. She was going to find

them after all. "Mr. Kelly, where were they headed when they left here? Do you think they're coming back?"

"Oh, they'll be back sure as certain, but who's to say when, me dear? Those boys show up maybe twice, three times a year. They've found it's not healthy to stay in one place, if you know what I mean."

She realized what he was hinting at, no doubt trying to spare her feelings about their outlaw status. But Juliana saw no need to sidestep the truth. "You mean because they're wanted men and must keep two steps ahead of the law, don't you, Mr. Kelly?" she said, facing him with lifted chin. "Well, that doesn't matter to me. I must find them. So please . . ." She gazed directly and appealingly into his eyes and, reaching out impulsively, touched his sleeve. "Please try to recall where they might have gone. I'm certain they must have mentioned something about what direction they were headed . . ."

The touch of this heavenly creature's hand upon his arm was having a dizzying effect on the giant bartender. His cheeks grew even redder with pleasure, and his blue eyes danced as he grinned down at the girl. Then something popped in his brain, and he chuckled and snapped his fingers. "Cooper Creek—that's where they were headed!" he exclaimed. "It's not more'n sixty miles from here . . ."

"Last call for the stage!" the driver's voice yelled from the street outside, and Juliana jumped.

"Thank you, Mr. Kelly," she cried, and whirled toward the door, but as she started forward three men surged up from the table near the center of the room and quickly moved to block her path.

"Hold on a moment, miss . . . Montgomery, ain't it?"

The man who grabbed her wrist was weed-thin and bony, but she felt the sinewy strength beneath his spare frame. He wore a patched red shirt and dusty breeches tucked into boots that were caked with mud. His narrow dirt-streaked face looked as if it hadn't been washed or shaved in days. His companions were worse, if that was possible, Juliana thought in disgust, as she stared into the unsavory faces of the riders she had observed from the dining room window.

"Let me go," she ordered, as firmly as she could. It was all she could do to keep the alarm from her voice as she tried to pull her wrist free. "Step aside, if you please."

"Not so fast, lady." The man tightened his grip. "Not till you answer the question. Your name's Montgomery? First name . . . somethin' fancy . . ."

"Julie sumpin, Cash," the tall, stringy-haired one piped in, grinning toothlessly at her.

"That's it." Cash nodded. Studying Juliana, he licked his lips. "That you, honey?"

"What if it is?" Juliana felt panic rising inside her. How did these men know her name? Through the one good window she saw the stagecoach driver climb into his seat. "Wait, Mr. Fitzsimmons! I'm coming . . ." she called out, but the third man, an apelike, shaggy-haired fellow with coal-black eyes and a jutting chin, and breath that smelled like pig droppings, shook his head as he leaned toward her, so close his nose nearly touched hers.

"No, ma'am. You ain't goin' nowhere," he crowed. " 'Cept back to Denver with Cash and Luke and me. Nothin' personal, you understand. We're just doin' our job. Takin' you in—alive, just like the notice said."

"What are you talking about? What notice?" Juliana had been trying in vain to break free of Cash's grip all this time, but now she froze, as a sudden dread swept over her in one great burst. "What . . . are you talking about?"

"The Wanted poster. This one." Pig Breath pulled a handful of torn, crumpled papers from the pocket of his grease-stained duster. "Let's see. Here it is."

He unfolded one page from the others and dangled it in the air before her. "See? The law in Denver wants you back real bad." He clucked his tongue at her mockingly. "Horse thievin' is serious business in these parts, ma'am. So's stealin'. You shoulda known better."

Juliana felt as if he had punched her in the stomach. She stared at the notice in sickened horror, trying to take in what was happening. The words were printed in large, bold type. Her name, a description. She was wanted for horse theft and robbery—there was a reward of two thousand dollars for her capture. She blinked, staring incredulously at the paper before her. Her body began to tremble.

No, it couldn't be. She felt a pounding in her head. But through the explosion of panic, she knew she had to try to stay calm, to think.

"You're lawmen?" she managed to ask.

They burst into loud guffaws. "Not exactly." The thin man—the one called Cash—answered her, still squeezing her wrist. "We're bounty hunters, honey."

She twisted about to stare at the bartender, watching the scene in grim silence. "Mr. Kelly, there's been a mistake. Please tell these men to let me go. I must get on the stage . . ."

Kelly's expression was troubled. He was a hardened man and had lived many years alone in Cedar Gulch, minding his own business with cheerful good sense and a strict policy of never sticking his neck out. But something about this young woman and her situation affected him. She didn't look like any damned horse thief he'd ever seen, but then . . . it really was none of his business. Still, pity made him say in a forced, jovial tone, "Lads, it's too hot for bothering about business today. Tell you what. Drinks are on the house. Why not let the little lassie go and—"

In an instant, Luke Curry had his Colt trained on the

huge bartender. "Two thousand dollars can buy a hell of a lot of drinks, and lots of other things, mister," he hissed. "So don't think of interfering. We're taking the little lady back."

"Damn right," Cash echoed, and suddenly yanked Juliana toward the door. As she glanced back in frantic appeal to the bartender, he shook his head in regret. Luke Curry kept his gun trained on him all the while that Cash and Bo dragged her from the saloon. Kelly scowled, but kept his hands flat on top of the bar. These hombres were of a type he knew well. Vicious coyotes, more animal than human. They'd just as soon kill a man as look at him. He'd have liked to help the girl, but he'd be digging his own grave if he interfered.

Outside, Cash dragged Juliana toward his horse. When the stagecoach driver, seeing her struggle, called out sharply to them, Luke Curry waved the Wanted poster at him. "You don't want no one like this on your coach," he called. "We're takin' this gal back for her trial." He pointed his Colt in a businesslike fashion at the driver, a grin splitting his face when several of the passengers screamed. "You folks had best be on your way," he sang out.

The driver glared, spat a wad of tobacco juice into the dirt, then flapped the reins. As the horses bounded away, and the stagecoach disappeared in a haze of dust, Juliana saw her last hope of rescue die.

She felt cold and hot all at once. Terror gripped her in a deathly vise. These men were savage, filthy brutes. How would she make it back to Denver alive? Even if she did, she thought on a wave of despair, what awaited her there? John Breen's fury. He must have been livid to have put up such a bounty—and to have claimed she stole from him. Would he send her to jail? Or force her to marry him? She trembled at the thought of being handed over to him, of being completely at his mercy.

Suddenly, as Cash released her arm for an instant to untether his horse, she saw her chance and grabbed it. She bolted past him quick as a jackrabbit. Lifting her skirts in one hand, she fled down the deserted boardwalk with every ounce of speed she could muster.

Behind her she heard Cash shout. "Put that thing away, Bo! The poster said 'alive,' dammit. Surely we kin catch a little girl like that without havin' to shoot her in the back."

Juliana's feet pounded the boardwalk as she spun around a corner and headed toward a group of ramshackle buildings up ahead. Her reticule flew off her wrist and went sailing into the dust, but she never paused. Her breath was coming in short, painful gasps as she ran ever faster. She stumbled once, regained her balance, and ran on, wanting to scream for help but knowing there was no one to help her, no one who would lift a finger against the bounty hunters, no one who cared.

A sudden gust of wind sent dust flying in her face, blinding and choking her, but she ran on, not knowing where she was going, only that she had to get away from those men, that she would rather die than be caught. With a little sob she staggered forward, her chest heaving, her eyes smarting, the clamor of their pursuit drumming in her ears.

Glancing back over her shoulder for one precious second, she saw all three men closing in on her, their faces purple with anger. Cash whirled a rope, sent it sailing out toward her, and with a scream, she dodged desperately to her right. The loop skimmed past her and fell harmlessly in the dust, but as she hurled herself sideways, Juliana tripped over a rock in the dust and went sprawling.

Wildly, with a low weeping deep in her throat, she scrambled to her feet and plunged forward once more, straight into a wall of solid rock.

Then with a gasp she realized that it was not a wall of

rock after all. It was a man's broad, solid chest, hard and immovable as granite. Before she could draw back, she felt powerful hands seize her arms and hold her fast.

Tears lined her eyelashes as she raised her head to stare into his face. The sun beat down into her eyes and she could barely see him, but from what she could see, she knew one thing. She would find no mercy here.

Cole Rawdon held her immobile before him. His face was a mask of ice.

She opened her mouth to speak, but no words would come. Gulping, she tried again. Her knees were weak as pudding, but this time she managed a whisper. "Please. Oh, please."

At that her knees gave out and she would have fallen if not for his arm swooping about her waist.

For the second time, Cole Rawdon stared down at this girl who had a habit of collapsing in his arms, and he swore silently at a fate that seemed destined to mock him. His attention left her flushed, terrified face and the tumble of pale hair that had come unbound from its chignon, and riveted itself on the three men coming up behind her.

Cole Rawdon studied them with cool detachment as the girl twisted about in fright. He had a firm hold of her wrist, otherwise he knew she would have bolted. He could feel her pulse racing like a runaway train engine beneath his thumb. He sensed, even more than he saw, the panic coursing through her.

"Howdy, Cash," Rawdon drawled after a long, taut moment when the sun seemed to blaze even more fiercely down upon his head. "What seems to be the trouble?"

· 8 ·

Cash Hogan skidded to a halt and swore under his breath. Rawdon. Damn it all to hell. Why did it have to be Rawdon?

Cash made sure the grin he flashed was at least outwardly friendly. Maybe if he was smart—and careful—they could work this thing out without a fight.

Behind Cash, Bo and Luke waited in uneasy silence, tugging at their neckerchiefs, squinting at the black-garbed man in their path.

"Uh, you've got our prisoner there, Rawdon," Cash chuckled nervously. " 'Preciate it if you'd give her back."

"It doesn't look much like she's your prisoner, Cash. Matter of fact, it seems to me she's my prisoner."

Juliana trembled. For just a moment, she had thought Cole Rawdon might help her. How stupid could she be, she chided herself as a tear slipped down her cheek. This man, like the others, was a bounty hunter. He was after her too. Dread clawed at her heart, for something told her he was even more dangerous than the others. Despite the hot sun, a chill spread through her, turning her skin clammy, her blood to ice.

"Yours? Hell, no, she ain't." Bo started forward, but Luke, stringy hair dangling in his eyes, grabbed Bo's arm.

"Well, she *ain't,*" Bo hissed furiously at his brother, then clamped his lips shut when he saw the deadly purpose in Cole Rawdon's face.

"Let's be reasonable about this, Rawdon," Cash went on, a wheedling note entering his voice. He pushed his hat back on his head. "We got her first. Caught her right back there in the saloon. The bartender will tell you that. Fair's fair, ain't it? Why don't you jest hand her back over to me, and the boys and I'll buy you a drink?"

"Go to hell."

Juliana held her breath, unable to believe that Cole Rawdon could speak with such arrogance to the three men facing him. They were dangerous and they were greedy and angry to boot—such a combination boded ill for anyone who got in their way. Yet this man with the iron grip on her wrist seemed totally unafraid, even contemptuous, and he must know he was enraging them. Luke's face had turned blood red, and Bo had gotten a dark, weasely shine in his eyes, which Juliana guessed meant he was ready to kill Rawdon on the spot.

Even Cash, who probably had more brains than the other two put together, now looked as though his anger was getting the better of him. "Not very sociable, are you, Rawdon?" he growled, and Juliana saw the muscles clench in his neck.

Cole stood relaxed and calm, yet his gaze never wavered from Cash Hogan's face. "I'd sooner eat a skunk than sit down to a drink with you and your pards, Hogan," he remarked conversationally. "And I'm sure as hell not going to turn over my two thousand dollars to you. Ride out now while you still can and save the folks of Cedar Gulch the trouble of burying you."

Juliana saw the change flood over the three bounty hunters' faces. The fear was still there, etched deep beneath the blustering facade, but now the men had been goaded and lashed into anger by Rawdon's scornful words and arrogant dismissal. Luke's lips thinned and his eyes glittered in the sun, Bo's thick shoulders hunched, and Cash seemed to turn to stone, every sinewy muscle tightening, readying, his thin face twisting into an expression of snarling, frozen fury.

"There's three of us, Rawdon, and only one of you," Cash hissed. "Reckon you're the one goin' to need buryin'."

Everything happened at once. Rawdon shoved Juliana into the dirt with such force that her hands, face, and knees were scraped raw in the gritty dust. She lay stunned, red sparks of light exploding in her head while deafening gunfire thundered above her. She covered her ears with her hands, screaming. Acrid gunsmoke clogged her nostrils as the air reverberated with gunshots. It seemed like an eternity before they ceased, and when they did there came a stark silence. Floating on this stillness, Juliana heard the groans of a dying man.

A tremor shook her. For a moment she couldn't move, then she forced herself to lift her head, forced her body to inch upward. Every muscle cried out in pain. Blood oozed on her cheek.

There was silence all around her now. Eerie, absolute silence. Juliana somehow managed to crawl to her knees, and she blinked against the glare of the sun.

No more than six feet from her, three men sprawled motionless in a crimson pool of blood.

"Oh, my God," she choked. She shut her eyes against the grisly vision. With an effort of will she fought the nausea that welled up in her throat and threatened to overtake her.

Cash, Bo, and Luke were all dead, bloodied bits of

sinew and bone and flesh spattered all about them. Juliana trembled, her body a mass of jelly. She flung herself away from the ghastly pile of bodies and willed her eyes to open once more. A shadow loomed over her.

She gazed dazedly up, up at the man who towered above her. The tall, black-garbed man, the one they called Rawdon, who held a smoking Colt .45 in each hand.

Slowly, as Juliana watched in sick terror, he replaced the guns in their holsters. Expressionless, he bent toward her.

"No," she breathed in a wisp of a voice.

He seized her arm and hauled her to her feet. "You're not going to faint on me again, are you?" he demanded.

Juliana could only gape at him in stunned fear.

He studied her. The sun glittered down. No sign of life came from anywhere in Cedar Gulch.

So this was the horse thief, Juliana Montgomery, the one he'd been tracking for the past two weeks. It was unbelievable, Cole mused—or maybe not. He sure hadn't figured her for a thief that day in Denver, with her fancy dress and plumed hat, with those big, bright green eyes of hers that he hadn't been able to forget. Even when he'd read the description on the Wanted poster, it hadn't occurred to him that the blond-haired thief was the same girl who'd fainted on him outside the Gold Dust last April. Yet remembering another girl long ago, one with almond-shaped brown eyes and thick ebony hair that felt like silk in his hands, he swiftly reminded himself that nothing a woman did should surprise him. Women could be every bit as greedy and dishonest as men, without a clue of it showing on the outside—and he had the scars to prove it. So this one, innocent and weak as she looked, would bear watching. Cole tried to ignore the fascinating beauty of her delicate features, which, combined with the curvy softness of her body, proved a delectable combina-

tion. He stared at her, exerting all his will to see not a
fragile golden-haired waif of a girl but a criminal worth
two thousand dollars cash when he brought her in. It
wasn't easy.

When he moved his hand up to her face, the girl
flinched, but he only traced the dirty scrape across her
cheek lightly with his thumb. "I didn't mean to push you
so hard." His tone was curt. "Still," he said, grasping her
wrist once more, "you'd have gotten a lot worse from
them." Instinctively, she followed the direction of his
gaze to the dead men in their pool of blood, and this time
her knees buckled.

"Oh, no, you don't." He steadied her, and shook his
head in exasperation. "C'mon, let's get out of here. We've
got a ways to go before dark."

"G-go? Where?"

"Colorado."

Juliana froze as panic flooded back. The first shock of
the shootings was draining away and she was left with
the reality of her own situation. She couldn't go back to
Denver and the fury of John Breen—he would throw her
in jail or . . . who knew what he would do now that she
had humiliated him? Dread clawed at her, giving her
strength to wrench free of Cole Rawdon.

"You can't take me back there," she cried, lifting a
desperate face to him. "You can't! Listen to me, please,
there's been a mistake. I'm not a thief!"

"Sure you're not. And I'm not a bounty hunter. I'm
the President of the United States. C'mon."

He grabbed her arm again, but Juliana tried to pry his
fingers away. "There's been a terrible mistake, you must
listen to me . . ."

But he wasn't interested. He held her easily, and
scanned the sky and horizon with steady, searching eyes
all the while that she babbled on, then he seemed to make
up his mind about something and started directing her

toward the stables at the far end of the street where a
pinto horse was tethered to a hitching post.

Juliana gave a shriek of pain and stumbled.

"What is it now?" he growled, but she was leaning
over to touch her ankle, her face a portrait of agony.

"My . . . ankle," Juliana gasped. "I must have
twisted it when you pushed me . . ."

He lowered her to the ground and knelt beside her.
When he touched her foot, she cried out. "Oh, it must be
broken." Juliana bit back a sob. "It hurts quite terribly . . ."

"Damn."

Rawdon looked about. At last the citizens of Cedar
Gulch were starting to emerge from their burrows to see
the results of the gunfight. Several men drifted around
the corner of the main street and peered toward the bodies. Rawdon stood up.

"I'll find out if there's a doctor in this hellhole. Don't
try to move it in the meantime."

"I won't." Juliana's voice was fraught with pain.
Frowning, Cole moved off toward the cluster of men.
What the hell was he going to do if she had a broken
foot? It would slow things down considerably, but he
couldn't just drag her off without letting a doctor set it,
or bandage it, could he? He'd never had a woman prisoner before and he didn't intend to treat her any different
from a man, except . . . except she seemed to be in a lot
of pain, and he figured he'd best get that foot seen to
before they started out. It could be a rough trip back to
Denver, Cole knew. Every bounty hunter for two hundred miles around would be after that reward. Cole's eyes
narrowed at the thought. He wasn't about to lose that
money. It just might be enough to help him outbid Mc-
Cray. Fire Mesa actually could be his again, he thought
with a little flicker of hope, it could come back into Rawdon hands, thanks to Miss Juliana Montgomery. But he'd

have to push her hard and fast across rough terrain to get back to Wells with the money in time. He hoped she could endure the ride ahead. She looked to be a weak, fragile thing, and she certainly had no stomach for bloodshed. Chances were she'd see more of it before this was over. Part of Cole almost felt sorry for her. Almost. He reminded himself that she was an outlaw, and that he'd better treat her like one. And he would, he vowed, once he got that foot of hers taken care of.

Juliana, in the meantime, watched him walk away from her with a frantically beating heart. She had fooled him. She had done it. She couldn't believe that he had fallen for her trick, but then, he probably thought her a perfect idiot anyway. Why wouldn't he believe that she'd have been clumsy enough to have broken her foot? Now, if she could only go through with the rest of it . . . She could scarcely believe what she was about to do next, but she had no choice. She looked at Cole Rawdon, walking in one direction, his back to her, and then swiveled her head to study the pinto tethered no more than twenty feet away in the other direction. She took a breath, readied herself. Not yet, not quite yet. Rawdon reached the group of men at the end of the street and started to speak to them. Now, she told herself, summoning her courage. *Now.*

Juliana thrust herself to her feet and ran. Her heart in her throat, she plummeted straight toward that pinto, trying to make as little sound as she could in the dusty road. Above her, a turquoise sky blazed, but below it was gray and quiet, too quiet, she thought, as her own footsteps drummed in her ears and the beating of her heart seemed like an explosion. She heard a yell as she grabbed the tether, and the next instant she had a foot in the stirrup.

Somehow she vaulted into the saddle, her skirts askew, and grabbed up the reins.

Cole Rawdon was sprinting toward her, his face black with fury. He went for his gun.

"Giddyap!" she screamed, and dug her heels into the pinto's flanks. They were off like a bolt of lightning, racing away from Rawdon, away from Cedar Gulch. A shot blasted to the right of her, but Juliana never flinched. Cole Rawdon wouldn't kill her. The poster had clearly stated that she was to be brought back alive. She laughed almost hysterically to herself as she bent over the horse's mane and urged him on faster. Cole Rawdon was trying to frighten her. He expected her to give up. Well, she wouldn't give up. She had a horse now, and, glancing down at the thick saddlebag tied on behind, realized she had supplies as well. There would be a canteen, maybe even food. Whoever this horse belonged to had been prepared for traveling. She owed its owner, whoever he was, a big debt of gratitude.

Suddenly the laughter died out of her throat. As the pinto swept over a rise that led into a high stretch of pine forest, it dawned on her that there was only one person to whom this horse could belong. There had been no one else about.

She gulped at the enormity of what she had done.

She had tricked Cole Rawdon and escaped from him. She had made him look a fool before the men of Cedar Gulch. And despite all her protestations that she wasn't a thief . . .

She had stolen his horse.

· 9 ·

Night was coming, and with it a storm. Her tracks would be washed away if he didn't find her before then—but he would, Cole vowed to himself. Come hell or high water, he would.

Anger flicked through him every time he thought of how he'd been tricked. Treacherous little bitch. She'd made a damned fool of him in front of the entire town. Riding Cash Hogan's bay through the pine forests above the Rim, he inspected every branch and twig, every print in the earth, reading the evidence of her passing like a clearly marked map. She hadn't had much of a start, just enough to keep ahead of him for a while. He'd let her think she was safe, that she'd given him the slip. When she least expected it, he'd take her. Rawdon smiled grimly at the thought.

He hadn't been smiling when he'd grabbed Cash's horse back in town and set out after her, all the while trying to ignore the expressions of the men in Cedar Gulch. Not one of them had dared say a word to him about being outwitted by a woman, or had had the nerve

to laugh out loud, but he knew they'd wanted to. They
had probably burst out with it when he'd gone. And that
bartender, Kelly, damn his eyes. He'd grinned when he
saw the girl ride away.

"The luck of the Irish, that's what that lassie has—aye,
that's what I think," Kelly had remarked to no one in
particular as Rawdon had swung himself onto the bay in
front of the Red Snake Saloon.

The man had kept grinning, even when Cole, rigid in
the saddle, had gritted his teeth.

"We'll see how lucky she is when I'm done with her,"
he had bitten off, and then he'd ridden out without waiting for the bartender's reaction. Kelly might be in sympathy with the girl, but that wouldn't do her one damn bit
of good once Cole found her. When he got his hands on
her . . . Cole's muscles tensed in anticipation. Nothing
would help her then.

Any ideas he'd had of showing Juliana Montgomery
mercy on the way back had vanished like night mist at
morning light. She didn't deserve mercy. Hell, she didn't
deserve anything but to have her pretty little neck wrung.
He'd never lost a prisoner before, not once in all these
years, not until she had come along.

That's what you get for going soft, Cole told himself.
*Because she's a woman, you let your guard down. You're
just damned lucky she didn't blow your head off.*

"I'm not a thief. There's been a mistake." How
damned convincingly she had spoken those words. So
now he knew something about her, besides the fact that
she was guilty as hell. Lies came easily to Juliana Montgomery. She could stare a man in the face and look as
soft and innocent as a woman could look, and lie through
her teeth. Well, he hoped she would enjoy this brief fling
of freedom because it was the last she would know for a
good long while. He'd turn her in to the law in Colorado
if it was the last thing he ever did, reward or no reward.

Even the two thousand dollars and the chance of getting Fire Mesa back dimmed beside the satisfaction he'd feel hauling her in to Denver, trussed up like a roped calf. When Cole spotted Arrow's tracks swerving up a trail that flanked White Canyon, he spurred the bay forward and gave a grunt of satisfaction. He cleared his mind of everything but the job before him, and let himself become wholly intent on his prey. All his energy and concentration focused on tracking the girl who was trying so desperately to elude him.

She was inexperienced, that much was obvious from the loco trail she was taking—and he'd bet his boots she was bone-tired by now. He'd have her by dark, easily. Another hour, at the most, he guessed, and then he'd give her a surprise she'd never forget. Beneath his hat, Cole's face wore an expression of taut anticipation. His eyes gleamed like shards of blue ice as he pursued Arrow's all too visible trail.

Juliana looked around her in bleary exhaustion. She had no idea where she was, except that she was on the lip of a limestone walled canyon that zigzagged dizzyingly down to a narrow ribbon of water far below. She'd been riding for hours, heading west, hoping to eventually hit Cooper Creek. But the trail was twisting and dangerous with unexpected drops and turns, and the mountains kept getting in her way. She could go no farther tonight. Storm clouds were gathering in a sky that had turned an odd, ominous shade of cobalt blue. A cold wind sliced through the trees, and every few moments heat lightning seared the sky.

Up on the plateau, overlooking the high canyon, Juliana was afraid.

"Don't worry, boy. We'll be all right." She patted the pinto's scruffy mane as she spoke to him, but it was really herself she was trying to reassure. There was a world of difference between traveling through this immense, mountainous country in a stagecoach, with a driver to look after her and a host of other passengers for company, and riding it alone. She felt as tiny and insignificant as a dormouse in this vast, fierce land. The endless expanse of sky, towering rocks and sculpted mountains, and the deep-shadowed, scented forests along the Mogollon Rim threatened to swallow her up, and she felt as though she might wander forever through the wilderness and never glimpse another soul, much less a town or outpost of civilization.

Stories of Apache atrocities kept creeping into her head, much as she tried to banish them. Every time a branch rustled in the wind, or a pebble rolled underfoot, she thought she was about to be attacked. If not by Indians, then by some wild creature or—and her heart pounded painfully in her chest every time she thought of it—by Cole Rawdon, who was no doubt ready to kill her without a second thought. She knew he was her most likely source of danger, if not an exclusive one, and she would have to hide from him with all the cunning she possessed if she was ever going to make it to Cooper Creek.

At least, he hadn't been able to set out after her immediately, she thought, clutching the reins more tightly between her sweating palms. That was something to be thankful for.

With any luck, she'd find a town and a place to hide before he could buy himself another horse.

With any luck. Yes, she would need luck. And she'd need her wits about her. Remembering the murderous expression in Rawdon's eyes when she'd wheeled the pinto about, she felt a twisting of apprehension in her stomach. If he caught up with her . . .

She couldn't let him. Despite the risks of Apache, snakes, mountain lions, losing her way, of being unable to find food or water, she knew with every ounce of her being that Cole Rawdon's getting his hands on her would present the worst danger of all.

Opposite the canyon, on the other side of the trail, stretched a ragged stand of aspen and pine trees that opened onto a flat, grassy expanse. This area was sheltered by the wall of yet another massive gray cliff rising up to a sheer point above. It looked like the best place to make camp that she'd seen in a while. *But why couldn't it be a cave?* Juliana thought in despair. She needed shelter from the storm. When the rain came, as she was certain it would at any moment, she would be at its mercy, completely unprotected. But there was nothing she could do about that now. There was no time to go farther, in search of one, for both darkness and the storm would close in on her any moment now. Besides, she was too exhausted to ride another step. Every muscle in her body cried out in agony, begging for rest.

At least this spot was secluded, she told herself, sliding from the saddle in one weary movement. Cole Rawdon could never find her here in the middle of this huge mountain, one among so many. Glancing about, she saw that there was no indication of movement from any direction. Only the leaves shuddering in the rising wind. Before her, far across the canyon, there were rising forests of pine, as deep and impenetrable as dark, looming clouds. Behind her rose the gray-and-red granite cliff, nearly touching the sky.

Well, at least the trees and the storm and the encroaching darkness would help to conceal her camp, she told herself, trying to be grateful for the isolation of this place. Cole Rawdon, if he was still following her, couldn't possibly track her here.

For tonight, Juliana whispered to the pinto, as she led him to an aspen, *we'll be safe. Wet, perhaps, and cold, but safe.*

Rest, how she needed rest. It was almost beyond her
strength to see to the pinto and then sink down onto the
grass with Cole Rawdon's saddle pack before her. The
wind had picked up. It blasted around her now in a rising
gale, whipping at her hair as she ransacked the pack, one
by one rifling through the bounty hunter's supplies.

This is better than gold, Juliana exulted as she eagerly
examined the contents. There was an oilcloth coat, which
she could cover herself with when the rain came, and also
a folded bedroll and extra saddle blanket tucked inside,
along with a canteen filled with water. Juliana's spirits
rose with the discovery of each treasure. She found two
flannel shirts and pairs of trousers, razor blades, and a
strange little wood carving of a horse, but she was mainly
interested in the food: strips of dried beef jerky, the remains of some hardtack biscuits, a tin of coffee, and some
campfire utensils, along with a knife and tinderbox.
Thank you, Mister Cole Rawdon, she thought, not without satisfaction, as she wrapped the blanket and the oilskin around her and settled down against the cliff wall
with the jerky and biscuits. Her stomach growled its hunger as she took her first bite. How many hours had it been
since that meal in the Cedar Gulch hotel? It seemed an
eternity since then, but at least she was free, free of Cole
Rawdon and Cash Hogan and John Breen and all the
other monstrous men in the world. *For the moment,* she
reminded herself. Fear sliced through her every time she
thought of the deadly fury on Rawdon's face when he
had seen her riding off on his pinto, right out from under
his nose. But she didn't want to think about what would
happen if he caught up with her. He wouldn't, she told
herself with forced bravado. She had outmaneuvered him
today, hadn't she? All she had to do was keep a sharp
lookout, stay one step ahead of Cole Rawdon, and steadily make her way west. She'd be bound to hit upon a
town sometime tomorrow, surely, and then she could in-

quire about the way to Cooper Creek. And as soon as she found Wade and Tommy, Cole Rawdon wouldn't be such a threat. With them and their gang, experts at eluding trouble, she'd be safe.

Safe. To think that her brothers and safety could be less than a hundred miles away filled her with a buoyant hope that could not be destroyed by the oncoming storm. As Juliana hugged her arms around her, a blast of wind ripped in from the north, sending ice-cold chills over her. She couldn't give up, she insisted to herself, shivering, while darkness fell over the clearing like a heavy woolen shroud. She would make it through this storm and this night, and tomorrow would bring her that much closer to Wade and Tommy.

She tried not to let herself think about what it would be like here in this desolate spot once the storm began. It was starting now, she realized, as a smattering of drops fell onto her head, and the grass began to blow as if it would be ripped from the earth. Huge drops pelted the trees, the cliff wall, the rocks and brush, striking Juliana's small figure as she huddled beneath the oilskin. Suddenly, lightning struck, so close that the pinto reared up screaming its panic, and Juliana cried out. She half rose, then froze in terror as from the darkness above, dropping down into the clearing directly before her like a monstrous phantom, sprang a dark, massive figure.

She screamed, but the sound was bit off by the roar of the wind. Then she saw with a gasp of dread that the apparition before her was not a phantom at all. While thunder crashed around her like cannonballs, she stared in transfixed horror into the gleaming eyes of Cole Rawdon.

Juliana bolted sideways and started to run, even as he lunged for her. His hands closed over the oilskin and it whipped from her back, but she never paused, crashing headlong through the rain, not knowing where she ran or how she would escape, knowing only that she had to get away from him. She slipped on the wet grass but stumbled on, unable to hear his pursuit for the wind and rain. She skittered desperately forward, seeking the path, the trail, but it was too dark to see . . .

Rain poured down her face, soaked her hair, her cheeks, blurred her vision. She whirled sideways, first one way, then another, searching frantically for the trail. She saw from the corner of her eyes that he was upon her. She threw herself forward into the murky darkness and realized too late that she had overshot the trail, she was at the edge of the precipice, hurtling over the lip of the canyon, and that there was nothing below but jagged rocks and stream. Her scream died in her throat. She knew in that instant she was going to die, even as she teetered backward, trying to save herself. The wind struck her, knocking her forward and she saw below a vast black chasm. The instant that she hovered there on the brink seemed an hour, a year, a lifetime. As she felt herself falling forward into the nothingness, she was grasped so fiercely from behind that the breath swept out of her, and Cole Rawdon hauled her back.

He dragged her backward and threw her down upon the ground and pinned her there with the weight of his body, gazing down in pure fury into her terrified face.

"Damned idiotic bitch. I ought to have let you fall," he shouted at her over the blast of the wind. He was as soaked as she; his black hair streamed into his eyes, but that only seemed to emphasize the ferocity of his appearance. Juliana, held helpless beneath him, with rain pounding into her face, streaming in rivulets down into her neck to soak her flesh, could do nothing but stare up at him, too stunned by what had almost happened to her to speak.

"You don't even have the sense to find shelter from the rain!" he yelled. "I should leave you here to drown!" As suddenly as he had thrown her down, he dragged her to her feet. Driving wind buffeted them but he managed to propel her along the track, around a sharp bend, and then they scrambled down a ravine. He half dragged, half carried her, and none too gently. Juliana lost track of all direction, but the next thing she knew they were at the mouth of a cave. He pushed her ahead of him and she saw at once Cash Hogan's bay horse tethered well inside the opening.

Shelter. She stumbled in gratefully, stooping a little due to the low rock ceiling. Outside, the vicious rain slashed, and thunder filled the sky with a deafening roar that echoed through the mountains, but here it was dry, blessedly dry, and she hurried in as far as she could get from the opening. Then Cole Rawdon grasped her, and before she even realized what was happening, he had tied her wrists together with rope. He forced her to the ground, ignoring her protests, and bound her ankles as well.

"You're just enough of a damned fool to run off again while I'm gone," he said. He pulled the knot about her ankles tight, and Juliana winced.

"Where are you going?" Panic shone in her face. "You're not leaving me alone—like this?"

"That's exactly what I'm doing."

"Where are you going?" she demanded, trying to shake the wet streaming hair from her eyes. "I insist that you untie me at once."

But he merely turned his back on her, and stalked out, vanishing through the cave opening and into the violence of the storm.

He's mad, Juliana thought. She struggled uselessly against the rope. *I've been trapped in here by a madman —a madman who despises me. He won't kill me,* she told herself, trying to stay calm. But there were other things a man could do to a woman, she knew, things that were

worse than murder. Remembering the expression on Cole
Rawdon's face when she'd stolen his horse, Juliana knew
he would be capable of anything.

She didn't know how long she sat there, terror building
as to what would happen when he came back. But eventually a new fear took hold: What if he never came back?
What if he had just left her to starve to death here in this
cave, as revenge for taking his horse? What if lightning
had struck him, or he'd tumbled over a cliff or been killed
by a falling rock or. . . . A dozen hair-raising possibili-
ties presented themselves, all of which resulted in the
same thing—she would be trapped here, helpless, to face
slow, agonizing death.

Juliana fought the urge to scream her terror and frustration at the top of her lungs. She clamped her lips together, bit back sobs, and wrestled against the ropes. Every time lightning zigzagged across the blackness outside,
every time the wind tore through the trees, and with each
passing minute of drumming rain, Juliana's fear
mounted. She twisted and turned, chafing against the
rough rawhide that bound her, but all she succeeded in
doing was rubbing her wrists and ankles raw. The ropes
stayed taut.

Just when she thought she would go mad with frustration, that she would start to scream and never stop, he
returned, stamping through the entrance of the cave with
the frightened pinto in tow, and the saddlebag and gear
he'd been able to recover from the clearing as well.

Oh. So that's where he had gone. Relief poured over
her, as well as a reluctant sense of admiration for his
coolheadedness. *She* had forgotten all about the horse
and the supplies—but then, she'd been the one who'd
almost died out there, thanks to Cole Rawdon. She
couldn't be expected to think clearly after something like
that.

She ignored the fact that he had also been the one to

save her life. If not for him, she never would have been anywhere near the edge of that canyon, Juliana reasoned. Sitting on the floor of the cave, watching him tend to the pinto with quick efficiency, she was struck by how smooth and capable each of his movements were. Dripping wet, no doubt freezing, as she was, he nevertheless saw to the animal with patience and ease, all the while totally ignoring her.

Anger pulsed through her. "Now that you're back, you can untie these ropes," she commanded. "I'm certainly not going to run off while you're here to guard me."

He didn't even glance her way. "Lady, you're loco enough to do just about anything." He began building a fire with a store of dried twigs and branches Juliana could only surmise he had gathered together before the storm. So, he'd had this all planned out, had he? He'd found this shelter, then waited until the storm had hit, to seize her. And then he'd tried to scare her to death besides, jumping down like that out of nowhere. The man had a mean streak. It gave her little satisfaction that he was as wet as she. He didn't look one bit uncomfortable, but her teeth were chattering, and she felt as if her skin were coated with ice.

Rawdon built the fire and soon the cave was lit by a golden blaze. Amber tongues of flame leapt up and outward, casting weird shadows on the rough rock walls. Warmth flowed outward from the fire's crackling center, tantalizing Juliana in her sodden garments. She wriggled as close to the glowing flames as she could. "It would be a great deal easier to get warm without these ropes," she remarked in an acid tone, wondering in helpless fury if he meant to keep her tied up all night.

"I reckon it would" was all he replied. He sent her one long, nonchalant glance. Then he began to strip off his own wet clothes, first his boots, then his shirt and pants.

Scandalized, Juliana averted her gaze, but not before

she had had a glimpse of his huge, dark-furred chest. She had never seen a man's naked chest before, and she wondered if they were all as broad and powerfully muscled as this one. Even in that brief instant, she had seen the muscles rippling . . .

Her fascination with his chest was outrageous, she decided—Aunt Katharine would say it was immoral. Yet she had to fight to keep from stealing another glance at him. Enemy or no, he had an undeniable virile beauty, as rugged and dangerous as the mountains themselves. She told herself that by now he was probably naked from the waist *down* and she certainly didn't want to see *that.* So she managed to keep her gaze fixed firmly on the dancing flames, until suddenly she became aware that he was hunkering down across the fire from her, preparing coffee.

He was fully dressed—to an extent. He had donned the blue trousers and flannel shirt she had seen in the saddlebag, but he had left the shirt open to the waist. That rippling, muscled chest was exposed, tapering down to a flat, hard stomach. Juliana swallowed. He was a compelling, infuriating sight—pure masculine power and ease, handsome as sin, and coldly indifferent to her own wretched discomfort.

"I think you've proven your point, Mr. Rawdon."

She met his cool gaze over the flames, and there was green fire shimmering in her eyes.

"My point? What point would that be?" He poured steaming coffee into an iron mug and lifted it to his lips. He sighed in pleasure as he tasted it, then reached for the jerky and biscuits in the pack.

"You've caught me." Juliana gritted her teeth. She was utterly miserable, fighting back tears, but she'd be damned if she'd let him see that. "I'm your prisoner," she managed to say in a calm tone. "You are clearly in charge. That doesn't mean you have the right to starve me—or let me freeze to death!" It was difficult to get the words out clearly, she was shivering so much, yet she refused to let a pleading note enter her voice. She spoke to him with an air of seething anger, pride preventing her from giving in to the temptation to beg. "Now are you going to untie me and behave in a civilized fashion or are you going to continue to play the role of a barbarian?"

He set down the coffee mug and the food and came around the campfire with the stealthy, catlike grace of an Indian. Juliana didn't like the look on his face.

With one smooth movement, he pushed her backward onto the rough floor of the cave and held her down with the weight of his body.

"I've seen barbarians, sweetheart. I know what they do. You don't know shit about barbarians." His hands tangled in her hair, tightening painfully. "If I was a barbarian, you wouldn't be sitting here with your pretty little dress buttoned up to your throat." His eyes glittered with iron-blue sparks. She'd never seen such ruthlessness as she saw in his face. He looked dark, wild, cold. It scared the wits out of her.

"If I was a barbarian, you'd be staked out on the ground. You'd be naked. And I'd be punishing you for stealing my horse in a way you'd never forget."

"Let me go!" No longer was her trembling a result of the cold. Terror beat through her, filling every pore, every muscle of her body. "Please, let me go!"

"Barbarians don't let their prisoners go," he snarled. "They don't show any mercy."

His face held no emotion except cold indifference. That terrified her more than if he had been furious with her. This was something she didn't know how to deal with, or to protect herself against. She bit her lip, and tried to blink back the tears that stung her eyes.

"Stealing a horse is a serious crime in this country, lady. Men hang for it. Maybe you think that being a woman, you won't get the same kind of justice. You're wrong. I could string you up right now and no one would say a word against it—a half-dozen witnesses saw what you did."

"I had to . . . get away."

"You didn't get away and you're not going to get away. Do you understand that?"

She was suddenly too weary, too miserable to fight or argue or even worry any longer. She went still, limp as a rag doll beneath him. Her slender form, weak and tired and aching from the rigors of this day, couldn't take any more. As Cole held her to the ground her pale face looked up at him in bleak despair, empty of fight, of anger, even of fear.

"What is it you want?" she whispered. "What do you plan to do with me?"

For a moment he just stared at her, taking in the dripping golden curls, the fragile, lovely face so weary and drained, the shivers running through her soft form.

He knew what he'd like to do with her. But it was unthinkable. She was his prisoner, completely at his mercy. He couldn't take advantage of that. Besides, she rightly hated him. She'd probably like to claw his eyes out right now, and he couldn't really blame her. But if she had been willing, he thought, his eyes darkening as he stared down at her, if circumstances between them had been different . . . For a moment, he imagined that she was just a girl who had fainted outside a Denver saloon, and not a thief and a liar and a wanted woman who'd do or say anything to suit her own ends. Thinking of her like that, he knew damned well what he'd like to do with her.

But she wasn't just any girl, he quickly reminded himself. And he wasn't a man to let his feelings interfere with a job. A tremor ran through the muscles of his body. He regained control of his thoughts with steely effort.

"Do you understand that you can't get away?" Delib-

erately, he kept his tone rough. "That you're going back
to Denver to face those charges against you?"

"Yes. I . . . understand."

Cole rolled off her. "That's better," he said, lifting her
to a sitting position. "You're learning."

He began silently working at her bonds.

Juliana was too tired to say anything. She was also
leery of angering him again. When she was free, she
rubbed at her wrists and ankles with shaking fingers, then
glanced up when Rawdon suddenly dropped the saddle
blanket in her lap.

"Get out of those wet clothes and put this on," he
ordered. At her wary look he nodded. "Don't worry, I
won't touch you—unless you try to escape again. Otherwise, I'm not much interested in drowned rats."

She actually thought she heard him laugh as he turned
away and went to the mouth of the cave, staring out at
the wild night.

Juliana realized that this was his way of allowing her
to remove her clothes in privacy. *Saintly of him,* she
thought bitterly as she faced the rear of the cave and
fumbled at her soaked gown. She was too cold and miserable to feel any gratitude at all to Cole Rawdon—and
that remark of his about her looking like a drowned rat
rankled, despite her shivers. Of course she looked like a
drowned rat. She was nearly frozen to death, her hair was
streaming into her eyes, and her skin must be blue with
cold—and it was all his fault. Moreover, she didn't give a
damn (there, Aunt Katharine!) about how she looked,
only about the quickest way to get warm. Still, wet as
they were, she couldn't bring herself to remove her cami-
sole and pantalets, not with a man like Cole Rawdon at
such close proximity. She also kept on the pouch tied on
a thin ribbon around her waist. Ever since she'd been
robbed, she kept her mother's locket and her other small
treasures, as well as her money, in a little silk pouch

hidden beneath her dress. Though she'd lost her reticule back in Cedar Gulch, she had her money still. It might come in handy yet, she thought, tossing her sodden dress down beside the fire. The pouch gave her some comfort, and a little more confidence. But she didn't have enough confidence to try to get those guns of his away from Cole Rawdon—at least, not yet. She realized that was the only way she would be safe—and, of course, the only way she would have a chance to escape. No matter what she had said to him, she was going to get away. She'd rather die of starvation in the mountains or of thirst in the desert than be turned over to John Breen.

She wouldn't actually shoot Rawdon, of course, once she got his guns, but if she could threaten him . . .

She almost smiled, thinking what it would be like when she was the one in control.

Later, maybe, Juliana thought as she pulled the blanket tight around her shoulders. Just now, she needed warmth and rest, and she needed it desperately. She inched to the fire, huddling once more as close as she could get to the flames. Rawdon must have heard her movements, for he turned back into the cave and strode toward her.

"Drink some coffee," he ordered, stooping to pour some into a mug.

"No, thank you," Juliana was surprised to hear herself say between chattering teeth. "I don't like coffee. I prefer tea."

It wasn't true, but now that she was dry and getting warm, her spirit was returning as well. Though she desperately wanted coffee, she wanted to defy Cole Rawdon even more. Not enough to get him angry at her again, but enough to annoy him.

Aunt Katharine had always accused her of choosing to be difficult. Juliana decided she was right.

"Too bad, your highness, but my provisions don't include tea," Rawdon responded dryly. His eyes were as cold as the granite walls of the cave, doing nothing to dissipate her shivers. "You'll have to make do."

"Well, then." Juliana shrugged. "I don't need any coff—"

He stepped toward her: "I'm not letting two thousand dollars' worth of flesh die of exposure because you're in the mood to be stubborn. Do I have to pour it down your throat? I'd be glad to oblige."

He would, Juliana realized, staring up at him in alarm. Her eyes flashed with anger, but she knew it would be foolish to try to resist him at this point. Besides, the coffee looked and smelled marvelous. Instead, she responded with all the cool dignity she could muster under the circumstances. She was nearly naked, alone on a storm-tossed mountain with a man who had already killed three people today (that she knew about).

"Fine, Mr. Rawdon, but I require cream and two lumps of sugar."

That much was true.

"Can't help you. It's black."

"You don't have . . . either of those items?"

"No."

"Well, then, I don't believe I care for any . . ."

"Drink it!"

Juliana drank. Despite the bitter taste, the searing heat of the coffee penetrated the cold in her blood even more than the blankets and the fire. Sharp warmth burned through her, deliciously comforting. She gasped, sighed, and drank the rest, draining the cup as Cole Rawdon watched impassively, his face lit by the glowing flames.

When the coffee was gone, he handed her some jerky and a biscuit.

"I suppose I ought to thank you." But Juliana refused to look at him, and instead concentrated on the food. She didn't care if she wolfed it down like some kind of savage.

She was starving. "I'm overwhelmed by your kindness," she couldn't help adding between mouthfuls.

"Can't let my prisoner die. They might withhold the reward."

She paused and look at him. "Greed is your master, then, Mr. Rawdon? Money is more important to you than truth? Than"—she searched for words—"than justice or the miscarriage of justice?"

"You'll have a trial, lady. Find your justice there."

"Not in Denver! You don't understand . . ."

He gave a curt laugh.

"How many times must I tell you? I am not a thief!"

His face went flat, still. "You have a bill of sale for the pinto, I suppose?"

She stopped short. Hot color rushed into her cheeks. "You wouldn't listen to me," she pleaded. "I had no choice."

"Just like you had no choice except to steal five thousand dollars and another damned horse back in Denver. Well, I'll tell you something, lady, and this is the last time we'll discuss it."

My, he was angry. Cool and controlled this time, but angry. The taut face that made him handsomer than ever, the electric fire in his eyes . . . did he hate all thieves so savagely, Juliana wondered, or just her?

He reached down and pulled her to her feet so that she faced him, clutching the blanket about her.

"I don't give a red-hot damn about any of the fugitives I bring back, and I don't waste my time listening to them claim their innocence. You know why? Because I don't care." His damp hair had fallen into his eyes, giving him an almost satanic look as he continued. "This is my job. I'm not a judge. I'm not even a damned sheriff. I'm a bounty hunter. I make my living bringing criminals back to face trial, and I intend to make a damned good profit bringing you back, sweetheart. If the reward wasn't so

damned high, I wouldn't bother with you." His gaze
scorched her with its intensity. He gave a rough laugh. "I
don't much care for women, except the kind you meet in
a saloon. And something tells me you're not that kind. I
don't talk much, and I can't stand a lot of chatter. Or
tears. So don't try any of that." He shook her. "You're
going back. Unless you can manage to kill me, because
that's what it would take for you to get away again. And
I don't think you're going to manage to kill me, because
others have tried who are a lot more capable of it than
you. So forget about telling me you're innocent, forget
about sweet-talking me into letting you go, forget about
escape, and save your tears and your begging for the
judge. You got that?"

Juliana drew a breath. Rain continued to pour outside
the cave, pounding the storm-tossed darkness like a hail
of bullets. She gazed up at Cole Rawdon with wide, cool
eyes.

"For a man who doesn't like to talk much," she remarked, "that was quite a speech."

His jaw clenched. She thought she heard his teeth
gnash.

"There's just one thing," she rushed on, before he
could explode at her. "You see, Mr. Rawdon, the difference between me and your other prisoners is that I *am*
innocent," she said triumphantly. "That is the plain and
simple truth."

For an instant, as she met his gaze firmly and with
unwavering conviction, he almost thought it could be
true. Then he remembered how she'd stolen Arrow from
under his nose, how she had gasped in pain over a supposedly broken ankle before sprinting for the horse with
the agility of a deer. Juliana Montgomery was good, all
right. She was very good. The lies poured from her lips as
sweet as molasses.

"Keep talking, and I'll gag you for the rest of the trip,"

he flung at her. He pushed her away, relieved not to have
to look into those luminous green eyes anymore, to
glimpse the beauty they held, a beauty filled with deceit.

Cole stepped around her, and fished a pouch of tobacco from his pocket. He fixed himself a smoke, feeling
restless and on edge, while the girl settled down in silence
before the fire. Wrapped in his blanket, staring into the
flames, she seemed unaware of how seductively lovely she
looked. But he wondered if she knew the effect she was
having on him, one that made him damned uneasy.

Amber firelight gilded the riot of heavy curls framing
her face, and revealed every delicate plane of her chiseled
features. Her skin had lost its icy-cold paleness, and now
glowed in the flames, making her look so vibrant and
alive, so tantalizingly soft and warm, that Cole had to
fight the urge to . . . to what? Grab her in his arms and
kiss her? Make love to her right here on the gritty floor of
this cave? He was disgusted with himself.

You'd think she was a regular woman, one of the girls
in the Red Feather, someone like Ina Day. She wasn't.
She was an outlaw. She might be pretty, she might talk
fine and smell good, and she might have the most enticing bare shoulders he'd ever seen, but she was as underhanded and dangerous as any of the scum he normally
lassoed.

And he'd better remember that.

Turning his back on her, Cole smoked and worked at
hardening his heart against the slender vision by the
campfire. He couldn't afford to let his guard down with
her, she was without doubt an expert at manipulating
men with her looks and her body. He wasn't going to fall
for her tricks. He summoned up the vision of Fire Mesa
as he remembered it from his childhood, and he thought
of that two-thousand-dollar reward and how it just might
tip the scales in his favor.

The sooner he dumped Juliana Montgomery in the

Denver jail, the closer he'd be to buying back Fire Mesa —if it wasn't too late already.

Think about that. Don't think about anything *but* that. Cole tossed the butt of his cigarette into the fire.

"Time to turn in."

He spread his bedroll on the ground and the oilcloth beside it.

"Come here."

Warily, Juliana rose and approached him. What now? She tried to draw back when she saw the rope in his hands, but he grabbed her wrists in one fist, and quickly hobbled them together.

"There's no need to keep me tied up—I'm not going to run out into that rain . . ."

"That's right, you're not. And you're not going to kill me in my sleep either." He fastened the remaining three feet of rope to his belt with quick precision, then lay down on his bedroll, forcing her to the ground by his movements.

"Sleep while you can. We've got a lot of ground to cover tomorrow."

Sleep? The oilcloth wasn't much protection from the drafty cave floor. Cold air buffeted her. The blanket had slipped off one shoulder and the rope bit into her skin. Juliana knew she wouldn't sleep a bit.

She twisted uncomfortably, trying to find a position where the blanket was secure and where the ground didn't feel quite so hard beneath her.

Cole Rawdon, three feet away, had his back to her.

"Stop squirming around and go to sleep," he growled.

She thought his voice had a strange edge to it. She wasn't sure why, but she didn't want to make him any angrier than he already was, so she went perfectly still and stared up at the rocky ceiling of the cave, weirdly lit now by the dying gold embers of the fire.

She would never, ever be able even to doze. Not with

the storm, the rope, the lightning, and, worst of all, Cole Rawdon's powerful form right beside her.

At least he had made no move to touch her. But what if he did? Tension worked its way through her aching body.

She hadn't a prayer of getting any sleep. She knew it. She would lie here, cold, miserable, and afraid all night.

But weariness swooped down on her like a hawk and carried her off before she even realized it, bearing her inexorably to the edge of slumber—and then beyond, deep, deep into the dark, limitless crevasse.

Curled unconsciously against her captor in a cave of black and amber, Juliana closed her eyes and slept.

· 10 ·

She awoke at dawn to find Cole Rawdon standing over her.

"It's about time," he drawled.

Behind him, one of the horses whinnied as if in agreement.

Rawdon was fully dressed, including gunbelt and boots, and looked clean, shaved, rested—and impatient. "We're breaking camp. Better hurry if you want breakfast."

What she wanted, Juliana thought, was to be a thousand miles away from here. She pulled the blanket over her head with a groan. She couldn't believe it was morning already. And she couldn't believe she had slept. She managed to sit up then, combing the hair back from her eyes with her fingers. Cole Rawdon was watching her, his thumbs hooked in his pants pockets, his expression becoming more amused by the second.

Damn him. She must look a sight. It was never easy for Juliana to wake up before ten in the morning, and in the past she had always preferred to have her chocolate in bed before speaking to anyone, even her maid. Now she was on top of a damned mountain at dawn, being scrutinized by the most infuriating man alive, who looked as if he was ready for anything. For a moment, she wished she *had* fallen off that precipice into the canyon last night.

Juliana gave a sigh. Pulling the blanket up over her shoulders in an effort to preserve what was left of her dignity, she managed to stand without his assistance, every muscle in her back and shoulders crying out in protest.

Morning sunlight streamed beyond the cave's entrance, flooding the fresh-washed world outside with clean, shimmering light. Looking down, Juliana realized that her bonds were gone, the bedroll was folded and packed, and fresh coffee had been made. It smelled heavenly. To her further amazement, a small animal of some sort was roasting on a spit above the fire, and the mouthwatering aroma of roasting meat permeated the cave.

He'd been busy this morning, hadn't he? Where in the world did he get the stamina?

The tantalizing smell of the meat filled her nostrils, and made her stomach growl, penetrating even her just-awakened fog. Lord, it smelled good. So did the coffee Rawdon had in his cup, steam rising fragrantly into the air.

"I didn't know you could cook," she muttered as she headed toward the fire and the food.

"I can do a lot of things," he commented with a grin, and raised one eyebrow. "Want me to show you some of 'em?"

"No," Juliana said hastily. But her stomach did a strange little somersault. He seemed different when he smiled like that—younger, almost agreeable, certainly less dangerous, and, if possible, even more handsome. She thought of asking him what kind of creature it was, there on the spit, but then she decided she'd be better off if she didn't know. As eagerly as if she were sitting down to a china-covered spread of poached eggs, sausage, biscuits, and marmalade, she took the greasy meat he handed her and ate it with famished gusto. Even the black coffee was the most delicious she had ever tasted. Ladylike manners were forgotten. Juliana gobbled every piece as quickly as she put it to her mouth.

Cole studied her when she was intent on her food and not paying him any attention. If possible, she looked even lovelier than she had last night, her eyes soft and dewy with sleep, her pale hair tousled about her face, her skin glowing with luminous beauty. Every now and then the blanket slipped off her shoulder and he caught a glimpse of a lace-edged chemise caressing her pale flesh. The chemise was pretty, delicate, just like her, he thought. And then he caught himself. No use traveling down that road. It could only lead to trouble. The problem was, he told himself, he was used to being alone—or else having some dirty outlaw scum trussed up before his campfire. Not a woman. Especially one as beautiful and dainty-looking as this one. Even the way she nibbled at the rabbit meat and took small, neat sips of coffee was elegant and graceful and somehow fascinating. How the hell did someone like her get mixed up in stealing? he wondered.

Easy, he answered himself quickly. He scowled, thinking of Liza, of how she and Jess had laughed when they'd left him for dead in the desert. The sound of that laughter still echoed in his head sometimes, hurting him more than the bullet ever had. The pain had never completely gone away. Maybe it had hurt so much because he'd only been a kid, and had still believed in friendship and goodness and trust. But Jess Burrows had taught him that friendship meant nothing when money was involved, that goodness was a myth and that trust—trust between friends, or between a man and a woman, led only to be-

trayal and pain, and probably death. Yeah, he'd learned
all right and he'd better not forget those lessons.

This girl looked nothing like Liza, Cole reflected, di-
viding the last of the rabbit meat between himself and
her. She was even more beautiful in her own way. And
she was most likely every bit as cunning—maybe more.
She'd probably gotten away with a lot before the law
started to catch up to her in Denver; that would explain
the unusually high bounty put out by Judge Mason. So
the less he thought about her as a woman, Rawdon told
himself harshly, the better. She was a prisoner, like any
other. As his gaze flitted from the dusting of freckles
across her nose, to those full, rose-pink lips she was licking, and downward, along the long column of her throat
to where the saddle blanket hid the curves of her slender
form, he swallowed. Like any other. He gulped down a
freshly poured cup of coffee, scalding his throat.

"There's something I want to ask you," he said, trying
to ignore the deep, burning pain the coffee had caused.

Juliana swallowed her last mouthful of meat and sent
him a scathing look. "I'd rather not talk to you, if you
don't mind." She tossed her head back. "Since you won't
believe a word I say, what's the point?"

"The point is, I'm asking you a question and you'd
damn well better tell me the truth." He reached out suddenly and gripped her wrist. That got her attention. Her
eyes went wide and met his head-on. "Are you related to
that Montgomery gang that's been holding up freight
lines and stagecoaches all over the place?" he demanded.

For a moment he thought he saw something go tense
and still in her face. She tried to pull away from him and
failed.

"No."

But her voice was weak.

"You're lying again."

"I am not! I don't know who or what you're talking about."

"Then why did you think that hombre I shot in Denver was someone named Tommy? There's a Tommy Montgomery heading up that gang."

"So?"

"You and he have the same last name."

Juliana shrugged. "So?" she said again, in a cool, haughty tone. "It's a coincidence."

"Then who's the Tommy you mentioned?" he persisted relentlessly.

"N-no one. A former sweetheart, that's all."

The narrow-eyed look he fixed her with made her lick her lips nervously. He spoke in a low, even tone. "You married to someone in that gang, lady, or kin in some other way? Tell me."

"I already told you . . ."

"Lies. You've told me nothing but a pack of lies." Disgusted, he hauled her to her feet so suddenly, the blanket slipped away. Her near nakedness was a shock for them both. Cole couldn't help noticing the lushness of her curves, or the way her full breasts strained against the thin chemise, just as he couldn't help the tension that hardened in his body at the sight of her. He pulled her close.

"When are you going to level with me?"

"I already have and you wouldn't listen."

She was struggling to get away, to reach the blanket, but he wouldn't let her. Cole stared down at her, breathing hard. Her face was raised to his, and her expression was so filled with anger, fear, and some emotion he couldn't quite read, that he could do nothing but gaze at her for a moment, caught in the spell of that heartrending, flowerlike beauty. Her hair spilled over her shoulder like sunshine, and he fought the urge to crush it between his fingers.

"Please," Juliana gasped, not struggling anymore but aware of how tightly he held her, of the strength in that tall, muscled form. She felt vulnerable beyond description.

"Please?" he repeated, his eyes glinting. "Are you asking me to let you go—or to do something else?"

Heaven help her, for one instant she didn't know. She despised him—didn't she? And yet, there was a current between them, a potent electricity that jolted her senses as she stood here in his arms, half naked and afraid—yet not afraid. Her heart was pounding wildly, her body tingled every place his body touched hers, and she could not stop staring at his mouth.

What was wrong with her? This was insane. Cole Rawdon was her enemy. He had her in his power more surely than even John Breen would have if she had married him. Yet, she wasn't frightened of him. Some instinct told her he would not hurt her, despite what he wanted her to believe. And especially not now, not the way he was holding her. Strange, she had never felt the smallest spark between her and John Breen: when Breen had touched her, it made her skin crawl. But Rawdon's touch made every sense spring to life. He made her ache deep down. She ached for something she didn't understand, couldn't name, couldn't figure out, yet she ached all the same. She wanted him to . . . to what?

Kiss her. Hold her. Stroke her cheek, her hair. Tell her . . . what?

"Crazy." She didn't realize she had said it aloud until she saw the smile curve his lips.

"You're right. But you still haven't answered my question." His voice grew husky suddenly. "Or maybe you have . . ."

She wasn't fighting him, she didn't want to get away. Without thinking, purely on instinct, Cole bent his head suddenly and kissed her. She might be an outlaw, but she was all woman in his arms. He kissed her hard and for a very long time.

Cole found her lips even more intoxicating than he had imagined. She tasted so sweet. Her scent was light and fresh, purely feminine. And that cloud of hair the color of spun gold nestled soft as flower petals in his hands.

Juliana couldn't breathe. His lips imprisoned hers, and set them afire. His mouth was warm and strong and as determined about what it was doing as Cole Rawdon was about everything he set himself to. He stroked her hair, his hands rough, greedy, yet somehow gentle as they tangled themselves in her curls. She quaked inside and out. She felt explosive little ripples surging through her. Oh, it was madness, but she didn't want it to stop. She never wanted it to stop . . .

Suddenly, he shoved her backward and she lost her balance, nearly falling. Cole drew his gun and wheeled toward the cave entrance in one lightning movement, even as a man's voice gasped out, "Whoa there, mister. We don't mean you no harm."

Two strangers crouched just within the entrance.

They looked to be prospectors. The older one had a pickax in his hand, and the younger carried a sack of tools slung over his bony shoulder. Cole stepped in front of Juliana, keeping his gun leveled on the elder of the two. He was a stooped man of about fifty, grizzled of face and with black, shining eyes, whose skeletal form was covered with frayed bib overalls and a tattered fedora that looked to have been through flood and famine. He had a gun stuck in his worn-out belt, and both his boots had holes where the toes ought to be. The other man, Juliana noted, was a gaping youth of no more than fifteen years, his flannel shirt and trousers in even worse condition than his companion's.

Cole studied them with a piercing glance.

"Who are you?"

"N-name's Jebediah Garsden, mister. This is my boy, Gus. Now lookee here, we don't want no trouble. No need for that there gun."

"You ought to know better than to sneak up on strangers."

"Wal, we wasn't meaning to, but we was passing by and saw your horses—our claim ain't far off." He peered worriedly at Cole from beneath his hat. "You weren't headed for it, were you?"

"Do I look like a prospector?"

"Nope, but that's not to say . . . well, never mind. Reckon me and Gus are just gettin' suspicious these days. Heerd about a fellow whose claim got jumped over near White Mountain. Kinda makes a body think. You know, you folks ought to be more careful. We coulda been Apache or something, 'stead of just a couple of miners. . . ."

"Outside." Cole still held the gun. "Let's give the lady some privacy."

The two backed out of the cave with Rawdon following right behind them. While she dressed Juliana heard the three men talking: of the storm, the shortest route to the nearest town, the latest rumors of Apache renegades hiding out in the mountains. Her muslin was still damp, but she yanked it over her head anyway and pushed her arms through the sleeves, trying not to think about what had happened a few moments earlier. She didn't know how she would face Cole Rawdon—or those other men. She didn't know what she had been thinking of. That was the problem, she fumed inwardly, fastening the buttons of her dress up to her throat with shaking fingers, she hadn't been thinking at all.

The word *passion* had never had any meaning for her before, but now she still felt warm with the heat of it. She was mortified, and furious with herself, and cringed with shame at the thought of facing Cole Rawdon beneath the merciless clarity of the sun. Why had she let him kiss her, and even kissed him back? Why did she feel passion for Cole Rawdon in the first place?

He was not an acceptable, civilized man. He was a bounty hunter, a dealer in flesh and misery. To add to that, he considered her nothing but a lying thief. So why had he wanted to kiss her? The answer made her burn with shame. Because men didn't care about anything but a pretty face and a . . . a comely figure. He didn't give a damn about her. He had just wanted to satisfy some horrid male lusting . . .

Her cheeks flamed with humiliation. She didn't know what her excuse was. Did women have this lusting too? Was it only his rugged male beauty that had drawn her to him and made her want to stay in his arms? She couldn't think of any other reason. Many handsome men had courted her. John Breen was handsome, and he had wanted to marry her.

But she had never felt anything for any of them remotely similar to what she had known when Cole Rawdon held her. None of the suitors who'd flocked to her door, none of the silly, smitten beaux who had sent her flowers and poems and begged her for a dance had ever set her heart to racing or blood pounding to her head. Cole Rawdon, with his cool, nonchalant face and his infuriatingly self-assured way with horses, caves, storms, and campfires, and his stubborn, domineering manner had affected her like the clash of cymbals in a musical piece, jarring her, jolting her, playing havoc with her pulse and her poise.

But she could have no more of that. She mustn't let this despicable lust, if that's what it was, get the better of either of them, ever again.

That still didn't help her with the immediate problem besetting her—how could she face him?

Juliana hesitated as long as she could. When she heard the prospectors moving off, she slipped out of the cave.

He was watching the two men and their pair of pack mules disappear down the mountain and didn't even glance at her. "Wait here." He sounded as curt and as cold as ever. "I'm going to follow them a ways and make sure they're really gone."

Juliana was grateful he hadn't looked at her. Yet his cold indifference made her feel even more foolish and ashamed than before. "Why don't you trust them?"

"I don't trust anyone." He didn't tell her that some of these old prospectors had been known to go loco occasionally and murder anyone found within fifty miles of their so-called claim.

He moved off on foot after them, so quickly and stealthily, Juliana could do nothing but stare after him in awe. Suddenly, she realized something. In his preoccupation with the strangers, he had left her alone with the horses. Both horses. If she took them both before he got back, he'd have no way to follow her.

He'd also be stranded in the mountains.

She stood torn for a moment, battling her conscience and her determination to get clean away. But there was really no choice.

She couldn't do it.

But she could take one of them, she told herself, starting into the cave with alacrity. Not his precious pinto, but the bay that had belonged to Cash Hogan. He was already saddled and ready to go. She had only to hurry, and she'd have a head start . . .

She led him to a rock, but as she began to mount she felt herself grabbed roughly from behind and yanked clear of the horse. Rawdon shook her by the shoulders, none too gently.

"At it again, lady? Don't you ever learn?"

Frustrated nearly to tears, Juliana thrust up her chin.

"What do you expect me to do?" she demanded. "Wait around to be mauled by you, and then packed off to jail? I don't know which is worse!"

The only sign he gave that her jibe had hit home showed in the flash of steel in those vivid blue eyes. "I don't expect anything of you, Miss Montgomery, except trouble. And you've already caused me plenty of that. You want to ride?" He gave a grim laugh that chilled her blood. "We'll ride. Come on."

Hours later, Juliana was to wish she had never set foot aboard the train leaving the St. Louis station all those months ago. She wished she had never come anywhere near a horse or a mountain.

She had long ago given up trying to remember their trail through the dense forested plateaus of the Mogollon Rim, but as hours passed and the hot afternoon sun blazed down on her head, she decided this could only be a road into hell. The pinto carried both her and Rawdon along a seemingly endless winding canyon trail. The sky was crystal clear, scrubbed clean of all the storm clouds that had descended the previous evening, and the earth was fragrant and damp with the aftermath of rain. It was hot and quiet enough to hear lizards gliding along the rocks. Quiet enough to hear the cry of eagles—or was it vultures?—echoing from distant hills. They dipped through a precarious rocky pass masked by jagged boulders and stands of hardy scrub oak, then picked their way up a steep gorge to a bald hilltop. Below raced a cascading mountain stream, and the sound of the water rushing through the rocks made Juliana's parched throat ache; but although she glimpsed the beautiful gurgling waters of the crystal stream when Rawdon turned the pinto to a cactus-studded trail headed north, the man sitting in the saddle behind her never paused for rest or drink. On they rode, climbing higher through a forest of fragrant pine, then suddenly descending a canyon so steep, it made her gasp in fright. She closed her eyes against the dizzying sight of jagged gray and purple rocks far beneath the sheer drop, trying to blot out her fear, her exhaustion, and the terrible aching of every muscle in her tortured body. *He must be made of iron,* she thought at one point when the sun had begun to dip in the western sky and pink shadows of impending sunset tinged the horizon. Throughout this endless day, from the moment they'd left the cave, Cole Rawdon had never slowed the steady pace of his horse, never faltered in his path or direction. It was as if he knew every crevice of the mountains, every pass, every chasm, rock, and tree.

From the tension in his body she sensed that he was very angry. He didn't speak to her once that entire day. Which was just as well, because after hours on horseback over grueling trails, Juliana couldn't have spoken a single civil word to him, and she knew that would have only made him angrier. Behind them on a lead rope came Cash Hogan's bay, bearing the gear and supplies. At first Juliana had wondered why Rawdon hadn't let her ride Cash's horse instead of forcing her to ride with him, then she had realized as the day wore on that he probably doubted her ability to survive the precipitous trails over which they were riding. He didn't want to see his two-thousand-dollar reward tumble over a cliff any more than he had wanted to see it die of exposure last night, and that at least, was something for which she could be thankful. He wouldn't kill her—she was too valuable to him alive. Now all she had to do was figure out how to get away from him. It shouldn't be too difficult, escaping a man much stronger, more experienced, and more familiar with the terrain than she was—eluding him in the middle of this godforsaken Arizona Territory, with nothing around for miles but mountains and cliffs and snakes and coyotes—and other bounty hunters searching for her

besides. Simple. Easy. Like baking a strawberry pie—
without benefit of flour, sugar, berries, or stove.

Hours passed, long, bone-crunching, scorching hours,
and still they rode in silence, with his muscular body,
solid as the rocks around them, pressed against her weary
spine, his powerful arms encasing her slender frame as he
held the pinto's reins.

At last, when deep gray shadows had nearly obliterated the rose and gold of the sunset-painted sky, they
halted. They were in a wide grassy valley beneath an
overhang of granite rock. A stream of water tumbled into
a shallow basin of smooth stones. Beside this pool was a
stand of blue spruce that rolled away to their left, disappearing into dark forest. A rabbit scurried away beneath
a piñon, grouse circled overhead, and in the distance,
Juliana, raising her weary head, saw an elk silhouetted
for a moment upon a bald plateau before it bounded
away into the shadows.

Rawdon swung down from the saddle with ease, then
pulled Juliana down beside him. Her sore legs sagged
beneath her weight and she groaned, nearly collapsing.
With one arm around her waist supporting her, he
frowned down at her flushed, weary face. "You'll get used
to it" was all he said.

"Another day like this will kill me. You'll never get
your filthy reward money if I'm dead," she muttered.

"Don't count on it. I could always bring back your
scalp for proof."

"My . . . scalp?" A sick, weak feeling churned
through her stomach. "You're . . . joking, of course."

"Think so?" He studied her a moment, then turned
away and began the business of making camp.

Juliana shuddered uncontrollably. She should at this
moment be on the stagecoach getting nearer to Wade and
Tommy every mile, instead of at the mercy of this impossible man who hunted human beings for a living. He was

a monster, she thought, watching him tend the horses with the competent movements of someone who had done this all a thousand times before. He had no feelings, no human compassion, no morals whatever. Had he shown one ounce of emotion after shooting those men back in Cedar Gulch? Had he shown the least bit of concern or even common decency for her throughout the torturous past hours when she had ridden without rest across this savage land? Suddenly, staring at him, she was overwhelmed with hatred of this man—and of John Breen, who was truly responsible for her plight. She vowed to herself never to go back to Denver, no matter what. She would get away from Cole Rawdon somehow, anyhow. Sooner or later. He would have to sleep, to let his guard down sometime. When he did, she would be ready. And, she thought, straightening her shoulders unconsciously, she would do whatever was necessary to get clean away.

Rawdon turned suddenly and looked at her. For a moment, while the sky blazed overhead, he studied her with a penetrating look that made her feel he could read her thoughts. "Forget it," he said, with a light, mocking grin that chilled her blood. "You've failed twice already."

It was all she could do to keep her mouth from dropping open. "I don't know what you're talking about," she said after only a moment, her chin lifting.

His grin deepened.

"Sure you don't, lady," he drawled. "And you never stole anything in your life."

With that he hunkered down to start a fire. Juliana sank down upon a rock under an overhanging cottonwood, as far from him as she could get. Glancing about the secluded clearing with its tufts of brown grass, cactus, and wilting wildflowers, she debated the wisdom of bolting while his back was turned. But much as she was tempted to put as much distance as she could between her and Cole Rawdon at the earliest opportunity, common sense told her such a move would be plain stupid right now. For one thing, she was exhausted and weak from thirst, and her muscles burned with pain. She wouldn't get far, and even if she could get a head start, elude him, and hide herself in the wilderness, she would probably die of starvation in these mountains without ever seeing another human face. No, she would need a horse and supplies if she was going to get away and live to tell about it. That might take some time and planning. But she could wait, Juliana told herself, glancing darkly at Cole Rawdon's broad back as he worked to start a fire.

As daylight fled, a bleak, cold loneliness seemed to descend over the valley. In every direction, all Juliana could see were towering jagged peaks stretching upward like giant's fingers toward the vast, purple sky. Leaves rustled in the sweeping north wind, which swirled through the clearing in sudden, sharp gusts that made the embers of the fire dance wildly. The air was laced with pine and its mournful wail echoed through the crevices of the surrounding rocks. Beyond the campfire, unseen creatures scurried in the brush, making Juliana distinctly uneasy as she huddled before the flames, eating the wild grouse Rawdon had shot and plucked and shown her how to cook. She would not look at him, but stared instead into the flickering flames, wondering if he would tie her to him again when it was time to sleep. She dreaded it, but there was little she could do against him. He was too big, too strong. And something told her that once he made up his mind about something, he didn't relent easily. The only thing in her favor was that he had so far shown no sign of trying to hurt her. She could only pray that would continue.

Juliana knew one thing. She would not beg for mercy or show any sign of weakness in front of him. She had nothing left now to use against him but her pride and her wits, and she would cling to those with all her strength.

Chewing the last juicy morsel of the grouse, Cole studied her across the fire, a queer feeling in his gut. It was as if he was hypnotized by the sight of this slender, fair-haired beauty with the haunting green eyes sitting so close to him in this lonely clearing. What the hell was wrong with him?

His eyes narrowed as she hugged her arms around herself, and he saw her shiver. Damn. This wasn't turning out to be as simple as he had first thought. The more time he spent with her, the more she got under his skin. Like this morning, he thought, feeling anger and self-contempt surge through him again. How had he ever let himself get to kissing her—and then get so caught up in it that he hadn't even heard those prospectors coming up on them until it was almost too late? *We could've both been killed,* he reflected, stung by his own carelessness. *If I'd been in my right mind, I'd have heard those hombres long before they got within shooting distance of the cave entrance. What the hell is she doing to me?*

No woman since Liza had ever had this kind of effect on him. It wasn't healthy. A man could get killed thinking about yellow hair and dazzling eyes, about a woman's mouth so sweet, he couldn't draw himself away from her. . . .

"Going somewhere?" he asked as she rose and brushed off her skirt, then stepped purposefully toward the shadowed stand of spruce.

"I require a few moments of privacy," Juliana retorted, gritting her teeth at the indignity of having to discuss such intimacies with him. As if she needed his permission! "I assure you I have no intention of trying to run off."

"Glad to hear it." He nodded. "You might have more sense than I gave you credit for."

She stalked away from him, staring straight ahead, and made her way deep into the pines, well away from Cole Rawdon. When she had finished tending to the needs of her body, reveling in the few moments of total privacy, she became aware of the sound of rushing water to her left and, turning, discerned through the growing darkness the wider path of the stream that fed the basin of water near their camp. She started toward it, her skirts gathered in one hand, determined to wash the day's dust and grime from her face and perhaps in doing so, revive her flagging spirits. But she had no sooner dipped her hands into the icy water than a sound quite close to her made her quickly turn her head to the right.

She screamed, the bloodcurdling shriek echoing through the forest in a crescendo of pure terror.

· 11 ·

Cole heard her scream as he was tossing another branch on the campfire. He swung toward the forest, every muscle taut.

Damned woman, what the hell has happened now?

With his gun drawn he sprinted toward the sound that had chilled his blood. There had been nothing but silence after that one shrill cry, and Cole didn't know what that meant. He moved silently through the brush and trees, every sense alert, not knowing if he was going to meet up with Apache or outlaws, not knowing if she was already dead, killed in her tracks, or if someone was going to spring at him out of nowhere. . . .

He heard her voice then, high-pitched, frightened, coming from the direction of the stream, but he couldn't make out her words. At least she was still alive. He ran soundlessly through the trees until he reached the water, then stopped short at what he saw.

Juliana Montgomery was clinging to the limb of a tree, while below her, pawing at the trunk, was the largest black bear Cole had ever seen.

"Get away," she was ordering the creature while holding to the tree limb with arms, knees, elbows, and bloody fingers. *"Shoo.* Go back wherever you came from and *leave me alone."* Then, "Aaaaa . . ."

She shrieked like a banshee as her grip on the branch slipped and she nearly toppled from her perch.

"You do have a penchant for trouble," Cole remarked, watching her struggles from a distance of ten feet.

At his voice, Juliana tore her petrified gaze from the bear and stared at him in frozen fear. "D-do something!" she gasped. "I c-can't hang here much longer, I'm s-slipping . . ."

The bear swung toward Cole, a growl in his throat and his black eyes shining. He reared up on his hind legs and appeared to be wavering between whether to rush Cole or stay with the prey he had trapped in the tree. His growl ripped through the falling darkess of the descending night.

"Don't shoot him," Juliana ordered, gasping as she concentrated on maintaining her hold. "Just . . . get rid of him . . . somehow . . ."

"Seems to me you're not in a position to be giving orders," Cole drawled, noting the interesting picture she made with her skirt hitched up around her thighs, revealing long, slender legs. "You sure as hell could've told me you were meeting up with a friend. Maybe I should just leave you two alone."

"Don't you dare make fun of me at a . . . time like this!" Juliana gave a shriek as the branch she was clutching began to crack beneath her weight. "Oh, dear Lord . . ."

The bear glanced up and swung a giant paw upward toward the girl hanging almost directly over him. Juliana screamed again.

"What's the connection between you and the Montgomery gang?"

"What?" Juliana couldn't believe her ears.

"You heard me."

Her fingers were raw with splinters from the branch, and every muscle in her arms burned with the effort of holding herself aloft. "This is . . . hardly the time . . ."

"Can't think of a better one. If you don't want to dance with that fellow, you'd better talk fast. And make it the truth."

"Cole . . . please!"

"What's the connection?"

"They're my brothers—but they have nothing to do with—"

"Tommy—that's your brother?"

"Yes, yes—one of them—now please . . ."

The bear started to shinny up the tree.

"Cole!" Juliana shrieked.

"Why did you faint outside the Gold Dust?"

Her hands were slipping. She clutched desperately, pressing with her knees, elbows, fingertips, everything she had. Less than ten feet away the bear snarled, showing her its teeth . . .

"For God's sake . . ."

"Why?"

"Because I can't bear the sight of blood! But I'd gladly shed yours right at this moment! Now get this thing away from me, but . . . don't shoot him . . . unless you have to!"

"Maybe you'd like *me* to dance with him," Cole remarked. He raised his gun.

The bear, as if sensing his intentions, swung down from the base of the tree and faced Cole on all fours, eyes shining.

Cole fired past the bear's head.

The animal swerved sideways with a growl. He seemed to be gathering himself for a lunge forward. Cole fired off another shot, and sprang directly toward the creature, letting out a piercing Cheyenne war cry. Startled, the bear rumbled deep in his throat, swung about, and lumbered off through the trees as quickly as his legs could carry him, disappearing into the inky shadows cast by the twilight.

Cole slipped his gun back into its holster and strolled forward, wondering why he hadn't just killed the animal. The bear could have charged him, instead of running off. Fool woman. *Don't shoot him.* And he had listened. He scowled at her, not sure if he was more annoyed with her, or with himself. "Well, Miss Montgomery," he drawled as he gazed up at her in her flushed, disheveled state. "Now I know you can ride, steal, *and* climb trees. I'm learning more about you all the time. The question is, can you say thank you?"

"G-get me down from here," Juliana gasped. "I think . . . I'm going to fall—"

Even as she spoke the branch snapped and she tumbled downward, but Cole caught her neatly in his arms. Her hands were scratched and bloody from scrambling up the tree, and he guessed her knees and arms were the same, but her face, bright red and furious, was almost comical in its dismay.

"Ohhh! Let me *go,*" she demanded as she felt the strength of his iron grip about her body. "Let me go this instant!"

"Anything you say, ma'am." Cole dumped her into a pile of pine needles without ceremony.

Landing flat on her backside, Juliana screeched in outrage. She was already unbelievably stiff and sore from the grueling day of riding—not to mention scrambling up the tree. She didn't know how much more she could take. She glared up at him as fury whipped through her. "You . . . you . . ."

"You're welcome." Cole smothered the urge to laugh.

Instead, he touched his hand to his hat, turned, and started back through the trees toward the campsite.

"Stick around as long as you want—maybe your friend will come back for another dance," he called over his shoulder.

He heard her scrambling to her feet. "Wait . . . for me!"

But he didn't slow down or glance back, and she had to run to catch up to him. "You . . . you are the most impossible, ungentlemanly, discourteous man . . ."

"And you're the most troublesome, ungrateful, complainingest woman . . ."

For a moment they glared at each other in the twilight beneath the spreading branches of the spruce, she with her tumbling curls dangling in her face, with pine needles stuck to her gown and fury glimmering in her eyes, and he with that cold, mocking expression that never failed to rile her. Then Cole reached out and seized her by the shoulders and started, he swore, to kiss her but at the last instant, with his mouth only inches from hers, he yanked his head back, silently cursed himself for a weak damned fool, and pushed her away. His back straight, he turned on his heel and stalked off without another word.

What the hell had almost happened, he wondered as fury and bafflement struggled within him. Hadn't he learned his lesson this morning? This woman was more trouble than a dozen varmints like Reese Kincaid. He had to stay away from her, as far away as he could get. Why the hell did he keep wanting to kiss her? Because she was so damned beautiful she put a sunrise to shame, and so full of pluck she hadn't the sense to be properly scared of him or a bear?

Don't shoot him, she had said. And she had fainted in Denver when she'd seen a dead man. So bloodshed and killing bothered her, but stealing did not. Odd. But then, so was this entire situation. For once in his life, Cole felt unsure of his own instincts, his own will. If he wasn't careful, she'd get the upper hand with him yet, not through pulling a gun or a knife on him while he slept, but by tearing down his resistance. Hell, he was a man, wasn't he? But she was one hell of a bewitching woman.

He made a decision. There was no way he wanted to drag her all the way back to Denver. It would take weeks of traveling together across the wilderness at close quarters and he'd be damned if he'd put himself through that. There was a quicker, easier way. Tomorrow he'd take her to Plattsville. Let Sheriff Rivers deal with transporting her to Denver. He could wash his hands of her once he brought her to jail. It would take longer to get the reward: Rivers would have to get it wired from Denver, and it might take up to a month before the paperwork was completed, the girl was turned over to the law in Denver, and the money was forwarded. In the meantime he'd ride down to Fire Mesa and see what he could do about stalling for time. It would be worth it, Cole decided with a grim twist to his mouth, to be rid of her, even though it wasn't the way he usually conducted his business. But he'd had enough of Juliana Montgomery and her shenanigans.

Juliana followed him back to camp with great thoughtfulness. She didn't know what to make of Cole Rawdon. He was the most unpredictable and infuriating man she'd met, but she was beginning to wonder if he was really quite as impervious to her as he would like her to believe. He had tried to make it plain that she was nothing to him but an object, a piece of property of value only because she could be exchanged for cash; yet she could have sworn back there that he was ready to kiss her again—even though he was angry, even though she had annoyed him and caused him a good deal of trouble. Kiss him! She'd as soon kiss that old black bear as kiss Cole Rawdon.

Still, if he *was* attracted to her, even the tiniest little bit, wasn't that something she could use to her advantage? She might be able to soften his feelings for her enough to convince him to let her go—or at least to let his guard down so she could find an opportunity to make a decent escape.

It certainly bore thinking about.

When she reached the camp, he was leaning against a tree, smoking one of his cheroot cigarettes. His face was unreadable. He looked very tall, strong, and forbidding, standing in the gray twilight, his hat slouched down over his eyes. Juliana took a deep breath. It was best not to waste any time in trying out her new plan of action. Though there was an inherent danger in her plan that she hadn't overlooked, a danger of encouraging more attention from Cole Rawdon than she desired or could handle, she was desperate enough to try anything.

She walked up to him, trying to hide her uncertainty, completely unaware of the sensuous sway of her hips as she moved along the thick grass. She had no idea of how enticing her thick, tousled hair appeared as it swung forward over her shoulders, or of how softly the shadows lit her oval face. She was nervous, thinking about the perilous game she was about to begin playing with this unpredictable man. But she swallowed her apprehensions, and with one hand smoothed her curls back from her face. She must look a sight, she knew, bedraggled and dirty, with her skirt torn from shinnying up the tree, but she was still a woman, she reminded herself, and that supposedly had a big effect on a man.

So she gave him what she hoped was a beguiling, apologetic smile and said in a soft voice, "I'm afraid I didn't behave very well back there, Mr. Rawdon. I owe you an apology—and a thank-you. I appreciate that you didn't kill that creature."

He took a drag on the cigarette. "Yeah? What about the fact that I saved your hide?"

"I appreciate that too."

In the gloom of the clearing, his eyes pierced her face. "What's up?" he asked roughly.

"I beg your pardon?"

He threw the cigarette down and stomped on it hard. "What are you up to now?"

Juliana spread her hands and tried to look indignant. "Why must you be so suspicious of me? I merely realized that I did in fact owe you my life—actually, you saved my life yesterday, too. If it hadn't been for you, I would have toppled right over that precipice."

"I almost let you."

This startled her so much that she forgot her calm facade. Her mouth dropped open. "You . . . did?" she squeaked.

"Yes."

Damn the man. He sounded like he regretted that he had grabbed her back from the cliff. Juliana fought back her anger. *Don't let him distract you. He's trying to bait you, to make you mad.*

"So it occurred to me," she forced herself to continue in an even tone, "that even though I don't want to go back to Denver, you're right about one thing. I will have a trial there, and I can try to convince the jury of my innocence. So there's no point in my being rude to you or . . . trying to get away from you. I've decided that I'll simply let you take me back to Denver and I'll face up to the charges against me."

"You'll let me take you back? As if you've got a choice?" He mocked her deliberately, enjoying the angry sparkle she tried to keep from her eyes.

"There's no need to taunt me, Mr. Rawdon," she murmured, wishing she could contrive to have her eyes fill with tears, the way Victoria did whenever Uncle Edward had scolded her. Instead she had to settle for a desolate shrug of the shoulders. "I've already conceded defeat."

Cole watched her flutter her eyelashes at him in silence. "So you have," he said after a moment. "Mighty prettily, too." Suddenly, he seized her by the arms, and Juliana's eyes widened in alarm, but he only spun her about so that she faced the campfire and the clutter of dirty plates and utensils piled around it. "I realized something too, lady, while you were gone. I shot that grouse we had for dinner, so you can have the honor of cleaning up. If you're going to be my traveling companion, you'll have to do your share of the work."

He spun her around to face him again, and frowned down into her eyes. "What do you think of that?"

It took great effort, but Juliana kept her expression meek. "I think it's only fair," she managed to say.

She offered him a sweet smile. "I'll get started right now." She tilted her head to one side, slanting a pert look at him. "Will that be all right, Mr. Rawdon?"

"You can forget the *mister. Rawdon* will do just fine."

"Rawdon, then."

"Yeah, that'll be just fine."

She started to move away, but he didn't let go of her. She realized that he wasn't even aware that he still held her, though his grip was so strong it hurt. He was staring at her, his blue eyes like daggers in the darkness, studying her not with warmth, as she had hoped, but with cool, hard suspicion. "Mr. Rawdon, you're hurting me."

"What? Oh." He let her go.

But his gaze followed her back to the campfire. Juliana would have traded every coin in her money pouch at that moment to know what he was thinking.

She was bone-tired from the exertions of this day, and still stiff from the discomforts of last night, but she forced herself to do what he had asked without complaint. She'd have liked to hit him with the long-handled frying pan, but instead she piled the dishes into it. When she had gathered up all the plates and utensils and carried them to the pool, Rawdon instructed her how to scrub them with the sandy dirt and then rinse them in the water. While she worked he filled the canteens, brought more wood for the fire, and finished tending the horses.

Darkness fell over the valley, a hushed velvet blackness broken only by stars and moon. An owl hooted from the trees, its call desolate in the stillness. Water gurgled into the pool, and the wind sang a lonely melody through the brush. Juliana, finished at last with her chores, huddled near the campfire, weary beyond belief.

Without glancing at her, Rawdon unstrapped his bedroll and threw it down on the thick grass, with the oilskin right beside it. Then he, too, moved toward the fire and hunkered down to gaze into the flames.

Having a woman, especially one so uniquely lovely as this one, so near in these desolate surroundings was proving more torturous than he had imagined it could. Despite himself, he was drawn over and over by her delicate beauty and by the artless grace of the way she moved and spoke. Even now, the play of firelight across her face was evocative and her hair, which looked as soft and enticing as silk, shone brighter than any gold he'd ever seen. Yet he knew full well that she wanted him to notice her, to be attracted to her. She was using her sex to weaken him, like Delilah had with Samson. She was pretending to be sweet, compliant, and cooperative just to try to make him forget that she had stolen his horse, caused him more trouble than a bronc with a burr under its saddle, and attempted twice to get away. Now she was trying to convince him that she was as tame as a kitten, with coquettish tricks he had seen employed a hundred times by dancing girls and whores trying to lasso his interest. Or at least she had been trying these little tricks a short time ago. Now all the steam seemed to have gone out of her.

She looked too worn out to be thinking of anything but sleep.

Which was just as well, because if it was his attention she wanted, he might just give it to her—and then turn her in to Sheriff Rivers tomorrow. There was no need, Cole thought with cold satisfaction, to let her know that her transparent efforts would get her nowhere, that she would have a new jailer tomorrow. Let her think she had a chance of manipulating him and she'd be less likely to try to run off tonight. He didn't want to tie her up again unless he had to. She looked like she needed a good night's sleep and they had a long ride to Plattsville.

He wondered, not without a certain amount of pleasurable anticipation, if she would try to win her freedom with a display of affection tonight. Maybe he ought to let her make full use of her charms, then inform her in the morning that he was turning her over to the sheriff.

He smiled grimly to himself, picturing her outrage.

Maybe she'd think twice before trying her games on another man, Cole reflected. But the mere idea of her fluttering those eyelashes of hers at another man made his jaw clench.

"Better get some sleep," he said curtly, breaking off that uncomfortable train of thought. "We ride out at daybreak."

"Will we be covering as much ground as we did today?" Juliana couldn't imagine another day like this one. Even the thought of getting to the oilskin bedding seemed an impossible task. Maybe she could crawl. Maybe she could just sleep right here on the grass. Except that it was so cold. But even the cold couldn't keep her eyes from drifting shut.

"More," he answered. "And we'll be crossing rougher territory."

"I didn't know there was any rougher territory."

"Today was an easy route. Tomorrow I'll show you what Arizona riding is all about."

I can scarcely wait. Juliana struggled to keep her shoulders from sagging. At that moment she no longer cared about her plan to attract Cole Rawdon, she no longer cared about anything. All she knew was that she had to get up and somehow get over to that oilskin. Then she'd at least be warm; he had left the saddle blanket for her. She didn't even care about the rope anymore. If he tied her up, she wouldn't feel it. All she wanted to feel was sleep descending upon her. Soft, beautiful sleep. All she had to do was move five steps, she told herself. Five little steps . . .

Cole heard a sound in the rocks above. Instantly, he was on his feet. The horses were quiet, apparently not disturbed by whatever he had noticed.

He wondered if there were Apache about. A peace treaty had been signed, but that didn't necessarily mean anything. There were still plenty of renegades who didn't give a damn about treaties with the whites, General Crook, or any number of cavalry patrols sent out to hunt them down. He scanned the rocks above, then moved stealthily to the smooth white boulder from where he had heard the sound. He watched and waited, listening with the skills he'd learned among the Cheyenne, but only the sound of wind and water reached his ears, only the spell of the night smote him. Then, suddenly, he saw a glint of tawny fur. A mountain lion leapt off the ledge twenty feet above Cole and bounded silently toward the forest. He spotted a doe darting away into the blackness of the spruce, pursued by the big cat. The horses started, whinnying their fright. Cole gave a sigh of relief. Not Apache after all, merely a mountain lion stalking its prey. Nevertheless, he listened for a while, standing in still, perfect silence before he was finally satisfied and turned once more back to the camp.

His prisoner was lying flat out on the grass near the fire. For one grim moment Cole thought she was dead, murdered by an Apache while his attention had been distracted by the mountain lion. He reached her in three quick strides and saw that she was asleep, peacefully curled upon the grass, her head resting against the crook of her arm, her hair flowing like molten gold across the earth. He stared down at her, breathing hard.

Hell, she looked innocent when she slept. She also looked completely exhausted. He knelt down and studied her in the moonlight, noting the delicate lines of her cheekbones and the proud curve of her chin, and felt a strange tightening in his rib cage. Suddenly he remembered the way she had looked up in that tree, with the bear right below her. He grinned to himself. He scooped her up in his arms and carried her away from the fire, over to the gear. On impulse, he laid her down on his bedroll, which was softer and thicker than the oilskin, and covered her with the blanket. She murmured softly in her sleep and snuggled into a more comfortable position. Cole just stared at her. After a few contemplative moments, he settled down beside her and rolled up in the oilskin, covering his face with his hat.

It was just for tonight, he told himself. Tomorrow she'd be spending the night in the Plattsville jail. And after that . . . well, it didn't matter what happened to her.

But maybe he'd have Hank Rivers ask a few questions about this business just the same. Not that he believed her story, but . . . it wouldn't hurt to get more facts. Then he could turn her in with a clean conscience and take advantage of his chance to buy back Fire Mesa.

Tomorrow, I'll get myself a room in the Plattsville hotel and a girl to share it with me. A black-haired girl with blue eyes, he decided. *Or maybe a buxom redhead. Anything, anything but a blonde.*

That's that, he told himself. *Tomorrow she'll be Hank Rivers's problem, not mine.*

He heard her soft even breathing beside him and couldn't resist lifting his hat and turning to look at her one more time. Damned if she didn't look just like an angel dropped right out of heaven.

But she wasn't an angel. She was an armful of trouble he wished he'd never met. Two days with Juliana Montgomery had been enough for him.

Soon as they reached Plattsville, he'd wash his hands of her for good.

But first, there was one more thing about her he had to know. Come morning, he'd find out for sure.

· 12 ·

A tiny sigh escaped Juliana as she cuddled beneath her flowered silk coverlet, delaying the moment when she opened her eyes. She was deliciously comfortable in her big lilac bedroom with the French silk drapes and Persian carpet and the antique looking glass above her dressing table. The plump pillows felt so lovely beneath her head, and the silk caressed her skin as she shifted in the bed, turning onto her side, with her hand cupped beneath her cheek. In a moment, Maura would come in with her chocolate and part the drapes to let the sunshine in, but for now Juliana delayed the moment of full awakening, letting herself drift peacefully on the edge of wakefulness. She sensed something beside her and realized she must have brought Charlotte into her bed.

Charlotte was the doll Mama had given her on her sixth birthday, a beautiful china doll with blue eyes and snow-white skin and black silken hair. Charlotte always looked resplendent in her dress of exquisite blue satin with tiny pearl buttons down the back. She had brought Charlotte with her from Independence when she went to

live with Aunt Katharine and Uncle Edward, and for a
long while Charlotte had shared her bed every night,
bringing the comfort of familiarity and warm memories
and love. But when Juliana was twelve, Aunt Katharine
had decided she was too old to sleep with dolls, and had
insisted Charlotte take her place on a shelf in the bedroom instead. Sometimes, when Juliana felt very lonely,
she would sneak Charlotte off the shelf and onto her pillow for an evening.

She must have done that last night. But why had she
felt so lonely? There was some reason . . . She had better return Charlotte before Aunt Katharine noticed she
was missing from the shelf. . . .

Juliana's fingers were still stroking the doll's hair as
she opened her eyes. Beside her was not the dainty figure
of her beloved doll, but the tall, well-muscled form of
Cole Rawdon. Her body had somehow rolled right up
alongside his. She was curled against him, as close as
could be, and her fingers were stroking not Charlotte's
silky doll hair, but Rawdon's black unruly curls, while he
lay grinning at her in the most unnerving way.

"Oh, good Lord . . ."

She snatched her hand away in confusion as Rawdon
lifted himself up on one elbow and gazed down at her, his
grin widening. "Don't stop now. It was just getting interesting."

He slipped a hand along the curve of her spine and
pressed her forward against him, while at the same time
one leg swung over both of hers to keep her from moving
away.

"Stay away from me," Juliana gasped, trying to roll
sideways, but he held her tight.

"You started it."

"I th-thought you were Charlotte," she stammered.

"Who?" His blank look made her feel like even more
of an idiot.

"My doll," she blurted out. Her cheeks blazed pink as carnations. "Never mind, you wouldn't understand," she said hastily, trying to wriggle away from him.

"Yeah. Your doll." Cole held her beneath him without effort and studied her, thinking she looked like a delectable doll herself, all soft and pale and delicate, lovely as any porcelain creation. But the rounded breasts beneath the faded muslin gown, and the slender neck and soft arms and shapely hips, all belonged to a real, live woman. Those wide green eyes were still a bit dreamy with sleep, making his insides tighten uncomfortably. He didn't know why she was babbling to him about a doll, but he didn't believe a word of it. This whole thing was probably an act of some kind, meant to drive him to distraction. Well, it was succeeding. She'd just have to take the consequences of her little scheme, for a man could endure only so much. . . .

"You're the one who rolled onto my part of the oilskin," he told her, his gaze sweeping over the tempting curves pressed against him. "You had the whole bedroll to yourself, but you spent the night huddled right beside me."

"I . . . must have been cold . . ."

"It still is cold."

He was right. A luminous pink was only now squeezing through the silver gloom of the night, and the air about them still held a bitter predawn chill. The fire had all but died out, and their little clearing in the valley was cold and quiet and eerie, as if there were no other life or light or warmth anywhere in the world. Juliana found herself trembling, but not from the nip in the air. Cole's nearness was alarming to her and intoxicating all at once. He filled her mind and her senses. She didn't know what it was about him, but he commanded all her sensations in a way no one else ever had—it was as if she was mesmerized by his muscular strength, his presence, the virility and purpose that infused him with some rugged, irresistible appeal she couldn't fathom.

When he leaned down toward her, gathering her close, she could feel his heart beating in his chest, and she was struck with a yearning so fierce that panic immediately broke over her. She sensed he would not be a man easily stopped; unlike her St. Louis beaux, polite restraint dictated by the bounds of society would carry no weight with him. Neither would gentlemanly manners. Her voice caught in her throat as she started to struggle, pushing against his chest. "No," she whispered, terrified that her plan, vague at best, would any moment career out of her control. But instead of listening to her, he slid his hand into the thick tangles of her hair and tightened it so she couldn't turn away.

"Yes," he said, and pinioned her with his body.

Juliana's lips parted in a gasp of half-frightened, half-hypnotized anticipation. She couldn't breathe. Her heart was hammering against her ribs. Against her will, her neck craned upward to meet him.

For just a moment she saw the glint in his eyes, and he almost smiled, then he kissed her hard, a kiss naked in its pleasure, as if he were conquering an enemy and reveling in every moment of it. He took his time with her, his mouth searching and insistent as he tasted her lips, her tongue, and took from her what he wished. What he was doing to her left her breathless, panting, and on fire with a need that terrified her even as it filled her blood like the headiest of potions. She did more than kiss him back. She tasted his mouth, and quivered with delight, and parted her lips to receive him. Moaning, she fought to quench the fire he had started by battling back with her own tongue, but the flames within her only grew and spread, roaring through her like an inferno as he caught her face between his hands and kissed her even more thoroughly than before. Juliana was consumed, driven by the fire he ignited all around and within her.

His thighs pressed down on hers, and he began to stroke her hair while his mouth burned a trail of kisses along her throat. Ripples of ecstasy fluttered downward to her belly and below. His hands were strong, sure. She clung to him, gripping at his strength, the muscular power of him, and as she did so, his mouth returned to her lips and he groaned in pleasure, and kissed her again, this time with slow, exquisite gentleness.

What was he doing to her mouth, to her body? Driving her to distraction, making her quiver and yearn . . .

She twined her legs about his powerful calves, and gasped as his body seemed to mold against her. When one of his strong hands cupped her breast, she gasped with pleasure and felt the tension coiled in every muscle of his body as he murmured something indistinguishable against her hair. He was arousing sensations in her she had never dreamed of before, and her eyes widened as his hand tightened on her breast. He gazed down at her with glittering and unmistakable desire.

"Juliana, you're so damned beautiful," he whispered. The husky passion in his voice sent waves of electricity through her. It was the first time he had called her by her name, and the sound of it on his lips thrilled her, but as his fingers began slipping deftly down the buttons of her muslin dress, leaving the bodice parted and her chemise exposed, years of ingrained modesty suddenly intruded. Her sanity swooped back upon her, banishing passion, recklessness, and every inkling of desire. She blushed a fiery red.

"Stop! Don't do that . . ."

She clutched the gown over her exposed skin as he froze, then drew back to stare down at her in disbelief. "What the—"

"How dare you!" Juliana tried to slap him, but he grabbed her wrist before she could connect with his jaw.

"Hold it, angel. Just what the hell do you think you're doing?"

"Get off of me! Get away! How dare you take such liberties . . . when you promised you wouldn't hurt me if I didn't try to escape again . . ."

"Who said I was planning to hurt you?"

"You were! You are! You attacked me."

"Attacked?" His skin was flushed a deep, sunburned bronze, but his laugh sounded deadly cold. "Ma'am, I know an invitation when I see one, and I saw one here plain as day. Just because you changed your mind . . ."

She sat up and pushed him off, scrambling to her knees. She still was clutching her gown to her chest as angry tears glittered in her eyes. "I didn't change my mind. I never wanted . . . you—all I wanted was to find my brothers! Oh, why wouldn't you ever listen to me? I told you I wasn't a thief, I told you I never stole John Breen's money . . . !"

"Breen? You mean that big-shot tycoon who owns half the country? *That's* who you stole from?" Rawdon gave an astounded laugh. He couldn't help staring at the beautiful, dainty girl before him. He had figured her for a small-time con artist and thief, a shrewd little easterner who probably got run out of Chicago or Philadelphia or St. Louis and had decided to try her luck on the poor suckers out west. But John Breen?

Like everyone else, Cole had read newspaper accounts of the man and knew the name was synonymous with self-made wealth and business genius. Juliana Montgomery was far more stupid than he had thought, or far more ingenious. To take on a man like that . . .

"Lady, you sure know how to pick 'em."

"I didn't pick anyone! He picked me! He wanted to marry me . . ."

"I'll bet he did." Cole hauled her up to a standing position and drew her to him with one arm locked around her waist. His narrow-eyed gaze was filled with speculation.

"Those brothers of yours. Were they in on this scheme with you?"

She glared at him. "There was no scheme . . . and I already told you they had nothing to do with what happened in Denver."

"Outlaw blood just happens to run in your family," he mocked.

The remark echoed so closely the kinds of things Aunt Katharine used to hint at that Juliana was suddenly overwhelmed with mortification. For the first time since she had learned that John Breen had actually put out a bounty on her head and accused her of all sorts of horrendous crimes, she wondered how her aunt and uncle were reacting to this turn of events. If they knew about this, it would humiliate them beyond words. If it ever reached the St. Louis papers . . .

Suddenly she jerked free of Cole Rawdon and whirled away from his cold blue gaze, from his mocking, distrustful face, toward the massive pine-crested rims to the west. They shimmered silver in the dawn, as majestic and awesome as any kingdom on earth, and she lifted her face to the mighty peaks, yearning to lose herself in them. It had all sounded so simple, trying to find Wade and Tommy, trying to reunite her family, which had been split apart for so long. How had it all gone so wrong?

Because one man had seen something he could not have and had wanted it badly enough to destroy another person's life to get it. More than one life, she realized, thinking of her aunt and uncle, of the harm that such a scandal could do to Victoria as well. Heaviness descended over her heart as she thought of the pain they were suffering now, thanks to John Breen. When she thought of the hopelessness of her own predicament, captured by a man as heartless as the very hills surrounding her, a man who believed the worst about her and who would not stop until she was delivered right back to John Breen's doorstep, she wanted to scream. But she wouldn't lose control in front of Cole Rawdon. Instead, she spoke bitingly without turning to look at him.

"You can leave my family out of this. What happened in Denver is between me and John Breen. You can believe his side of it if you want to, but don't expect me to tell you one thing that would help you find Wade and Tommy."

"I suppose they're going to try to rescue you?"

Rescue her? They had probably forgotten her very existence. She was the sister from a childhood home that at the moment seemed even to Juliana like a hazy, distant dream.

She turned toward Cole Rawdon, glad at last that she could say something that might alarm him, that might make him sleep just a bit less easily in the coming nights. If he were nervous, on edge, he might make a mistake. And a mistake on his part would be to her advantage.

She regarded him in her haughtiest manner. "They might. That wouldn't be too healthy for you, Mr. Rawdon."

To her infuriation, he laughed. Juliana resisted the urge to slap the smile from his face. "You've sure changed your tune from last night and from a little while ago," he commented, his expression filled with contempt. "I could've sworn you wanted to make friends."

"I don't! I didn't! I just . . ."

"Wanted to charm me into trusting you enough to turn my back on you. I know." He did turn his back then, and started toward the horses. "Pack up and make it quick, angel. We're leaving pronto."

As he walked away she glanced down and started to

tremble. A strange queasiness ran all through her. His
gunbelt was lying on the ground just beyond the oilskin
where he'd been sleeping. Both of the big Colt pistols
were in their holsters.

Her throat tightened. From the relatively short time
she had spent in this brutal, violent West, she had learned
one thing: Guns were power—and power, in her case,
would bring freedom. If she could bring herself to grab
that power and use it, she just might make it to Cooper
Creek yet.

She swallowed. She had to try. And if she had to shoot
Cole Rawdon to get away from him, then she would.

She stooped down and slipped one of the Colts from
the holster smooth as silk. Then she covered the other
one and the gunbelt with the oilskin. The Colt was
heavier than she had thought it would be, and it felt
ominously cold in her hand. She repelled the urge to drop
it on the ground, and instead closed her hand around it.
There was no doubt in her mind that she could hit Cole
Rawdon if she fired at him. Tommy had taught her how
to shoot tin cans without missing a one of them—he'd
said she had a good eye. But she'd never thought to use a
gun on a human being, especially not since that day in
Independence when she'd come home to find—

Juliana's knees grew weak and she forced those memories away. All she had to think about now was Cole Rawdon and getting away. Not one thing else.

Juliana took a step forward. Then another. She approached him warily, her hair fluttering in the morning
breeze, the gun raised before her as she stepped across the
matted grass.

He was intent on saddling the horses and never
glanced up at her approach. When she was a dozen feet
away from him, she stopped. Sunshine poured down
upon her head, making her feel hot despite the iciness of

her palms. Perspiration beaded at her temples and her heart thudded painfully against her ribs.

"Don't move, Rawdon." Juliana's voice sounded high-pitched and breathless, not at all like the strong, clear tones she had hoped to achieve. She tried again as he turned slowly to look at her, those keen blue eyes noting the gun in her hand.

"Saddle the packhorse for me." This time she managed an authoritative note. "I will be kind enough, you see, to leave you your precious pinto. But I want all of the supplies. Pack them."

To her chagrin, he didn't look the least bit alarmed—or even surprised. His eyes were frosty as he gazed at her, and the darkly handsome face that a short time ago had been gazing at her with passion now wore a mask of nonchalance that infuriated her.

"You're stealing my supplies?" he inquired in a drawl that made her eyes snap. "But I thought you weren't a thief."

"Don't talk," she ordered through clenched teeth. The gun felt heavy as a cannonball in her hands, and the perspiration dampening her palms didn't help. "Just do what I say and you won't get hurt."

He hooked his thumbs in his pockets. "And if I don't?"

"I'll blow your damned head off."

Juliana marveled at her own coolness. It was a bluff she prayed she wouldn't have to live up to, but she had observed enough in the past days to understand that weakness was despised out here in this savage land. Strength and ruthlessness were respected, and if she didn't quite have all those qualities, it wouldn't hurt to pretend she did. Cole Rawdon already thought the worst of her. If he believed she would shoot him, then she most likely wouldn't have to do it. So she gestured with the gun, and barked at him the way she'd heard John Breen bark at his men: "Get moving and don't try anything funny."

"I am moving." Cole Rawdon took one deliberate step toward her, his lean, hard gaze boring into her face. Then he took another. Juliana's fingers tightened on the gun.

"Get back," she snapped. "Don't come any closer."

"Why not? You're going to shoot me?"

"You bet your boots I'm going to shoot you—if you take one more step."

He did.

"You're lying," he remarked in a pleasant tone, almost as if he were discussing weather or crops. "You're the girl who fainted outside the Gold Dust Saloon because you saw a dead man. You nearly puked when I shot those hombres in Cedar Gulch full of holes. And you wouldn't let me kill a bear, of all damned things. Lady, you're not going to shoot anyone. You don't have the stomach for it."

She felt her knees wobble as he took yet another step toward her. Good Lord, she was going to have to kill him after all. Her stomach churned as if it were stuffed full of greasy rags. Her hands were so clammy she feared she'd drop the gun, and then where would she be? Juliana was waging a tremendous struggle within herself, and splinters of tension pierced her skull.

"You're willing to risk your life on that?" she cried frantically.

Cool eyes mocked her. "No risk involved. You're too damned chicken to shoot."

She gritted her teeth. How she hated this man. He was within three feet of her now.

"Stop!" she yelled, sick with desperation.

"Go ahead, pull the trigger."

She willed herself to do it. He deserved to die. He was a killer. He was going to keep her from Wade and Tommy, he was going to hand her over to John Breen.

She could have her freedom back. She could have the horses and the supplies and provisions, enough to last her until she found a town and got her bearings.

It would be so easy—Cole Rawdon would be dead, like Cash Hogan and his two horrible companions. For an instant the memory of those bloodied corpses swam into her mind's eye, and she shut her eyes to block it out. The thought that this gun could do such a thing to Cole Rawdon filled her with revulsion. The next instant she opened her eyes and saw him right before her, less than a foot from the barrel of the gun.

He made no move to take it from her. He stood perfectly still, daring her, challenging her, mocking her.

The pistol was pointed at his chest, but her hand was shaking so hard, she realized she was in danger of shooting him in the shoulder or the neck or the stomach instead of the heart. It didn't matter, she told herself. It would stop him. She could get away.

Shoot, she told herself. *Shoot him anywhere. It'll stop him. Do it. Now, before it's too late.*

She took a deep breath, and tried to squeeze the trigger, but something inside her kept her hand frozen, the fingers refusing to function as she wished.

"No!" Juliana shrieked in sheer frustration as Cole Rawdon at last reached out one hand and twisted the gun from her lifeless grasp. He tossed it down on the ground, never taking his gaze from her as Juliana, white-faced, backed up until she reached a boulder and then sank down upon it.

"Don't ever draw a gun on anyone unless you're prepared to use it," Rawdon said. "And make sure if you do that the safety catch is released and that the gun is loaded."

It was then that she noticed his calm, amused smile.

"L-loaded?"

"With bullets." He grinned.

Slowly, the meaning of his words and of his amusement dawned upon her. Juliana went stock-still. Her lips felt numb. "You mean . . ."

"I was pretty sure you wouldn't go through with it, but for insurance I emptied both Colts before you woke up this morning. I'm afraid I've got all the bullets, Miss Montgomery."

She didn't know how she had the strength to do it, but she flung herself off that rock and straight at him, as if she were a bullet herself. Flailing her arms at his chest, his face, she screamed, "I wish I had killed you! You're despicable! You don't deserve to live!"

Her fingers clawed at his eyes, his cheeks.

"Maybe not," he muttered as he grabbed her flailing arms and pinned them to her sides. "But I found out what I wanted to know. You're no killer."

"I wish I was! I wish to *heaven* I'd shot you!" Her eyes blazed at him like jade set afire. Rawdon almost lost himself in the glow.

"I'll put in a good word for you to Sheriff Rivers when we reach Plattsville today. Maybe he'll give you an extra nice little cell."

"Cell?" His words stunned her enough to make her stop struggling and stare at him instead.

"Yeah. I figured it's time for us to say *adiós*. The sooner the better, right? I'm turning you in to Rivers. He'll see you get to Denver for trial eventually, but you might have to sit in the Plattsville jail for a while until he can arrange transportation."

Jail. She'd be in jail—by tonight?

"Anything will be better than having to endure your company!" Juliana choked. But she was in shock and more upset than she would show. The thought of jail terrified her. But at least it would be better than being the prisoner of this man with his unpredictable moods and cruel jokes, she told herself. Suddenly, she wanted to cry.

He had left that gun there to test her—or maybe to torment her into thinking freedom was at hand, but all the time he had known that whatever way she chose, it would be useless, and he would be the victor.

Juliana hated him with a passion that vibrated through her like a thunderbolt. She hated him almost as much as she hated John Breen. She'd like to see them both dead, she vowed to herself as tears welled in her eyes. And the more gruesome the manner, the better.

How ironic that here in the wide-open spaces of Arizona she was far less free than she had ever been back in straitlaced St. Louis. By tonight, she wouldn't even have the open skies and endless mountains to comfort her but would be trapped in the filthy confines of a two-bit town jail.

She dropped her head so he couldn't see the tears gathering on her lashes and heard him say, "We've wasted enough time here. Let's ride."

He gathered up his guns, reloaded them, and went on with his preparations.

Juliana readied herself with slow, trancelike movements, dreading what lay ahead. At least she'd be free of Cole Rawdon come evening. That was the one thing to which she could look forward.

But for some reason, that prospect did nothing to lessen her sense of foreboding and deepening gloom.

Years of solitary living and a learned distrust of every other human he encountered had bred in Cole the ability to hide his thoughts and his motives, to suppress his feelings and keep them under rigid control. He knew all too well that he would never have survived the years in the orphanage if he hadn't. And only when he'd let his guard down enough to trust Jess Burrows and Liza White had he nearly lost his life. So the lesson had been doubly learned. Now, as he covered the traces of their camp and watered the horses, he struggled against his feelings regarding Juliana Montgomery. This woman was as combustible as dynamite. Trouble was, he wanted her, even though he knew better. She had knocked him off balance with her beauty, with something courageous and indomitable in her spirit, with the unpredictable quirks of her behavior, but when he'd touched her, kissed her, and held her in the circle of his arms, something even more confounding had happened. He wasn't sure what that was, and he didn't want to know. What he had to do, Cole told himself as he obliterated all traces of their campfire and of the camp itself, was to get his balance back. To think calmly and clearly about Juliana Montgomery. Which meant keeping as far from her as he could get until he had a chance to sort her story out.

Something wasn't right about this business. Though Cole had never broken his rule concerning prisoners before, never discussed the guilt or innocence of anyone he captured, never paid attention to their protestations of innocence, he found himself intensely curious about what had happened between Juliana and John Breen. Either she was a damned good con artist and liar and thief or she was . . . what? Some kind of victim.

He didn't exactly believe what she said about John Breen, but he couldn't completely discount it either. Yet, he had no reason to believe a word she said. Her actions ever since he had snatched her away from Hogan and his men had caused him nothing but trouble—and her words were as full of deceit as a tonic peddler's guarantees. So why this nagging feeling that something was wrong? Why the doubt?

Because he wanted to believe her, Cole realized in disgust. That's why he had tested her with the gun. Even though he'd had every reason to believe she wouldn't shoot him, based on her distaste for blood and killing, he'd had to know. Liza had fooled him, fooled him well, proving that he wasn't proof against a woman's wiles.

Hell, no man was. So he had played that trick on her, something she probably thought of as cruel, pointless, but Cole had needed to know if she could kill him to get what she was after. Now he had his answer. Trouble was, it led him to a whole lot of other questions, questions as prickly as a cactus.

Rivers was a good man, though, and Cole intended to have a lengthy talk with him about Juliana Montgomery, John Breen, and this whole stinking business before the day was out. He ignored her as best he could while he tied his pack onto Arrow's saddle. Yet he was all too aware of Juliana's every movement.

Part of him wanted to kiss her again so badly it hurt, but the other part wanted to cleanse her memory, taste, and scent from his mind. The farther he kept from her, the easier that would be to do, so he helped her mount Cash Hogan's bay and kept his face closed and impassive when she glanced at him.

It would be a relief to turn her over to Hank Rivers, to not have to meet those deep, expressive eyes again, and keep from drowning in them. Cole reckoned they'd reach Plattsville by suppertime and that over a good meal in the Peterson Hotel, with Juliana safe in jail, he and Hank could talk things over.

· 13 ·

Sheriff Lucius Dane spit a gob of tobacco juice out the open window of his office, chuckling when it landed on the skirt hem of old Mrs. Wiggins, the doctor's wife, who happened to be passing by.

"Beg pardon, ma'am," he sang out cheerily, his broken-toothed grin widening when she scowled at him. He slammed the window shut and laughed. The old hag looked as ferocious as a coyote, he thought gleefully. But she wouldn't dare open her mouth.

He saw the pair of strangers heading into town from the direction of Bone Creek, and his grin faded like daylight before the first stars. Pushing the strawlike gray hair out of his eyes, he edged closer to the window to better appraise them, but from this distance all he could see was that they were a man and a woman, and their horses looked tired. But he couldn't let it go at that. As sheriff of Plattsville, it was his duty to keep the town clear of troublemakers and those who would get in Mr. McCray's way. Naturally, he didn't want to tangle with any real outlaws or gunmen. Keeping the shopkeepers, ranchers,

and merchants who didn't like what was happening in
Plattsville quiet was much more in his line. If McCray
wanted someone to deal with a professional gunman who
was skilled at his business, he'd have to call in Jackson
and his boys.

From the look of the pair riding into town, Lucius
Dane thought with a grimace, Jackson would have his
hands full. They were definitely not some banker and his
wife back from a Sunday social.

He swore under his breath as the couple drew nearer,
wondering if they were just passing through. He had a
feeling this wasn't going to be one of his better days.

The man was tall and tough-looking—with a dark,
savage face, Lucius thought. Not a desperado, his demeanor was too cold and sort of dignified for that, and he
didn't have that air of furtiveness most wanted men carried around with them. A gunfighter, probably, and if
Lucius guessed right, a good one. The woman, worn and
bedraggled-looking in a gown that had seen better days,
was still a damned sight prettier than any woman Lucius
Dane had ever seen. She had an amazing cloud of golden
blond hair and a figure that made his mouth water.

When Lucius realized they were headed straight for
the center of town, he felt sweat dribbling down his arm-
pits. If it was the woman alone, he'd have been more than
eager, but that ruggedly grim hombre wasn't one he'd
like to tangle with, especially not knowing if the business
bringing the stranger to Plattsville branded him friend or
foe.

He sighed aloud with relief when several of Jackson's
boys appeared suddenly from the saloon, peered at the
newcomers, and lined up alongside the boardwalk to
head them off. In a moment, Jackson himself strode from
the Long Arm, eyeing with surly appraisal the man
who'd just ridden into town.

Lucius Dane leaned against the dirt-streaked window of his office and watched.

Juliana shuddered in the saddle as the bay trotted into Plattsville beneath a queerly yellow-gray sky. Another storm was brewing, and soon rain would come slashing down from the Rim, but that wasn't the reason for the chills that darted over her now. Neither was the fact that she was bone-tired from the past excruciating hours on horseback, with only one brief rest all day. The cause of her dread was this place, Plattsville, and the people in it. An air of fear and gloom hung over the town, with its boarded-up storefront windows, empty streets, and its eerie silence. The few men and women she saw hurrying about their business wore glum, anxious expressions on their faces, and did not speak to one another. No children played in the shady glade across from the newspaper office, no dogs lounged under porch chairs, nor were there any young, smiling faces in sight. Instead, several swarthy-looking men had come out of a saloon and were staring at her and Rawdon. They were men who looked even more evil and murderous than Cash Hogan, Luke, and Bo, something she had thought would be impossible.

What kind of a place had Cole brought her to?

Her stomach muscles twisted deep within. How could he abandon her in a town like this?

Rawdon could almost smell the fear in the air as he rode past the blacksmith's shop and the stables and sent Arrow trotting toward the sheriff's office in the center of town. He didn't know exactly what was wrong here, but he had a feeling he was going to find out fast.

When he saw the reception party coming out of the saloon, a hard glint entered his eyes. He wondered what the hell was the matter with Rivers, letting vermin like that into the town? He didn't know any of the men personally, but their type was easily recognizable to him.

Hired guns and bullies, second-rate, the kind that wouldn't be particular about who they killed or why. When he saw Knife Jackson come out of the Long Arm, he sucked in his breath. Jackson he knew.

Cole rode on, keeping the corners of his eyes fixed on the big man with the tar-black eyes who was fond of carving an *X* with a bowie knife on the foreheads of the men he killed.

"It's been a long time, Rawdon." Jackson planted his big hands on the hitching post in front of the sheriff's office as Cole swung down from the saddle. In his holster was a Walker Colt, and stuck inside his right boot, Cole knew, was a razor-sharp bowie knife that he could whip out in a flash.

"Say, Rawdon." Jackson grinned. "You ever catch up with the Hardin boys?"

"Someone knifed them down by Blue Creek before I could get them, Jackson. Any idea who that might be?"

"Nope. But I think it's a damned shame. They died without saying where the money from the bank job was hid, didn't they?" The tar-black eyes shone beneath shaggy brows. If not for the pockmarks and scars on his face, he might have been a handsome man. "All that cash, just plumb disappeared."

"Your brand was on them."

"My brand?" Jackson slapped his thigh. "No, you don't say! Wal, someone's trying to frame me!"

The men on either side of him broke into loud guffaws. One of them spat into the street, inches from Cole's booted foot.

"Just a word of advice," Cole remarked as he helped Juliana down from the bay. There was no sense beating around the bush with a man like Jackson. "Get in my way one more time and I'll kill you."

A silence gripped all the men. Jackson's face worked convulsively as he struggled with a sudden flood of rage, and Juliana's stomach flipped over and back as she waited for him to draw on Cole. But Jackson must have known he was no match for the bounty hunter in a fair gunfight. He swallowed back his fury, glared with those black eyes of his, and said in a raspy tone, "Maybe I'll be the one to kill you someday, Rawdon."

"Not unless you learn to shoot straight, Jackson." Cole took Juliana's arm and started for the sheriff's door, but Jackson stepped into his path.

"Who's your ladyfriend, Rawdon? Ain't you going to introduce me?"

He reached out toward Juliana, as if to grasp her shoulder, or maybe her hair, but instantly Cole blocked him, his eyes hard as agates. "Don't touch her, Jackson," he said quietly. "Not one finger. Or I'll blow holes in you till there's nothing left for the undertaker to stick into the ground."

"Hey," one of the other men growled suddenly, swinging forward with his teeth bared like a wolf's. "You can't talk to him like that. Knife, you going to take that? Who the hell does he think he is?"

Through the thunderous pounding in her ears, Juliana heard someone say, "That's Cole Rawdon, you durned fool. Shut up."

Cole pulled her along with him, and the men stepped back, out of his path. No one touched her, or spoke, but she could feel their stares upon her, and she sensed their hostility. But they wouldn't make a move—because they were scared of Cole. Scared of his name, his reputation, as well as the assured and deadly way he carried himself —as if he could shoot down any or all of them with no apparent effort or concern. She was glad of his hand upon her arm, of his tall, lean form beside her, especially as they passed the glaring figure of the man called Jackson.

Before she knew it, she was past them all, past the rocker and the spitoon outside the sheriff's door, and inside the low-ceilinged little office, Cole still holding her arm. It was dim inside, for the windows were so filthy, only a smattering of light could penetrate from outside, and no one had bothered to light the kerosene lamp. Juliana took a deep breath and nearly choked on the cigar fumes and the stench of human sweat.

Lucius Dane pretended not to have heard the commotion outside and even ignored the creak of the knob as his door swung inward. He refrained from looking up until the pair was actually in his office, then greeted them with raised brows and his most solemn, professional lawman's stare, the one he had practiced in front of the mirror for hours after he'd won his first local election five years ago. It hadn't been the first time he'd bought votes to win an election, and most likely it wouldn't be the last, but that election had taught him the value of looking the part. The sheriff's badge and a Navy .45 helped, but the cold-eyed Dane stare worked wonders on doubtful, weak-kneed citizens who got a little too curious about a man's background at a time when it wasn't convenient to answer questions.

"What can I do for you folks?" Lucius demanded, resting his nail-bitten hands on the arms of his chair. He was about to say, "Speak up, I don't have all day," but when he saw the frowning expression on the stranger's face he thought better of it. He clamped his mouth shut instead and waited in growing uneasiness for some inkling as to what this was all about.

Rawdon noted the weasely man's badge with a start of surprise.

"Who the hell are you?"

One look at him was enough to tell Cole that this short, spindly man with the protruding dark eyes and coffee stains on his vest was no model of honesty and virtue. The man looked like scum, smelled like scum, and had the shifting eyes and braggart posture of scum. The sheriff's office and the cells behind it looked filthy and unkempt, not at all the way Rivers normally kept them. Cole glanced around slowly, noting the lumpy unmade beds in the prisoner cells, the rats gnawing old bread in a corner, the dirt ground into the floor. In the dim light he could see cigar butts and ashes littering the desk, as well as filthy crumpled handkerchiefs and a pile of poker chips half hidden by a sheaf of papers.

One glance at Juliana, frozen by his side, showed him that she had not failed to note the filth—or the rats.

Dismay was written all across her face.

"Where's Rivers?" Cole went on before the man in the sheriff's badge could speak. "Answer me, damn you."

Dane puffed out his chest. "Hank Rivers?" he drawled. "Why, he's dead, of course." The sheriff shoved back his chair and got to his feet, jabbing a thumb against his badge.

"I'm Lucius Dane, Plattsville's new sheriff. Who might you be, mister?"

"Cole Rawdon." Cole didn't bother shaking hands, or even nodding. He saw that Dane recognized his name. The man's face turned ashen and his hands, loose at his sides, started to tremble.

"I've . . . heerd of you." Dane tried to make his voice sound normal, but it was a shade hollower than it had been before. He swallowed convulsively as he stared into the cold blue eyes of the infamous bounty hunter.

"What happened to Rivers?" Rawdon asked curtly.

Dane dropped his gaze and shrugged his shoulders. "Shot in the back. Poor bastard. Heard tell the Montgomery gang did it. Actually, fellow name of Wade Montgomery."

Juliana, who had been too weary from riding all this time to do more than gaze in horror around the filthy office and into the reaches of the jail cells, felt shock vibrate through her at these words. She stared into the sheriff's face, her eyes growing wide and furious.

"No!" She jerked loose from Cole's grasp and darted forward, suffused with an overwhelming rage. "You're lying. Wade would never shoot anyone in the back!"

Dane let his gaze travel up and down the sensuous young beauty before him. It didn't matter that she looked as if she'd like to eat his heart for supper; she was still the most dazzling female he'd seen since the time he'd paid a small fortune at a brothel in San Francisco for a night with the house's prime beauty. But this girl made that exquisite whore seem ordinary in comparison. This one was a peach, ripe, luscious, perfect—the other, a plain old apple, polished and rosy maybe, but nowhere near as delectable a morsel. Everything about her was delicate and feminine.

Except the way she was glaring at him.

"You know that young killer, missy?" Dane inquired, raising one eyebrow at her. "Maybe you can tell me where to find him."

"Wade is no more a killer than I am!"

Rawdon pushed in front of her, addressing Dane. "When did this happen?"

"Maybe two months ago. The Montgomery gang robbed a gold shipment headed from the Sanders mine to Timber Junction. Rivers took a posse out after 'em. The posse split up. Rivers and two other men, including his deputy, got bushwhacked in their camp. Rivers took a bullet in the back—never even got the chance to draw his gun. One of the men survived, though, and told us who done it." Dane plumped himself back down in his chair; his knees felt none too steady under the bounty hunter's hard gaze. "So Rivers was a friend of yours?" he asked, picking up a pencil and beginning to tap it against the iron coffee mug at his elbow.

"No."

Cole spoke the truth. He considered no man his friend, hadn't since the time when Jess Burrows had betrayed him. Yet he was sorry about Rivers, who had been honest and decent and had the courage to put on a badge and fight the vermin inhabiting much of the West. He was of a very different breed than Lucius Dane.

Dane cleared his throat. "Not that I mind having company, but you folks come by for any particular reason? Or did you just want to say howdy to Hank Rivers?"

Cole glanced at the girl beside him, who hadn't taken her gaze off Sheriff Dane. "This woman is wanted in Denver," he said slowly.

Something inside Juliana withered at his words.

"The reward is two thousand dollars. How long will it take to get my money?"

Juliana closed her eyes against the pain that burned her eyelids.

Dane whistled through his teeth. "Two thousand? Who is she?"

She forced herself to stand up very straight as Cole pointed to the board next to the window where the Wanted notices were posted. A poorly etched drawing of Juliana was displayed along with a bold-faced description of her and her alleged crimes. Though she kept her eyes fixed straight ahead, and her shoulders stiff, she couldn't stop the humiliating flush that crept up her neck and into her cheeks.

"Juliana Montgomery?" Dane's ears pricked up. His feral eyes swiveled toward the girl once again, this time with a sharper kind of interest. "Missy, air you kin to that terrible Montgomery gang?" he inquired.

Juliana lifted her chin, proud as a statue. At least she was trying to look proud—proud and tough and contemptuous, but inside she was fighting against a choking panic. She couldn't believe Cole Rawdon was going to leave her here in this awful place with this beastly little man. She was icy with fear, her hands as cold and heavy as marble. What had Wade and Tommy gotten involved in now? Murder? It was impossible, she told herself, thinking of the handsome, fun-loving brothers she had adored. Her heart was sick with worry for them. She didn't know which was worse, the trouble the boys were in, or her own plight, locked up here in this foul little town in the custody of Lucius Dane.

At least she'd be rid of Cole Rawdon. But suddenly, the thought of him walking out that door and leaving her here with this sheriff caused suffocating fear to rush through her.

"Air you goin' to answer me, missy, or not?" Dane demanded, and reaching out, grabbed her by the arm.

"I'm not answering any questions until my trial," Juliana shot back, wrenching her arm away.

Cole Rawdon watched in silence.

"Mouthy little troublemakers get no favors here." Dane scowled at her from beneath his brows. "I'll wire Denver in the morning and find out how Judge Mason wants to handle this. Meanwhiles, come along. I've got work to do and can't stand here jawin' all day."

She flinched away from him as he came around the desk. Her skin was as white as a seashell bleached by the waves.

"You're going to lock me up now?"

"Naw, I'm going to throw a shindig in your honor." Dane sent Rawdon an amused smirk, but the other man returned his look in stony silence. With awkward haste, the sheriff turned back to the girl.

"Course I'm going to lock you up, missy. Now don't make things difficult on yourself."

Once again he grabbed her arm. His fingers pinched her flesh like crab claws.

Late afternoon sunlight slanted weakly through the office window as Dane dragged Juliana toward the first of the dank tiny cells at the rear of the building. The light made thin amber bars on the floor as she stumbled along beside the sheriff. Feeling empty and sick inside, she fought back paralyzing despair and willed herself not to cry.

Dane's hand on her wrist was warm and sticky. His fetid breath hung in a cloud about him, assaulting her nostrils. She could feel Cole Rawdon's piercing gaze upon her back, and as she reached the door of the cell, she spun about to gaze at him.

Mute appeal flickered in her eyes. She didn't know why she should expect him to help her—he was the one who had captured her and brought her here. He had never said or done a single kind thing for her—except that he hadn't shot that stupid bear. All he cared about, she reminded herself bitterly, was his precious reward money. No doubt he was as glad to be rid of her as she was of him. She felt hot tears gathering on her lower lashes. Once he walked out that door, she'd never have to see that cool, nonchalant face again, never have to deal with him or his maddening self-assurance, or worry about her heart turning to jelly when he came near her or . . . kissed her. Now she'd only have Lucius Dane, John Breen, and a host of other narrowminded, blind, deaf, and dumb men to deal with.

Her gaze locked with Cole's as she stood with a hand on the cell door. For a moment he stared back, his lean, bronzed face unreadable. He looked remote, as unreachable and uncaring as a granite peak jutting high above the desert.

Juliana wanted to say something. Her lips parted but the desperate words would not come out. Something was closing tight and hard around her heart.

Then it was too late—he turned on his heel and left the office, slamming the door shut behind him with a thump that sounded all too final.

Not even a good-bye. Emptiness rocked her. But what had she expected?

Anger at herself for the pain in her heart made her bite her lip until it bled.

"Here you go, missy. Not too fancy, but it'll hold you till I get instructions from Denver."

Lucius Dane chuckled at the dazed expression the girl's face wore when he turned the key in the lock. She sank down upon the narrow cot with its stained, smelly mattress and tattered blanket as though she were in some kind of dream. Or more likely a nightmare.

"I'll send for your supper soon. If you're a good girl, I'll let you eat some of it." He ran an eye over the curves apparent beneath the crumpled dress. "Then, later on, you and me kin get acquainted. And you can tell me about the Montgomery gang. It'd be a real feather in my cap if I could find 'em. And if you help me out, maybe I can do something for you along the way—put in a good word for you with Judge Mason, maybe get him to drop the charges."

Juliana didn't waste her energy answering him. She wouldn't help him regardless, but the man was lying. Lucius Dane wouldn't help his mother out of a ditch unless there was something he could gain from it. But, she reflected, trying hard to concentrate through the fog of exhaustion and despair that shrouded her brain, if she could convince him that he had something to gain from helping her, he might prove useful after all.

Wearily, she closed her eyes. She would have to try.

Even as he returned to his desk, Lucius Dane was planning the note he'd send to McCray. Mr. M would be mighty interested in what this little filly had to say. She wouldn't be going anywhere until they'd gotten every last bit of information from her.

Getting her to talk wouldn't prove too difficult from

the looks of her. She looked like she'd break if you pinched her. Jackson would do more than that to find out where the Montgomery gang was hiding out. Oh, yes, McCray would be mighty relieved to have them rounded up at last.

It was turning out to be a fine day after all—thanks to Mr. Cole Rawdon.

Dane chuckled to himself as he folded and sealed his letter. He could hardly wait to start the fun.

· 14 ·

A tiny wren of a woman brought Juliana's supper. Since the sheriff hadn't returned from his own meal in the hotel yet, she left it on the desk and started to hasten out, but Juliana, pressed against the bars, begged her to bring over the food.

"I can't. Oh, I just can't." Chalk-faced, the woman tiptoed toward her with the slow reluctance of someone treading on quicksand. "Sheriff Dane wouldn't like it one bit."

"Please, ma'am, I'm awfully hungry. Won't you bring me the tray?"

"I can't give it to you. Not without the sheriff here. For one thing, I don't have the keys."

"But you know where they are."

Juliana saw that the woman was homely and leather-skinned, with a lined, apprehensive face beneath stick-straight brown hair. Beneath the fear that stamped her plain features and pointed chin, Juliana saw kindness, a timid, wary kindness that she knew she had to try to draw out. She wasn't hungry in the least, even though it had been hours since she and Cole Rawdon had eaten. In these dismal surroundings, with rats scurrying in the corners, she doubted she could eat a morsel, but if the woman bringing her food could also bring her a chance to escape, she'd behave as if she were on the brink of death by starvation.

"Sheriff Dane left me strict orders. Yes, indeed. Leave the food on my desk, that's what he said." She peered pityingly at the slender girl behind the bars who stared at her with such an imploring expression. "What did you do, anyhow, girl? He said you were very dangerous and I was to stay far away from you."

Dangerous? Juliana gave a bitter little smile. Maybe the truth would serve her well in this instance. She sensed an inherent decency in the woman on the other side of the bars. "I stole a horse so that I could get away from a man I didn't want to marry," she replied quietly. Shocked eyes met her own. "If the sheriff sends me back to Colorado, I'll have to marry this man and . . . and I'm afraid of what he will do to me for having left him like that. Do you understand?"

The woman swallowed hard. Indecision flitted over her face. She smoothed her calico skirt with work-roughened hands that shook a little. "You don't look like a bad sort. Pretty thing like you—I'll bet all manner of men would want to marry you."

"This one was no prize," Juliana muttered. Every second that passed increased the chances that Lucius Dane would return. She decided to lay all her cards on the table at once. "Please, if I could only get out of this cell. Won't you help me? Is there an extra set of keys in the desk drawer? Or . . ." She hesitated only briefly. "A gun?"

The little wren's mouth dropped open. "Do you want to get me killed, girl? Listen, Lucius Dane would skin me alive if—"

"If what, Henny?"

Both women froze at the harsh grate of the sheriff's voice. So intent had Juliana been on persuading the woman to aid her that she hadn't even heard him come in.

"N-nothing, Sheriff," Henny stammered. "I was just leaving supper for your prisoner. Reckon I'll be on my way."

Dane walked toward her, slow and easy. There was a queer light in his eye. A light rain had begun to fall outside, and his clothes were damp with it. "You feeling sorry for this gal, Henny? Thinking that mebbe she don't belong behind bars? Wal, that's just the kind of poor thinkin' that got your boy Bob shot and killed. Remember? He thought Mr. M didn't have no call taking over the hotel after Isaac got killed. But Mr. McCray knew all along it'd be too much for you alone, what with two young sons to raise. And he was right, wasn't he? Wal now, Bob got himself killed, but you've still got that other one. What's his name, again, Henny?"

"W-Will," she whispered in a low voice choked with fear.

"That's right. Will. Now he's a fine boy. All of nine, ain't he?" Sheriff Dane grinned at Juliana, listening in horror. "We sure wouldn't want no harm to come to him. So now you just go on back to the hotel, go on about your cooking, and leave the complicated thinking to me. Sound about right, Henny?"

The woman nodded wordlessly, her face pinched and white. She was shaking from her narrow shoulders down to her tiny feet. She threw one terrified glance at Juliana, trapped like a pale, lovely bird in a cage, and then scurried toward the door without a sound. As she passed him Dane jerked his foot sideways and tripped her. Henny hit the floor with a cry of pain.

"Why, Henny, don't be so clumsy." Chuckling, Dane

pulled her to her feet, none too gently. "Can't abide a
clumsy woman," he said as she backed away from him.
"Women should be pretty and graceful, like that one
there." He waved a hand toward Juliana. "Yessirree,
women should be light on their feet and flat on their
backs. That's how I like 'em."

He threw back his head and laughed at his own joke.

When the door thudded shut behind Henny, Dane
turned to Juliana with a broad smile. "Hungry, missy?
Henny's a good cook. You'll enjoy your dinner."

*I'd enjoy seeing you locked up in the cell next door, or
better yet, a dungeon, where no one would find you for a
thousand years,* she thought, eyeing him in disgust. Not
only was he cruel, he was abhorrently filthy as well. He
had gravy down the front of his shirt, and dark crumbs
still clung to his scruffy mustache. His bandanna had a
greasy smear blurring the dark red color.

Juliana swallowed back her revulsion and tried to
speak in a level tone. "Did you really kill that woman's
son?" she asked. He merely grinned at her. "And just
who is this McCray?"

"You'll find out soon enough. First, why don't you tell
me about the Montgomery gang. Those boys are damned
hard to find."

"I know that, Sheriff. I've been trying to locate them
myself—or I was—until Mr. Rawdon showed up."

"Just where was you headin'? You got a notion where
they air?"

My, he was eager. The lust for information shone all
over his face.

Juliana pretended to waver. "Nevada," she said at last,
in a quiet, resigned tone. "That's what a bartender in
Cedar Gulch told me."

He eyed her suspiciously. With small steps he approached the bars. "Nevada's a mighty big place, missy.
Whereabouts, exactly?"

Juliana bestowed on him a sweet and hopeful smile. "If I tell you, will you write to the judge in Denver on my behalf?"

"Mebbe."

She pouted, then brightened. "Will you at least let me out of here while I eat my supper? I . . . I don't think I can tolerate a bite of food behind bars. Besides, there's a rat in my cell."

Suspicion still clouded his gaze, but she looked so pretty, and she was so dainty and fragile-looking, like a porcelain statue, that he knew she couldn't possibly be any danger to him. Besides, he had a feeling that she'd be fairly easy to trick into thinking that he was working in her best interest. If she thought he'd help her go free, she'd be real cooperative later on, when he cornered her in her cell tonight. Then, in the morning, he'd let Jackson and the boys at her and see if she was really telling the truth. She was giving in too easily about those Montgomerys, but that was Mr. M's problem, not his. His was lonesomeness, and this prime little filly could solve that real fast.

"All right," he said, reaching into his pocket for the keys. "Spill it and I'll open these here doors."

Juliana looked at him from beneath her lashes. Where in Nevada? Her mind searched desperately for a name.

"Pueblo," she pronounced. And held her breath.

His eyes narrowed. He paused directly before her, keys dangling. "That's in Colorado."

"No, is it? Goodness me, there must be another one then. Unless that bartender *meant* Colorado . . . oh, dear."

She shrugged delicately. "All I know is what the bartender told me. Pueblo, Nevada, he said."

He fit the key into the lock, lips twisting. "That there Montgomery gang has caused an awful lot of trouble, missy. Stubborn, fire-eatin' rascals, that's what they are.

But their days are numbered. Mr. M can't have thievin', murderin' troublemakers in these parts no more. No, sir, he's going to see to it that Plattsville grows into a real fine, civilized town."

His guffaw defied his words and sent an icy shiver down Juliana's spine.

She stepped out of the cell as he swung the door wide.

Darkness was falling like a black cloud over Plattsville, and with it came the first rumblings of the storm. Rain pattered steadily against the windows. Lightning ripped across the open sky. The sounds of horses and wagon wheels and voices had all died away. Faint piano music floated on the breeze, drifting in from a saloon. For a moment it reminded Juliana of when she had first stepped off the train in Denver, and had heard similar music from the Gold Dust Saloon—just before she met Cole Rawdon.

Cole Rawdon. Where was he now? she wondered with a bitter aching in her heart.

Probably riding far away from here, planning what he'd do with all that reward money. Part of her hated him. And part of her wished he'd come crashing through that door right now and take her away from this dreadful place.

But she didn't need him, she reminded herself as she steeled her nerves for whatever might happen in the next few minutes. She could escape all by herself. She had made it this far, all the way from Denver, despite everything, hadn't she? She still had her money pouch, her wits, and her determination. If that couldn't get her to Cooper Creek, nothing could.

Nothing but a little luck.

"Don't try nothin', now. I'd get mighty angry if you was to pull anythin'."

"Sheriff, I'm only interested in my supper."

And in getting my hands on your gun.

·15·

"Royal flush! Whoopee! Drinks are on me, boys!"

Cole scarcely glanced at the ecstatic cowboy scooping his poker winnings into his hat. He needed answers and he needed them fast. He hoped to get them here in the Ten Gallon Saloon.

This whole business about Hank Rivers stank, especially since, if Cole was any judge of men, Lucius Dane was as crooked as they came. Cole ordered a whiskey from his corner table, then engaged the sloe-eyed saloon girl who brought it in private conversation.

She wore a purple-and-red-striped dress that revealed a narrow body beneath breasts that were small and round. She kept dipping down as he spoke to her, enabling him to see inside her dress. It was almost as fascinating as what she had to say.

Within a short time he knew that Line McCray was up to his old tricks again, taking over yet another town. This time it was Plattsville. He pictured the iron-eyed McCray with his gray suits and string tie, and scowled. Poor Rivers—he hadn't stood a chance.

Cole took a slug of his whiskey and set the glass down. While the liquor ran down his throat like wildfire, the girl wrapped her skinny arms about his neck.

Cole pictured McCray ensconced at Fire Mesa. Slow, hot rage licked through him. Not this time. Not Fire Mesa. McCray would just have to find out you don't get everything you want.

Cole was only vaguely aware of the girl's oversweet perfume assailing his nostrils. The bright light of the chandelier as it glittered and swung overhead hurt his eyes. He stared at the scarred table, thinking of how he had left Juliana Montgomery alone across the street with that slimy old coot Dane.

Until he had this figured out, she was safer there than out in the open with him. There was one more thing he needed to know before he could think about going back and getting her out. The name of the men in the posse who'd been with Rivers when he was shot, particularly the one who'd claimed Wade Montgomery did the killing.

Cole looked up, his face tightening. The bartender was frowning at the girl, probably annoyed that she was spending so much time with him and not seeing to the other customers. She caught his look, and quickly picked up Cole's glass and brought it coaxingly to his lips.

"Here, drink up, honey and let me bring you another. Or Fred will holler at me til his face turns blue, and take back half my pay."

Cole took the glass from her, took another swallow, and set it down.

Grasping her wrist in a light but firm hold, he asked her about the names of the men who were with Hank Rivers when he died.

"I don't know nothing about that. C'mon, you finish your drink. Maybe we can have some fun later."

Cole stared up at her as she hovered beside him in the noisy, crowded saloon. She looked funny. Skin ashen beneath all the cheap paint, eyes glassy and bright. Scared? he wondered. Of me, or of Fred?

He glanced over at the bartender once again, remembering his low, coarse laugh, his habit of smacking the girls who worked for him on the fanny whenever one passed by. Just now he was pouring whiskey for a hunched-over miner at the bar. Fred had been pouring drinks at the Ten Gallon for as long as Cole could remember. Maybe he would know who had been with Rivers that day.

"Thanks, beautiful."

Cole pressed several greenbacks into the girl's palm. He pushed back his chair, surprised by a sudden surge of light-headedness. He must be hungrier than he'd thought. Liquor on an empty stomach was no good. He'd better stay away from it. Had to get Juliana safe away from Plattsville. Couldn't leave her with Dane. Didn't want her mixed up with McCray. Had to find out if that member of the posse had lied about Wade Montgomery.

He had a hunch that McCray—

Cole's legs buckled as he reached the bar. He collapsed against the smooth wooden surface, clinging to it for support. Fred grinned at him, and set down a glass already full of amber liquid.

"On the house, Mr. Rawdon. You've always been a good customer."

"Don't want a drink." Why was it so difficult to talk? His tongue was as thick and greasy as a lump of rags. Cole felt icy cold, then hot. Damn. What the hell was wrong with him?

"Who . . . who was with Hank Rivers when . . ."

Cole was sweating. As he looked into Fred's broad, smiling face, the bartender's features grew blurred.

"He wants to know, Fred, who was with Sheriff Rivers

when he died?" the saloon girl said beside him. She was speaking in a low, honeyed tone, so low, Cole could hardly hear. But he heard the edge in her voice.

Turning his head to look at her would take too much effort. He stared straight at Fred, but Fred's features were wavy and indistinct, as if he were seeing them underwater.

"Oh," Fred said, leaning toward him, his voice as quiet and soothing as the girl's. "That's easy." He placed both hands on the bar. "I was there. I saw the whole thing."

Cole heard him chuckle, and through the fog of dizziness that ensnared him like a lariat, he realized too late what was wrong with him.

Juliana. He had to get to Juliana.

Desperation seized him. His eyes burned with it.

The girl's hand was on his arm. Cole shook her off, sending her stumbling backward into a thin gambler in black. Fred came around the bar and caught him under the shoulders. "Wal, now, too much to drink, eh, Mr. Rawdon? I'll fix you right up. Come along."

He half carried, half dragged Cole into a back room. Cole was too weak to resist. His muscles had all turned to water.

When the door was closed, Fred pushed him up against a wall and made a fist. Cole tried to fend off the blow, but the room spun and ice-cold nausea gripped him.

The bartender's blow struck him square on the jaw. Cole went down hard. Fred kicked him in the back. Then in the face.

Cole swallowed his own blood.

Agony ripped through him. He was blinded by pain and dizziness. Like that day at Fire Mesa . . .

He was going to pass out.

Juliana. He had to get to . . .

"When Knife and the boys are finished questioning the girl, they'll be back for you. Don't go nowheres now."

Knife. Juliana. He had to . . .

Fred kicked him again.

The last sound he heard was the bartender's coarse, guttural laugh echoing through the room like a black vulture circling for the kill.

Juliana forced herself to eat several bites of food while Dane stood over her at his desk. Seated in his chair, she chewed slowly and thought desperately. The only weapon she could see was the one Dane wore in his gun-belt. She had an idea how she could get it, but it wasn't a plan she relished. Still, if it worked . . .

Perhaps Henny's cooking was good, but everything tasted like paste. If she tried and failed, Dane would be furious. Remembering his callousness with Henny, the way he'd tripped the poor woman for no reason, made her wonder what he would do if she gave him cause for brutality. Cole Rawdon, for all his strength, had never actually hurt her. This mean little man would hurt her without a qualm if she crossed him.

But she had to cross him.

"Would you like some, Sheriff? I'm not as hungry as I thought."

"I've got a different type of appetite, missy." Again, he laughed at his own humor, and Juliana forced herself to join him. She tilted her head back provocatively, and leaned toward him with a tantalizing smile.

She saw his eyes glint. He tensed, took a step toward her, stopped.

"Maybe you've got the same kind of hunger as me," he suggested softly, watching every plane and angle of her oval face.

"Maybe I do," Juliana managed to whisper. She moistened her lips with her tongue, nervous at this dangerous game, but her unconscious gesture served as the catalyst for the uncouth sheriff's desire. Before she even realized it, he snatched her out of the chair and into his arms. Juliana cried out. Then he planted his lips on hers and began to kiss her, and her next cry was muffled against tobacco-reeking lips. The next instant, he grabbed her breast and squeezed hard.

Juliana bit back the scream in her throat. She forced herself to stay perfectly still. Willing herself with every ounce of her strength, she allowed that long, greedy kiss to go on and on, while Dane fondled her painfully, then ever so slowly she draped her arms about his neck, let them slide languorously downward toward his hips, and . . .

Oh, how she wanted just to lunge for that gun—but she forced herself to move with sensuous deliberation. She felt wet and slimy from his kiss, and both her nipples hurt from being pinched. He was pressing her back against the desk—in another moment she'd be lying atop it, with him over her. She squirmed sideways, resisting being forced backward. She wanted to kick him as she had kicked John Breen, but first she had to get the gun. . . .

Her hand slid lower.

"Why, Sheriff," she whispered, to distract him, and giggled. She felt the pistol against her palm, cold and hard. What was it Cole Rawdon had said? Don't draw a gun on a man unless you're prepared to use it. Well, she would if she had to, but she was getting to be a better actress by the moment. She'd bluff if she could, fire if she had to, and then retch all over this damned office if need be. But Juliana was praying it wouldn't come to killing. Though she hadn't been able to bluff Cole Rawdon, she was sure she could convince Lucius Dane she was a trigger-happy outlaw who wouldn't hesitate to pull the trigger.

She had it. Her hand tingled with a sudden surge of power. Suddenly, she kicked Lucius Dane, just as she had kicked John Breen. She kicked him so hard, he screamed. At the same time, she whipped the gun from his holster and jumped back. Dane shrieked twice more, and slumped to the floor, clutching at his injured anatomy.

Juliana clicked off the safety as she'd seen Cole do. Aside from the primrose color in her cheeks, she looked perfectly calm.

"I hope you can walk, Sheriff, but if you can't, you'll have to crawl. Quick, into the cell."

He was gaping stupidly up at her, his face a mixture of raw pain and incredulity. "You . . . sneakin', lyin' bitch," he rasped. "I'll fix you good for this . . ."

Juliana kept the gun trained on him with one hand, copying Cole's nonchalant pose. Her heart was thudding like a runaway train, but outwardly she schooled her expression into one of flawless composure. "My brothers— the Montgomery gang—taught me to shoot, Sheriff. I can blow your head off at fifty feet." Her tone hardened. "At this range, I wouldn't miss if I wanted to. And I assure you, I don't want to. Now I'm going to count to five. If you're not in that cell by then, you're going to your Maker, and I hope you're prepared to answer for the death of Henny's boy Bob. Say your prayers, Sheriff. One . . . two . . ."

His face contorted with pain, the lawman half staggered, half crawled toward the cell.

"Three . . . four . . ."

"For cryin' out loud, I'm doing the best I can!" he gasped, sweat breaking out on his face.

"Five," Juliana announced as he collapsed into the cell. She swung the door shut and it clicked home. She quickly turned the key, then flung the ring to which it was attached across the room. It landed with a shrill jangle beneath the windowsill.

"You'll swing for this, missy!" Dane called after her as

she dashed toward the door. "By all that's holy, I swear I'll hang you by your toes!"

"You'll have to catch me first," Juliana retorted over her shoulder. She opened the door, began to spring out into the cool Arizona rain, then stopped short, her heart lurching into her throat.

Three men in heavy coats, silk bandannas, and Stetsons blocked her path.

"Miss Montgomery?" Knife Jackson inquired, smirking as he pushed her back inside.

"Guess we got here just in time," his companion remarked. Despite the blood pounding in her temples, Juliana recognized him from the street that morning. The third man had been there, too, watching with dark-eyed hostility when Cole brought her into the sheriff's office. The smallest of the three, with a scar below his right eye, he spoke next, shooting an amused glance at Lucius Dane in the cell. "The boss'll be real sore with you, Dane. You almost let this little filly slip away."

Terror slashed through Juliana.

Then, before she could move, Knife Jackson reached out huge fingers and grasped her by the throat.

"We've got some questions for you, Miss Montgomery," he said in an amiable tone. His fingers started to squeeze.

"And if you answer them real nice and polite," he went on, his smile widening into a grin, "we just might let you live to see the morning."

· 16 ·

The questions came at her faster than pistol shots.

"Where are the Montgomery brothers hiding out?"

"What does Rawdon want from Mr. McCray?"

"Where'd the Montgomery gang stash the gold from the Sanders mine?"

"What's Rawdon's interest in Fire Mesa?"

"Is Wade Montgomery planning to rob the Henshaw freight payroll?"

"Is Tommy Montgomery still in Arizona?"

"How much is Rawdon planning to bid for Fire Mesa?"

Bruises covered her arms and neck. Her lip bled, dripping down to stain the frayed bodice of her gown.

Knife Jackson's face loomed above her like a nightmare, smirking, snarling. His eyes—tar-black, monstrously cold, savage—glittered with the pleasure of inflicting pain.

Juliana knew she'd never forget those eyes. She'd see them forever after in her nightmares. If she survived . . .

The other two held her. Knife did the beating.

After a while, she couldn't even scream. She whimpered when Knife knocked her to the floor with the back of his hand. The room crashed in on her. So much pain. Blinding lights exploded behind her eyes. A clamorous pounding slammed through her ears, ringing again and again. Juliana heard Knife's voice as if from very far away.

"Answer me this time. If you say you don't know again, I swear I'll take the bowie knife to you and cut your face so that your own mother won't recognize it. *What is Rawdon after?*"

Rawdon. Through the salt of her own blood and the tears on her lips, through the agony crashing through her head and body, she saw a cool, handsome face, smelled his clean pine-and-leather scent, felt his lips on hers. The hard floor faded away. The boots of the men standing over her blurred.

Rawdon.

"Yeah, Rawdon."

Knife Jackson's fetid breath rushed into her face as he grabbed her by the hair and hauled her to her feet. The glint of his knife shone in one hand as Juliana stared at him through pain-dazed eyes.

"What is Rawdon after, damn you?"

Juliana struggled to draw breath through the pain in her ribs. Her cut lip bled anew as she formed the words.

"If I knew," she whispered, fear making her teeth chatter, "I wouldn't tell . . . you."

The knife streaked toward her.

Juliana passed out.

Cole came awake to find something wet and sticky soaking his face, neck, and shirt. He forced his eyes open, despite the pincer-needles of pain that pierced them. When he lifted his head, groaning, he saw the ruby stream winding its way across the sawdust floor. Blood. His own blood. He was lying in it.

Where? Through the torture of bruised ribs and muscles, memory oozed back. His mind was still groggy with whatever evil concoction Fred had put into his whiskey, and it hurt when he blinked, but at least he remembered what had happened to him. Or at least some of it. Fred. The saloon girl. His drink.

He tried to get up and flopped back down into the red, sticky puddle.

His hands were tied behind his back. His ankles were bound together tightly by rawhide. Fred had done a damned good job.

Cole gritted his teeth. Sheer determination got him to his knees. Everything hurt like hell, but he managed to stay upright and to glance around the room. It was bare except for a filthy cot against the far wall, an old chest of drawers so scarred and chipped it might splinter into a million pieces if you kicked it, and a three-legged cane chair in the corner. A pair of half-burned-down candles flickered in tarnished sconces on the wall over the cot, casting the only light in the room. Breathing hard, Cole noted the window was covered by a burlap shade, which prevented him from seeing outside. Was it night? Day? How long had he been here?

Suddenly the room, which had been spinning slightly, straightened. Everything came into sharper focus, hurting his eyes. At that moment he remembered Juliana and what Fred had said about her just before he'd passed out.

He struggled with his bonds, swearing in frustration because there was no slack, no room to twist free. But there had to be a way. He had to cut these ropes, to get out of here.

Once again Cole surveyed the room, this time with Cheyenne thoroughness. The words of Sun Eagle came back to him: "See with the eyes of a hawk, my friend, not a man. The mouse always hides beneath the snow."

And that was when he saw it—what he had not even paid attention to before—the cracked pitcher atop the chest of drawers, and beside the pitcher, two glasses and a bottle of whiskey.

Squinting against the pain, Cole started slowly and torturously to jackknife himself across the room.

It seemed to take hours. Sweat poured down his face, mingling with the blood. From outside the room came the raucous noises of the saloon, shrill shouts, laughter, off-key piano music. Inside there was only the buzz of flies and the sound of his own breathing. Cole concentrated all his energy on getting to that chest. When he reached it, he slammed his body into it with all the strength left in his muscles. It took three tries before the bottle and pitcher toppled over and smashed onto the sawdust floor.

He worked as quickly as he could, taking one of the shards of splintered glass between his fingers, working it against the rawhide. Again and again he sawed at the rope, trying not to think of Juliana, of what Knife was doing to her, and then, just as he felt the cords of the rope beginning to fray, just a little, he heard it—the sound of boots outside the door.

Something tightened inside him. An instant later, the door swung open and Fred stared at him as he sprawled before the bureau, surrounded by shattered glass.

The bartender flushed with anger as he met the other man's stony face and realized what he was trying to do. Despite Rawdon's bruises and the blood smearing his face, he looked as cold and arrogant as ever, making Fred want to stomp those handsome features right into the ground. He wiped his hands on his stained and crumpled apron, and a wide grin stretched from one ear to the other.

"Still thirsty, Rawdon?" The door slammed behind him with a resounding thud. "And here I thought you'd had enough liquor for one day."

Cole watched him stoop to pick up a glittering shard of glass, study its deadly edges in the murky light, then straighten, the shard clenched in his hand like a dagger. Blood pounded in Cole's temples. He'd faced death many times, and here it was again. Always before, he had managed to cheat it. This time he wasn't sure he would.

Fred advanced upon him, grinning.

"I was kinda hoping to repay you for your hospitality," Cole drawled, straining desperately at his bonds. He couldn't break them, though he flexed every muscle in his body. His face strained with effort, blue eyes fiercely glittering.

"Too bad, Rawdon. You ain't repaying me for anythin'. You ain't gonna do nothin' but bleed."

Fred's laughter exploded in his ears as the bartender lunged at him again.

Knife Jackson paced around the sheriff's office with seething impatience, his temper deteriorating by the moment. It was taking forever for the girl to come around. Didn't do no good to cut her when she couldn't feel it, couldn't know the pain, the fear. He'd have to wait.

Knife hated waiting.

"If she don't come to soon, we'll have to bring her with us. Can't stay here all night—jails make me nervous, even if I'm on the right side of the cell." His scowl was answered by chuckles from the other two men, kneeling beside Juliana. Their faces shone with sweat in the weak light of the kerosene lamp that broke up the shadows in the filthy office. They'd already dumped cold water on the woman, and slapped her cheeks, all to no avail. She was out cold.

"Carmen's waiting for me back at Delinda's," the scar-faced one muttered. He wiped his palms on his trousers. "Mebbe we should finish this business there."

"So long as we finish it before morning," Knife growled. "Mr. M doesn't like delays. If we don't catch up to the Montgomerys soon, there'll be hell to pay for sure."

"How 'bout lettin' me out now, Knife?" Lucius Dane's wheedling plea was met by silence from all three men. No one seemed the least inclined to release him from the cell.

"I kin bring her round," Dane cajoled. "Quick-like, too. Smelling salts, that's what you'll need."

Knife spun about to smile at him, showing cracked yellow teeth. "Why, that's a good idea, Dane." He stared at the other two men. "Why didn't we think of that?"

"Want me to get some, Knife?" The other man, with a lined face and thatchy brown hair, raised one ragged eyebrow. "One of the gals over in Fred's place must have somethin' like that, don't you think?"

Knife was scowling down into Juliana's battered face, the long, curled eyelashes lying like velvet fringe against her cheeks. "I'll go—I want to see if Fred nabbed Rawdon like he said he could. That's one hombre I'm itching to get my hands on."

"But Knife—what about letting me out? After all, you said it was a good idea . . ."

Jackson turned, one hand on the doorknob. "I'll think on it, Dane. You think on how you almost let this little filly slip right through your fingers."

As the door banged behind him, Dane's face fell. "Aw, boys, c'mon . . ."

But the scar-faced man snorted, "Shut up or we'll ram those keys down your throat—Sheriff!"

"Yeah . . . Sheriff!" Fingering Juliana's dress, the other man sighed. "Sure wish we had time to have some fun with this one. Lordy, just look at her . . ."

"This is business, Clyde. Knife'd skin you if he found out . . ."

"I'm only thinkin' out loud, Pritchard. C'mon, help me get her into that chair. Let her sit a minute once those smelling salts bring her round. She cain't answer no questions if she's half dead."

Through a haze of throbbing pain, Juliana heard their words, and shuddered inwardly. Her ribs felt as though they'd been run over by a locomotive, the splintering pain in her head was so excruciating, she could scarcely keep from moaning; but she fought to remain as still as possible, to put off as long as she could the rest of the questions—and the rest of the beating.

Why don't they just kill me and get it over with? she wondered, but she knew the answer already. Because they wanted information from her and would keep her alive—just barely—until they had it. So what could she do? Lie. Give them a tale that would satisfy them and pray that they wouldn't kill her when she was done.

But when she tried to remember the questions so she could prepare false answers to deceive them, her mind wavered in and out of consciousness, and she could not remember what they wanted to know. Something about Wade and Tommy—and Cole Rawdon.

Where is he? The bleak question ran through her in waves of hopelessness. *Why doesn't he help me?*

Probably because he was far away from here by now, no longer thinking of her, or of anything but how he would spend his reward money. He was gone, he didn't care. . . .

Tears stung her eyelids but she forced them back. A heavy, dragging weakness possessed her. Every part of her, even her toes, hurt. She couldn't withstand much more. Oh, why wouldn't they just shoot her and be done—

"Hey, she's coming round. Her hand moved. See?"

"Yeah." Pritchard jerked her upright in the chair and slapped her lightly on the cheek. "Wake up, honey, we're not finished with you yet."

A moan escaped her lips. She couldn't help it. It was all going to begin again. The questions, the blows, the shouts . . .

"Hey, Knife'll be real glad if we could get her to talk by the time he gets back," said Pritchard, the man with the scar. He yanked Juliana's hair, forcing her head back, and stared down into huge green eyes that were dazed with fear.

"All right now, girlie. Where's that hideout? Tell us and we'll go easy on you. We won't let Knife cut you, will we, Clyde?"

"Naw. Not if you tell."

Knife. She hadn't thought she could feel any more fear, but at the mention of his name, dread crawled through her. Juliana ran her tongue over dry, bruised lips, trying not to cry. Her throat hurt all over from the cruel pressure of Knife's hands.

"Water, please," she managed to whisper.

"Unh-unh. Not till you talk, girlie. Where's the hideout?"

"I need water . . ."

"Let me out of here," Lucius Dane called desperately, rattling the bars of the cell, "and I'll make her talk."

Thunder crashed outside, drowning out the men's response, but they were angry, she could see that even through her bleary, pain-racked eyes, angry at Lucius Dane and his incessant nagging, angry at her for refusing to answer their questions.

Pritchard, who smelled like onions and rancid sweat, struck her another blow to the side of the head and bent over her again, glaring.

"Tell us about Rawdon, then. . . . is he going to make a bid for Fire Mesa?"

"Rawdon . . ." Juliana croaked as her lip started bleeding again, and both her tormentors leaned closer, faces alight with eagerness. "Never heard of him . . ."

Clyde kicked the chair out from under her, knocking her to the floor. What was left of a scream tore from Juliana's throat as he lifted his foot to kick her. But the kick never came. One moment she saw his boot coming toward her face, and the next instant gunfire rocked the office, shot after shot, until Juliana lost count and lay half conscious with her hands over her head, waiting at any moment for the next blow to fall or the next bullet to take her life.

Someone leaned over her and she flinched with fear, but did not even have the strength to push away the strong hands reaching down to her.

Knife. He was back. He was going to stab her now . . .

"I hope you don't mind my shooting them, angel, but it's all I could think of at the moment," Cole Rawdon said in a hoarse voice she scarcely recognized. She opened her eyes in hazy disbelief, peering through a mist of agony into glinting cobalt eyes so furious, they made her gasp—then immediately she thought, *It isn't him. This man is covered with blood.*

Grayness clouded her vision, then she felt herself grasped in powerful arms, lifted, and the next thing she knew, rain was pelting her face, her neck, her gown.

"Hang on, sweetheart, we've got to get away from here."

His voice. His arms around her. And cold, icy rain. There was lightning, too, which seared her eyes. Like the night Cole Rawdon had found her, the night he'd pulled her back from that cliff. . . .

"Cole . . ."

"I know it's cold, sweetheart, but we can't stop, not yet."

She hadn't been trying to say *cold.* It was *Cole* she had murmured, unaware of where she was or what was happening, unable to comprehend the galloping motion of the horse, or the swiftness with which the stormy night ripped by.

All she knew was that Cole was with her again, holding her in his arms, keeping her on this horse, and whether it was dream or reality, she didn't care . . . he was there and she was safe . . . safe . . .

"Cole," she whispered again, her words lost on the wild wind. Deep within the streaming mountain gorges through which they rode at breakneck pace, on a pinto horse as swift as the streaks of lightning that burned the sky, with a man holding her who was covered with almost as much blood as she, Juliana passed out.

· 17 ·

Sunlight caressed Juliana's eyelids, sending waves of golden light beneath her lashes to tease her from her slumber. Something scratchy and vaguely familiar tickled her chin. Murmuring, she curled sideways and felt the softness of bedding beneath her. She opened her eyes with great reluctance, and a little trepidation, to find herself lying on a neatly made up feather bed, with Cole Rawdon's saddle blanket tucked around her. And nothing beneath. Not a stitch of clothes.

Just a bandage around her ribs.

She lurched up, then fell back with a groan as every muscle busily reprimanded her for her foolhardiness. After a moment she tried again, this time raising herself up carefully and gazing about the tiny, square cabin in which she found herself.

It was a modest one-room structure. There was a crude fireplace on the north wall, an old dented stove beside it, and a bench beneath the window with one small cupboard standing open to show a meager assortment of plates and mugs. Three cane chairs and a small roughly

carved table of pine were set near the stove and were the
only other objects of furniture besides this bed. No curtains, no rug, no ornamentation of any kind, nothing but
a broom in the corner, an ancient-looking iron kettle on
top of the stove, a wood box, and some kindling.

Where was this place? How had she come here? She
struggled for a wisp of memory, something to tell her
what had happened to her. The last thing she recalled
was the men beating her in the Plattsville jail . . .

The door opened and Cole Rawdon walked in just as
she was trying to get down from the bed.

"Whoa, there, what are you trying to do?" he demanded, sprinting forward and seizing her as her legs
wobbled. He caught her carefully in his arms and eased
her back onto the bed, scowling beneath the shadow of
his hat.

"I reckon Knife Jackson and his boys didn't knock any
sense into you after all. . . ."

"Where are my clothes?" Juliana cried, clutching the
blanket around her. Why was she always near naked
around this man? What was he doing here? And exactly
where *was* here?

"Your clothes are gone," he told her abruptly. "With
the bloodstains, they weren't worth saving. I've got a
shirt and trousers you can wear if you don't have a hankering for my saddle blanket."

"Who . . . took my clothes . . . off me?"

"Bounty hunter. Nice fellow. Rides a pinto horse that's
partial to yellow-haired women. Maybe you know him."

"How *dare* you undress me! You . . . you . . ."

"Isn't that just like a woman?" Cole mused, pushing
her back on the bed with one hand as she tried to rise and
wrench herself away from him. "You bring her to the
prettiest spot on earth and all she worries about is what
she's going to wear."

Juliana stared at him, speechless. For the first time, she

was able to have a clear view of his face, and shock bolted through her at the sight of the bruises around his jaw and left eye. Most chilling of all was the wicked cut across his cheek, jagged and tender-looking, the tissue not yet mended and sure to scar. "What happened to you?" she gasped, horror and concern rising in a rush, but he merely shrugged and laughed grimly.

"I got lassoed by part of the same outfit that got their hands on you," he said. His face changed, softening. "I owe you an apology for that."

He reached up a hand and gently touched her cheek. Despite the softness of his touch, Juliana winced. "And for that—and that"—he pointed to the various bruises on her bare arms—"and that." His finger lightly circled the marks on her neck. She saw the remorse on his face.

Sunlight had turned her emerald eyes to glowing gems, brilliant and incandescent in the pale, bruised face. He thought of that split second when Fred had come at him, slicing him with that shard of glass, and how his one thought had been for Juliana—who would save her after he died? Then, miraculously, some final burst of strength had rent the ropes apart, and he had been free to fight Fred to the death with his bare fists, free to get Juliana out of that jail. Too bad Knife Jackson was nowhere to be found, but he had shot the other two. Dane had been behind bars, cowering like a rabbit. Disgusted, angry as blazes, Cole had left him to rot. He had brought Juliana here, cared for her, agonized over the sight of each of her hurts. All of it was his fault. Cole hadn't ever believed he could feel such pain over another person's suffering, but this girl affected him like no one he had ever met. Seeing her now, hurt and confused, made him want to enfold her in his arms. The fact that she was naked beneath that blanket made it even more tempting.

Easy, boy, he told himself sternly. *Settle down and let*

the lady catch her breath. But he had to fight a powerful urge to ignore his own advice.

Juliana, for her part, couldn't stop staring at the gash on his face. She suddenly wanted to hold him, stroke his hair, and comfort him as if he were a little boy. All the while she had thought he'd abandoned her, but he had been undergoing far worse than she. "Did Knife Jackson do that?" she whispered in dismay.

"One of his hired thugs. It's a long story." Cole shook his head. "How much do you remember?"

Juliana groped to bring back the events that seemed so long ago. She shivered a little as she recalled the endless questions, the fists, the black boot aimed at her face . . .

"You got me out of there, didn't you?" she said slowly, the icy cold panic dying out of her as she looked into his face. "I thought it was a dream. . . ."

"Some dream." A muscle clenched in his jaw.

Words floated back to Juliana: "I had to shoot them, angel . . ."

"So you did come back for me. Why?"

His eyes razored in on hers. He had cleaned her up, washed away the blood from her bruises, bandaged her ribs, and seen her safely tucked into bed. That had been two days ago, and she still looked so deathly pale and drawn, filled somehow with a haunting sadness, that he almost told her he'd always meant to come back for her, that he never intended to leave her with Lucius Dane. But he couldn't bring himself to do it. That would be exposing too much of himself . . . she might get the wrong idea. He set his jaw and tried to harden his heart against the open innocence of her face. "I went hunting for answers in Plattsville and got bushwhacked. By the time I found out that Knife and his boys had gone after you, it was almost too late. I got you into that mess—I thought it was up to me to get you out."

Obligation. That's what had motivated him. Some

strange code of honor. She supposed she should be grateful, but she had been hoping for something more. What, exactly, she didn't know, and she pushed away the silly tears that threatened behind her eyes. Sunlight touched the scar showing clearly against his bronzed skin, delineating the raw, dried-blood edges.

Juliana swallowed, feeling weak. "When . . . how long have we been here?"

"Two days."

"Two days!" Shocked, Juliana stared at him in disbelief, as if he were making up a tale to tease her.

"I recall my sister reading a storybook once—my grandfather had sent all the way to Boston for it. All about a girl named Sleeping Beauty. That's all I could think of while you were lying there—you looked just like the girl in those pictures." A grin lightened his face. "But as I recall, *she* was sweet and obedient, and didn't spend every day of her life getting into trouble."

She was lost in the deep sea of his eyes as he smiled at her, and it took a moment for his words to penetrate. But when they did, she looked at him.

"*You* have a sister?" she blurted out.

Immediately she regretted her words, for the smile vanished, the familiar shuttered expression came over his face once again, and he drew back from her a full step. Secrets. This man was full of secrets, and he had no intention of sharing any of them with her. As if to illustrate the point, he spun about and stalked to the window.

"This discussion isn't about me, it's about you. You're going to have to give me some answers, Miss Montgomery."

His muscular frame seemed to fill every corner of the one-room dwelling. Beyond him, through the cabin's only window, a tiny slit in the chink of the log walls, she caught a glimpse of hazy emerald mountains and open sky. *The most beautiful spot on earth,* he had said. She longed to see it. After being in that jailhouse she needed open space. But she was his prisoner once again. Weariness washed over her. She had hoped . . . What had she hoped? It was too foolish even to explore.

"I've already told you all I know." She rubbed a hand across her eyes. "You didn't believe my side of the story before . . ."

"It's time I listened a little better."

Her hand dropped. She stared at him, bewildered. But it was hard to see; her eyelids felt heavy and thick.

He must have seen the exhaustion in her face. "Later, when you're feeling better," Cole said, "you'll tell me again. Everything. And maybe we can figure out why you and those damned brothers of yours are so important to Line McCray."

Line McCray. The name was familiar, but the dizziness seeping over her again made it difficult to concentrate. She closed her eyes. "I want to know some things too . . ."

"Sleep first. Then we'll talk."

"I'm hungry."

"Sleep first."

He hadn't changed. That same air of command, so infuriating, so . . . comforting. At least it was right now. She didn't feel capable of dealing with anything at all at the moment. Cotton wool clogged her brain, her body was still tender and sore, and the light-headedness drifting over her in waves made it impossible for her to argue . . . for now.

Juliana opened her eyes once and saw Cole standing over her. There was a strange expression in his eyes. He didn't look one bit dangerous for once. He looked . . . anxious? About her? She was hallucinating, that was it. Cole Rawdon hated her. Yet he had returned for her, injured as he was, he had fought—killed—to get her away from those men.

She brought herself up short. It wasn't as if he truly cared that she had suffered. He felt responsible, that was all, because he had left her at the mercy of savages. Decent of him to feel this regret, but he would have felt the same for anyone whom he had left vulnerable to attack. Even a liar and a thief who was wanted in Denver for a two-thousand-dollar reward.

"Where did you bring me?" Her voice was subdued, weary. "Where are we going from here?"

"We're not going anywhere until I'm sure McCray's men have lost the trail. And until I've got a handle on what's going on here. So sleep."

"But—"

"Later." He sounded irritated. "Get some rest or I'll have to knock you over the head with a frying pan."

"This place doesn't have a frying pan," she murmured.

It didn't seem to have much of anything, but it was shelter. Shelter from Knife Jackson and his friends, from Lucius Dane and that horrible Plattsville jail. Cole was going to listen to her, give her a chance.

She wanted to talk, to figure everything out, but somehow the knowledge that he was there watching over her made every limb in her body go slack, and she relaxed. Her troubled mind stilled. Her breathing slowed and she let the cascade of weariness pour over her in great, gentle waves.

Juliana slept until the sun set.

When she awoke she was alone in the cabin once more. Daylight had fled, replaced by a soft, blue-gray dusk. She heard a bubbling sound, and smelled something delicious. Soup. No, a stew. Great plumes of fragrant steam sailed up from the huge pot over the fireplace. Juliana's stomach grumbled noisily.

She managed to sit up and peer around the cabin without too much discomfort this time. Immediately she noticed the man's clothes folded across one of the cane chairs, along with a pair of boots.

Maybe not the latest Paris fashion, but they sure beat the saddle blanket. Wincing only slightly, she put on the yellow and blue plaid shirt and dark trousers, then grimaced at their huge size. She had to roll up the sleeves of the shirt and tie the hem in a knot at her waist to keep it from dwarfing her. The trousers were even worse; in addition to rolling up the cuffs, she had to fashion a belt from a bit of rope she discovered in the wood box in order to keep the pants from falling down around her knees. She frowned as she stuffed old dishrags into the boots to approximate a near fit. It irked her to know she must make a comical sight, but the delicious aroma wafting from the stew pot distracted her. Examining the cupboard at close range, she found that the cabin was better stocked than she had imagined. By the time Cole Rawdon walked in the door, she had a pot of beans heating on the stove, biscuits warming inside it, and the table set for a meal. The stove had given her some trouble at first, but she'd finally managed to light it after several unsuccessful tries had finally spurred her to kick it with all her might. That had done the trick.

"It's not fancy, but it's the best meal I've ever eaten," Juliana declared between mouthfuls of the venison stew. "Where have you been anyway? I thought you were standing guard. That's why I slept so well." She broke off, embarrassed. He pretended not to see the pink flush that blossomed on her cheeks.

"I'm asking the questions around here, remember?"

But there was a teasing gentleness in his voice that she hadn't heard before. Looking up quickly, Juliana saw him studying her. Embarrassed, she tried to smooth her hair.

Loose, wild, it glinted in the light of the kerosene lantern he had removed from the wood box, fascinating him.

His old plaid shirt was ridiculously large on her, he observed, his chest tight, and so were the trousers, but their bulk only emphasized her femininity. She looked adorable. More fetching than the pictures of Sleeping Beauty in Caitlin's storybook. More fetching than any woman he'd ever seen.

Cole knew himself to be in unfamiliar territory here—dangerous territory. Best to stick to business, he reminded himself in alarm. That meant to stop looking at her, stop thinking about her. Sticking to questions and answers, facts, information. Yet when she leaned over him with the soup ladle, spooning more stew into his bowl, and her hair accidentally brushed his cheek, he felt a tightening in his loins.

Dangerous, that's what she was. She could blast a man's resolve to smithereens more effectively than any dynamite he'd ever come across. Just his luck that the woman wanted in Denver hadn't been some tub-bellied cow with a leathery face and dirty fingernails instead of this porcelain-skinned hellion who could alternately rile or entrance him with a single word or gesture.

"Maybe you ought to tell me exactly what happened between you and this John Breen." He set down his cup of coffee and regarded her in the growing shadows that spilled in through the window slit. "The whole story this time, angel."

So she told him. Leaning forward across the table, her always expressive face flushed and animated even more than usual, the words spilling out one over another, she told him how she had come west to find her brothers, how her uncle had arranged the marriage to John Breen without her knowledge, how she had disliked Breen from the very first moment.

"So you ran away? All alone?"

His stupefaction made her mouth tighten with defiance. "Well, not all alone. I had Columbine. The horse I stole from John Breen," she explained, and added quickly, "If you think I'm sorry about that, or I deserve to go to jail for it, you're wrong! I only took her because there was no other way, and I wasn't about to be sacrificed for any man, however much *he* might desire it. I control my own destiny—or at least I did, until you came along. But I never stole five thousand dollars. John Breen made that up so he could trick men like you into bringing me back. You never would have bothered with a mere horse thief, would you?"

Cole didn't answer. She had a point. His blood was boiling. Fury, cold and deep as the thrust of honed steel, pierced through his chest until he could hardly breathe. He'd been used. Used to capture and torment a woman who had just wanted her freedom, used to satisfy another man's selfish will. Years ago he'd sworn never to be used by any human being ever again—and now this bastard Breen had framed Juliana Montgomery, put every bounty hunter west of the Missouri on her trail by dangling that filthy two-thousand-dollar reward for her capture, and in so doing had snared him into this ugly, private game of vengeance.

Why hadn't he listened to her in the first place?

Because Jess Burrows and Liza White had soured him on believing in anyone ever again. Because even his own father had betrayed his family's trust, because his years in the orphanage had taught him that cruelty ran deep in human beings, and that appearances were always deceiving.

Excuses. He had plenty of those. But it didn't change the ugly part he had played in this.

Now he was in it deeper than ever—they both were—and it wouldn't be over for her until this mess with the Montgomery gang was settled, McCray was out of the picture, and this confounded tycoon John Breen was dealt with. He swore savagely to himself that when this was over, Juliana Montgomery would be free to do as she pleased. But not until then.

Cole didn't pull any punches. "You're in danger," he told her, eyes narrowed. "Until we figure out what Mc-Cray is up to and why he wants your brothers so badly, you've got to stay hidden. Can you think of anything that was said when they were roughing you up, anything that might give us a hunch what kind of burr is under Mc-Cray's saddle?"

Chin on fist, Juliana stared straight ahead, concentrating. It was hard to summon up the memories of that night without shuddering, hard to recall the angry torrent of questions—and fists—without feeling fear knot in her throat. But then she nodded suddenly, nearly jumping from her chair with excitement.

"They asked me if Wade was planning to rob a freight payroll . . . the Henshaw freight payroll, if I'm not mistaken."

"That payroll will be coming through north of Plattsville in four days time. If the Montgomery gang does plan to waylay it, and we can figure out where they plan to stage the holdup, we might catch up with those brothers of yours yet."

"Why are you so interested in helping me find them all of a sudden?"

Juliana couldn't hide the suspicion edging her voice, or the worry that knit her brows together. If he thought she would do *anything* to help him capture Wade and Tommy and then turn them in for a reward, he was dead wrong. She would fight him every step of the way. But Cole sent her an exasperated look.

"Settle down, Juliana. I'm not your enemy anymore, McCray is. He's opened fire on both of us, as far as I'm concerned, and what I want to know is why."

"Do you know this Line McCray?"

"We've met." Hard lights glinted in his eyes. "I don't

think much of him, but he's been mighty successful. Owns some valuable property in southeastern Arizona and down in New Mexico. Now," Cole said, swinging away from the window to pace restlessly about the room, "it seems he's taken over Plattsville lock, stock, and barrel."

Juliana recalled what she had learned from Henny, and told Cole about it, trying to put the pieces together. "So McCray forced Henny to sell him the hotel after her husband died—or rather, was killed," she said slowly while Cole frowned down at her in silence, "and when her son objected to his tactics, he died too." She jumped up from the chair, distraught once more as she recalled the scene in the jail. "And Sheriff Dane was threatening her other little boy, Cole, as sure as I'm standing here. He had the poor woman terrified of even peeking at him sideways."

She wheeled about and marched up and down the small width of the cabin, her oversize boots scraping the floor. "I wouldn't believe one word that awful man uttered," she exclaimed furiously. "If Dane claims Wade shot Hank Rivers in the back, the truth is that he probably did it himself—so he could take over the sheriff's job or . . . or because McCray wanted him to . . ."

In spite of the seriousness of the situation, Cole couldn't help but grin at the sight of her all worked up and stalking the cabin floor furiously. "You'd make a pretty good Pinkerton detective," he commented. "I think you're right."

Silence. He did?

"You do?" For a moment she thought the beating she had endured had affected her hearing. This man who had never done anything but argue with her and order her around—he was actually agreeing with her about something?

Then he grinned and came forward, grasping her by the shoulders. "The man who gave me this"—and he pointed to the gash on his cheek—"admitted to me that he was the witness with Rivers when he died, the one who swore it was Wade Montgomery who did the shooting. He also slipped his own special concoction in my drink and beat the hell out of me afterward, all on orders from either Line McCray or Knife Jackson. Some witness. His testimony was all part of the setup. For some reason, McCray wants to pin Rivers's murder on your brothers, along with whatever else he can find—and get the Montgomery gang out of the picture. When we track them down, we can find out why."

"I remember something else," Juliana said, her heart hammering against her ribs with painful thuds as she stood before him, so close she could feel the heat and tension rippling through his body. Kissing close, she realized, conscious of his firm hands on her shoulders holding her lightly, of his eyes searching hers, not as if she were a piece of outlaw scum, but as someone who counted, someone to listen to and consider.

"Knife . . . and the others." She moistened her lips with her tongue, trying to keep her mind running in a straight path. "They asked me about you—and about someplace called . . . Fire Mesa."

In the absolute silence that followed, she could hear his breathing, shallow and harsh. From outside came the sound of wind blowing through trees, of birds singing faintly in the distance. Was it a cactus wren? Or a grouse? She saw the tension bite through the powerful muscles in his neck, saw the narrowing of eyes that suddenly looked like chips of sapphire ice. This mattered. She didn't know why, but it mattered. Maybe more than anything else.

"What did they ask you?" His voice was deliberately casual, but it didn't fool her for a moment.

"If you planned to make a bid for Fire Mesa." Juliana stared up at him. "What is Fire Mesa?"

For answer, he gripped her arm suddenly and led her

to the door. Then they were outside the cabin and Juliana caught her breath. She stared through widened eyes at the stunning rose-kissed beauty of a world so radiant, it tore her breath away.

"This," Cole said, still holding her arm, "is Fire Mesa."

From the tiny window facing south she had glimpsed mountains, but she had not guessed at anything like this. For who could imagine paradise? The cabin before which they stood was an insignificant twig cupped at the foot of a great red rock mountain so immense it seemed to touch the clouds. Steep gray- and red-hued canyons wound their way to the north, and to the distant south and east stretched a breathtaking panorama of golden green mountains so majestic, so like spires in a king's jeweled crown, they took her breath away. Nearer, luscious valleys dipped and wound their way around buttes and mesas, which climbed gradually into soft purple and gray foothills that rolled gracefully away. And far below the rocky mesa on which the cabin was perched, a glint of silver shimmered in the dusk. A river, racing, jumping. Flashing like quicksilver through the cottonwoods below. Juliana, turning slowly in a circle to see every angle of the spectacular view, saw great lonely rocks in the distance, shimmering lavender in the sunset, spruce and fir and pine high above, gilded by the last dying rays of the sun. The mossy-green foothills were alive with wildflowers, and wild goats roamed through the north canyon walls. It filled her with awe, this wild, splendid land of distant purple sagebrush, of towering ponderosa pine that rose and dipped in a zigzag line as far as the eye could see.

Fire Mesa.

The name suited it well. The rocks, the buttes, were all the marvelous colors of fire, ruby and amber and gold. The land itself seemed to catch the light, to glow with spectacular beauty so powerful and overwhelming, it was almost dizzying to behold.

"This," Cole added, watching the wonder on Juliana's face as she studied the horizon from each glorious direction, "is the southernmost tip of Fire Mesa. There's a whole lot more."

"How did you ever find this place?" she whispered. "I feel . . . as if we are all alone in the entire world."

"We are. This particular spot is known to only a handful of human beings. No one can see this gorge from the trails over the mountains. There's a secret route in, and another one, even more hidden, out on the other side, closer to Flagstaff. Fire Mesa has countless canyons like this one. The horses live here."

"Horses?"

"You're looking at wild horse country. Mustangs. Hundreds of 'em. Maybe thousands . . ." His voice trailed off. "This is some of the most beautiful, blood-stained country in the world. I loved it here when I was a boy—and then for years I hated it. I haven't been back to this spot for twenty years. But it's still the same." He tore his gaze from the vista of rocks and spruce, and let his glance rest on her for a moment.

"You're safe here." He was matter-of-fact. "McCray's men would have to search for months to find this particular cabin."

She wanted to ask him the connection between him and this place; there could be no doubt that there was some deep, significant connection. In his lean face she detected the pride of ownership, a pride that had nothing to do with vanity or boasting, but was instead something keen and fine and inborn that stemmed from his heart and soul. Yet, lurking in his eyes, behind the obvious appreciation for the unspeakable beauty of this paradise, was pain. What had happened here? What was it about

Fire Mesa that brought that haggard look to a face so young and handsome?

"Thank you for bringing me here. It's lovely . . . and if you say it's safe, I believe you. But . . . you say you were here as a boy. Did your family live here? Why did you leave?"

Sunset glowed like a candle flame about them. Incandescent lavender light shimmered on the mountains, the dying sun drenched the treetops with gold. A deer darted across the river far below, and in the cottonwoods that stood like sentinels behind the cabin, Juliana heard the song of birds. But she saw nothing except Cole Rawdon's face, the scar vivid in the fleeting light, as he answered her, his voice oddly drained of emotion.

"My family lived here. My grandfather owned Fire Mesa—thirty thousand acres of Arizona treasure, he called it—he passed it on to my father. They caught wild horses, broke them, sold them . . . it was a good, free life, a fine life for a boy growing up. My sister, Caitlin, could ride like the wind. She sensed where the horses would run. It was in her blood, I reckon. She and I would sit at Grandfather's knee at night when the coyotes would howl in the darkness and lightning raced across the sky, and he would tell us legends about the king of the mustangs."

Juliana remembered the wood carving she'd found in his pack the night he'd first tracked her down. The horse's head, every detail carved in wood, magnificent in every line and angle. That carving had captured a sense of strength, pride, and wildness in the animal, and could only have been lovingly wrought.

"But my grandfather died when I was six, and my father took over Fire Mesa. He used to ride to town nights—he loved saloons even more than horses. And he loved to play faro—and poker—a lot more than he should. One night, my father hit a losing streak. But he couldn't stop, he kept thinking his luck would change. It didn't. He lost everything, all his money, his pocket watch, ring—and he was ashamed to come home. So . . . he put up the deed for Fire Mesa as collateral and gambled some more—and lost."

His eyes became flat, cold. Juliana shivered as she stared up at him. Night was creeping in, bringing a rich amethyst darkness to the beauty all around them. But Cole saw none of it; he was seeing the past, a time of pain, of loss and sorrow . . .

"But that wasn't enough for him. He was frantic to get Fire Mesa back. So he rode three hours to the next town —and started gambling some more. Again, he put up the deed for Fire Mesa—though he had already turned it over to Joseph Wells. Again, he lost." Cole's mouth twisted. "But this time, he couldn't pay up. There was no deed to give over. There was nothing left. He'd already forfeited Fire Mesa."

As he paused, sucking in a deep, painful breath, Juliana felt the stirrings of fear inside her. Bleak, chill air touched her shoulders, her neck. Cole's face was ashen in the gloom of falling night.

"What happened?" she whispered, sensing all the while that it was something she did not want to know. But she had to know. Maybe it would help her to understand him. Maybe it would help her to fathom some of the dark, secret side of this most self-reliant, solitary man.

"What happened was that the next morning a rancher from the next county named Barnabas Slocum rode up to our front door, along with some of his hands, and demanded the deed my father had promised him. Fire Mesa was a prime piece of land, pretty well known in these parts. Slocum had had his eye on the place for years.

"My father had come home drunk just after dawn and

was sleeping it off when Slocum arrived. My mother answered the door. My mother was a pretty woman."

His voice broke, but only for a second. He went on, in a tone so low and deadly it sent shivers down Juliana's spine. "My mother didn't know anything about what had happened that night. Until Slocum started shouting for the deed. Then my father told her, and he told Slocum that he couldn't pay his debt—that another man already owned the deed to Fire Mesa. Slocum got angry. Angrier than I've ever seen any human being. You don't want to know what happened after that."

She didn't. Heaven help her, she didn't. But she had to know. Something haunted and agonized in his eyes told her that whatever it was, it had been horrible, more horrible than she could imagine. And he had been how old at the time? Seven? Eight?

"What did Slocum do?"

At the hushed, fearful tone in her whisper, Cole looked at her, studying the small, bruised face illuminated by the night's first stars. He hesitated, then spoke again, all in a rush.

"He killed my parents and sister. Raped my mother and Caitlin first. Forced my father to watch. Then he and his men killed them, each of them, one by one. I was the last, held down the entire time, a stupid, fighting, screaming kid, useless . . . but I saw, I heard. When they had choked the life out of Caitlin and left her naked in the dust beside the well, Slocum had his men beat me to within an inch of my life. They left me for dead at the bottom of a ravine half a mile from the house. First, they dragged me there behind Slocum's horse."

"No. Oh, no, no, no." She wept. Her hands covered her face while tears soaked through her fingers, and her shoulders shook with the savagery and horror of it. What he had described was unspeakable. She couldn't imagine such brutality—and a picture of him as a child enduring what he had just so dispassionately described burned in her mind and her heart. Something broke inside her. She reached blindly for him then, not thinking at all, merely needing to touch him with gentle hands, as if to soothe away every hurt, even those that could never be soothed, and before she knew it she was swept into a hard embrace.

"It's all right." His mouth was against her hair. "No need for you to cry—it was twenty years ago. Twenty long years," he said, wondering at her response, stroking her hair, her soft, elegant nape as she wept in his arms.

"I shouldn't have told you."

"I . . . want to hear the rest. What . . . happened after that?"

"Juliana . . ."

"You started the story—please, you must finish it for me," she urged in a low, desperate tone.

He took a deep breath. "Slocum made it look like the Apache had done the killing. He and his men must have paid witnesses to place them somewhere else that morning. No one believed me. A kid of eight, broken, battered, half loco with rage and grief. A judge passing through town sent me east, to an orphanage in Iowa. I lived there for the next eight years of my life. And that's the end of the story."

An orphanage. At least she had had Aunt Katharine and Uncle Edward. And the hope of being with Wade and Tommy again. He had had nothing. No one.

"And Slocum?" She hesitated. "You never saw him again?"

"What do you think?"

Her heart began to hammer at the lethal look in his eyes. "You found him?"

"I found him." Cole's lips tightened as he stared out at the falling darkness, scented with sage. "Eight years I

had to wait, but I found him. I made sure he'd never rape
or kill anyone ever again."

"So you killed him."

He didn't deny it.

She shook her head, dazed. She couldn't blame him,
but . . . it frightened her. Yes, he had witnessed and
suffered from terrible violence as a young child. And yes,
he had confronted violence later, choosing a profession
that required it. He had come away from his ordeal
toughened in a way she could never understand. How
different they were. What had happened to her own parents had given her a dread of blood and brutality that
made her abhor any act of savagery. He dealt with such
acts every day. She could not condemn him, but for just a
moment she was afraid of him. Afraid of the darkness
that might lurk in his soul, of the need to strike out at
every enemy, every opponent, with a killing lust. But
then she looked at him again, looked deep into that
strong, toughened face, and knew in her heart that his
soul was not tainted. His eyes might grow cold and hard,
but there had never been a glint of cruelty in them. He
derived no pleasure from killing. His actions might be
deadly at times, brutal, it seemed to her, but this was a
brutal land filled with brutal men. He survived. He
walked tall. He knew his own power and used it not to
bully the vulnerable, as Lucius Dane and Knife Jackson
did, but to cut down the savage men who would attack
anyone of lesser strength.

Cole Rawdon gripped her arms suddenly, his eyes
glinting like blue sparks in the moonstruck darkness.
"Yes, I killed Slocum, Juliana. I've killed many men, so
many I don't even know the number. Do you despise me
for that? I don't blame you. You're a woman, you're from
the East, what do you know of life out West? From what
you've seen so far, I would think you might understand.
But, no. I can see by your face you don't. You're scared

of me. Maybe you should be. Maybe I am no better than an animal."

"No!" Juliana clutched his arm as he started to turn away. "I do understand . . . in a way. I hate guns and I hate killing . . . but I see the need. You . . . are not an animal. You are not like Knife Jackson or Cash Hogan or those others. Don't you think I can see that, Cole? Don't you think I know what kind of man you are?"

Furious tears sparkled suddenly on her lashes. "You think I'm a complete fool, don't you? That I can't understand anything about you or this wild country or the men who inhabit it."

For a moment he just stared at her, seeing her trembling lips, her lashes moist with tears, her eyes brilliant in the pearly gleam of the moon. And then he started to laugh, a husky, desperate laugh. "Oh, God. I think that you, Juliana, are the damnedest woman I ever met—and if you don't stop looking at me like that, I can't answer for the consequences."

"Consequences?"

The wind caught her hair, sending it dancing like a golden halo about her head. Cole captured it in his fingers, crushed the fine, velvet-soft curls in his hand.

"I warned you," he managed to say in a deep, breathless tone as she continued to gaze at him with the most hypnotizing luminosity in those beautiful shining eyes. "Back off, Juliana, before it's too late or—"

For answer she stepped closer and threw her arms around his neck.

"Or what?"

Her voice was a purely feminine invitation. Soft, playful, the voice of an irresistible minx. Cole felt his control slipping dangerously.

Juliana smiled, feeling as though she was on the verge of a sweetly perilous adventure. The most delicious pleasure surged through her at the surprise in his face, followed immediately by a darkening of those keen, vivid blue eyes. There was no mistaking the passion in his voice when next he spoke.

"I do believe you're calling my bluff, Miss Montgomery . . ."

"Never threaten—or promise—a woman something you're not prepared to follow through, Mr. Rawdon," she began in a softly lecturing tone, but her words were cut off by powerful arms imprisoning her with a suddenness that snatched her breath away, and in the same instant, his mouth clamped down on hers with a sublime impact that left her shaking.

He kissed her hard. It was a fierce, powerful kiss. He didn't need her, damn it, he didn't need anyone, but he sure as hell felt like he did. A savage desire pounded through him as her honeyed mouth kissed him back with startling abandon. It wasn't fair, Cole thought desperately, what she'd been doing to him since the first moment they met, dogging his thoughts, distracting him, making him want her. He'd make her want him just as badly, even if it was just for tonight. She'd asked for it, she'd practically dared him. What kind of a wild woman was she, this fragile easterner who burned like a candle flame in his arms, kissing him bold as any saloon girl, her mouth open, her body squirming against his. Tenderness and wonder warred within him. Pressing his mouth over her lips, his hands moving up and down her body, rough and heedless and demanding, he drank in the scent and heat and feel of her. His mind reeled, he knew only driving need and a deeper emotion, something tangled and confused, but strong as whiskey, and he swept her off her feet, into his arms, and carried her into the cabin with single-minded purpose.

· 18 ·

Cole carried her to the feather bed, set her down, and leaned over her, his hands sliding inside that damned shirt. . . .

Juliana lost herself in his eyes, in his arms. Passion rained over her like a summer storm, growing more insistent, pounding, pounding, until she was drenched in the downpour, and the wetness was everywhere, even between her thighs. She opened her body to him like a flower and begged him to taste the pollen. Legs flung about his legs, thighs pressed together, both of them naked now, she scraped her hands over the muscular power of him, caressing that broad powerful back, touching him everywhere, gasping at the strength and size and beauty of him. She felt driven by wonder and a rapturous curiosity that made her forget girlish modesty. Tenderness radiated from him, in the way he held her, touched her, even when his mouth and hands seemed rough and hungry. She was not afraid. She was caught up in a tide of eagerness that bore her along a turbulent, sizzling river, uncontrollable, unstoppable, plummeting deeper and deeper into the raging waters. Her nipples were hard and taut beneath his probing fingers, she strained to meet him, every part of him, her breath coming in long, heated gasps, and when he entered her, she gave a scream at the sudden flash of pain, then felt herself soothed by a kiss as tender as a feather against her lips.

"Juliana. You're so beautiful, oh, angel, so damned beautiful . . ."

He was the beautiful one, but she had no breath to tell him so. He was moving inside her now, thrusting, and the sensations that drove through her melted her tongue and made her want to burst. She was going to burst, to burst into flame, yes, any moment now—and the shudders of delight that gripped her carried her to a plateau higher than any mountain she'd ever seen, hotter than any sun that ever shone. Floating, floating on a cloud of fire, so vibrantly alive, she rocked and tossed with him in the cabin bed until the peak of bliss left her soaring, shuddering, and then she was floating downward, feeling as still and whole and perfect as a dove who has completed a graceful, perfect flight.

She lay naked in his arms, dazed and dreamy, her temples damp, her skin glowing. In the golden warmth of the kerosene lamp, she saw the black curling hair of his chest, felt the bulge of muscles beneath her cheek. How could a man be so fierce and strong, and at the same time so loving and gentle, he melted your heart? She didn't know, she only knew that she was happy. For the first time in so many years, she was happy.

Cole lay with eyes closed, breathing in the scent of her. She was incredible. Beautiful, spirited, and so amazingly gentle. She had given of herself with such abandon it stunned him, and she felt so exquisitely right in his arms it terrified him. He never wanted to let her go, and yet he feared that if he moved or spoke, she would vanish like a puff of smoke, and he would never see her or hold her again.

"My Aunt Katharine is a very stupid woman," she whispered suddenly, drawing him from his reverie.

"What made you think of *her*?"

His bewildered expression elicited a giggle.

She pressed a teasing kiss into his neck, feeling strangely comfortable, at peace, as if she'd known him all her life. "The night before I ran away from Twin Oaks, Aunt Katharine told me that I would have to perform my wifely duties after I wed John Breen, and she described to me—in a very unappealing way, and with a great deal of embarrassment—what I had to look forward to, or rather, not look forward to, when we began our honeymoon."

"Did she now?"

"Yes, and she did not make any part of it sound the least bit enjoyable."

Cole's muscles tensed at the thought of Juliana in bed with another man. His arms tightened protectively around her. "But this was?" he asked with a slow grin. Damn, she was soft. Her body was all sensuous curves and silken flesh, arousing him with every breath she took, every tiny movement she made against his own rock-solid frame.

She struggled free, laughing up at him, batting her eyelashes in the adorable way that made his insides fire up.

"Whatever gave you that idea, Mr. Rawdon?" she teased, then giggled as he grabbed her around the waist and drew her down on top of him once again.

"Certain clues," Cole said purposefully, his eyes gleaming into hers. His grin made her shiver all over with heady anticipation. "Reckon I'll have to show you what I mean."

"Is that really necessary?" she cooed, rubbing his calf with her foot.

"Absolutely necessary."

They forgot they were exhausted. They forgot they were sore, battered, hurt by more than fists and boots, bruised by the emptiness of the past.

Each found what they sought in the other's arms. An hour after dawn, with peach light edging across the sky, they slept at last, curled together in the narrow bed, cleansed of sorrow and pain, spent but whole, like sailors who have found safe harbor from the raging storm.

Cole woke several hours later, lying with Juliana snug in the circle of his arms, pondering that everything good he'd ever wanted or possessed in his life had been taken from him, thinking with taut fear in his chest that she was the best gift, the most prized treasure he had ever known.

Storm clouds gathered over Twin Oaks as John Breen reread the telegram from Plattsville.

"Sheriff Lucius Dane," he spat, tapping it against his palm. "I reckon he's hungry for the reward."

"What's that you say, darlin'?" Jet Reeves, the newest dance-hall girl from the Lucky Dog Saloon, purred from his bed.

Breen scowled at her, then folded the telegram and flung it on the Louis XVI bureau. "Nothing. I guess this weather has me talking to myself."

"It's that telegram that has you talking to yourself, honeykins. Ever since Bart brought it up here you've been . . . different. On edge, all upset about Lord knows what. I guess it's up to me to think of some way to relax you."

Relax? That was the last thing on Breen's mind. He felt fired up in a way he hadn't in months—not since Juliana Montgomery first vanished from his life. Unbelievable that in all that time no one had found her. None of the bounty hunters had turned up with her in tow, none of his men had uncovered a trace of where she'd gone after she'd sold that mare in Amber Falls. It was as if the woman had disappeared into thin air—until today. Until that telegram arrived.

Well, Sheriff Lucius Dane—whoever the hell *he* was— would have his reward, if this tip proved valid. And if it led him at last to that gorgeous little bitch's capture. That snotty little golden-haired debutante who'd turned up her nose at him right from the start. No one turned up her nose at John Breen—no one had dared in the past twelve years.

It rankled deep within that he'd been bested by a woman—but, of course, he hadn't. He'd only been de- layed by her. He'd have Juliana Montgomery back, he vowed to himself as Jet held out her arms to him. He'd have her in his bed, in his complete control, on his own terms, and before the month was out.

He was leaving for Plattsville himself in the morning, storm or no storm.

As if to challenge him, a blast of thunder shook the sky, and heavy splatters of rain smashed down against the leaded windowpanes.

"Sweetie pie, come to bed." Jet's black hair, from which she took her name, swirled over her shoulders and partially hid her large, drooping breasts. "I know how to keep you safe and warm," she promised with a sidelong smile.

"Get out of here, Jet." Breen had no patience with her. Just seeing Juliana Montgomery's name in that telegram —after having had no sign of her for months—had him wrapped up in her all over again. She was like a fever in his blood. "I've got thinking to do," he dismissed the dark-eyed girl curtly. Her perfume, as gaudy and over- powering as the dresses she wore in the Lucky Dog, was clogging his nostrils, making him want to retch. "And I need to pack. I'm going on a trip tomorrow."

"But honeykins, it's so early—not even eight o'clock—
and it's starting to pour. You can't send me all the way
back to town in this weather."

Breen reached her in three strides. The back of his
hand caught her full across the face. She fell sideways
across the bed with a scream.

"Don't tell me what I cannot do, you two-bit slut." His
shout rang through the house like a steel gong. "I said get
out and I mean it. Now. And if I call you back in an
hour, you'll come. You'll come on foot, if I tell you to—
you hear me?"

She started sniveling, her cheek blotchy where he'd
struck her, the vivid fear stark in her narrow, painted
face. Breen seized her by the arm and literally threw her
out the bedroom door, then hurled her clothes after her.

Seething impatience pumped through him. He'd had
his fill of Jet and her ilk. What he wanted was that eastern vixen with her snooty airs and emerald eyes so deep
you could drown in them. He longed to see on Juliana
Montgomery's face that same fear Jet had shown. He
longed to have her in his bed, doing what *he* told her to
do.

And he would have her there, right where he wanted
her. Unless this fool sheriff Lucius Dane was drunk or
lying, he'd have his hands on her very soon.

· 19 ·

It was a vision out of a dream, Juliana thought as she lay in the long grass of the valley beside Cole, watching as the wild white stallion grazed along the opposite stream bank with his herd of mares. "He's magnificent," she breathed, unable to remove her gaze from the proud figure of the snowy mustang, ghostly in the morning light. Beyond him was Eagle Mesa, and beyond that a series of rocky outcroppings dipping among aspen and sage, but along the streambed, junipers and piñon pines flourished, and the horses watered and grazed peacefully, momentarily vulnerable, in the open spaces beneath the tranquil opal sky.

The wind was blowing north, so the herd had not yet caught the human scent in the sage-tinged air. Juliana and Cole lay side by side for long moments, watching the shaggy-maned mares and the stallion keeping such careful watch over them.

A slight awkwardness had been between them until, after breakfast, Cole had taken her riding, showing her more of the rugged beauty and glorious isolation of this land he called Fire Mesa. The wild, indescribably gorgeous countryside somehow soothed both of them, forging an unspoken bond of appreciation between them. She hadn't known what he was tracking at first, or why he kept switching trails and directions, until he brought her here to this lonely spot on foot, leaving the horses tethered in a rocky dell some fifty feet back.

They had settled down and not spoken until the wild band showed itself, and Cole had shared with her at last this miracle of the proud and tough wild horses who roamed among the valleys and buttes and lower canyons of Fire Mesa. Something inside Juliana quivered with awe at the sight of these hardy and brave creatures. There was no doubt that Cole, for all his toughness and experience, felt as she did about these fascinating creatures. His eyes glinted, and his face shone in the hazy light as he studied the watering band. Their shared pleasure in spying the herd and secretly watching its movements eased the remaining awkward feelings between them. Juliana could have stayed here forever, side by side with Cole, watching the horses in that near-mystical setting. But suddenly the wind changed and the stallion caught their scent. Instantly, his head came up, and he snorted in anger. He caught sight of them, low in the grass across the stream, and charged forward, stopping at the riverbank. Head up, he tossed his silvery mane and stomped the ground in fury. Then he reared up, forelegs pawing the air.

"*Adiós,* my friend," Cole muttered under his breath.

Then, as if hearing him, the stallion gave a harsh, screaming whinny, alerting the band of mares to danger. Their heads flew up, and almost as one they scrambled toward Eagle Mesa, guarding their colts close, nipping, bumping together, streaming around the shimmering gray rocks toward the safety of the secluded canyons beyond. The stallion stayed behind, rearing up, screaming, giving the mares and foals time to flee. Only then did he wheel about and depart after them, his hooves flying over the grass like sparks of white fire. An old gray mottled mare, slower and weaker than the rest, waddled behind the pack, and the stallion nipped her rump ferociously as he caught up with her. That sent her galloping. As the sun sailed overhead through the cloudless arc of pale blue, they disappeared in a flurry among the rocks and brush and aspen.

"That was wonderful! Thank you for bringing me here," Juliana exclaimed as he helped her to her feet. "That stallion was magnificent. Have you ever seen a horse as pure white as he?"

He was quiet for a moment before he answered her. "Not for many years."

She wondered at his grim tone, then rested her gaze on him questioningly. Unsure what had brought that tight line to his lips, she regarded him in silence and waited.

"A man I used to know had a white horse much like that one. No dark markings, pure white. A mustang, hardy as even that stallion, though he was a gelding."

"You didn't like this man very much, I gather," Juliana commented as he cupped a hand beneath her elbow and led her down the path to where their horses were tethered.

"Oh, I liked him well enough, until he and the woman he was working with—a woman I imagined myself in love with—shot me in the back and left me for dead in the desert," came his casual reply.

She stopped, staring at him in horror. "Who was this man?" she asked.

"It doesn't matter anymore. He's dead. So is Liza. Not by my hand," he added quickly. "Though if I'd found them alive, it would have been my doing. They died in San Francisco, killed over the gold they stole from me, and from some poor old prospector left murdered in the hills."

His eyes were haunted, despite his calm tone. She sensed that this hurt and the old hate that accompanied it ran very deep within him, as deeply perhaps as his grief over the atrocities committed at Fire Mesa. "Why did they try to kill you?"

He lifted a hand as if to dismiss the question, then saw the soft compassion in her eyes. Something about that tender, intent look stopped him from avoiding the discussion, as he had intended to do. He had not talked about this with anyone in twelve years. So why, now, Juliana?

Maybe because last night had been the first night of peace, true peace, he ever remembered. Maybe because her kisses, her voice, her silken arms tight around him made the shadows retreat, the stone-cold loneliness he had taught himself to live with, even to enjoy, go away—if only for a little while. No one except Sun Eagle, who had saved him in the desert and allowed him to live among The People for a time, a brother among brothers, knew the story of how Jess Burrows had betrayed him. But he told it to Juliana now, on that quiet hillside, seated beside her on a slab of red rock beside the yuccas and agave. While the sun shone bright as fool's gold, and a tiny wild geranium poked its scarlet head between two small boulders at Juliana's feet, he told her the dark tale of murder and betrayal that had haunted him for the past twelve years of his life.

He had met Jess Burrows in California about a month after he'd hunted down Barnabas Slocum. Burrows was a strapping, good-looking fellow, congenial and generous, for all that he was as dirt-poor as Cole. It was Burrows who introduced him to Liza, working at the time as a dance-hall girl in one of the hundreds of saloons that had sprouted up in the wake of the gold rush. And it was Burrows who introduced him to Abe Henley, the flinty-eyed old prospector Burrows was supposed to protect but eventually murdered in order to steal his gold.

Henley had hired both of them, Burrows and Cole, to help him work his claim near Yuma, Arizona, and to help him protect it from claim-jumpers. He promised them a share in his treasure if they were lucky enough to hit a rich find. They struck gold, plenty of it, but Burrows double-crossed the old man. He murdered Henley while Cole was away from their camp. And Liza, who had left her saloon job to journey with them across the wilds of Arizona, told Cole a story about bandits who had raped her before murdering Henley, convincing him that Burrows was away from camp as well when the murder took place.

Cole had wanted to set out after them right away. Liza remembered their saying something about Bear Pass. But she hadn't let him go alone. With no sign of Burrows's imminent return, she had clung to Cole and begged him to take her with him. She was terrified, she said, of being attacked again and would only feel safe with him. In the tumultuous emotions of that scorching, bloody afternoon, she had told him it was really him she loved, not Jess Burrows.

"And I was just young and stupid enough to believe her," Cole told Juliana dispassionately as they sat together while prairie grouse squawked overhead. "Only it wasn't me she loved after all. It was Henley's gold, and my share of it. She led me into a trap at Bear Pass, where Burrows was waiting to ambush me. He shot me in the back, stole my horse, and left me to die in the desert, at least fifty miles from any town. I would have died if not for Sun Eagle. And that's another story."

Juliana thought of the way Uncle Edward and Aunt Katharine had betrayed her, selling her in marriage to a man she detested. She remembered how hurt and disillusioned she had felt, realizing that they cared so little for her happiness that they could dispose of her to the highest bidder, regardless of her feelings. But all that, painful as it had been, could not compare to what Cole must have suffered at the hands of this pair. Betrayed by both his friend and the woman he thought he loved, left to die a horrible death, she wondered that he was not hopelessly embittered to the rest of the world. And to women in particular. What was she like, this Liza? How much did he love her? she wondered, but couldn't bring herself to ask. It seemed that there would always be things about Cole she would not know or fully understand; his past had been too tragic, too crammed with violence and the dark side of human nature. Maybe if she had time, she would eventually learn more, but she sensed it would take years and even then there would probably always be something held back. It didn't matter. All she wanted was to be with him, to erase that tough, iron-hard expression from his face for just a little while, to bring him away from the pain of the past and to heal his hurts in whatever small way she could.

It was time for him to find some happiness, Juliana thought, reaching for his hand. She wasn't sure what to say about Jess Burrows and Liza, she could only say what was in her heart.

"It wasn't wrong to love that woman, Cole. What *she* did was wrong. You mustn't blame yourself or . . . or fear love."

His hand closed over hers, but his grin widened, making his face suddenly boyish. "What makes you such an authority on the subject, angel? I suppose you've been in love a hundred times."

"No. Never. Men used to chase me all over ballroom floors to dance with me, court me at picnics and parties, flirt with me over tea and in the park and in drawing rooms over champagne and candle-lit suppers. But I never cared a fig for any of them," she said matter-offactly. Her tone changed, and her hand crept up shyly to touch his cheek. "Until now," she said in a low voice he had to strain to hear.

Cole stared at her. Her beauty was so intense, it took his breath away. Only that impish dusting of freckles saved her from icy perfection, imbuing her with that delightful, sensuous warmth that was such a vibrant part of her charm. But it was her words that hypnotized him. What did she mean by *until now*?

Juliana swallowed and forced herself to go on, to get past the shyness so uncharacteristic of her. But she'd never spoken these words to any man before, never even imagined the powerful emotions that would summon them forth. But those emotions compelled her now to speak to Cole of what was in her heart.

"I love you, Cole," she said simply. "And I promise you from the bottom of my heart that I will never hurt you."

He dropped her hand and stood up. "There's something you need to understand. I'm not like any of those men who chased you around ballrooms."

"I know that . . ."

"I'm like that stallion we saw by the stream. Wild, Juliana, needing to be free. I can't romance you with candle-lit suppers or waltz with you around fancy ballrooms—and I can't make any promises. None at all. Do you understand that?"

Because I don't want to hurt you either. But he kept that part to himself.

"I understand, Cole," she said, rising alongside him, gazing up at him with naked hope in those vivid green eyes. "But I'm not talking about promises. I'm talking about love."

Love. It scared him more than Apaches, prairie fires, cornered outlaws, and a rattler's bite all rolled together. He'd rather face a Texas norther or a mountain flood than the expectation in Juliana Montgomery's all too vulnerable eyes. Nothing he had loved had ever survived. How could he let himself love this beautiful, kindhearted girl?

"I've got to ride over to the ranch house at Fire Mesa today to see Joseph Wells," he said, as if she hadn't spoken. "Time we headed back."

He moved away from her before he could wrap her in his arms. He didn't look back. What she was thinking, he didn't know, he only knew that he had to stop this madness growing between them before he destroyed her.

She followed him to the horses, silent, hurt. Well, better she feel a little hurt inside than end up dead like everyone else he cared for. Cole held the bridle for her and helped her mount, then without a word sprang onto Arrow.

They headed back to the cabin with only the drone of insects and the rustle of the breeze breaking the silence between them.

"I'll be back before sunset. Stay inside the cabin."

Juliana rubbed her palms on her trousers, squinting in the brilliant afternoon light. "But didn't you say there was a stream down there in the valley? I won't go a step farther."

"You'll go nowhere near that stream—or anywhere else. Stay inside the cabin!"

"You're not my captor anymore—I'm a free woman and I'll do as I please!"

All the intimacy between them had vanished, as well as all the tender feelings. Anger blazed in her eyes as she faced him in the cabin doorway, sunshine pouring through to light her face with gold. After what had happened this morning, she was damned if she'd let him tell her what to do. He wasn't the only one who needed to be free. He might have made love to her last night—all night

—but that didn't give him the right to keep her locked in this cabin all day—she was no servant, no saloon whore, no prisoner. She had given of herself willingly, given him everything she had to offer with all the love and passion in her heart, and offered it again to him this morning—only to be thrust aside like a stranger who has put oneself in the way. If Cole Rawdon thought he could dismiss her whenever he chose, yet rule her life whenever it suited him, he had better think twice.

"Maybe you've forgotten," Cole bit out, grabbing her by the arms so forcefully, she gasped. "Knife Jackson and his outfit will be combing the mountains for you. Line McCray will have them searching every inch of land between here and New Mexico. Not to mention the fact that renegade Apache are on the loose. And *you* won't fire a gun."

Her chin lifted, giving her delicate face a proud tilt. "I would if I had to."

"You probably couldn't hit a log cabin if you put the muzzle up against the logs."

"Then take me with you."

Cole released her with a groan, knowing he would shake her until her teeth rattled if he didn't step back that instant. "I already told you. I've got business that doesn't include you. Stay inside. Promise you will and maybe I'll bring you back a surprise."

"I can't make any promises today either!" she shot back, and congratulated herself when his eyes narrowed.

"This kind of promise you can and will make to me. Or do I have to hog-tie you and keep you inside that way?"

He'd do it, too, she thought, fury making her clench her fingers into fists. He talked to her as if she were a child! Tipping her head to one side, Juliana regarded him coldly. "What kind of surprise?" she asked with all the dignity she could muster.

But he wouldn't tell her.

"Promise, angel."

"Oh, very well." Sliding her hands behind her back, she crossed her fingers and promised.

"Kiss me good-bye?" she asked sweetly, her anger with him fading as she recognized the grim concern on his face. His eyes looked shadowed and dark in the bright glory of the summer's day. His anxiety on her behalf touched her then, filling her with shame at her dishonesty, and with a rich sense of wonder. Did he care about her? Truly? Did he merely want to protect her as he might any woman who had fallen into his bed, and might again—or was it something more, something like what she felt whenever he was within ten feet of her.

He didn't appear to be afflicted with madness, which she was certain was her own fate. He had acted downright cold and sane and rational this morning, hadn't he?

But last night . . .

When he touched her again, his grip was gentle. The kiss was not.

"Behave yourself—if you can," he ordered. "Don't forget where you are. This isn't St. Louis."

Wise words, but she scarcely heard them. Her senses were swimming from the kiss, from the warm, intoxicating taste of his mouth on hers, from the way his hands moved up and down her back when he held her. It was not the embrace of a cold and uninterested man.

"Mmm-hmmm." Unaware of the effect her dreamy eyes were having on his insides, she smiled, feeling hopelessly foolish but happy in a deliriously silly way. Maybe Cole Rawdon was not as much a free man as he thought. Maybe she should think some more about his reaction to her pledge this morning.

"Hurry back," she urged, longing in her upturned, eager face.

"I reckon I will."

It was all Cole could do to mount Arrow and leave her, but he had to see Joseph Wells and it couldn't wait.

The moment he was out of sight, Juliana closed the cabin door and strolled off, searching for a cool stream, a long bath, and the tattered shreds of her emotions.

He loves me. He loves me not. He loves me. He . . .
The delicate petals of the daisy lay like a spattering of white jewels in Juliana's lap as she concentrated intently on her task.

He loves me not.
She frowned, holding the naked flower between her fingers. No more petals. The answer was there for her to see. He loves me not.

She brushed the petals from her lap and stood up, biting her lip. The afternoon sun had swept far into the western sky. The air, laced with pine, was becoming cooler. Where had the day gone?

She had enjoyed the solitude and freedom. Here, by the mossy edge of this lovely, crystal-blue stream, with junipers overhead to shade her from the sun, she had bathed naked and frolicked in the cool waters. She had sprawled on the grass, reveling in the silken caress of the meadow flowers on her bare skin, daydreaming about Cole and all that had passed between them last night. Happiness washed over her. Remembering the way he had kissed her and touched her and united his body with hers made her quiver with a warm delight that had nothing to do with the golden sunshine splashing down all around her. She was certain that beneath that tough exterior, and all his protestations, despite the horrors of his violent past, Cole Rawdon was capable of intense tenderness—yes, of love—but the question plaguing her was whether or not he felt love for her. It was too soon; they hadn't known each other very long, and most of that time they'd been enemies trying to outwit each other. Yet her own feelings were so powerful, rocking her whenever he was anywhere near, that she couldn't help wondering if he didn't feel the same way, if the lightning current that kept jolting her could possibly run in only one direction. From the way he had held her and made love to her last night she was tempted to believe that it couldn't, that he matched her feelings with equally strong ones of his own, that his passion was as reckless and heartfelt and unstoppable as that which rushed over her whenever he touched her or smiled at her or even looked at her with those unforgettable fire-blue eyes.

But . . . He loves me not.

How stupid. It was only a silly flower, a foolish game. It didn't mean anything. Yet she was dismayed. Uncertainty spoiled the exquisite peace and beauty of the day.

Buttoning her shirt, and tucking it into the oversize trousers with their makeshift rope belt, Juliana was suddenly in a hurry to get back to the cabin. Cole had said he'd be back by sunset. He'd be furious if he returned and found that she'd disobeyed him, but really, she had needed the relaxation of the bath, needed the lush beauty of Fire Mesa to enfold and soothe her and help her sort out what had happened this morning, and it had done just that. Twisting her hair into a knot in back of her head, she secured it with a tortoiseshell clip that had been in her preciously guarded money pouch with some other small pieces of jewelry. Cole had handed it to her this morning, reminding her that he had removed it from around her waist while she slept after reaching the cabin, and the glint in his eyes had made her blush down to her toes, for she remembered that last night when they made love had not been the first time he had seen her naked.

Was that part of the reason why he had wanted to make love to her—because he had seen her when he'd undressed her that other time, and desire, maybe even curiosity, had caused him to set his mind to having her?

Maybe that was all he had wanted, maybe it would never happen again, maybe he wouldn't even come back for her . . .

But here she managed to halt the fearful direction of her thoughts, racing like a runaway locomotive into a tunnel of gloom.

No, Cole would never leave her when she was in danger. He had too much sense of honor for that. As for the reasons why he had made love to her, she would have to wait and discover those in time, along with the secrets he kept locked in his heart.

Time. It was growing later with each moment that she dallied here, and Juliana, stooping to gather a fistful of daisies for a centerpiece on the cabin table tonight, realized she'd have to race back and start that damned stove again.

But as she stepped past a juniper tree and headed toward the little dell that separated this part of the valley from the cabin, she heard a sound in the brush. She froze.

Was it an animal, a deer, perhaps? Or something— someone—else?

Glancing around uneasily, she could see nothing but the lilac-gray sweep of sagebrush hills, the staggering red rock escarpment rising to a sheer cliff beside her, and the trickling stream, its clear dancing water aglisten in the sunlight, behind her.

All was quiet. Maybe too quiet. She put a hand to the rock to steady herself. She had the eerie, skin-prickling sensation that she was not alone. Her heart in her throat, she moved forward again.

The Apache dropped down from the sheer cliff above her with incredible grace, his moccasined feet making only a soft scrabble in the grass.

Juliana's scream echoed through the tall rocks. She turned and tried to run, but he grabbed her, holding her in muscle-corded brown arms. Fighting him, scratching,

biting, she felt herself lifted in arms far too strong to
resist, carried to a paint horse, tossed up into a saddle.
Wild panic flooded over her, closing her throat. He
sprang up behind her before she could move, and they
were off, galloping like the wind itself across the stream
where she had bathed, crossing the summer-soft valley
floor and then climbing a rocky embankment, which led
to an overgrown trail that twisted and turned and led
them impossibly far from the cabin.

A sob broke from Juliana's throat. Stark terror had
taken possession of her. So far, the Apache had made no
sound, had not spoken one word to her, not even a grunt.
All the stories she had ever heard of Indian atrocities
flashed through her brain at once, and she wondered with
a sickening lurch of her stomach if he was bringing her to
a camp where there were other braves, if they would all
watch while he killed her or . . . or whatever . . . if
they would each take their turn torturing her.

On and on they rode, while the fading sun burned like
a bronze disc above them, and mesquite and wildflowers
whipped by. How far they had gone, even in what direction, was impossible to tell. Juliana, in her terror, could
think of nothing but that she would never, ever see Cole
again, that if he ever found her after this Apache was
finished with her, he would doubtless find only a scatter-
ing of broken bones and bloodied flesh.

She wondered in agonized sorrow if he would even
mourn her death or if he would simply ride on and return
to his own violent and personal business without more
than a fleeting regret.

The cabin appeared out of nowhere, a rundown pine
structure larger than Cole's, but in far worse condition
from the outside, stuck in a slab of mountain that rose,
sheer and stark, to the sky. There was a clearing of about
fifty feet around it, with a spring behind the cabin, and a
row of scattered piñons alongside. But everywhere about

was desolation. Wild, beautiful, lonely desolation. For miles she could see nothing but rocks, brush, open mountain, and cacti.

When the Indian pulled her down from the horse, she tried to run, but he seized her about the waist, his black eyes slitted and intense.

Fear closed around her heart tight as a vise. Every muscle was tense; her throat seemed to be stuffed with flannel. Yet she screamed. Out of pure terror, she screamed. Loud and long, the scream echoing among the rocks, bouncing off the mountain walls, trailing through the crevices where wildflowers poked their bright heads.

All hell broke loose.

The cabin door was flung wide and a group of men rushed out.

"Gray Feather, what the hell . . ."

"Lord, Wade, it's *her* . . ."

The Apache released her, grinning. But Juliana was no longer looking at him—she was staring dazedly at the two men nearest her. They had stopped ten feet away, while the others hung back, and they were staring at her as if searching for something . . . something lost or forgotten or perhaps something that never existed at all.

Wade. Tommy. Could it be?

Her breath quick and shallow, Juliana stared from one to the other. The taller man appeared to be in his early twenties and had wide shoulders and light brown hair beneath a hat of pearl gray. His eyes were a keen, piercing shade of green, riveting in a handsome, square-jawed face that was just now frozen in shock. The second of the two had hair of the richest gold, worn straight to his shirt collar. Rangy and muscular, he cut a dashing figure in a fine blue linen shirt and dark trousers, with a silken neckerchief knotted about his throat. But it was his eyes, dancing, bold blue eyes set within a merry, good-looking face that captured Juliana's attention. They were fixed on

her with an expression of pure happiness, sparkling blue
light seeming to fly from them as their owner started
forward at a run.

"Aw, shucks, Juliana—it's us. Wade and Tommy.
Don't you recognize us, peanut?"

"Hold on, Tommy." Wade seized his brother's arm before he could reach the stunned girl. With a stern look,
he said something quietly to the other man, and then
took a halting step forward.

"Juliana. I'm sure this is a shock for you. Gray Feather
must've scared you pretty badly bringing you here like
this—but hell, we've been searching all over for you and
all I can say is: Thank God he found you." Wade hesitated, then went on, the silence in the clearing loud as
thunder.

"We've been . . . we want . . . oh, hell, there's so
much to say, but it doesn't matter. All that matters is
that you're safe. You are safe, you know. We'll see to that.
We're your brothers, honey, and whatever you may have
heard about us, well, it may or may not be true, but we've
come clear across Arizona to find you and . . . you may
not want anything to do with us after all the stories, you
may not have forgiven us for not writing to you in so
long, but . . . We'll take this real slow and let you get
used to us again and try to explain . . ."

With a sob of overwhelming joy breaking from her
throat, Juliana rushed headlong into his arms.

Wade hugged her tight, still dazed by the joy and
unquestioning acceptance in her face.

"Whoopee!" Tommy pounced on her then like a wild
young cougar. He grabbed her and whirled her in the air
until she was dizzy, then wrapped her in a giant hug. "I
told Wade you wouldn't be some prissy, snooty little
thing. Didn't I tell you, Wade? But, peanut, you sure did
grow into a beauty! And Keedy—no wonder he's been

like a lovesick calf all this while—where the hell *is* Keedy?"

From the doorway of the cabin came the tall, red-headed figure of the cowboy she'd met at Twin Oaks.

"Howdy, Miss Juliana. Sure is good to see you again!" he said, sweeping his hat off his head and grinning from ear to ear.

"Gil!" Her mind whirling in confusion, Juliana hugged him as if she couldn't believe he was real. "Oh, Gil . . . I don't understand. How did you get mixed up with Wade and Tommy? How did you find me? How . . . Well, I don't care, really! What matters is that we're all here—I can't believe it."

"Come inside, Juliana." Wade, his handsome face somber but his eyes lit with a warm glow as he stared down at her, took her arm. "Skunk has supper just about ready and we can explain everything while we get some grub. I'm sure you'll have a lot of questions—and so do we. Such as where Gray Feather found you, and how you got those bruises you're wearing." Ever so gently, he touched the faded marks upon her face. "It looks like you've had a bad time of it. But never mind. You'll rest first and we'll talk later. The most important thing is, no one is ever going to hurt you again, Juliana. Not while Tommy and I are alive."

"Oh, Wade," Juliana gasped, still scarcely able to believe that this tall, keen-eyed handsome young man was her eldest brother.

Just saying his name, feeling the touch of his hand on her arm, made Juliana's eyes swim with tears. "It's really you." She was babbling like an idiot, but she didn't care. She was too happy. "And Tommy." She smiled a brilliant, tremulous smile, drinking in the sight of each of them in turn and rubbing her wet eyes with the back of her hands. "It's a miracle. There were times when I thought I'd never see you again."

Wade enfolded her in a strong embrace. He smelled good, of leather and spice, and he felt so solid, so real, that Juliana felt all her cares fading away as he held her. She leaned against his chest and closed her eyes, filled with an exhausting relief.

"Skunk!" Tommy yelled suddenly, shattering her tearful reverie. Juliana opened her eyes and couldn't help laughing as he grabbed ahold of the short, wiry little man closest to the cabin and shook him off his feet. "Better whip out some of that elderberry wine 'cause we're going to celebrate something fierce tonight. My little sister's here, and damned if she isn't the prettiest, finest girl you ever did see! Dancing! That's what we'll do! Juliana, will you dance with me? Skunk has a fiddle, and Keedy can call the steps and we'll just tear this little old cabin to pieces!"

Grabbing her hand, he raced with her into the cabin and lifting her, spun her about again, round and round until Juliana shrieked, caught between laughter and tears, and Wade ordered him to stop. But Juliana clung to him after he set her down, gazing with soft, loving eyes into his mischievous face.

"Tommy," she said, tenderly stroking her fingers through his gold hair, the same shade as hers, soft and thick as velvet, "you haven't changed." Her voice broke. "Oh, thank God, you haven't changed."

· 20 ·

There were five members of the Montgomery gang—not counting Gil Keedy—and Juliana met them all that evening over Skunk Moses's roast venison feast. And what a feast it was, with potato soup, corn bread biscuits dripping with butter, beans sweetened with molasses, elderberry wine, sugared coffee, and peppermint candy for dessert. Her brother Tommy, she learned, had a sweet tooth and purchased stick candy by the pound whenever he passed through a town. Before she entered the cabin on Stick Mountain—for that is what the place was called—she knew virtually nothing about the young men who were her brothers. But by the time that rollicking, festive meal was over, she knew a great deal indeed.

Wade was perhaps the most astonishing to her. When last she had seen him, a self-sufficient and intelligent boy of fifteen, she might have guessed that he would grow into a formidable man, but she could not have guessed that he would be so quick-witted, keen-minded, organized and yet so daring that he could mastermind the exploits and escapes of a gang of bandits that had never once in all these years been apprehended. Wade, with his deep-set eyes and square jaw, listened more than he talked, she observed as she relished each mouthful of Skunk's delicious cooking, and when he did speak, his words were crisp, definite, and well thought out. Tommy, on the other hand, every bit as bold and brash as those long-lashed blue eyes of his would suggest, blurted out whatever was on his mind, giving no heed to the consequences. He was as blunt and direct as his brother was contemplative, but his heart, Juliana saw at once, was open and giving, as big as the canyons themselves, and there was never a hint of malice in any word he uttered. Tommy, who had forever worn the same blue and yellow plaid shirt as a boy, who had waded through mud puddles and piles of horse manure without a second thought, was now a rake, immaculate in his cleanliness and personal appearance, his hair always brushed and slick, his clothing as spotless and as dashing as he could find. Skunk told her all this while he brewed more coffee, and though Tommy swatted the top of his head and called him a dog-faced liar, Juliana could see for herself that it was true. In his expensive pale blue linen shirt and silken neckerchief, with his boots polished so brightly, he could see his own glossy reflection in them, her golden-haired twenty-two-year-old brother was as impeccable as he was handsome. A ladies' man, Skunk next whispered in her ear, with his lopsided grin spreading from one side of his homely face to the other. Women always swarmed over Tommy, he added, like hornets around a bowl of sugar—and Tommy, he fell in love with them all, one right after the other, sometimes two or three at a time—and then, lordy, the pickles he found himself in.

Juliana listened and learned much from all that went on at that rowdy table while the sun drifted lower in the sky outside the shuttered window and plumes of pink and lavender swept delicate arcs across the horizon.

There was so much to discover, to savor. And there were gifts—after the meal, Tommy and Wade showered her with an assortment of plumed hats, pearl earbobs, a fine silver hairbrush, a jeweled reticule, and gowns . . . a fetching, daffodil-yellow organdy with narrow sleeves and waist, and a low cut, seafoam-green silk with a sash adorned by pearls set within tiny ivory rosettes, and a full, graceful skirt falling in diaphanous folds over a cream satin underskirt. Wherever did they find such creations? Overcome, she had merely gazed in spellbound wonder at all these treasures. She'd been reduced to wearing the same crumpled muslin day after day, and then this dreadful oversize shirt and trousers, only to find herself now the recipient of lovely and feminine items designed to gladden any woman's heart. The most touching part of all was the discovery that all this time she'd been thinking about her brothers, struggling to find them, Wade and Tommy had been thinking about her too. They'd been gathering up these gifts, packing them in along with all their other gear, and dragging them about the West just so they could shower her with presents when they finally found each other again. Tommy, seeing the glisten of tears in her eyes as she stroked the silken skirt of the gown and glanced about at all the other lovely things, quickly told her that all of these were just silly little trinkets, which they had purchased since Gil Keedy had told them of her plight and they'd first started searching for her.

"There's a whole lot of birthdays we missed while you were growing up from a little freckle-faced peanut into the loveliest girl ever to take the West by storm. We're meaning to make up to you for all those years we lost."

She cried, throwing her arms around him and then hugging Wade, clinging to them both with a fierce need and longing for her family that was finally being answered after years of denial.

"I have nothing for you," Juliana gulped at last, wiping her tears on the big neckerchief Wade handed her. His eyes were moist, too, Juliana noted, though she refrained from embarrassing him by mentioning it.

"You've brought sunshine back to us. You've made our hearts whole again. I reckon that's enough." Wade looked a little startled by his own sentimental speech, and ruffled her hair to cover his own discomfiture. "Tell you what, peanut. Go in that back room and put on one of these fancy new dresses. You'll find some other things in there, too—thanks to Josie."

"Josie?"

Her brothers exchanged glances. Gil Keedy started to say something, then stopped. To Juliana's surprise, Tommy shot him a glowering look.

"We'll tell you all about Josie later," Wade said after an awkward moment when Gil and Tommy glared at each other. "First, run along and fix up your hair and try on those fancy earbobs. We haven't had much feminine company in a while and it'll do us good to see you all gussied up and gorgeous."

So she did what he asked, slipping into the seafoam gown, suitable for a ball or the opera, ridiculously out of place in this Stick Mountain cabin—yet, she wanted to celebrate her happiness by looking her best, and to please her brothers by showing off their gifts. The mysterious Josie, whom she wanted very badly to learn more about, had left a parcel on the bureau for her containing undergarments, shoes and a chemise, as well as hairpins and a comb. The dressmaker who had sewn the gowns for "a young lady of slender and perfect proportions," as Gil Keedy had described her (he being the only one to have seen Juliana in recent years) had done an excellent job— the gown fit remarkably well, and she fastened the pearl buttons across her bodice with gay pleasure. There was no looking glass in the small bedroom with its straw cot and cedar bureau, but glancing down at herself, she felt delight at the sight of the cascading skirt, the snug bodice, the lovely sash that accentuated her tiny waist. Next came the fine pearl earbobs, and then she brushed and brushed her hair until it glimmered like fire.

With her thick curls arranged in a pretty cascade about her face, she at last emerged from the back room to smile dazzlingly at the roomful of men.

Tommy was the first to speak, in a subdued, admiring voice matched by the appreciative shine in his eyes. "Well, you sure do look like mama. Little sister, I never thought to see another woman as pretty as her—but you do match her and maybe then some—no disrespect intended."

"Bless mama's soul, but I never saw her look so radiant," Wade said. He came forward and took Juliana's small hands in his strong grip. "She had a hard life and it showed. Her eyes always had a shadow over them, even when she was happy, which she was whenever Pa was near. But you . . . Juliana . . . you'll steal the breath away from every man who looks at you."

Gray Feather nodded, his dark eyes shining. Skunk snatched his hat off his head. "Yep, Miss Juliana, that's no exaggeration. You surely are a sight to behold."

Gil Keedy stepped forward, his freckles standing out in bright relief against his flushed face. "I never reckoned a dress could look so pretty on a woman. I'm mighty glad John Breen didn't get his chance to slip that ring on your finger, Juliana."

"If you think you're going to start up your flirting with my sister, Keedy, you're dead wrong," Tommy burst out, striding forward with fists clenched. "It's bad enough the way you keep dangling after Josie, but—"

"I'll thank you to steer clear of my business, Montgomery," Gil fired back, "unless you want to step outside and eat some dust . . ."

"Try and make me!" Tommy growled, his blue eyes dangerously narrowed.

"Enough," Wade ordered, shooting his brother an irritated look, then shaking his head at the riled Texan. "Simmer down, Tommy. And you, too, Keedy. I've had enough of you two squawking like a couple of roosters over Josie Larson, and I'm not going to let you spoil Juliana's first night with us."

"I think we ought to have a toast," Juliana interrupted hastily, alarmed by the angry rivalry she'd just witnessed between Tommy and Gil. She was more curious than ever to learn about this Josie Larson, but at the moment she felt it best to change the subject quickly. "To the Montgomery gang!" she exclaimed gaily. "To Gray Feather for bringing me here! To birthday presents—especially late ones! Tommy"—and she bestowed on her still glowering brother a brilliant smile—"you may pour. Please?"

Forming a circle, they all toasted, Wade and Tommy touching their tin cups to hers.

Juliana stared around the motley little group and wondered that she felt perfectly at home. In addition to Wade and Tommy, there were Skunk, Gray Feather, and Yancy, each man so different from the others, yet she felt as though she'd known them all her life. Criminals? These men were all wanted outlaws, but from what she had seen, there was nothing savage or vicious or dangerous about any of them. Looking at Skunk as he downed his second cup of wine, she couldn't imagine him hurting anyone. He was an odd, funny creature with a great talent for cooking—not at all the kind of man she could imagine holding up banks and stagecoaches. Skunk. So named not for any undesirable odor, as she at first anticipated, but because of his unusual hair coloring, he was a swarthy, good-natured little man. His thin black hair tended to stand straight up on his head, and in one patch had turned a pure shade of white. Gray Feather, the

Apache who had brought her here, was a mute—when he first seized her, he could not have told her he was bringing her to her brothers, for his tongue had been cut out as a boy when he had been captured by an enemy tribe.

Gray Feather, whose silken dark hair, sharply chiseled face, and shining black eyes had so frightened her before, became for Juliana an object of intense sympathy after this story was told. But Tommy threw back his head and gave a shout of laughter when he saw the compassion on his sister's delicate face. "Don't feel sorry for him, peanut, he talks with his knife far better than with any old tongue. He's quick as a hawk, Gray Feather is—he can throw that knife of his faster and straighter than a man can shoot a gun. And when it comes to tracking, or covering up tracks, no one is better than Gray Feather. He's no poor babe to be pitied, now, are you, my friend?" He said something in Apache that brought a quick smile to the Indian's dark face.

The Apache's eyes gleamed at her. There was a not unkind amusement in his face as he watched the fair-haired sister of his companions blush prettily.

"Tommy, don't tease Juliana," Wade said sharply. "She's been gently raised and it's only natural she'd be shocked by what happened to Gray Feather."

Tommy sank down on one knee beside her. "Juliana, you don't mind my teasing, do you?"

His tone was light, but she could see that in the depths of his eyes he was searching to see if he had really offended her.

She reached out and ruffled his hair, her heart tightening with a rush of love. "Not in the least—but I hope you won't mind if I tease *you* about a certain lady—Josie, isn't it?" She raised her slim brows at the hot color that rushed into his cheeks.

"Who told you about her?" Tommy jumped up, all six lanky feet of him, and glared about the room, his big fists clenched. "Skunk, it was you." He yanked the cook out of his chair. "I reckon I'll roast you over that soup pot, damned if I won't . . ."

" 'Twas me, boy." Yancy, the fifth and most unobtrusive member of the gang spoke up from the bench at the end of the long pine table. He was a barrel-chested, round-jawed Irishman, older than the others, with pale ghostlike wisps of hair and sad eyes the faded color of an old blue shirt.

"That lassie needs a friend, and I was thinking that your sister here might be a good one for her. If that troubles you, lad, we can always step outdoors and settle the matter, now can't we?"

But there was a smile in his eyes as he said these words and Tommy quickly grinned and shook his head. "You know I'm no match for you, Sergeant, but why'd you have to blabber about *her*? Josie isn't like the others, and you know it."

"That's what he says each and every time," Skunk whispered in Juliana's ear.

"And as for needing a friend, I'm her friend and I'll take care of her. She doesn't need *anyone else.*"

This last remark seemed pointed not at Yancy or even Juliana, listening in keen silence, but at Gil Keedy, who rose from his place on the pine bench and bestowed on Tommy another one of those glowering, all-too-ready-to-fight looks.

"Yancy's right," Gil said, evenly enough. "I reckon Josie does need a ladyfriend to talk to her. If you weren't such a peacock-headed fool, prancing around feeding her a lot of sweet talk, you'd see that she needs another woman to guide her and help her. Someone fine and sensible like Juliana. What she doesn't need is you hanging around bothering her all day long. . . ."

"You're the one always hanging around her like some

damned lovestruck calf, with that pitiful expression on your face . . ."

Both men sprang toward each other, fists swinging, and Juliana cried out in alarm, but Wade jumped between them and shoved Tommy back. Yancy grabbed ahold of Gil's shirt and pulled him into a far corner, while Skunk and Gray Feather watched in wry amusement. Juliana was horrified.

"I won't have violence under this roof!" she stormed. "Look at the two of you—acting like a couple of tomcats, not grown men! Tommy Montgomery, I'm ashamed of you! And Gil, why, you know better than to behave like this! Whatever happened to those gracious Texas manners?"

Gil, beet red, mumbled profuse apologies, and after being released by Yancy, came forward to press Juliana's hand. Tommy had the grace to hang his head.

Wade said, "I think it's time we all sat down and talked. Juliana must have a lot of questions, and so do we. Let's get 'em answered. And then tomorrow we can take Juliana to meet Josie and the baby."

Juliana felt herself being drawn into something that grew more mystifying by the second, but before she could interrupt with a question, Wade had taken charge of the group. She found herself seated on the battered hardback sofa before the stove, with Wade beside her and the other men pulling up chairs and benches and crates, all except for Tommy, who sprawled comfortably on the floor with his head propped on his chin. There was still an angry, defiant glint in his beautiful eyes, but he waited patiently enough while Wade launched into a concise explanation of the brothers' past, from the time they'd left Independence up until the present. Juliana listened in wonder and amazement, forgetting everything else, hearing only the smooth, pleasant tones of Wade's deep voice, seeing only the picture his well-chosen words conjured up. And what a picture it was.

She saw not two savage, violent criminals, as Aunt Katharine and Uncle Edward would have had her think of them, but two young men searching for adventure, whose high principles and basic decency had ensnared them in a way of life as dangerous and exciting as it was illegal. Bandits, yes, Wade and Tommy were indeed outlaws, but according to her brother, they stole only from those who cheated and connived to get their wealth, and never touched a penny belonging to an honest man.

It was an incredible tale—a tale of adventure, daring, and sheer steel-edged nerve. Wade and Tommy had reached Texas all those years ago, but along the way to their dream of a horse ranch they had found a town called Skye. A town where a greedy man rustled cattle without anyone being able to catch him at it, a town where that same man grew rich and bought up business after business, cheating the townspeople, raising prices, milking the citizens dry. Where a female saloonkeeper had begged their help because the greedy man, one Amos Long, was trying to force her out of business, and if she couldn't come up with a hefty sum of money to pay the mortgage on her saloon—a mortgage he held—he would close her down and take over the place himself.

It was Wade who had come up with their first plan. Tommy had been only too willing, for he'd been head over heels in love with the voluptuous saloonkeeper from the first moment he laid eyes on her. The brothers had donned masks and held up a stagecoach carrying Amos Long's payroll gold. They'd split the loot fifty-fifty with the saloonkeeper, enabling her to buy off her mortgage and thrive, despite Amos Long. For their trouble, they'd gotten five sizable sacks of gold all to themselves, and the excitement of surviving the chase of their lives. Long had organized a posse to track them down—they'd had to flee

Skye, flee Texas, but eventually they moved on down through Arizona and New Mexico, and "situations," as Tommy called them, always seemed to find them.

It didn't really surprise Juliana, once she started to think about it. The West was filled with lawless, corrupt men who would run over everyone and everything in their paths to get what they wanted. John Breen was such a man, and so—from what she had heard—was Line Mc-Cray. Wade and Tommy had moved from town to town, and when they found one where greed and ruthlessness had made one man rich at the expense of others, they took their time finding out enough information about him and the operation of his business to make their holdup successful. Such as when the payment was coming through, how many guards there would be, where the likely trouble was expected. Then they would do the unexpected—attack at a surprise point, when the horses were most tired, when the guards were least alert. Patience and the passage of time, Wade told her with a grim smile, revealed all things. One of the things they learned while spending time in the various towns, was who had suffered most at the greedy man's expense, who was most in need of aid, and who would help them by supplying information. These people all received a share of the haul from whatever job was pulled, while the brothers kept the rest for the risk and effort involved. Along the way, and through the intervening years, they had allied themselves with Skunk, Gray Feather, and Yancy, all of whom possessed unique abilities. Gray Feather knew the land as well as he knew every line and knuckle of his own hand. He was an expert guide to the most secluded hideouts—and famous for covering every vestige of their tracks in such a way that even the most skilled trackers couldn't detect them. Skunk, in addition to being an excellent cook, was a skilled rider and marksman, with aim almost as good as Tommy, who was considered the best shot in the gang, and was able to ride hard and fast for days on end over the most savage country without tiring. Yancy, a former sergeant with the Union army, was a munitions expert, with dynamite his specialty, a skill that had come in handy many times for the Montgomery gang. Wade's area of expertise was his cool head for planning and a genius for organization, while Tommy brought enthusiasm, unequaled quickness with a gun, and more daring than most ten men put together. One time, cornered in Lost Creek Canyon, surrounded by a posse large enough to kill or capture them all, Tommy had managed to sneak away, shoot a round of rifle fire that startled the daylights out of the posse, and then lured them all in hot pursuit of him, enabling the others to get away. He'd led the posse a wild chase, over ravine, hill, and valley, down into the brakes beneath the Mogollon Rim and up steep escarpments, and finally lost them deep within the forests of ponderosa pine, while Wade led the others to the hideout. Tommy joined them several days later, exhilarated, triumphant, and unscathed. It was only one adventure of many, Wade told her, where his younger brother had saved the day.

"But you still look like something's gnawing at you, little sister." Gently, Wade tugged one gold curl. "What's wrong?"

Juliana gazed up into her eldest brother's face. She bit her lip. "I understand how it all got started, Wade. I also understand why you felt you couldn't drag me into all of it or even keep much in contact with me. I don't like it, but I understand. But whatever your reasons, it's still stealing, Wade. No matter how you explain it, it doesn't change that fact. It's still wrong."

Wade stared at her a long time. The other members of the gang did not meet her eyes. Then Tommy sat up, drawing his long legs before him, and spoke, his voice low.

"We know that, peanut. Sort of. I guess you could say that deep inside we know it's wrong, but . . . we help people . . . and ourselves. The only ones who get hurt are the men growing rich from rustling, or land schemes or cheating—stealing in other ways, just not outright holdups."

"And lots of 'em do worse things than we ever do," Yancy added in a somber tone.

"But we've been planning on quitting—all of us," Tommy assured her earnestly. "It's time. Matter of fact, we were having a look-see around by Cooper Creek to find us a neat little spread where we could start raising horses—or maybe cattle—when Keedy found us and told us you were in trouble."

"Which brings us up to the present," Wade finished for him, placing a hand over Juliana's as it rested on the faded cushion of the old sofa. "A friend—actually a fellow we pay handsomely to let us know when someone's asking questions about us—told us that some hombre named Gil Keedy was hot on our trail. He wasn't a known bounty hunter, and he didn't look like any Pinkerton detective we ever saw—so we arranged a little meeting with him. And," he finished, flashing Gil his calm, steady smile, "that's how we first heard about this marriage with John Breen that Aunt Katharine and Uncle Edward were forcing you into."

"Yeah," Tommy broke in, jumping up to squeeze beside Juliana on the sofa, "so we started toward Colorado and we'd only gone halfway across Arizona when we heard that there was a bounty on your head—two thousand dollars." He whistled through his teeth. "That's a whole lot more than anyone ever paid to find *us.* So what'd you do, peanut, rob the First National Bank of Denver?"

"All I took was John Breen's horse—and his pride, I

suppose. I ran away from Denver the night before our wedding."

Wade chuckled appreciatively, Yancy and Skunk and Gil laughed aloud, but Tommy lifted her in the air and whirled her about yet again. "I'm damned if this sister of ours isn't the pluckiest filly I ever did meet—along with Josie," he amended quickly. "But," he told her, setting her down gently on the floor, "it's your turn now. We've been searching high and low for you ever since we heard about the bounty, but we couldn't find any trace. Not until Keedy heard some word about you a few days ago in Plattsville. McCray's men are searching for you—and us—like crazy, but we figured Gray Feather could find you before they did."

Then it was Juliana's turn to relate her own experiences since she had left Twin Oaks. When she reached the part where Cash Hogan and his companions had grabbed her in Cedar Gulch, only to be shot by Cole Rawdon, Tommy interrupted her.

"Rawdon! He's more dangerous than any of 'em. We heard he brought you in to the sheriff in Plattsville. Was that true? How'd you manage to break away?"

And here Juliana froze. The entire room blurred. The plain shuttered windows, the rag rug on the floor, the still-warm stove, the men all leaning forward eagerly waiting for her to continue, all of it swam before her eyes. Even the flies buzzing through the air seemed strange, unreal, moving in slow motion. The sharp, sweet tangy scent of elderberry wine and Yancy's pipe tobacco became forever engraved together in her brain.

Rawdon.

Her gaze flew to the window. Darkness. The sun had set long ago.

What had she done? What in the name of heaven had she been thinking of?

Stupid, idiotic . . . she cursed herself even as she

jumped up from the sofa. How she had managed to forget all about Cole, all about the cabin where he would be returning by sunset, expecting to find her, she didn't know. Her hands turned ice cold. She started to shake. Yes, she had been overjoyed to see Wade and Tommy, and yes, there had been much to tell and learn, but how on earth could she have forgotten about Cole?

He had made her promise she would stay in the cabin. So that she would be safe. But she had broken her promise, and Gray Feather had carried her off, and . . .

And Cole would surely think her dead—or nearly so, for the obvious conclusion he would draw when he returned and found the cabin empty would be that Knife Jackson and his companions had found her.

She had to go back. Dear Lord, she had to go back.

But she didn't even know if he would be there. He could be looking for her; he could run smack into Knife and the others while trying to find her. And they would kill him. Deep down in her heart she knew that if they caught him again, they would kill him. She had the most horrible feeling that he might already be dead.

A faintness came over her. She fought it back, her face white as parchment. She darted from the cabin before any of the men realized what she was doing, running out into the midnight-blue darkness in blind panic.

"Juliana, what the hell has got into you? Where do you think you're going?" Wade pounded after her and grabbed her arm as she peered frantically about in the starlit darkness.

"I need a horse. And a guide. Gray Feather . . ."

"You're not going anywhere. Are you loco?" Tommy tried to catch her as she yanked her arm free of Wade's grip and started to move away from them both.

"Oh, no, you don't! You'll kill yourself here in the dark." He caught up with her and was starting to pull her toward him when a shot rang out, knocking his hat off his head.

"Let her go."

The deadly threat in the voice that rang like cold steel through the night made the hairs on Juliana's neck stand on end. But she recognized that voice, and a sudden rush of exhilaration and relief flooded through her.

"Cole! Cole, I'm all right," she gasped. "Don't shoot!" She hurled herself like a shield in front of her brothers. "It's Wade and Tommy!"

There was a tiny sound of brush rustling somewhere on Stick Mountain, and then a shadow emerged from the deeper shadows of the rocks, a shadow that detached itself from its cover and moved toward them. Faintly lit as the night was by the glow of a thousand burning stars, Juliana recognized Cole's tall, muscular frame, the shape of his hat, the strong, tense line of his jaw as he stopped in front of her.

"Thank God!" she cried on a little sob of happiness, and threw herself into his arms. But the next moment she gasped as he gripped her shoulders hard and held her at arm's length away from him.

"So you're safe, after all."

His voice was odd. Cold. Hard. The way it used to sound when she first met him, when he always thought the worst of her.

"Cole, I'm truly sorry. I forgot all about everything else—we were celebrating—isn't it wonderful? Wade and Tommy found *me*—at least, Gray Feather did, and there was so much to talk about. You must come inside and have some wine and let me introduce you . . ."

Her voice faded away. She was beginning to be able to discern his face in the darkness now and what she saw frightened her. His expression was as deadly and formidable as when he had faced down Cash Hogan, Luke, and Bo. The glitter in his eyes turned her blood to ice, and she felt her knees trembling as his harsh gaze swept over her with no visible sign of emotion, then shifted to study Wade and Tommy, just behind her, fixing each of them in turn with that hardened detachment.

"Take your hands off my sister." Turning, she saw that Wade had his gun drawn. So did Tommy. In the ivory-frosted darkness that shrouded the trees, tipping everything with an eerie faint silver light she realized that Yancy, Gray Feather, Skunk, and Gil were all fanned out in a semicircle, their guns drawn and pointed at Cole.

"Back away from her, Rawdon." She scarcely recognized Tommy's voice. Her handsome, roguish brother sounded every bit as hard and dangerous as Wade, even as Cole Rawdon himself.

"And then throw your guns down nice and easy," Wade added crisply as he stepped forward and with one hand jerked Juliana back, out of Rawdon's grasp.

Cole let her go, his lips curled in a snarl. He never shifted a muscle.

"Wade, Tommy, no!" She shook herself free, turning to them with her arms spread in a gesture of appeal. In the seafoam-green gown, with starlight shimmering on her pale hair, she did look like an angel, or a mermaid swept from the depths of the sea, a delicate figure of unearthly beauty, whose lovely face was marred only by an expression of distress. "Put your guns away! Cole isn't here to harm me! He's been helping me. He saved me from Line McCray's men in Plattsville. In fact he's saved my life more times than I can count. Put your guns away, damn you. Now."

And then she flung herself in front of Cole as a slender, lovely shield against all the men lined up against him. "Do as I say, or I'll leave with him this minute and never come back."

"Juliana, whatever he's told you or done for you—or made you think he's done for you, it's a trick." Wade spoke quickly, never removing his alert gaze from his adversary's face. "Rawdon's a bounty hunter. He's only after the reward—the one on your head and on ours."

"Go inside and let us deal with him." His voice flat and cold, Tommy sounded nothing like himself. "He's lied to you, Juliana—that's plain. We'll sort it out later, but first, for Pete's sake, get in the cabin and leave him to us."

"So that you can all kill each other? I don't think I will."

Staring angrily at her brothers and the men behind them, and then spinning about to see Cole's hard face in the darkness behind her, she felt the bubble of wrath inside her explode. "Men! You're all alike! You think violence is the answer to everything, don't you? Well, the men who killed Mama and Papa and left them lying in their own blood thought that way too. And look where it left us! Maybe none of us would be on this godforsaken mountain right now, Wade, if it hadn't been for that. Maybe we'd all still be back home in Independence, eating Sunday dinner with Mama and Papa. I've been running away from violence ever since. But I've seen enough of it in the past few months to last me a lifetime. I'm sick of it, do you hear me? Sick to death of shootings and beatings and threats."

Her voice broke, and as he listened to her a shock ran down Cole's spine. So that was what had spooked her, made her faint at the sight of a dead man, made her wish to avoid even killing a damned bear. Her parents, like his, had been murdered. It was a grim fact they had in common. Poor kid. He suddenly felt some of the red-hot fury seeping out of him. Something ached between his temples. Pity. Or maybe just tension, raw and ugly. He'd been loco ever since he'd come back to the cabin and found her gone. He'd assumed that Knife had her, and the panic that had roared through him, ripping at his heart and guts, had been worse than anything anyone had ever done to him. Driven by a flailing desperation, he'd searched for her for hours, until down by the stream he'd finally found that damned comb she'd wound into her hair this morning. He'd felt like someone was tearing his insides out then. The tracks had been almost impossible to follow, and he'd lost the trail twice, but he'd hooked onto it at last. To find her here, safe with her brothers, pretty as a seashell in this fancy dress, not even thinking twice about him—or what he had suffered when she disappeared. Cole felt a gut-wrenching pain. No longer from anxiety or fear for her safety. Something else. Something he couldn't define. All he knew was that she didn't need him anymore. She had quickly forgotten him—as soon as she found these brothers of hers. It hurt more than he cared to think about. But he wasn't going to cause a bloodbath over it. Even though it seemed those brothers of hers would like nothing better than to blow his head off.

Juliana, he was about to say. *Settle down. I'll have a few necessary words with your brothers, clear a few things up—and then go on my way.*

But she rushed on, never giving him the chance.

"Throw down your guns, every single one of you," she ordered, her breath coming quickly in the cool night air. "And do it right now. Because if any one of you gets shot or hurt—I'll . . . I'll . . . I'll jump right off this mountain, I swear I will!"

As if to illustrate her words, she took a step into the perilous darkness toward the uncertain ledges beyond, but Cole's strong arms reached out and seized her around the waist. "I already pulled you back from one precipice, angel. Don't tempt fate by dangling yourself over another."

She was stunned to hear that the harsh edge was gone

from his voice; it was lighter, amused almost, and his arms around her waist were tight and reassuring.

"Wildcat," he whispered in her ear, and then said to Wade, "maybe we should call a truce until we can straighten a few things out. It strikes me that we might be on the same side on this one."

"I don't trust him, Wade," Tommy blurted out.

"Tommy!" Juliana cried in exasperation, but her eldest brother interrupted.

"Our little sister is no fool, Tommy. We'll give Rawdon a chance." He slipped his gun back into its holster. "Everybody inside. We're going to talk."

Cole held on to her as the others edged cautiously toward the cabin. "Tell me one thing. They found the cabin?" He had thought it safe, virtually undetectable to anyone not raised on Fire Mesa. Her answer confirmed what he had suspected.

"N-no. I went down to the stream for a bath."

Slate-blue eyes pierced her with a look that chilled her heart. "I see."

"Cole . . ."

"So much for promises."

He released her, stepped past her as though she were nothing but a tree or a rock, and went inside the Montgomery gang's cabin.

·21·

Two hours later Wade Montgomery glanced somberly at the blue-eyed bounty hunter leaning against the pine table and said, "Rawdon, it appears that my brother and I owe you one big apology."

He thought: *The poor bastard hasn't taken his eyes off Juliana for more than an instant. He's in love with her.* Strange that he should see that right off, Wade thought. But then he was unusually perceptive about people, tending to see what went on beneath the facade they put up every day, sensing their secrets, their lies, piercing right through the outward layer of civility to the real core beneath. When it came to Rawdon, though, he was stunned by what he saw. It had never occurred to him, during all the years he'd heard of the infamous Cole Rawdon, that when he finally met the most dreaded bounty hunter in the southwest territories, he'd see not a cold, relentless hunter (although from outward appearances, Rawdon was indeed that) but a strong man wrestling in the throes of love. Never having been in love, Wade thought such a fate nearly as fatal as dying, but he quickly reminded himself it was Juliana whom Rawdon loved, and that made him one lucky hombre—if she returned his feelings. Wade reckoned, from the way she'd rushed to his defense earlier, and in the way her eyes lit up whenever he said something—hell, whenever the fellow drew a breath—that she did. If Juliana wanted him, he decided with typical Montgomery determination, she would have him, even if Rawdon had to be tied up and lassoed like a bawling calf till she got him to the altar. Somehow or other, Wade didn't think it would come to that. With Juliana looking so damned beautiful she might have stepped right out of heaven's gate, he couldn't imagine Rawdon resisting her for long—so long as Tommy kept his mouth shut and stayed out of it.

Juliana, when she heard her brother's words, let out a sigh of relief.

Peace. Maybe there would be peace between Cole, Wade, and Tommy yet. The expression on Cole's face wasn't exactly warm and friendly, but it wasn't nearly as coldly unnerving, as implacably set as it had been when he'd first appeared outside the cabin.

Not that she could blame him for being furious. Her heart trembled when she thought of her own role in what had happened today. It was her own fault, for she sensed that it was concern for her that had made him so fiercely angry. He must have been very, very worried. Out of his mind, almost. Maybe old superstitions didn't always hold true after all, she told herself with a flicker of hope. *He loves me not.* What did an old daisy know?

She found herself smiling a little to herself, and just at that moment Cole's gaze touched hers. He seemed to be taking in everything: her softly pinned curls falling artlessly around her shoulders, the gown that emphasized her long neck and hugged her curves. His eyes narrowed, and it seemed to her that their expression, deep within those blazing depths, became suddenly more intense, yet he allowed nothing more to show in his face. Still, she had come to realize that he was a master at concealing his emotions. Like a gambler, he played his hand close. Maybe he felt more toward her than she'd thought, maybe even more than he would admit to himself. Hadn't he come to her rescue time and again? Hadn't he found her even tonight despite Gray Feather's skill at covering his tracks? She thought of the scar on his face. He'd endured that, and a beating, and had still come for her in Plattsville. He'd fought and killed to get her out of that jail. He'd come back to Fire Mesa, with all its gruesome memories, to bring her to a place where she would be safe.

And she had repaid him by running off the moment his back was turned, disappearing with Gray Feather and forgetting all about him.

Sitting there, with Wade beside her once more on the sofa, she felt a stab of remorse so powerful, it made her head hurt. She had to speak to Cole. Alone. And without delay.

In the back of her mind she heard Tommy say, "I reckon we're in your debt, Rawdon. You've taken good care of our little sister."

And then Cole was straightening his hat, coming toward them, speaking in that cool way of his. "No trouble. Anything I can do to spoil McCray's day is fine with me."

"Well, we'll handle McCray and his men," Tommy assured him. "No one will have to worry about them again when we're through."

That made Cole pause. He stared into the tall young man's face with a look of warning. "You and your brother had best stick to taking care of Juliana," he said very deliberately. "That bounty is still out on her head and until you clear that up, she'll be a target. Leave McCray—and Knife Jackson—to me."

Then he was walking toward the door, leaving—without even glancing her way.

She sprang off the sofa in a flash and blocked his path, a golden slip of a girl with a spine tight as a steel rod. "I need to talk to you outside, Cole. Alone."

His expression as he stared down at her was distant and polite, as though she were a stranger he had just encountered in a shop or along the street. "Our business is finished, angel. You found your brothers—that's what you wanted. They seem pretty capable of keeping you safe. Now it's time for me to be moving on."

His casual words cut her to the quick, until she realized that this too was part of his facade, part of that wall he built up around himself. She willed herself to remember the tenderness in his eyes when he had caressed her last night, when he had held her and made himself a part of her and she a part of him. "No, it's time for me to apologize," she said, taking his strong hands in her small, slender ones and pulling him toward the door. "Come on. I'm not going to humble myself in front of all these men."

"Juliana." Gil Keedy loomed suddenly at her side. There was a fervent desperation in his face. Beneath the shock of red hair she read three things: jealousy, concern, and a deep yearning. *No, Gil,* she thought sadly, *save all that for Josie, whoever she might be. I want one man and only one. And if I don't prove that to him, he'll walk out that door and leave me forever.*

"Gil, this is between me and Cole."

"Let him go, Juliana. I'm begging you," Gil urged in a low tone. "He's trouble. You don't need him anymore. We'll take care of you now . . ."

She saw the quick flash of anger spark in Cole's eyes as he stared at the other man, then he quenched all emotion and jerked his hands from her, his lips tight. "He's right," he drawled evenly. "*Adiós,* Juliana."

"Out! Everybody out!" Juliana ordered suddenly, whirling toward her brothers and the other men. "If Cole won't step outside with me, we'll have to talk here. Leave us for a while!"

Yancy guffawed at the sight of this slender female issuing orders like many a general he'd seen during the war. Gray Feather grinned and sauntered toward the door, while Skunk elbowed Gil in the ribs, then hustled the red-faced cowboy across the room.

"Hold on, Juliana," Tommy began, shooting Rawdon a suspicious glance, but Wade clapped a hand on his shoulder. "Let's go, Tommy boy. Our very determined little sister has spoken."

"You're going to leave her here alone—with him?"

"Yep."

The anger rising in him at being made the object of ridicule by every grinning man present, Cole stared at Juliana with murder in his eyes. "What's to stop me from walking out that door with the rest of them?" he demanded in a low tone.

It was Wade, overhearing, who answered him from the cabin door. "Won't do you any good, Rawdon. You can't leave anyway. While we were talking, I had Skunk hide your horse. You're not going anywhere until my sister gives her permission."

And with that, he shoved Tommy out the door before him, then slammed it shut behind them both, laughing into the Arizona night.

Juliana reached out a hand toward Cole's cheek, but he brushed it away.

"Say what you have to say and get it over with. I've got work to do and if you think I'm hanging around here to play nursemaid to you one minute longer, you're wrong. Dead wrong."

"Is that what you think I want?" Her chin lifted, and fury danced in her emerald eyes, but then, remembering

her goal, she tried to swallow back her own anger.
"Cole," she said softly, soothingly, placing a hand on his
arm. It was corded with muscles beneath his black shirt,
but she thought she felt it quiver at her touch.

"The least you can do is to let me apologize."

"For what?"

"For breaking my promise. For not coming back tonight to tell you I'd found my brothers. I know it was
awful of me, but we were so excited to be reunited, and
there were so many things to discuss and settle between
us—"

"Look," he interrupted, his voice raw, "that's real nice
about your brothers. I'm glad for you. You're back with
them where you belong." She had started caressing his
arm, rubbing her fingers back and forth lightly, provocatively, and it was having a damned strange effect on him.
He felt his insides go from tight and knotted to something else . . . something like melting iron. Damn her
and her tricks.

Suddenly he reached out and seized her by the wrists.
"That fellow Keedy. He's right about me. I am trouble.
More trouble than you can imagine."

"So am I." She tossed her head, sending a wayward
wisp of curl tilting over one eye. "At least that's what
you've been telling me all this time. I reckon that means
we're a good match."

"You've got me wrong, Juliana. I'm not the kind to
make any kind of match." Cole felt sweat breaking out
on his brow. She looked so beautiful, so fragile and sweet.
He had to use all his willpower to keep from reaching out
and smoothing that golden tendril back from her brow,
from yanking all those pins from her hair and letting the
entire pale mass of it spill like fool's gold into his hands.
He wanted to clasp her in his arms and never let her go.
But that would be the worst thing he could do. He had to
say good-bye to her forever.

Cole knew with bleak certainty that he wasn't the type of man to settle down. He wasn't the type ever to find the kind of peace and contentment she'd be looking for, that she deserved. Better she should stick with her brothers, and maybe eventually marry Keedy or someone like him —not a man who'd lived his whole life alone, who'd mastered the art of not needing anyone, not trusting anyone. He could never make her happy. Disaster followed him— and so did death. There was no way out of the violent cycle of his life. Deep down, Cole knew he was fated to an existence of brutality and danger. Juliana had been running from such violence ever since she was a child and had lost her own parents. She needed someone who would protect her from pain and difficulty, not someone whose entire life had been a chain of violence and confrontation, who had learned to survive by being more deadly, more ruthless, more dangerous than any opponent he might encounter. Juliana would want a house with curtains on the windows, and a garden, a place with books and matching china dishes—and babies. He couldn't give her that. He could only give her trouble.

"Look," he said as evenly as he could, trying to keep the pain that was tearing at his guts out of his voice, "I know you think you owe me something because I got you out of Plattsville. You don't. I did it because I wanted to do it, and you don't need to understand my reasons. But it's over. Wade and Tommy will take care of you. I'm going to take care of McCray."

The pile of daisy petals floated in her mind once more. *He loves me not.* Could she be so very wrong? Was she making an utter fool of herself? Desperately, Juliana searched his face.

He looked as cool, as handsomely, ruggedly detached as he had that day in Denver when she'd fainted in his arms. It wasn't at all the way Gil Keedy looked at her, or the way any of the young men in St. Louis had looked at her. It wasn't the way he'd looked at her last night. But she didn't know how to bring that tender expression back. It seemed to have vanished forever.

Because I submitted to him. He was curious about what it would be like to make love to me, and we were all alone at the cabin, and it happened. But it meant nothing to him. I mean nothing to him, except as something, someone he had to see safely disposed of. And now he's done that, so he's leaving.

A thousand jagged splinters seemed to pierce her heart. The anguish made it nearly impossible to breathe. She studied his lean face with an aching gaze, trying to memorize every line and angle, the strength and courage she read in his eyes, the kindness buried deep beneath the steely surface. There was a tightness in her throat so painful, Juliana couldn't swallow, and she was afraid she was going to cry. She searched in her mind for something to say, something that wouldn't betray her own foolish dreams any more than she already had, and her distraught mind came up with something idiotic and totally unrelated, but she blurted it out anyway.

"You . . . you said you would bring me back a surprise. M-may I have it . . . before you go?"

She wouldn't cry in front of him, nor in front of Wade and Tommy. She wouldn't. She would behave . . . in a sophisticated manner. She would let him go without bawling like some pathetic, drooling fool.

Standing there, seeing her in that elegant pale green gown that emphasized the emerald vibrance of her eyes, Cole thought of the cheap Mexican peasant skirt and blouse he had bought from Joseph Wells's housekeeper this morning. The woman had a daughter about Juliana's size. The skirt was brightly colored, a gay, pretty thing, and the plain white blouse had a scooped neckline with a tiny edging of lace. He had also bought from the girl some red and yellow hair ribbons, and a slim gold bracelet. Gifts for Juliana. The first gifts he'd ever bought for a woman.

But they were silly, secondhand offerings. He hadn't wanted to venture into the nearest town, for it would have meant leaving Juliana alone too long, so he had planned to bring back those few trinkets for her as a surprise. He had even imagined her wearing the clothes and the bracelet and the ribbons in her hair while they had supper, sweeping gaily about the cabin with the skirt twirling about her legs, making it seem more like a home than a place of hiding. And then afterward, he had anticipated the enjoyment of removing each article of clothing with leisurely pleasure. . . .

But here she was in the Montgomery gang hideout, dressed in a gown so fine and exquisite, it made little Lucita's skirt and blouse look gaudy and cheap by comparison. Juliana wore earbobs, too, he observed, his chest tight, pearl pieces that were lovely and expensive—gifts apparently from her brothers. When he thought of the paltry items in his saddlebag, items only half a day ago he had thought would delight her, he felt as foolish as a puppy begging for crumbs.

"I couldn't get you the surprise," he told her. He tried to let go of her shoulders but found himself gripping them even more tightly. "Sorry, angel."

"It doesn't matter." Juliana tried to smile. Tears threatened behind her eyes, and she was waging a tremendous struggle to keep them back. "Where . . . will you go now?"

"I'll head back to Plattsville and find out from Knife Jackson where to find McCray. Then I'll settle up with both of them."

"Don't," she begged suddenly. The fear that slammed through her heart made even the anguish seem dull by comparison. "Just . . . go away. Go to . . . New Mexico or Texas. I'm going to get Wade and Tommy to take

me away from Arizona, too. Then none of us will have to
worry about McCray or John Breen or anyone anymore . . ."

"I learned a long time ago, sweetheart, that running
never leaves behind the trouble. It always follows you."

"That's not true. I ran away from John Breen, and
escaped."

"You didn't escape. You got caught by me. And you're
still a target for some other bounty hunter who'd try to
bring you back to Breen so he could collect the reward."

"Then maybe I should go back and face him," Juliana
said slowly. The thought of it made her stomach churn
uneasily, but she was completely serious. "Maybe"—she
licked her lips as the idea grew in her mind—"I should
get rid of John Breen and those ridiculous charges once
and for all."

No! Cole wanted to shout. *Stay away from Breen. I
want you safe.* It shocked him how dearly he wanted to
protect her, to keep her far from any possible harm.
"Maybe Wade or Tommy could confront Breen—and
force him to give up the search." Even as he said the
words, he knew that he should be the one to do it. Suddenly her welfare, her protection, seemed to be the only
things in the world that mattered. Not Fire Mesa. Not
even evening the score with Jackson and McCray. Only
staying near Juliana and making sure that no one and
nothing harmed her.

Something must have shown in his eyes, some glimpse
of the powerful emotions possessing him, for her lovely
face lit up, the light dusting of freckles making her look
adorably like a child, a child who has been promised a
rare treat, and she clasped her arms around his neck before either of them realized what she was doing.

"Cole, you *do* care about me, don't you?" she
breathed. "You're afraid of what might happen if I fell
into Breen's clutches."

Somehow he found the strength to disentangle her arms from around his neck. "I reckon I feel somewhat responsible for you," he admitted, struggling for words. "The same way I feel responsible for my saddle and my horse. . . ."

"Your . . . horse?" The seed of hope that had bloomed magically inside her only a moment before withered and died a swift death. Her eyes were wide with dismay, and she felt as if she were choking. "Your horse," she repeated dazedly, humiliation burning into her cheeks.

"I mean . . ." Cole found himself stammering like a schoolboy. Confound her and those mesmerizing eyes anyway! "I mean that I couldn't leave Arrow saddled and lathered up and out in the middle of a storm somewhere, could I? And I can't leave you, I reckon, until this Mc-Cray business is cleared up." He was pleased with his comparison; it made perfect sense to him. "I'm beginning to see that I'd better stick around and help your brothers deal with this—and then make sure Breen doesn't bother you anymore. If your brothers venture all the way to Denver, someone's likely to lock them up. I'll have to go with them."

"You'd do that for me?"

"The man suckered me into something that wasn't any of my business by offering that sky-high bounty on you. Now I'm making it my business to set things to rights." It sounded convincing enough. Hell, it almost convinced him that that was all there was to it. He'd take care of McCray and Breen and then he would leave. Ride out of her life for good. He'd be able to do it, Cole told himself, when he knew there were no more threats hanging over her head—and when he was certain those brothers of hers would give up their outlaw life and look after her the way she deserved.

"That's most kind of you." Juliana stepped back from

him, then turned and walked toward the stove. Warmth still emanated from it, seeping out into the rough corners of the cabin. She realized she was shivering. The mountain air was cool, biting right through the silk of the dress. Or maybe it was her heart that was cold, she thought dully—cold and dead.

She had given Cole Rawdon every opportunity to tell her he loved her, even that he cared about her, and he had only admitted that he felt responsible for her—in the same way he felt responsible for his horse. The hurt of it flared inside her like pricking needles. She had thrown herself into his arms, she had practically thrown herself at his feet, and he had calmly told her she meant nothing more to him than his damned horse.

Fine, then. She had been wrong, wrong about everything between them. Her woman's instinct had betrayed her after all. He loved her not.

"Of course, my brothers and I will pay you for whatever work you do on our behalf. I have money in my pouch—" She broke off. "I left it at the cabin."

"I'll bring it here tomorrow."

"You're going there, to the cabin? Now? Alone?"

Despite himself, he grinned in the darkness. "I'm a big boy, angel. I'm not afraid of the dark."

"How much money do you want—for helping me?"

Inwardly, he groaned. *Nothing,* he wanted to shout as he recognized the hurt expression on her face, and realized how hard she was trying to appear detached. He had hurt her, even though he'd never meant to do it. He wanted to enfold her in his arms and kiss her until neither of them could breathe, until she could never again mistake exactly how he felt. But he knew now what he had to do—convince her that this was just business, that he was doing a job for pay, discharging a responsibility that would also line his pockets, and then maybe she'd forget about him and stop whatever foolish daydreams he had encouraged her to begin. Maybe she'd look to a man who could give her the steady, safe life she needed, the children and home she wanted. He couldn't. It wasn't in the cards for him. His fate was a life of solitude and danger, a rider of the plains and mountains, hunter of men—dealing out and being dealt trouble.

"Maybe you didn't hear me." Her voice was trembling, but her face was rigid in the moonlight bathing it. "I asked you how much money you want to help me."

Cole forced the words from his mouth.

"How much do you have?"

"About forty dollars—but I'm sure Wade and Tommy have more."

"Fine." He took a deep breath, hating himself. But it was for her, he was doing it for her. "One hundred dollars strikes me as fair."

"Oh, yes," she murmured faintly. "Quite fair."

She took a step forward and clutched the back of a chair for support as he stalked once more to the door.

Business. This was only business for him—just as it had always been. How could she have been so stupid?

Her knees shook. Her hands felt limp and cold against the rough wood. As Cole opened the door, his large figure disappearing into the darkness outside, she heard him say casually over his shoulder, "Good night, boss lady."

Then he was gone, and she was alone in the cabin, shaking like an autumn leaf caught in the bitter throes of winter.

In a moment Wade and Tommy and the others would come streaming back in, there would be laughter and jokes, the easy banter that seemed to characterize this gang flowing around her. Tommy might even still want to dance. But she had never felt less like dancing. Even though she realized that this was the night she ought to be deliriously happy, the night she had dreamed of for so long, the night she found her brothers, desolation shrouded her.

All the gaiety and warmth, the sense of belonging and of being loved that had bolstered her before, had fled. Cole was gone, taking her happiness with him. The intimacy and gentleness and sheer powerful passion that had exploded between them last night might never have been. Juliana was left drained, humiliated, and alone.

She felt dirty, and impossibly stupid. She never should have believed her feelings. She never should have let herself imagine that he might consider her any more seriously than he considered the dancing girls and whores he no doubt frequented in every town he passed through. Naive, that's what she was. A silly girl who thought that simply because a man saved her life, and kissed her for his trouble, he actually could care for her—more than he cared for his horse.

By the time her brothers and Skunk, Gray Feather, and Yancy trudged back into the cabin, Juliana had her outward appearance well under control. She was clear-eyed and straight-backed, and her smile was brilliant, if a shade too wide. She even danced with Tommy, her feet skimming lightly over the floorboards, and convinced herself that no one was the wiser, that no one guessed the torment strangling her heart.

Once she caught Wade's intent gaze on her and shot him a dazzling smile. But he didn't smile back. He was too smart, that brother of hers, too perceptive to be fooled by anyone for long. But she desperately had to try.

Because if she couldn't fool Wade and Tommy and the others, how could she possibly fool herself? How could she possibly get through this night, and the days to come —days when Cole would be near at hand, torturing her— if she couldn't somehow convince herself that she didn't care, she didn't care, she didn't care.

· 22 ·

One night of devastation, that was all Juliana was determined to allow herself. She may have cried herself to sleep the night before, filled with an acrid, bitter sorrow, but by the morning, when she opened her eyes in the back room to a day full of sunshine, she had made up her mind that she was *not* going to allow Mr. Cole Rawdon to ruin her life. She sat up in bed, tossing her hair over her shoulders in a defiant gesture. She didn't need him—she didn't need anyone but her family, and now that she had them back, Cole Rawdon could . . . could jump off Stick Mountain if he wanted to and she wouldn't blink an eye.

Forget him, that's what she was going to do. Forget about the way he looked and walked and smiled, the way his skin tasted against her lips, the spicy masculine scent of him. Forget the silky feel of his midnight hair between her fingers. Forget his muscular warmth when they had lain in that feather bed together, the way his hands stroked and aroused every intimate part of her body. Forget his voice, the way his eyes smoldered when she said something he took exception to, and the way they blazed right through to her soul when he was about to kiss her. Forget him!

Oh, yes, she was certainly going to forget him.

It wasn't so very difficult at first. There was breakfast to see to, and she was kept more than busy helping Skunk with the bacon frying and biscuit-making and coffee-pouring. There were good-morning hugs from Wade and Tommy that helped fill the emptiness inside her, a warm greeting from the usually taciturn Yancy, and Gray Feather in his buckskin tunic and leggings sent her that wry, slight smile of his that she found so endearing and at such odds with his sharp features and generally fierce appearance.

Gil Keedy was especially attentive. She felt him watching her all through the meal, while the friendly banter was going on, while she was helping Skunk scrub the plates and frying pan.

Afterward, Wade suggested that he take her to meet Josie, promising that he would explain all about the girl and her baby along the way.

Juliana agreed only too eagerly. She wanted to get as complete a picture as possible about this entire McCray business. The sooner they removed the threat he posed to Wade and Tommy, the sooner Cole Rawdon could leave for Denver and settle the business with John Breen. Then she'd be free of both Breen and Cole for good.

I can scarcely wait, she told herself, drying her hands on a dishrag and following her brother outside into the open air. She had donned the trousers and shirt from yesterday since she had figured she'd be riding today, and her hair was swept into a long golden braid down her back. Out in the sunlight, Wade noticed that her cheeks were quite pale, and there were hollows beneath her eyes, hollows as gray as the rocks that made up the buttes crowning the mountain. But he made no comment, for

Juliana still wore that brilliant, pasted smile of last night and obviously didn't wish to discuss what had occurred between her and Rawdon. Wade wanted to punch him, but when, just as Juliana pulled herself into the saddle of Skunk's mustang, Rawdon came riding up the trail looking cold as a pitcher of ice water in all-black garb, his hat low over his eyes, Wade forced himself to offer a curt greeting but nothing more.

Juliana had already informed him that she had hired Rawdon to help sort out this damned awful mess with McCray, and then with Breen, which was fine with Wade. They could use another man, seeing as now they had Juliana to protect, as well as Josie and the baby.

The whole thing had become too damned complicated, and far too dangerous for Wade to take lightly. Usually they were in and out quickly on a job—this Plattsville business with McCray had gotten out of hand and he knew it wouldn't end now until either McCray, or the Montgomerys, were dead.

"Come ride with us awhile," Wade addressed Rawdon. He noticed the wary look that had come into Juliana's eyes, but she held herself rigidly straight in the saddle and did no more than nod a greeting. Dignified as a princess, that was Juliana. She had a gentle heart, her brother reflected warmly, but plenty of backbone. Wade couldn't help but be proud of her, even though pity swelled through him. That damned bounty hunter was breaking her heart; when this bloody business was all over, maybe Wade would give in to his instincts and beat the hell out of him, but for now they had to remember they were working on the same side. If they wanted to stay alive, and keep the women safe, they'd all have to stick together.

Rawdon's horse fell in behind Juliana's mustang as Wade led the way down the rocky trail. After a while they reached a level grassy basin where they could ride three abreast, and Wade had the opportunity to ask the bounty hunter just how familiar he was with this vast piece of land called Fire Mesa.

A ghost of a smile touched Cole's lips. "Familiar enough," he returned in his usual laconic manner.

"Cole's family used to own Fire Mesa," Juliana said quickly.

"Oh—Rawdon!" Wade snapped his fingers as if just recalling something. "That *was* the name I'd heard about." He shot a piercing glance at the profile of the man beside him. "Seems there was some kind of story about the family losing it years ago—then an Indian raid —old Joseph Wells never felt quite comfortable on the place."

"Wells won it fair and square from my father in a poker game. No reason he shouldn't stay."

"He's planning to sell. You know that?"

"I know that."

A silence fell. Golden aspens rustled in the sharp morning breeze, a hummingbird sang, unseen but lovely, from a hidden branch. Before them stretched a vista of purple mountains, misty in the shimmering brilliance of the August sun. A pair of rabbits chased each other beneath a saguaro, and birds chittered overhead. There was no hint of the danger that seemed to hem them in on every side, a danger that all three sensed keenly. McCray and his men were desperate to frame and kill the Montgomerys. Cole still didn't understand why. But he knew that McCray's hired killers were out there searching, that being here in the relative openness of this plain exposed all three of them to ambush. Why hadn't he insisted that Juliana stay back?

Strange that they should end up here, on Fire Mesa. Cole felt a tingle down his spine when he thought about the Montgomery gang hideout being here, on his grandfather's land. Or Wells's land, he corrected himself swiftly. He hadn't come back in twenty years, and now all of this business was centered here. Why? Cole had a hunch, one that made his scalp prickle. Maybe it was his fate to die on Fire Mesa. Maybe he had cheated fate all those years ago when his entire family was wiped out. He should have died then, too, alongside Mama and Caitlin. Fire Mesa should have been his burying ground. Maybe it still would be. Maybe that was the reason for all this.

Cole wasn't a superstitious man, but he had a powerful belief in Fate, or perhaps God—some higher power that had created all this spectacular beauty in the West, who tested men's courage and mettle and honor, who dealt out life and death, pain and laughter, according to some secret plan that Cole couldn't fathom but that he knew with every fiber of his being did exist. Maybe this was all part of His plan. Maybe he was destined to die here on the land his grandfather had loved, the land that had already soaked up so much of his family's blood. If that was his destiny, it was fine with him. But he would take McCray and Jackson and their whole rotten outfit down with him when he went. He'd keep Juliana safe if it cost him every breath in his body, every last ounce of blood.

Seeing her this morning, being with her now, was torturing him. It would be different if he could tell her how he felt and explain the reasons why he was no fit husband for her or for anyone—but he knew that would only make it worse. She had a fiercely loyal heart. She was too headstrong for her own good. She probably thought she loved him. She would argue and resist him and use all her wiles to keep him by her side. And it would only make it more difficult when he had to ride away—or when she had to watch him lowered into the ground in a pine casket.

Better to break it off now—let her start turning her thoughts to Keedy or someone like him, as soon as possible. If she had started to hate him, so much the better.

But oh, damn everything to hell, what he would give to hold her again, to feel her softness against him, to kiss her lips, the pink nipples of her breasts, to feel her wrapped around him.

Juliana.

Never had he imagined a name could sound so sweet, or feel so warmly sensuous on his tongue. Never had he imagined he could feel so deeply, painfully for anyone ever again. He had thought in the orphanage, when night after night he'd endured beatings, hunger, and the virulent hatred of that institution's administrator, that he had learned how base human beings could be—and that he was forever safe from being hurt by any one human again. He had stopped feeling pain, hunger, the need for love. Later, his experience with Jess Burrows had confirmed his opinion of human beings. Only fury and a relentless belief in himself had remained. It was these same qualities that had enabled him to survive the bloodbath on Fire Mesa, the cruel years of the orphanage, and being left to die in the desert when Jess had shot him in the back. Then Sun Eagle had taught him the ways of the Cheyenne, ways of strength and cunning, and he had become nearly invincible.

But not quite. A woman, delicate and lovely as a flower, had pierced his shield. A woman with emerald eyes that could sparkle and flash brighter than any gem, a woman with stubborn ways and a laugh as mellow as fine wine, and a heart that was open and giving.

She had taught him that he was not proof against love. She had taught him that arrogance was the way of fools. She had given him the only moments of real happiness he had known since his boyhood.

He wouldn't repay her by saddling her with his troubles, and whatever dark fate lay in store for him. He would steer her in another direction, like a line rider driving a calf away from a dangerous precipice, and leave her free to love someone who would bring her far more than he ever could.

Wade's voice broke into his reverie. "If you're familiar with these parts, you may know the old Simpson place down by the river. The land borders Fire Mesa on the south. That's where we're headed. It's deserted now, except for the woman we're going to see."

Cole glanced at Wade, deliberately avoiding Juliana's silent form to his right. "And who is she?"

"Josie Larson—and her baby. They've left the place pretty much as it was, so that no one riding by could tell it's inhabited. So far, McCray hasn't found them. One of these days, I'm afraid he will. But Josie won't come and stay with us at Stick Mountain. She's stubborn, insists on staying on her own. We've been trying to protect her as best we can."

The story Wade told them then about Josie Larson almost made Juliana forget about her own problems. When a scant hour later, they rode into an overgrown, weed-strewn yard and pulled up before a dilapidated one-story adobe house with the windows all boarded up and a tumbledown barn and well behind it, she was so intent upon meeting the unfortunate young woman Wade had described to her that she almost forgot about Cole Rawdon's presence.

Almost.

When she stepped down from her horse, her foot caught in one of the long, tangled weeds strangling the front yard, and she nearly fell, but suddenly he was at her side, gripping her elbow, steadying her, the clean, masculine scent of him filling her nostrils.

She jerked her arm away. "When I need your help, I'll ask for it," she heard herself snapping.

"You'd have been asking from facedown with a mouthful of dirt and weeds."

"I'm perfectly capable of looking out for myself."

He touched a hand to his hat, then followed Wade to the door. She was right. He should have kept his distance. Trouble was, he was used to looking out for her now. It was a habit he'd have to break.

Broken steps and peeling paint, and more weeds sprouting right up to the threshold, gave the house a run-down air. Juliana wondered how anyone could live here as she picked her way after the men, her curiosity growing strong about Josie Larson.

A tall, willowy young woman was waiting for them inside, her baby boy clutched in her arms.

"I thought at first you were McCray," she said, smiling with relief as she came toward them. The only light came from a kerosene lantern on the mantel, and from the open door, so it was difficult to see her face until she approached. "Then I realized it was you, Wade. I put on some coffee." Gazing back and forth between Juliana and Cole, studying them with a swift, keen scrutiny, her smile widened suddenly. "You must be Wade and Tommy's sister!" she exclaimed, her brown eyes meeting Juliana's gaze warmly. "I'm so glad to meet you at last. They've done nothing but talk about finding you! And whoever you are, you're welcome, mister, since you're with Wade," she said easily to Cole. "Come in and try to make yourselves comfortable."

The inside of the house was more inviting and habitable than the outside, clean and free of dust and dirt, though it was a sparsely furnished little house with shuttered windows and bare floors and little in the way of adornment. But it was the young woman who had greeted them who drew Juliana's attention. She liked the friendly, plainspoken girl at once.

Josie Larson was as unaffected as a robin. She was perhaps twenty, slightly taller than average, and thin as a reed. Short amber curls spilled down about a pretty, heart-shaped face made most interesting by her wide-set brown eyes. She was not beautiful but, rather, warm and appealing with a direct manner and a calm, matter-of-fact voice that sat well with Juliana. Yet there was a troubled sorrow lurking in those clear brown eyes that touched Juliana. Knowing something of Josie's story, she understood the reason behind the young woman's care-worn air.

But the baby, little Kevin, only seven months old, was a treasure from whom she could scarcely draw her eyes. While Josie served coffee to the men in the small, homey kitchen, Juliana settled down in a corner rocker with the baby on her lap, and found herself totally absorbed in his antics, chuckling over his every attempt to pull her hair, to poke her eyes out with his tiny stubby fingers. She cooed with laughter each time she ducked her head away just in the nick of time. This, of course, made him squeal with joy and immediately encouraged him to try again.

But as Wade and Josie talked, interrupted now and then by a question from Cole, she drew the baby close to her and listened. Gradually, all the pieces of the McCray puzzle began to slide into place, and the picture it made was a chilling one.

Like Henny, Josie had been victimized by McCray's greedy takeover in Plattsville. She had been married to Clint Larson, the young owner of a livery stable, who had vociferously opposed many of the ideas McCray put forth for the town's expansion, sensing that these plans would be for McCray's benefit and no one else's. Two nights after the town meeting when he had spoken out, Clint had been working late when a fire broke out in his stables near the far end of town. Seven horses had died, and along with them, Clint's body was found among the ashes, his remains charred so badly, they were barely recognizable. Maybe an accident, maybe not, Sheriff Rivers had commented. He would certainly investigate.

But Josie had known deep in her heart that it was murder.

The story grew worse. McCray had had the gumption to show up at Clint's funeral, ostensibly paying the widow his respects. Somehow or other, the willowy, amber-haired young woman with the infant clasped in her arms had caught his fancy. He had begun pursuing her, sending flowers, gifts, calling on her—despite her state of mourning. Of course, she had rebuffed him at every turn and the sheriff had even warned him off on her behalf. But one night when Rivers was away from Plattsville on business, several men who worked for McCray had shown up at her house on the fringes of town and tried to drag her off. They told her that their boss was waiting for her in his suite at the hotel, that he'd been patient long enough.

Fortunately, Wade and Tommy had been heading out of town after a night of gambling at the saloon and saw Josie being dragged down the street. They'd interfered, wounding one man in the ensuing gunfight, killing two others. That's when the vendetta between the Montgomery brothers and Line McCray had really begun.

Wade and Tommy, after hearing her story, had helped Josie and her baby move out of town to this abandoned ranch. Not long afterward they had heard that Sheriff Rivers was dead, and that they were being hunted for his murder.

Juliana interrupted at this point to question Wade. Kevin had fallen asleep in her arms, his soft little cheek resting against the curve of her shoulder. "Sheriff Dane told me that you and Tommy robbed a gold shipment from the Sanders mine. Was that much true?"

"Sure was. That happened months ago, long before we came across Josie. We'd already met up with Gil and started heading back to Denver for you. When we reached Rimrock, we heard about the bounty and realized you must be on the loose. The Southwest is a mighty big place. We didn't know where to look, so we decided to lay low in Arizona for a while, hoping to get some word about your whereabouts. When there's a two-thousand-dollar reward offered, a lot of rumors tend to fly around. We spent a good while checking them out. Tommy even rode all the way to the Colorado border trying to pick up your trail, but all he heard was a lot of talk. While he was gone, Yancy and Skunk and I were nosing around about McCray. Everyone for miles around was talking about how he was buying up every piece of property and business he could find, that Wells was planning to sell him Fire Mesa, that he meant to build a railroad clear through to Texas. One of the things Yancy found out was that McCray owned the Sanders mine. He'd forced Jed Sanders to sell out to him secretly. So two months ago, waiting for Tommy to get back, we robbed the shipment on its way to Timber Junction, then gave a portion of it back to Sanders. Tommy got back from the border, still with no word about you, Juliana, and so we laid low for a while longer, waiting for our luck to change. Then one night Gil Keedy reported that Rivers was away. We had sent Skunk and Yancy and Gray Feather as far away as New Mexico trying to get a lead on you, but so far, no word from them. Tommy and I were going stir crazy up on Stick Mountain, so we decided to sneak into the Ten Gallon Saloon for the evening. We always wear masks during holdups, so we didn't worry too much about anyone recognizing our faces. Anyway," Wade finished, "that's the night we met Josie. Once we heard about her troubles, we got caught up in this whole mess and figured we had to stay and see it through until it was finished." He grinned over at his sister, comfortably reclining in the rocker with the baby sleeping peacefully against her shoulder. "Lucky thing you showed up in the vicinity. Now, as Tommy would say, we can kill two birds with one stone."

"And what might those two birds be?" Cole asked, setting his empty coffee cup down on the table. He tried to keep from staring at Juliana with that tiny baby in her arms. She looked downright natural holding him. She loved it, too, he could tell that by the glow on her face. Cole tried not to think about the little son or daughter he could have shared with her one day—if things had been different. They weren't different, he reminded himself angrily. Juliana would just have to have some other man's baby. . . .

But that thought made him scowl even more blackly.

"The two birds were to rescue Juliana from you and any other greedy bounty hunter who might have his eye on that damned reward," Wade retorted. "And to keep watch over Josie until McCray is dead or driven out."

"Men like McCray don't get driven out. He'll have to be six feet under before this is over," Cole said as though discussing the chance of an afternoon drizzle.

"Then he'll be six feet under." Wade met the bounty hunter's skeptical look with a determined set to his mouth. "He's hurt enough people already. It's the only way."

Juliana swallowed. Violence. She knew McCray was evil, that he deserved to die, and yet something inside her cringed at the easy way both Wade and Cole turned to killing for the answer. She took a deep breath. Maybe it wasn't easy for them after all. Maybe they had just seen enough of lawlessness and greed and brutality to know that sometimes it was the only way to put an end to such evil. She shuddered as a tremor worked its way down her spine. It might be the only way, but she couldn't bring herself to like it.

"Let me get this straight," Cole said, rising to stare from Wade to Josie, choosing his words carefully. "After

you helped Josie clear out of Plattsville, long after the
Sanders job, that's when Rivers got killed? We heard he
was out with his posse hunting for you when it happened."

"That's right. He had tracked us right after the robbery, of course, but found no trace. Gray Feather had
already found us the cabin on Stick Mountain, and Rivers hadn't a clue where we were holed up. But after we
helped Josie, McCray got word of it and learned who we
were. He realized that the Montgomerys hadn't only
pulled the Sanders job but had also ruined his fun with
the lady. He decided to seek his own revenge. My guess is
he made sure Rivers got a false lead concerning our
whereabouts, then he had him killed. That allowed Mc-
Cray to put his own man in as sheriff—that idiot Dane—
and also gave us a murder charge to reckon with. We've
been forced to stay pretty much away from any town ever
since. Except for Keedy. He's the only one not actually
associated with the gang—yet."

At the mention of Gil's name, Juliana noticed a light
enter Josie's dark eyes. But she had also seen the girl perk
up when Tommy's name had been mentioned. Apparently, Josie Larson was having a difficult time choosing
between the two young men competing for her attention.
Of course, it was still only a short time since her husband's death, but Juliana realized that here in the West,
people couldn't mourn for as long as custom considered
proper in the East. Life out here just kept going right on,
like a huge, raging river, and if you didn't keep up with
it, you were swept under. She had a feeling that Josie,
despite missing her husband, needed someone to lean on,
someone to love. It must be terribly lonely for her here all
alone. In addition, she had the responsibility of raising
her child. She would want a father for him, someone to
love and protect him in this untamed country. It was
only natural, Juliana reflected as the baby stirred and

whimpered in her arms, that Josie would seek out the companionship of another man. But which one did she prefer? Juliana, despite her fondness for Gil, felt a strong loyalty to Tommy. Couldn't this girl see how wonderfully handsome and fun-loving and dear he was? Of course, Josie certainly might feel that Gil, though not as lankily good-looking or charismatic as Tommy, nevertheless had his own special brand of charm. His gentle, drawling sense of humor, courtly Texas manners, and easygoing demeanor must have had an effect on Josie. Still . . .

Her musings were broken by the sound of the baby's wails. Startled, she rose and hurried to Josie, who reached for him with a weary smile.

"Looks like my little one wants his mama's arms. Can't say I blame him." She sighed, stroking the little boy's bald head with a work-callused finger. "Sometimes I wish for my mama's arms, too."

"Don't we all," Juliana murmured softly, thinking of the mother she had lost when she was nine, and whom she scarcely remembered. If only she had a mother to confide in now, to pour out all her doubts and hurts over Cole. Suddenly she felt a strange bond with this young woman, who like herself seemed destined to fight for survival alone in a world of men. "Don't we all."

The two young women smiled at each other then, each taking the other's measure with eager interest, more than ready to become friends.

"Tommy has talked of little else except finding you ever since I met him," Josie offered a little while later as they cleared away the coffee cups. Cole and Wade had gone outside and the two women found themselves alone in the kitchen, able to talk together without the men listening in.

"Come with me and I'll show you where Kevin and I spend most of our time," Josie said. "There's a little parlour in back that I've fixed up nice and homey."

Sure enough, tucked behind the dark wood staircase was a spotless, cozy chamber, perhaps originally a little sewing room, where the lace-edged pillows on the chintz sofa were arranged neat as a pin, where the cedar floor was swept and polished to a high gloss, and where the iron stove in the corner was as clean and bright as a newly minted government coin. Josie settled Kevin down in a crib she'd discovered in the former nursery upstairs.

"Gil carried it down here for me—in fact, he helped me fix up this entire room. I didn't want to make the rest of the house look too lived-in, but I needed some little place where I could feel at home."

"Why didn't you stay down at the hideout on Stick Mountain?" Juliana asked curiously.

"It just goes against the grain with me to stay in a cabin with a bunch of men and not be married or related to any of 'em. My folks raised me strict, I guess." She shrugged. "So every day or so one of them is kind enough to ride down and visit, seeing if Kevin and me need food or supplies or anything, and in the meantime, we just wait."

"For what?"

Josie glanced up from where she was busily folding a pile of the baby's newly washed clothes. "For word that McCray is gone, so me and Kevin can go back to Platts-ville. Tommy promised me we'd be able to go home again soon."

"Did he?"

Noticing the interested manner in which Juliana waited for her to continue, Josie gave a self-conscious laugh. "Tommy has been real nice, real concerned. He's here to visit almost as much as—"

"Gil Keedy?" Juliana suggested with a smile.

When Josie blushed and nodded, Juliana added, "They're very different, aren't they?" She couldn't help wondering what Josie's assessment was of her two suitors and hoped the question would prompt some insight, which it did.

"Tommy is . . . well, *Tommy*," Josie chuckled. "He acts without thinking sometimes—just plunges right into mischief and to heck with the consequences. Lucky for him, he shoots fast as lightning, so he can get away with it. That night those men tried to drag me off," she explained, her expression sobering, "it was Tommy who saved the day. Wade would've been shot in the back by one of McCray's men, but Tommy saw him and plugged him before he could get off a shot. If you've never seen him shoot a gun, Juliana, you ain't never seen any real shooting."

Thinking of how expertly Cole handled his Colt .45 pistols, Juliana wondered fleetingly if her brother could possibly draw any faster. But more on her mind at that moment was the admiring glow on Josie's face when she discussed Tommy.

"He thinks a lot of you, too," she said by way of a reply, and studied the girl's reaction.

Josie flushed the color of baby rosebuds, shook her head vigorously, and said, "Oh, Tommy's just a big tease."

"And Gil?"

"Gil . . ." Josie's confusion grew. "Gil is sweet, too. All the boys are dears—I don't know what Kevin and I would do without them."

Suddenly she turned to Juliana and lifted her hands helplessly. "To tell you the truth, Juliana, both Gil and Tommy have been more than just sweet. They've been downright attentive . . . and though they wouldn't neither of them be disrespectful enough to Clint's memory to actually court me yet, I can tell that they both want to."

"How do you feel about that, Josie?"

The girl stood over the baby's crib, staring down at the

sleeping child, whose breath came in slow, light beats, calm as sunrise. "It's too soon after Clint to say. And even though Clint . . . well, our marriage wasn't exactly a Sunday picnic—" She broke off, hesitating, then something in Juliana's expression, a glimmer of compassion, of interest touched by genuine caring, spurred her suddenly to continue in a rush: "He drank sometimes, you see—and when he was very drunk . . . he would sometimes . . . beat me . . . but not often, and it wasn't really so very bad—not usually."

Her voice trailed off. She was still staring down at the baby, but Juliana could see tears on her cheeks.

For a moment, Juliana was speechless. Then she went swiftly to the girl and put her arms around her. "But that's terrible, Josie. Even if it only had happened once— it would have been one time too many. Why didn't you leave him?"

"Leave him?" The girl looked blank. "He was my husband. I took a marriage vow to love and obey him."

"Pledging to put up with beatings isn't part of any marriage vow I know about."

"I was scared," Josie whispered in a tortured voice. "I . . . wanted to run away sometimes. . . . Oh, I didn't know what to do. And then there was Kevin . . ."

Juliana struggled to understand. Compassion for the girl crying in her arms warred with her fury at the man who had beaten her, and indignation that any woman could find herself caught in such a cruel trap. What frightened her most was that Josie had hardly realized she had had a choice. She *could* have left. It might not have been easy, but she could have done it—just as she had left Plattsville when Line McCray's attentions became too threatening.

"I'm not trying to say I'm glad Clint died in that fire," the girl added quickly, lifting a tear-streaked face. "I would never have wished such a thing on him in a hun-

dred years, but if it hadn't happened . . ." She took a
deep breath and went on. "I would never have met Gil or
Tommy, and wouldn't have known how . . . how truly
nice and kind a man could be. And that's why," she said,
plunging ahead with a determined glint in her dark eyes,
"I'm not going to rush into marryin' anyone again—I
don't want to make any more mistakes. I'm going
straight back to Plattsville and start over—and I'm going
to just sit tight and see."

"Let's just hope Line McCray gets what's coming to
him," Juliana muttered. And John Breen, too, she
thought as she picked up a flowered china vase from the
desk, studying the wildflowers arranged on it. She
couldn't help being struck by how similar her predicament was to Josie's. Both of them had been forced into
hiding by men determined to possess them at any cost.
Both only wanted the freedom to live in peace. Of course,
she sighed, unlike Josie, she had found a man she *did*
want to spend her life with—but he wasn't sweetly lovestruck the way Tommy and Gil were; he was by turns
unpredictable, arrogant, rude, indifferent, and heart-
breakingly gentle and tender, not to mention entirely too
self-sufficient to need or want her or anyone else. . . .

She found herself wishing suddenly, for the first time in
her life, that she didn't have these infernal freckles
marching all across her nose. And that her mouth was
not quite so wide. It did ruin the symmetry of her face.
Maybe if she was prettier, with the classic, perfect porcelain beauty common in so many girls she'd known in St.
Louis . . .

What would it take to make Cole love her?

Idiot, she chided herself in silent fury, *you're supposed
to be forgetting him!*

His voice at the door shook her out of her thoughts,
jarring her so badly, the vase dropped from her hands
and crashed onto the wood floor into a thousand delicate

shards of china, waking little Kevin, who immediately started to cry.

"Oh," Juliana gasped, "I'm so sorry." As she knelt and began hastily collecting fragments of broken china, she cursed herself for a clumsy fool—she who had whirled so gracefully about countless ballrooms and never trod on a partner's toe. She had always thought that love made one happy, whole, and perfect—not that it reduced intelligent, able young women to fumbling idiots!

"It's all right," Josie told her as she picked up Kevin and soothed him in her arms. "Don't trouble yourself. I'll fetch a broom . . ."

"Ouch. Damn."

Cole was by her side in three quick strides, frowning as she stuck her cut and bleeding finger into her mouth. "Let me see that."

"It's nothing . . ." she protested.

"Let me see it, Juliana."

He forced her to hold her hand still and studied the gash in her finger, from which blood spurted like a small crimson fountain. Snapping off his neckerchief, he quickly bound up her hand while Juliana ground her lip.

"You're not going to faint are you?" he asked quickly.

"Don't be ridiculous." She was tougher now, since she'd started traipsing through the West. She had to be. Still, she was feeling a trifle light-headed. Maybe because he was standing so close to her, holding her hand, taking care of her.

"I guess I'm clumsy today," she offered in a faint voice to Josie, who was watching the little scene with one brow lifted.

But Cole cupped her chin in his hand. "Today?" His face softened. Then he sent Josie a wry look. "Every day," he informed her.

"That so?"

"I beg your pardon . . ." Juliana fumed.

"First time I met you," he murmured, ignoring Juliana's outrage and continuing to hold her hand in his large one, "you fainted in my arms. Next time, you fell down in the dirt in Cedar Gulch right at my feet. After that, you stumbled over the edge of a canyon so deep, you'd have aged five years before you hit bottom. And this morning, you nearly fell just getting off your fool horse . . ."

"That's enough!" Juliana gasped between clenched teeth, humiliated, and wondering what on earth Josie was thinking. She yanked her hand from his. "And do you care to tell us why I almost fell over that canyon? Who was chasing me, scaring me half to death before I even got anywhere near the edge of that cliff?"

"Maybe we should tell the whole story," Cole suggested with a grin. "What about the bear—maybe you could demonstrate your tree-climbing ability."

"I prefer to forget every minute of the time I spent with you," she flashed.

"You sure about that, angel? You didn't enjoy any little part of it?"

"No!"

She saw Cole's eyes glint beneath his dark hat, but before he could embarrass her further, Wade's voice interrupted from the doorway.

"We'd better be heading back."

"Fine with me!" Juliana snapped.

She jerked her hand away from Cole's, swept past him with all the hauteur of a royal princess, and sailed out the door with a low-voiced farewell to Josie.

She was so angry, she could scarcely breathe. She didn't catch the amused glance Josie shot Wade as Cole stalked after her, didn't hear the girl whisper, "What's that all about?"

She didn't see her brother shake his head with rueful

resignation. "Love or hate, I'll wager. You tell me which one."

All during the ride back to the cabin, Juliana forced herself to look straight ahead. She refused to glance at either Wade or Cole. Instead, she fixed in her mind the image of Gil Keedy and reached a decision. She would make herself fall in love with Gil—beginning tonight. Josie Larson was unsure of her emotions, and besides she still had Tommy—so she wouldn't be crushed to bits at losing Gil. He was a fine man, a brave man, one who had already traveled hundreds of miles to locate her brothers in an effort to help her. Surely that deserved some reward. And she was not going to pursue Gil only to make Cole jealous, she told herself. That was the last thing she would ever do. She thought such tricks immature and beneath her, weapons of a desperate woman.

That was the last thing she was—desperate. She didn't need any man, much less Cole Rawdon. In fact, she told herself as she recognized the juncture in the trail that led to the cabin and spurred her horse ahead of her companions for the last stretch, he was the very last man with whom she would ever consider a permanent alliance.

She had a bath in an old washtub Skunk filled for her in the back room, with heated water from the stove and a cake of lilac soap Josie had given her. She washed her hair vigorously and brushed it until it shone in a pale cloud that drifted about her shoulders. She dressed for dinner in the yellow organdy gown Wade and Tommy had given her. She primped and arranged and adjusted, adding hair combs, pins, earbobs, then tying and retying her sash. She made herself as beautiful as she knew how to do.

She made up her mind that by the time she finished with him, Cole Rawdon would be *begging* for her attention. But she would not give it to him. No matter what.

Then she sighed, called herself a pathetic liar, and finally faced the truth. She sailed out to the main room of the cabin with the single-minded purpose of bringing that man to his knees.

· 23 ·

"**I**f you don't tell me where Juliana Montgomery is right now, I'm going to blow your damned head off."

Line McCray stared in incredulity at the tall, elegant man with the strange yellow-tan eyes who had just burst into the parlour of Belle Mallory's boardinghouse in Plattsville and pointed a double-barreled Winchester at his head. Three men in long dusters and muddy boots, brandishing their pistols as if they meant business, had charged in with him, effectively getting the drop on Knife Jackson, who didn't even have time to reach for his gun, much less draw it. Belle Mallory bit back a scream, then stayed frozen beside McCray on the velvet sofa.

McCray could do nothing but gulp for a moment as he stared down the barrel of that gun. Then he recovered his voice—and his temper.

"Who the hell do you think you are?" he bellowed in the manner of men accustomed to inspiring fear in others.

John Breen shot the whiskey glass out of his hand.

"I asked you a question, McCray." Breen's voice could have cut through rock. "If you want to live long enough to appreciate the charms of that lady there ever again, you'll answer it. Pronto."

"I never heard of this Juli—"

Breen's next shot struck McCray in the shoulder.

He fell back against the red velvet sofa, blood spurting out all over Belle, the cushions and the floor. She bit her lip but said nothing, shifting away from McCray and the blood dripping from his wound and turning a flinty gaze to the man with the gun.

McCray was sweating now, his pale gray eyes bulging from an ashen face. He clapped a hand to his wounded shoulder, trying to ignore the pain burning through it. The stranger had winged him; next time he might not be so lucky. The handsome, sunbrowned face of the man with the rifle was so set and determined, so filled with deadly purpose, that McCray was convinced there would be no reasoning with him, no putting him off, or stalling until Knife figured out a way to make a move.

"All right, you son of a bitch," McCray rasped. "I'll tell you what I know. But it isn't much. . . ."

"Start talking. Where is she?"

And so John Breen listened, the Winchester pointed directly at McCray's head, while the other man poured out a tale of frustration and failed effort. McCray explained how the Montgomery gang had been robbing him blind, how he was certain they would continue to do so until they were caught and thrown in jail—or, better yet, hanged as they deserved. And the girl, Juliana Montgomery, she had been a lucky stroke, an opportunity that had somehow slipped through their fingers. Sheriff Dane had hoped she could lead them to the gang, but then that bounty hunter, Rawdon, had run off with her before they could question her. And no, McCray admitted with pure aggravation seeping from every pore, they didn't have the smallest idea where she, Rawdon, or the Montgomery gang were hiding out.

But his men were searching. They were combing the area and it was only a matter of time . . .

Breen's fingers relaxed on the rifle trigger. McCray's words corroborated what Lucius Dane had already testified to in hopes of receiving the two-thousand-dollar reward. Breen had warned the sheriff that he'd get his money only if the information actually led him to the girl. But John Breen felt in his bones that he was close. A banked excitement flickered within him. As he studied the stocky gray-haired man before him, noting the receding hairline, the gray mustache, the heavy jowls, his own lips twisted in faint contempt. He'd heard of Line McCray from time to time, and what he knew about the man didn't impress him overmuch. McCray was doing the kinds of things *he* had done on his way up—but doing them poorly. Breen judged him stupid and shortsighted. Didn't he know that a man had to move secretly, applying pressure only behind the scenes in his acquisitions? Preserving one's name and reputation was crucial, or else when a man finally achieved the wealth and power he wanted, no one worth knowing would ever associate with him or think of doing business with him. Keep the gunplay, the coercion, the underhanded tactics to a minimum, and always as secret as possible—then kill anyone who could link you to them. That's how you built an empire and a name men respected. McCray might have money, and he had a degree of power in small towns like Plattsville, but if he wanted to be an important man in America, to achieve a position where he could really influence things—could buy men, elections, and companies the way most men bought a sack of grain—he had at least to *appear* honest.

Lack of respectability, that was McCray's problem. Breen dismissed him with scorn. Breen didn't give a

damn about McCray—all he wanted was Juliana. He had
a feeling, though, as McCray talked, that in order to get
her back, he'd have to join forces, at least temporarily,
with this man. McCray had an outfit here that was well
trained and knew the territory. He also knew something
about this bounty hunter, Cole Rawdon, whom they were
apparently up against. Rawdon was hanging on to the
girl for some reason Breen couldn't fathom. His actions
were strange. First he'd brought her in to jail, then he'd
killed two men to get her out. Why? It was loco. Maybe
he wanted to hike up the reward. Greedy bastard, Breen
thought, half admiringly. Or, he reflected as he kept the
rifle trained on McCray, maybe Rawdon was using Juliana as a way to get accepted by the Montgomery gang,
figuring if he joined forces with them against McCray
and robbed enough freight payrolls and gold shipments,
he'd pile up more money than any bounty would bring.

Hell, Breen didn't care what his motives were. All he
wanted was Juliana Montgomery. McCray wanted her
too—as a tool for locating her brothers. Well, working
together they would find both Juliana and the Montgomery gang. Whichever they located first could be forced to
lead them to the other; then he and McCray would each
have what they wanted.

When McCray stopped talking, a little silence fell on
the parlour, except for the clock ticking on the mantel.
Belle Mallory didn't move, neither did McCray or Knife
Jackson. Then Breen nodded.

"All right, your story makes sense to me. You're not
going to die just yet after all, McCray."

Knife Jackson, held all this time to silence by the fact
that Bart Mueller had a Colt revolver pointed at his
heart, could contain himself no longer. "Now tell us who
you are and what you want," he snarled. His black eyes
glinted with rage. "Nobody busts in on Mr. McCray like
this—you hear me? No one."

Breen's gaze was nailed to the sweat on McCray's face. "You may have heard of me, McCray," he said quietly. "John Breen."

McCray sagged back against the sofa cushions once more, as if he had been struck by another bullet. He gaped for a full minute at the tall, wide-shouldered man before him. *John Breen.* Breen was a legend. He was McCray's idol, the man he had tried to emulate in building his fortune. He himself had amassed a fair bundle of prosperity, but John Breen—why, he was the master of a kingly empire. Above all, he was a man McCray had always dreamed of someday doing business with, and that alone would mark the pinnacle of his achievements.

But Knife Jackson was spoiling everything.

"I don't care who the hell you say you are," Knife spat, his fingers flexing open and shut convulsively as he resisted the suicidal impulse to go for his gun. His scarred, pockmarked face looked hideous in the glare of the afternoon sunlight spilling past Belle Mallory's parted velvet curtains. His tar-black eyes shone malevolently as he stared in turn at Breen and each of his three men. "Put your gawdamned guns away and let me get a doctor for Mr. McCray or—"

"Shut up, Knife," McCray bit out. He raised himself unsteadily to his feet. Blood still gushed from his wound and his face was abnormally pale, but he held out his good hand with a smile pasted on his face. "It's a pleasure, Mr. Breen, a real pleasure. If I'd known who you were, all this unpleasantness could have been avoided. I'm only too happy to assist you in any way that I can, sir."

"I'm pleased to hear it."

"I understand there's a bounty out on the Montgomery girl." McCray's knees buckled, and he recovered his balance and his composure with visible effort. "That's all I know, Mr. Breen, but does that by any chance have something to do with why you want her?"

"My reasons are none of your damn business, McCray." But Breen lowered the rifle. He smoothed his mustache, glancing about the garish, overfurnished parlour with a scornful eye.

"I'm hoping to buy a ranch in these parts," McCray informed him quickly. Suddenly the velvet curtains and overstuffed sofa and chairs, the gilt-framed paintings and flocked wallpaper, even the sweetly perfumed air of the two-story boardinghouse, which before he had thought elegant and fashionable, now seemed cheap, ridiculous. "This ranch I'm buying—it's a magnificent place—soon as I can set the deal with the current owner, I'll be moving in," McCray assured him. "In the meantime, I've taken up temporary residence here—of course, I've rented out the entire house for my men," he bragged. He glanced over at the blood-spattered woman sitting like a tainted statue on the edge of the sofa. Belle Mallory had been through fire and flood in her life, and she knew she could get past an encounter with a Winchester, if she didn't make any stupid moves.

"Belle, don't just sit there," McCray said impatiently. "Where are your manners, woman? Get some whiskey— or maybe brandy—for our guest. Mr. Breen is a very important man."

"Line, it seems to me the first thing *you'd* want is a doctor . . ." she remarked quietly, getting to her feet after Breen's nod of approval.

"Don't need one. This is nothing but a flesh wound. He barely nicked me." McCray gave a slight, forced laugh. "Good shot, by the way, Mr. Breen."

Breen didn't bother to reply. Line McCray and his bootlicking ways, his ambition and nauseating conceit, were of no interest to him—except as they helped him track down Juliana. "Bart," he said suddenly, with a glance at his foreman, "why don't you and the boys show this fellow"—he jerked his thumb toward Knife—"over to the Ten Gallon and buy him a drink. And don't come back or let anyone in here until I say so. Mr. McCray and I have business to discuss—alone."

To the woman, waiting stony-eyed for orders, he said politely enough, "You can bring that brandy in here right away. Along with some bandages and liniment for Mr. McCray's shoulder. Can't have him bleeding to death before he's served his purpose, now can I, ma'am?"

He turned to McCray when they were alone and regarded the stocky gray-haired man through glinting topaz eyes. "We're going to go through every detail again, McCray, down to the color of Wade Montgomery's hat. And then I'm going to figure out a way for you to catch this pesky band of thieves."

"I appreciate your help, Mr. Breen, I truly do. And let me just assure you now that whatever I can do to repay you . . ."

"Oh, you will repay me, McCray. Believe me, you will."

From the cold-as-a-coffin smile on Breen's face, Line McCray had no doubt of the truth behind his words.

At the precise moment when John Breen fired his gun into Line McCray's shoulder, Cole was subduing the urge to blast Gil Keedy full of holes.

The young Texan's offense was plain for everyone to see: He was dancing in the cabin on Stick Mountain with Juliana, one tune after another. Grinning like a fool, he spun her around the floor, his arm encircling her waist, his eyes twinkling like summer stars, his Texas drawl grating on Cole's ears like sand across marble.

The other men danced with her, too, of course—all except Cole—but it was Keedy who really infuriated him. Maybe it was the way Juliana looked at the red-haired cowboy, her eyes all sparkly one minute, then soft and dreamy the next. Or maybe it was the way she laughed so delightedly at everything he whispered to her, or the fact that when she was dancing with him, she didn't appear aware of anyone or anything else.

It's what you wanted, isn't it? Cole asked himself angrily as he sprawled on a chair in the corner and watched the slender girl whirl like a graceful butterfly across the room. *She's turning her attention elsewhere, setting her sights on Keedy. And why not? He's all the things you're not—steady, good-natured, the settling-down type.* He'd take good care of her.

But would he make her happy? Remembering the rapturous way she'd stared up at him in the feather bed, the glow and happiness radiating from her eyes, Cole wondered if she could really feel for Keedy the way she'd seemed to feel about him. It hurt just thinking about it. But he hoped so, for Juliana's sake. Keedy would bring her security and peace.

So why was he having so much trouble resisting the urge to jump up and shove his fist down that scrawny Texan's throat?

I don't belong here. Cole took a deep breath, studying Juliana's brothers as she collapsed in a chair beside them at last, taking a sip of the wine that Skunk handed her. This cabin full of people, full of warmth, comradeship, a sense of festivity. Even with the danger surrounding them on all sides, a danger Cole smelled the way he smelled coffee when it was fresh-brewed and hot—even with all that, the Montgomery gang, Juliana, and Keedy too—all seemed to belong, to feel comfortable and at ease with one another, to be able to shed their cares and enjoy the companionship of an evening dancing and laughing and warming themselves before a fire. Cole didn't know how to do that. It had been years since he'd had any sense of family, any real link with another human being, and he felt cramped and stifled here. He wanted to be out there in the mountains, staring into a campfire beneath the stars, with the wind and the night creatures for company, and—

He stopped short. He'd been about to wish that Juliana was part of that picture too. He'd like to have her out there in the mountains with him, lying beside him on the fragrant grass, her hair waving in the night breeze and the moonlight cool, soft upon her face. He'd like to kiss each one of those adorable freckles marching across her nose, then undo the buttons of that dress she was wearing, and slowly, relentlessly make love to her beneath the Arizona stars.

What had happened to his urge for solitude, pure and simple? He was a loner, right? He didn't need anybody.

Damn, what had she done to him?

His throat dry, he had a sudden vision of her the way she'd looked this afternoon, holding that baby. The sight of it had done queer things to his heart. Tender feelings were new to Cole. He couldn't afford them, not in his line of work. A wife and a baby were loco things for him to wish for.

Besides, wishes didn't come true. He'd learned that years ago in the orphanage.

I don't belong here, he thought again, with even more bitter certainty, and he stood up, drawing the glances of Gray Feather and Yancy from their hotly contested checkers match. Without looking at Juliana, whose head was bent close to Keedy's before the fire, he stalked to the door of the cabin and left.

Juliana's heart fell when she saw him leave. Secretly, the entire time she'd danced with Gil, flirted with him, and chattered like a mad parrot with everyone in the cabin, she'd kept waiting for Cole to come over to her, to invite her to dance, or even simply to glare at her in that cool, infuriating way of his—anything to show her that somewhere deep down he did care. But he didn't. Not once had he tried to speak to her or even glanced at her with more than passing interest. She felt as though a huge weight were sitting on top of her heart, pressing out all her breath, all her life's blood.

Just because she'd been a belle in St. Louis, did that make her think she could snare the interest of any man she wanted? Cole Rawdon had merely made use of her while she was near at hand. Then his interest had waned. She'd better accept that and forget him.

But she had to swallow hard to choke back a sob of pain.

"Come here, little sister." Wade drew her to the corner. His hand clamped her shoulder firmly, but it emanated loving warmth. It was the first time he'd ever been called upon to offer advice for this particular type of ailment—Lord knew, Tommy would have slugged him for it—but the look of misery on his sister's face left him no choice. He couldn't bear to see her so unhappy any longer, and only prayed, even as he prepared to scold her, that he would never be afflicted with these despicable pangs of love. "You don't have to put on any playacting with me. I can see what's troubling you, Juliana—the same thing that's gnawing at Rawdon." Wade sighed. "Hell, why don't you just go out there and talk to him? Or better yet, give him a kiss and tell him all is forgiven!"

Juliana's mouth fell open. Then she shut it with a snap. "Wade, you'd do well to mind your own business. There is nothing to forgive. There is nothing between me and Cole Rawdon at all. Except perhaps . . . gratitude. He did save my life on more than one occasion."

"Ahuh."

The skeptical expression on his face made her sputter, "Oh, you're almost as insufferable as he is. Men—how do women ever learn to tolerate you? Even my own brother . . ."

"What's this?" Tommy loped up, throwing an arm across her shoulders. "Is big brother giving you trouble, peanut? Say the word and I'll wipe the floor with him."

"Think you can?" Wade's impatience at having this private conversation interrupted showed in the cool sparkle of his eyes.

"Easy," Tommy returned. "Just watch me . . ."

But Juliana threw herself between them. "I remember when Mama used to have to send you to opposite corners of the store and give you both chores to do till nightfall to keep you from fighting. Do I have to do the same thing?"

The challenging look left Tommy's face. "Do you remember her, Juliana? Mama, I mean. You were so little back then . . ."

"I do." Strangely, her mother's memory was with her now stronger than it had been for many years. Being with Wade and Tommy, so different in some ways from the rambunctious boys she remembered, yet in other ways so much the same, was bringing the memories back as strongly as good warm kitchen smells wafting out an open window, beckoning her back to a childhood before death and loss had left her alone.

"She used to sing while she was cooking supper. All different snatches of songs, all mixed together. They sounded pretty, the way she did it. And I remember how her hair felt like satin when she used to brush it out at night. We'd take turns. She'd brush mine, and then she'd let me brush hers—oh, a hundred times."

Tommy's eyes had taken on a faraway look. "She smelled like lemon verbena. I swear I never smell lemon verbena without thinking of her."

Wade's usually keen expression had softened as the memories flooded over him as well, warm as summer rain. "She was a fine woman," he said in a low tone. Of the three of them, he probably remembered her best. "She was sad a lot of the time. I think . . . she was always grateful for Pa marrying her and taking her away from that saloon where she used to work. She hated it there, she told me once. It's hard to imagine Ma in a place like that, but I guess she had no one to help her and she needed the money. But Ma—a saloon was the last place she belonged. Ma was always gentle, quiet. When I fell off Elam Potter's roof and broke my arm, I remember how that night she tiptoed in my room when she thought I was asleep and just stroked her hand across my cheek, over and over. It was light as a swan's feather."

"You're right," Tommy said slowly. "Even when she'd be so angry with us you'd expect her to shake us, she'd just tell us how disappointed she was and set us some chore to do, but she never laid a hand on us in anger."

"Pa didn't either, but more times than not he was sorely tempted," Wade put in dryly. "Do you remember when we decided to teach Juliana how to row a boat after Sunday school, and she fell in the creek and got her new dress muddier than the Mississippi?"

"I remember that day!" Giggling, Juliana stared from one to the other of them. "Mama had just finished sewing the dress the night before. It had pink and white ribbons on the sleeves and a cunning little pocket made of lace. By the time you fished me out of the water, the pocket was torn and there was a tadpole inside it!"

"And you were muddy from head to toe!" Tommy finished, groaning.

"And mad as a hornet! You kicked both of us in the shins and accused us of dunking you on purpose!"

"We did." Tommy grinned from ear to ear.

Juliana gasped and grabbed him by the shirt. "I always knew it," she cried. "But you two denied it up and down for days."

"Pa punished us by making us chop wood for old widow Dodd for a month. Without accepting a cent of payment. When I think of the blisters I had . . ."

"Pa could have done a lot worse," Wade retorted. "When I think of some of the pranks we pulled . . ."

Suddenly, Juliana's eyes filled with tears. Happy tears, mingled with those of sorrow. Their parents were gone, murdered by drunken outlaws ransacking the store, but Wade and Tommy were *here*. They were living reminders that once she had had a home, a family all her own, maybe not the grand house in St. Louis that belonged to Uncle Edward, but a cozy place that had been all Montgomery, with love and kindness and shared talk and meals and dreams. How different their lives might have been if only that day hadn't happened, if only she had not come home from school all alone and found the blood . . .

"You never let me see them," she said suddenly, and Wade shot her a sober glance. "Mama and Papa. I remember coming up on the porch—and there was blood seeping under the door. You and Tommy were behind me, playing tag, and you ran up suddenly and saw me just reaching for the door. You grabbed me back and wouldn't let me go in."

"Good thing too." Tommy cleared his throat. "It wasn't anything too pretty."

"As it was you had nightmares for a week following. Maybe longer. We don't know all that happened after you went to live with Uncle Edward and Aunt Katharine."

I still had nightmares. But my imaginings were far worse than anything I might have actually seen. Those dreams . . . She wouldn't let herself continue the thought. Not seeing what those outlaws had done had perhaps been worse than if she *had* seen. Her mind had visualized it all a thousand times, each scene more bloody and gruesome than the next. Maybe that was why the very sight of blood always affected her so intensely. It always reminded her of that puddle seeping out under the door. . . .

"Wade, Tommy." She grasped both of them by the hand. "You've never . . . hurt anyone in any of your holdups, have you?"

"No, Juliana." Wade squeezed her hand. His expression was fixed intently upon her as he looked down into her earnest face. "We've never hurt anyone, except some gun-totin' polecats who've tried to shoot our heads off first. There seem to be a lot of 'em out there."

"That bounty hunter of yours," Tommy put in darkly. "Did you ever ask him that question? He's the kind of hombre who might harbor a mean streak."

"You're wrong, Tommy." Wade shook his head. "Rawdon's not the mean kind—just fast. Fast as he needs to be."

"Think he's faster than me?" Intrigued, Tommy raised his brows.

"That's one thing we'll never need to find out," Juliana informed him firmly. "We're all working on the same side, remember?"

"I reckon so, but it sure seems strange. I'm used to avoiding bounty hunters, not inviting 'em to sleep in my hideout." He gazed about through suddenly narrowed eyes. "Where is Rawdon anyway?"

"He left." Juliana would have let it go at that, but Wade wasn't ready to give up.

"He said he'd be camping out down by the gully. I gather he's not used to a lot of company," he remarked, trying to catch her eye.

Gil Keedy appeared at Juliana's elbow at that moment. "Another dance—or are you too tuckered out?"

She hesitated, gazing into his flushed, eager face, reading the warmth in his eyes. Maybe Gil was just in love with love—maybe he didn't yet know if he preferred her or Josie—or if he fancied himself in love with both of them, as she'd heard Tommy was fond of doing.

Why couldn't it be Cole? she asked herself miserably.

*Why couldn't Cole be looking at me like this, with puppy
dog eyes, and his arms outstretched, waiting?*

Because that isn't the kind of man he is. He doesn't
show his emotions, he locks them away. Except for that
night . . . the night he had told her about Fire Mesa,
shared the horrible ordeal of his childhood, and turned to
her for comfort. That night he had made her feel loved,
trusted, desired. Cherished in a way she had never felt
before.

"Juliana?" Gil's voice recalled her to the cabin, to
Gray Feather and Yancy absorbed in their checkers
game, to Skunk repairing his saddle, to Wade and
Tommy looking at her as though she were drifting on a
sea a thousand miles away. And to Gil, dear Gil, waiting
for his dance.

"I'm sorry," she said quietly, meeting his gaze directly.
Sorrow filled her heart. She wished she could return his
feelings, she wished she didn't have to hurt him. "I don't
feel up to dancing anymore." She made a decision. "I
need some air."

Wade smiled. Tommy regarded her through narrowed
eyes.

"Excuse me . . ."

And she was gone, flying through the cabin door and
out into the star-frosted night. Letting her eyes adjust to
the dark, she moved off toward the gully. Down the trail,
past the clump of rocks, beyond the rise where the piñons
stood like sentinels and the ground dipped, she worked
her way through the darkness until she saw the faint
glow of his campfire up ahead.

Cole was on his feet at the first sound of her approach,
gun drawn. When he saw her slender figure, her yellow
organdy gown shimmering in the moonlight, the breath
caught in his throat. She came toward him like a ghost in
a dream.

The gun went back in his holster. "You shouldn't be

out here," he said. What he really wanted was to seize her in his arms.

Juliana forced a smile. "That isn't for you to decide." She couldn't resist adding, "I'm not your prisoner anymore, remember?"

"Wade should have more sense than to let you wander around in the dark alone. Hell, even Tommy should have more sense than that."

"I make my own decisions," she reminded him.

"Then maybe you should be sure they're the right ones."

She let that hang in the air between them for a moment, then whispered, "I am sure, Cole."

A muscle worked in his jaw. He was fighting the impulse to kiss her. If he started, he wouldn't stop. And all his resolutions—made for her own good, as well as his—would go up in smoke.

"Where's Keedy?" he asked in a hard voice as he hunkered down cross-legged before the fire once more. Joining him, arranging her skirts prettily upon the blanket she sat on, she saw that he had been doing another carving, similar to the horse's head she had seen in his pack that other time. This horse was a beauty, too, a replica of the white stallion they had watched together. With a regal flowing mane and proud neck, the chiseled figure, though incomplete, showed promise of graceful, powerful lines.

"What did you say?" she asked absently, absorbed by the fine work he had done.

"I said, where's Keedy?"

"I don't really know—or care."

"Could've fooled me."

A flame of hope leapt to life within her, glowing in the very center of her heart. He was jealous, after all. Maybe. Maybe she wasn't making a complete idiot of herself, then, coming out here like this, ready to throw herself at him. Just maybe, he wanted her here more than he could admit.

"Have you thought of a plan to get McCray?"

"I'm working on it."

"As far as I can tell, there's no one around. You can tell me . . ."

But in glancing facetiously around the small clearing where he had made his camp, her gaze fell on his saddle pack just behind him, faintly illuminated by the glowing flames of the fire. Protruding from the pack was the lacy edge of a blouse. What in the world . . .

Juliana reached back and pulled the pack forward, staring into it in amazement. When Cole groaned and made a move to take it from her, she pushed his hand away and then withdrew the creamy blouse and bright Mexican skirt folded inside. As she did so, a small raw-hide pouch spilled out, and she heard a jangle from within.

"You might as well see it all," Cole said between clenched teeth, and dumped the contents of the bag into her palm.

A gold bracelet, and blue and red hair ribbons. What was all this?

"Cole—is there a naked woman lying in the brush waiting for me to leave?" she demanded, only half joking.

The look he gave her made her heart quake with fear that it was true. "Come on out, Maria," he called, then burst out laughing at her dismayed expression.

"Don't be an idiot, Juliana," he told her, running both hands through his hair. Part of him wanted to laugh at her crazy assumption, and the other part wanted to curse the fact that now he'd have to tell her the truth.

"I lied the other day when I told you I didn't get that surprise I promised you. I did get it. Only . . ."

"These are for me?" Delight swept across her face. Even in the firelight, her green eyes glowed with pure feminine wonder. "Oh, Cole, they're *beautiful*. But why didn't you tell me? Why did you lie?"

Embarrassed, he turned back to stare into the flames, unable to meet her gaze another moment. "I . . ." Damn, his voice sounded as hoarse and choked as a strangled prairie dog's. "I didn't think you'd want 'em. They're nothing much compared to those things your brothers gave you . . ."

Suddenly she understood. "But they're beautiful," she said quietly. "I wouldn't trade them for diamonds and silks. How could you keep them a secret from me?" She held up the skirt, the bright folds sifting through her fingers like a kaleidoscope of gorgeous colors. "This is so lovely. And the lacework on the blouse is exquisite."

She jumped up and began working at the long row of pearl buttons on her dress.

"What are you doing?" he growled. He came to his feet, regarding her in shock and a good deal of fascination as she began stripping off the fancy dress, wriggling as it slid down her arms, to her waist, over her hips.

"I'm going to put them on."

His eyes narrowed. He knew that too sweet air of innocence. She was trying to drive him mad, that's what she was doing, standing there in her chemise, bold as brass, that delectable smile curving her lips. He could see the rosy tips of her nipples beneath the filmy chemise. Her skin glowed with the pearly luminescence of the moon itself as she stood before him, daring him to touch her. His heart galloped in his chest. As she gazed up into his eyes, her expression was so hopeful, so loving, that his insides turned to fire, and all his resolve withered like old bones in the dust.

"Unless you have a better idea," she whispered.

He pulled her up against his chest. "I just might, Juliana."

He snaked his arms around her waist so tightly, she

gasped, but he silenced her with his mouth. He kissed her hard and thoroughly, saying with his mouth what he could not put in words, his arms clamped around her as if he was afraid she would disappear into the clear, cold air in a puff of smoke. But she was soft and real in his arms, and she smelled of lilac.

He never stopped kissing her until her mouth was sore and swollen. He felt her trembling as he gathered her close in his arms, and buried his face in the rippling, scented waves of her hair.

"Oh, Cole, make love to me," she whispered. Her mouth burned from his kisses, and triumph made her dizzy. Her heart rose as she saw the yearning in his eyes, the tenderness that she had feared she'd never see again. There was doubt, too, tempering his passion, and she knew suddenly, instinctively, what he was thinking, what was holding him back.

"I don't care about tomorrow—don't think about it," she begged. "Let's just have tonight. One night—for us, Cole. I love you. Please, let's have one night just for us."

"One night won't be enough," he said, his voice so low and fierce it sent shivers down her spine. His mouth was hot against the pulse at her throat. She could feel his breath, the pounding of his heart against hers. "Juliana, you would tempt a saint." He laughed suddenly, an exultant, tortured sound caught between savagery and tenderness. "And if there's one thing I'm not, it's a saint."

I love you. That's what she'd said. He ought to send her packing and then ride as far as he could go. But he only held her tighter.

His eyes were dark, silvery blue in the moonlight. Glinting with a desire Juliana could not mistake. But beneath the desire, she saw the longing, the gentleness that she had never seen when he looked at anyone else. *He needs me too,* Juliana realized, *as much as I need him.* Overwhelmed by an almost painful rush of warmth and love, she melted against him, cupping his face in her hands, kissing him with all the fervent love in her heart. That he wanted her as much as she wanted him was all that mattered. There were the two of them, the stars, soft earth, and the wild Arizona night.

They needed nothing else.

Hot kisses. Sweet, sweet words.

Snow-puff clouds drifted overhead through a sky dark as blood, while beneath the towering shadow of the mountain, deep within the velvet-grassed gully, Cole and Juliana spoke the language of lovers in a poem as timeless as the earth itself. The air was cold, sharp with the biting tang of pine, but their passion was hotter than the scorching plains of the desert.

Morning stole in, shell-pink radiance dusted with lavender and gold, and caught them entwined, sleepy, sated.

The world looked different somehow.

They awoke, sat up, stared at each other. Juliana wished the dawn away; she'd have given anything to live the night again. Her words from the evening before came back to haunt her. Thinking of them, she chewed her lip.

"Well," she said, almost to herself, "it's over."

He reached for her, trapping her hand between both of his. "What is?"

"Our one night."

"Looks like it is." Cole sent a sardonic glance at the lightening sky, the creatures beginning to stir around them.

"Yep, it's over."

He realized too late what that sounded like. She jumped up, her cheeks bright pink, brighter than the dawn. "I . . . I'll go back now . . ."

She shook. Embarrassed. No, humiliated. What had she done? Thrown herself at him, promised it would mean nothing afterward. She had vowed to leave him alone and never bother him again—not in precisely those words, but that's what it had meant. Just for tonight, she had said. How could she have been such a fool? She wanted to stay with him forever. But in the cold, clear light of day it seemed impossible that he could want the same thing.

Naked, he was even more ruggedly beautiful than he was with his clothes on. She found herself staring as she always did at his muscled, dark-furred chest. She reached for her chemise. No. Time to go. Time to preserve what was left of her pride, her dignity.

There wasn't much left worth preserving.

Cole fought the urge to catch her in his arms and make love to her all over again. Lord, she was beautiful. And so sweet, a sweetness that was real and honest and whole, that came from the very core of her soul. He wanted to grab her, hold her, tell her she was stuck with him forever . . .

But he had to think. He didn't want to make a promise he couldn't keep. And he couldn't keep any promises if he was dead. He didn't know if he'd live long enough even to try to make it all work, so better to say nothing.

Come live with me and be my love. Words from a poem, half remembered, danced suddenly through his brain as the sun washed the sky with sunlight and Juliana tugged on her gown. His mother had read that aloud to Caitlin many years ago. The words had always stuck in his mind, probably because he had never ever thought they would apply to him. *Come live with me and be my love.*

He wanted suddenly, fiercely, to say them to Juliana, to beg her to stay.

He'd have to deal with McCray—and eventually John Breen. If he survived that, then maybe . . .

She deserved to be loved. Protected. Cherished. If he ever thought he could give her the life she deserved, he would do it in a moment, but Cole wasn't sure he'd ever get a chance at that kind of life. That kind of happiness was for other people, not him.

She was on her way before he realized it, half running from the gully, a slip of a girl whose every movement tore at his heart.

He could have caught her easily, but he just stared after her. If he survived what lay ahead, maybe they'd have a chance—if she still wanted him. If he could make her happy.

But first he had to settle things with McCray.

He did have a plan, and it was time to share it with Wade Montgomery.

Cole set his mind to the dangerous task ahead and tried not to think about Juliana. It wasn't easy. The woman was a thief, after all.

She had stolen his heart.

· 24 ·

Silence filled every corner of the hideout on Stick Mountain as Wade finished outlining the plan.

"Questions?" he asked, letting his glance fall briefly on each person in the room.

Juliana rose. "I have one. Why can't I go with you?"

Meeting her determined gaze, Wade sighed, but it was Tommy who answered.

"Because, little sister," he said from the bench at the little pine table, "we're not letting you risk your neck in the heart of this battle. And that's that."

"So I'm supposed to sit here doing nothing all day while the rest of you are risking your lives?"

"Yep." Tommy's grin received no answering response from the tight-lipped girl.

"You and Skunk will have to keep an eye on Josie. Make sure she's all right. Besides," Wade pointed out, coming to her and putting his hands on her shoulders, "if something does go wrong, you and Skunk and Gil are going to have to take care of Josie and Kevin—and all of you are going to have to get to New Mexico pronto. Skunk and Gil know the best trail."

His words filled her with alarm, but that only made her more determined. "I'm not going anywhere without you and Tommy," Juliana informed him.

"Course you're not." Wade flicked her cheek with his finger. "So wait here like a good girl and we'll celebrate like blazes tonight when this thing is over."

Skunk sighed dramatically. "My one chance to be alone with a beautiful gal and she'd rather get shot at than stay with me."

Everyone laughed—except Juliana.

He sent her such a beseeching glance that she relented with a tiny, reluctant smile. "Well, I suppose someone has to keep an eye on Josie and Kevin, after all. And make sure you don't burn the biscuits."

Wade turned to Gil Keedy. "You all set? Seems to me you've got the most dangerous part in all this."

"Pshaw. I reckon I can drop a hint in those varmints' ears and get back in one piece." Gil smiled, unconcerned.

"Well, be careful. Yancy, get together the equipment you're going to need." Wade was already moving to his pack, checking it for supplies and ammunition. While a bee buzzed in through the open window, then zoomed out again into the summer heat, Tommy and Gray Feather did the same.

Suddenly, Juliana realized that Cole had disappeared from the cabin. When had that happened? He'd been there when Wade had first started explaining the day's plan, and she hadn't even noticed him slip away.

"Where's Cole?" Her voice sounded loud to her own ears.

She hurried to the window and peered out. Arrow was gone, too.

Wade replied calmly, "He wanted to start out ahead of the rest of us. Don't worry, we'll meet up with him."

He hadn't said good-bye. Emptiness settled in the pit of her stomach, cold and heavy as a great stone. What if he never came back?

What if none of them came back? She watched in growing trepidation as her brothers readied themselves for the day's confrontation. They didn't know if they'd be facing one man—or ten. Juliana shuddered. She couldn't lose either of them. And she couldn't lose Cole either.

Clammy fear possessed her as she watched them ride off.

Finding herself alone in the cabin with Skunk and the breakfast dishes, worry knotted her stomach. She came to the realization that by the time sunset came to Fire Mesa, she could very possibly have lost them all.

Line McCray was pacing up and down Belle Mallory's carpet when Knife Jackson ran up the front steps of the boardinghouse and banged open the front door.

"Word in town has it that Joseph Wells is selling out to Cole Rawdon. Today," he announced, fairly exploding with the news.

"What?" McCray choked back a string of epithets. What else could go wrong? Fire Mesa must not be allowed to slip through his fingers. It was the prize piece of land in this entire territory. He was going to build his ranch there—a ranch to rival John Breen's legendary Twin Oaks. Not to mention the railroad that was to be built through one section of it in a deal already negotiated, guaranteed to bring him a small fortune. McCray's fury zeroed in on that wishy-washy fool Joseph Wells. He had enough to think about trying to guard his damned payroll tomorrow, without having to whip Wells back into line as well. He was certain the Montgomery gang was planning to hit the gold shipment, but he didn't have a clue as to where or when. All he knew was that he couldn't let them get away with another holdup. He'd be a laughingstock if he did—and it would be damned hard to meet the month's expenses without that gold.

The Montgomerys had to be stopped. And when he had them, he'd make them pay for all the trouble they'd cost him—and for stealing that widow woman right out from under his nose. McCray couldn't understand how a bunch of second-rate outlaws could outwit a man of his resources—but somehow they had. Luckily, John Breen was in the picture now. It was Breen who had recommended they post men in all the saloons, waiting and listening. The gang had to get information on the payroll shipment from somewhere, and when they made their move, McCray would find out about it. If they could capture just one of them—anyone asking questions about the payroll shipment and the movements associated with it—it would be an easy matter to force him into revealing the whereabouts and plans of the rest of the gang. . . .

Knife's gravelly voice broke into his thoughts.

"There's something else, Mr. McCray. Bart Mueller was in the Ten Gallon with me a few minutes ago and he hightailed it out of there to find Breen. Said you'd better meet 'em over at the hotel pronto. Something's up. Don't know what it's all about, but he was pretty fired up."

"Damn." McCray didn't know what that was all about either, but he had a feeling he was going to find out. He only hoped it was good news. He and Breen could use a break.

"Let's go." McCray grabbed his hat. "Get the boys ready to ride. Bring Dane along, too. Soon as I meet with Breen, we're going to pay a visit to Mr. Joseph Wells. I'm not playing games anymore—the deed for Fire Mesa will be in *my* hands by the end of the day—whether Mr. Wells lives to hand it over to me himself or not."

Gil Keedy had already spread the rumor about Fire Mesa in the Ten Gallon Saloon. He guessed it wouldn't take long to reach McCray's ears, and only wished he could see the expression on the man's face when he learned he was about to lose that prime piece of property. Gil knew he should leave town immediately, now that his part in Rawdon's scheme was done. But he didn't really feel he was in any particular danger. No one identified him with the Montgomery gang, and he had passed on the rumor in such a way that it would be difficult for anyone to trace it back to him. Besides, he wanted to go over to Miller's store and pick up a few supplies for Josie. She needed some flannel and wool to start sewing winter clothes for the baby. Gil felt the urge to buy her a little something, too. And of course, he told himself, something for Juliana.

Striding across the deserted streets of Plattsville, Gil fretted over his feelings for these two very different women. Juliana was like a moonbeam. Beautiful, magical, elusive. He couldn't quite catch her in his hands. Even when she was with him, Gil reflected wistfully, her thoughts were elsewhere. He could sense it. When Rawdon was near, Juliana seemed to come alive.

Josie was as solid and real, as warmly attentive and attuned to him as a willow tree rooted to the earth. His heart didn't buck like a wild bronc every time she smiled at him, the way it did with Juliana, but at the same time, he did have a nice warm feeling when she plunked the baby into his arms while she poured him a cup of coffee. When they had worked together in the house, making that one little room comfortable for her and Kevin, he had found himself imagining how nice it would be always to come home to that warmly smiling face, to the pleasant sound of her voice and laughter.

The more he thought about Josie, the more he felt a sudden urge to see her. But he'd better ride by the cabin first, he decided, and make sure everything was all right with Juliana and Skunk. Then he'd go to Josie with some tins of chocolate from the store, the fabric she'd been wanting, and whatever else he saw in Miller's that looked as if it would appeal to a lady.

Gil was so immersed in his thoughts as he came out of the general store a short time later with a parcel tucked under his arm that he didn't notice the cowboy lounging across the street, watching him from beneath the wide brim of his hat. Nor did he see the men staring at him from behind the curtains of the window above the saloon. He headed toward the hitching post where his horse was tethered, pleased that the rumor about Fire Mesa had already reached the merchants in the store, and surely by now, he assumed, Line McCray. He prayed Rawdon's plan would work. But in the meantime his part in it was over. All he had to do was keep an eye on both Juliana and Josie today until this thing was finished.

Not exactly a chore to Gil's way of thinking.

He was whistling as he headed out of town.

But Gil wasn't the only one pleased.

John Breen's topaz eyes were gleaming with excitement as he turned from the window overlooking the street. "It's Keedy, all right," he said to Bart Mueller. "This couldn't possibly be a coincidence." He slapped his foreman on the back. "Good work, Bart. We've just about got her."

Half turning, he smiled at Line McCray. "If we follow that fellow's trail, he'll lead us straight to Juliana Montgomery—and possibly the entire Montgomery gang as well."

"How do you know that?"

But Breen was already opening the back room door and answered without a backward glance. "No time to explain. Just take my word for it that he's hooked up with that girl. Get your men together and meet me downstairs pronto. My man Samuels is following him and will leave us a clear trail, but I don't want to fall too far behind."

"Hold on, Breen." McCray cleared his throat as the other man wheeled, frowning. "I've . . . got a little problem."

A frown creased Breen's face as McCray explained about Fire Mesa, and his need to "persuade" Wells to sell to him and not Rawdon before it was too late. Breen heard him out, though he was clearly impatient to be off.

"Take Jackson here and some of the other men, if this is so damned important to you. You can meet up with us later, after you've taken care of Wells. Since Keedy headed south, we'll rendezvous at the river. Someone will meet you there to show you the way. Unless of course," he added sarcastically, "you don't want the Montgomery gang as badly as you want this piece of land. In that case, I'll just grab the girl and be done with it, and the gang can rot in hell for all I care."

McCray followed him down the murkily lit stairway, his determination mounting. "I'll have Fire Mesa, Cole Rawdon, and the Montgomerys, Mr. Breen." Confidence nearly made him do a jig, but he kept his zeal in check. "See you at the river by midafternoon."

John Breen's brain was already clicking ahead, to what the rest of the day would bring. All this time, he'd waited to get his hands on Juliana Montgomery. And now that jackass Keedy would lead him straight to her.

"I want fifteen men at the stables within the quarter hour," he told Bart Mueller as they paused in the noisy, smoke-filled cave of the saloon. "No one's coming back to town or getting within a yard of a bottle of rotgut until we've got the girl."

· 25 ·

An ominous air seemed to envelop the mountains as Juliana helped Skunk with the horses and the chores, trying not to think about what was going on at the main house of Fire Mesa. Even the birds twittered with high-pitched excitement, and the leaves of the junipers crackled nervously in the wind. Or so it seemed to Juliana. Every time a branch snapped outside as some creature stirred across it, every time the wind howled down from the hills, blowing bits of dust and leaves, she jumped.

Had Cole and Wade and Tommy outsmarted Line Mc-Cray, or had something gone very wrong?

She told herself again and again that in a little while, they would all come riding back down the trail, rowdy with victory. But her fingers shook as she swept the broom about the cabin and scrubbed the little pine table where they'd all eaten breakfast a few hours ago. She wondered how Skunk could whistle so lightheartedly and hum little snatches of songs as he chopped firewood for the stove beneath the blazing sun. She wanted to scream with frustration.

At noon she could bear it no longer. She whisked herself outside and down to the gully, over Skunk's protests. She sat alone on a smooth white stone jutting out from the wild grasses, and strained her ears, listening. Foolish to think she could hear gunshots or shouts, foolish to think she could discern anything that was going on at Fire Mesa. But the need to know something was burning a hole inside of her.

All the people she loved, all the people she had left in the world, were there, facing danger. She felt useless and helpless in this peaceful neck of the mountain, hidden from the enemies who would destroy all those she loved.

Love. She had come west looking for it, in a fashion. She had wanted to find her brothers, to build a life with them in the glorious freedom of this vast, untamed land. If Wade and Tommy returned today having rid themselves of the threat posed by Line McCray, she could still do it. Yet, when she tried to picture herself in that cozy little home she had once envisioned inhabiting with Wade and Tommy, baking that rhubarb pie she had imagined, a hollow feeling spread through her. Much as she loved them, dear as they were to her, she kept picturing herself instead with Cole—welcoming him home at the door with a kiss that would show him how glad she was to have him there, sitting down to a hot breakfast with him each morning, pouring his coffee, curling under warm piles of woolen blankets with him at night.

Cole. Love. She hadn't meant it to happen—she had never imagined herself needing, wanting any man so desperately. But this man was so different from all others. When he was near she felt all her responses heightened. When he was beside her, she felt safe.

Pain knifed through her when she thought that maybe

he didn't need her as much as she needed him—that maybe he didn't love her at all.

She remembered what had happened between them last night right in this very gully, and that other night, in his cabin, that bleak little place that had been transformed into a blissful paradise consisting of the two of them and a narrow feather bed. It had all been too beautiful and too meaningful to be merely an outpouring of lust. Some stubborn instinct inside her still clung to that belief. When she considered Cole's past, the brutal tragedy of his childhood, his tormented years at the orphanage, and that vicious betrayal by Jess Burrows and Liza White, she realized it must be nearly impossible for Cole to believe in another human being or in love ever again. Any other man would have been scarred for life, scarred with hate and bitterness, with the ravages of the pain he'd known. But Cole was too strong, too tough for that. His inner strength and goodness had enabled the fine qualities he possessed to survive, to keep him sane and whole. Oh, he was lonely, he was distrustful, and he thought he didn't need anyone or anything at all. He probably didn't believe for one moment in love—but Juliana did.

I believe enough for both of us. If only I could explain that to him. All I need is a chance.

Maybe, if Line McCray walked into Cole's trap and gave up without a fight, she would get it.

Hoofbeats broke the burning stillness of the afternoon, firing across the dry dust of the land like rifle shots.

"Sounds like company," Tommy chirped, shooting an eager look at Cole as he bolted toward the window.

"Better lay down the welcome mat," the bounty hunter returned calmly.

Gray Feather took up his position at the far left parlour window; Wade and Tommy each moved into place behind curtains along the rest of the main floor.

Cole paused in the hall, trying to shake off the ghosts drifting around him. He had been here to see Wells that one day he'd left Juliana, but they'd talked outside. It was the first time he'd come back inside this house since the day his parents and sister had been killed.

Wells had made changes over the years, yet the rooms —two parlours, kitchen, study, and the winding oak staircase—were all eerily as he remembered, and he knew the sunny bedrooms above would be familiar too. A few pieces of furniture remained, tugging at his memory: the armchair where his grandfather had sat when they played chess, the little Queen Anne desk in the parlour where his mother had copied down favorite recipes for Caitlin's future use, the delicately painted seascape over the mantel, peach and yellow and blue shades—sunset colors, his mother had always said—all blending together in a tranquil scene. The rest was different. Different furnishings, different knickknacks. Yet it was home, unmistakable, immutable.

He was surprised to find that the ghosts felt friendly, at peace. The memories conjured up the moment he had stepped across the threshold this morning were not memories of death, as he had feared, but memories of life—of the days when this had been a grand and happy house, when his grandfather had run the ranch with his unique brand of wisdom and vigorous energy, and the wild horses had stormed through the canyons and arroyos like thunder, and when delicious cooking smells and his mother's and sister's laughter had filled the air with feminine delight.

McCray's voice outside in the yard blasted away the sweet, distant memories of his youth. Cole's senses jerked back to the present, and every muscle went tense, alert with that keen-edged vigilance, that ice-cold deadly concentration that was second nature to him.

"Wells, come on out here," McCray bellowed.

Pompous ass.

"We've got to have ourselves a little talk."

Not glancing sideways at Wade, Tommy, or Gray Feather, Cole opened the front door and strode out.

Sunlight slanted across the open yard, outlining in bright citrine relief the shock on Line McCray's face when he saw not the stooped, gray-haired man of slight build and watery voice whom he expected, but the tall, black-garbed bounty hunter who nailed him with a look of pure scorn.

One of McCray's riders went for his gun, his motion a blur in the sultry air. Cole drew faster, and shot the man between the eyes. The rider catapulted backward off his horse with a low, keening groan of agony, then died in the dust without another sound. Seven others, among them Lucius Dane and Knife Jackson, froze in the silence of the yard. Sweat broke out on a number of leather-skinned faces as they stared at the compelling figure that was Cole Rawdon.

Each one smelled in that instant the stench of his own imminent death.

Rawdon was not a man to take lightly. Tall, muscular, his reckless face as hard as a bullet, he skewered them all with that vividly intense blue gaze.

"Wells is gone, McCray. He sold out to me days ago. Said he'd rather sell to a dog than to you, matter of fact."

Fury and incredulity darkened McCray's face, turning his skin a mottled purple. He jerked a shaking hand at his string tie, trying to think past his outrage. He had encountered Rawdon before on occasion, but never like this, as enemies, opponents, ready to spill blood. He wanted to ask the man why in hell he had snatched that girl out of jail, why he was trying to buy this property out from under his nose, why he was making McCray's life miserable, but Line was too busy thinking about that dirty, cheating, back-stabbing Joseph Wells to bother.

He struggled for a moment with his emotions. "We had a deal," he rasped, his voice trembling with the hot fury flicking inside him. "He agreed to sell to me."

"Free country." Cole shrugged. "Man can change his mind."

He remembered Wells's relief when he'd ridden up, approaching slowly, letting the memories and feelings wash back. He had tried not to look at the corner of the yard where his mother had died. Wells had come out to greet him, smiling, wiping his brow against the heat of the day.

"Never wanted to sell to McCray, but he scared off any other buyers," he'd explained. Then he'd shaken his head. "Burned down one fellow's barn that was interested. Dirty bastard." He had shrugged. "I need to go east for some specialized medical treatment, doctor says New York or Philadelphia is the best place. Don't think I'll be coming back."

Cole had told him quietly he couldn't match McCray's price.

"Hell, I don't care about that, boy. I'd rather sell to you than to anyone—you've got a claim to this property no one else on this earth can match. I never felt quite right, the way I won it from your pa. I'll take what you've offered for it—it'll do just fine. Won't McCray be sore, when he finds out? I shore as hell don't want to be the one to tell him."

And Wells had chuckled, slapped him on the back, and packed up that very afternoon.

He'd be halfway to Philadelphia by now, Cole figured. But McCray was here, mad as hell, and there were two ways this whole thing could end. Either he could scare McCray into backing off, vamoosing out of Fire Mesa and Plattsville, leaving the Montgomerys and Josie safe or—

Or there'd be a lot of dead bodies rotting under the sun on Fire Mesa today.

Lucius Dane kicked his horse forward, his face working nervously. The sheen of sweat made his ashen skin seem to ripple. "Rawdon, why the hell are you mixed up in this? I've heard about you—you never stay in one place long enough to shine your boots. Why the hell do you want this ranch?"

"I reckon, Dane, I should have shot you that night when you got yourself locked up in your own jail cell. Puzzles me why I didn't."

"How much?" McCray rasped. "I'll buy the place from you. Right here and now. Name your price."

"Fire Mesa is not for sale."

McCray's mouth was an ugly slash in his face. "Every damn thing on this earth is for sale! Name your price, I said!"

Cole returned his frantic gaze with an expression of contempt. "Listen up, McCray, because I'm only going to make this offer once. I'm prepared to let you and these fleabag vermin of yours ride out of here alive—if you clear out of Arizona for good."

"You're prepared . . ." McCray sputtered. "These men could shoot you down right now, Rawdon, no matter how fast you are. You can't beat all of us!"

A gunshot blew his hat off his head as he finished speaking the words. Wade Montgomery's voice yelled, "He's not alone, McCray! We could cut you down like lumber right now, unless you swear to get the hell out of the territory."

"Montgomery!"

"You bet your ass!" Tommy shouted, firing rapidly into the air to punctuate his words.

Rage then surged through Line McCray in a torrential rush that swept aside caution and good judgment. A part of his brain told him to back off, to retreat, keeping his enemies hemmed in while he sent off a man to the river to summon Breen for help. Reinforcements would help him wipe out these hombres once and for all. But it stuck in McCray's craw to rely on Breen—the Montgomerys and this damned bounty hunter had pushed him far enough. He sensed the tension in all of the men around him, and knew that none of them—with the possible exception of Dane—were cowards. They'd follow him, and he'd never led them wrong yet. He'd reward them richly for victory —their only alternative was death. They'd fight like hell when he told them to start shooting. All he had to do was say the word.

One glance at the implacable set to Cole Rawdon's face triggered the fuse of McCray's frustration. He'd wipe out these bastards here and now—John Breen be damned.

"Kill 'em, boys!" he roared, spurring his mount forward with a vicious kick. Then he was shooting at Cole Rawdon, along with every other man on his side, but Rawdon dived forward into the dust and fired from the ground, the spray of his bullets killing the two men on either side of McCray, and missing McCray's head by inches.

Pandemonium broke out as gunfire erupted from inside the house and from the rocks behind McCray's outfit as well, panicking the riders. They started shooting wildly at windows and doors, then lunging for cover all about the yard as the deafening shots exploded in a cacophony of death. Horses shrieked in terror, and the fight was a blur of noise and action, grunts, shouts, shots, confusion.

From inside, Gray Feather killed a man just as he was jumping through the dining room window.

Tommy saw Lucius Dane sprint behind the shed, and went after him.

Cole, meanwhile, with a revolver in each hand, was working his way backward into the house.

Three of McCray's men suddenly made a run for the hill over which they had climbed just before descending toward the ranch house, and a mighty explosion followed them. Yancy waved an arm in triumph as the stick of dynamite he'd thrown from high in the surrounding rocks found its mark.

How many left? Cole crouched beneath the parlour window beside Wade and cast a glance around the yard. Bodies strewn everywhere. No sign of McCray. An unnatural silence descended.

Tommy crept around the shed, his boots making practically no sound in the dust. He listened, his own breath light and quick. A soft shuffling. Dane. Springing around the corner, he confronted Dane and fired. Lucius Dane fired back. The sheriff's shot zinged into the dirt, but Tommy's was true. It struck Dane straight through the heart, and he toppled face first into the dirt without uttering a sound.

The next instant, McCray and Knife Jackson both converged on Tommy at once, firing in rapid succession. He dropped to the ground, grunting at the pain slicing through his arm. A fountain of blood sprayed from his shoulder and down the expensive sleeve of his shirt. *Damn.* Rolling sideways to dodge the bullets, he sprang into a crouch and fired again, but even as his finger squeezed the trigger he saw that he was too late. Both McCray and Knife Jackson were very, very dead. Standing ten feet away, side by side, Cole Rawdon and Wade stared back at him.

"I had 'em. Didn't need any help, but as long as you're here, damn it, Wade, look what that bastard did to my shirt." His handsome young face, beneath the scowl, was pale.

When it was over, one of McCray's men escaped. The other seven lay dead beneath the glare of an amber sun. Gray Feather, too, had been wounded, a bullet piercing his chest, but Yancy, who'd seen a good many such

wounds in the war, announced that the Apache would
survive.

"And so will this varmint," he said as he gave Tommy
a playful punch in his good arm. "But we'd better load
them both on a wagon and get them to the doc in Plattsville."

They loaded up the bodies, too, in another wagon for
burial in town, since Cole didn't want McCray and his
outfit resting permanently on his land.

Wade offered to drive them into Plattsville, alongside
Yancy.

"With McCray dead, as well as that weasel Dane,
things should start getting back to normal in Plattsville,"
he reflected, wiping an arm across his perspiring face.
"And I don't think anyone's going to hold it against us
that we killed 'em."

"Hell, no, Montgomery, you and your brother will be
heroes," Cole assured him.

It was true. He'd seen it happen many times. Despite
the fact that the Montgomery gang was wanted by the
law, killing McCray had freed the townspeople from the
unscrupulous businessman's tyranny. The folks in Plattsville, once out from under his filthy thumb, would welcome the Montgomerys now with open arms, probably
give a dance in their honor.

"This means Josie can go home finally," Wade remarked, handing Tommy and Gray Feather their water
canteens before the wagons set off.

Tommy's eyes lit thoughtfully. "In that case, I might
want to stick around these parts awhile." He took a long
swig of water. His blue eyes fastened on Cole, standing
quietly beside the wagon as Yancy took up the reins.

"You're a pretty cool customer, Rawdon. I've only got
one bone to pick with you."

"What's that, Montgomery?"

"You made my sister cry." Both Cole and Wade stared

at him. It was the last thing they'd expected from the happy-go-lucky, good-natured Tommy.

"You thought I didn't notice," Tommy told Wade as he shifted more comfortably into the hay scattered through the wagon to cushion their ride to town. "But I see more than you give me credit for. I've seen her when she thought no one was looking. And I know those tears are all Rawdon's fault. Hell, anyone can see Juliana's out of her head in love with him."

Cole's eyes narrowed. "You don't know what you're talking about."

"For once, he does," Wade retorted. "Well, Rawdon, what exactly are your intentions toward our sister?"

Cole couldn't believe this. The two of them, confronting him, demanding to know about his feelings toward Juliana. He'd never answered to any man for anything in his life—now these two young outlaws, every bit as stubborn and outrageous as their sister—were trying to pin him down, make him sweat, get him to answer their questions.

Funny, he didn't mind it as much as he'd have thought.

"If you boys had any sense, you'd see right off that I'd make a terrible husband," he returned flatly. "I'm not exactly a family man . . ."

"You could be if you had your own family. Damn it, you *would* be if you married Juliana. We'd make damn sure of that," Tommy growled.

A laugh choked in Cole's throat. Cocky youngster. These Montgomerys had spunk. And gall. He thought of Juliana stealing his horse. And his gun. And demanding that he not shoot that bear.

Suddenly, something lifted inside him. Why not? Why the hell not? McCray was dead. The immediate danger was over for good. Marrying Juliana would certainly protect her from John Breen. Once he went to Colorado and dealt with Breen—as Juliana's husband—the man would have to back down. Maybe it could even be accomplished without bloodshed. No other bounty hunter would dare try to get to her if they knew she was Cole's wife.

As his wife, Juliana would be safe. But would she be happy? Did he really have it in his power to live a steady, regular life, to break old lonesome habits and carve out a piece of happiness with a woman, a home, perhaps even a child?

Not just any woman, he reminded himself. Juliana.

"Maybe you'd rather see her marry Keedy. He'd jump at the chance, I can tell you that."

These words produced such a flood of fury inside Cole that for a moment he couldn't even breathe. But the picture they conjured up—of Juliana living with Keedy, kissing him, cooking for him, sleeping with him, were like ice water being dumped on Cole's head. Suddenly, deep within his heart, he knew that he could never let her marry another man. He could never let her go at all. There wouldn't be any kind of life without her. Even today, fighting McCray, he'd scarcely been able to keep his mind on the job at hand. His thoughts had kept straying to where she was, what she was doing, wearing, thinking. He needed her, the way the earth needed rain, and the growing things needed sun. He needed her beside him every night and every morning, and he decided— filled with a sudden joyful determiration that seemed to cast off the shackles of uncertainty he'd been struggling under for days—that he'd make damned sure she needed him just as bad. She'd had her chance to get away—and she'd only come back to him in the gully, asking for more. Begging.

Well, she'd never have to beg again. The decision came clearly to him then, answering the longings of his heart. He'd love her and protect her until the end of their days, whether she liked it or not.

Cole grinned to himself. Something told him she'd like it just fine.

Wade and Tommy were still looking at him, waiting for some kind of answer. They probably thought he was loco.

He was. Loco with happiness.

One glance at the two-story adobe ranch house outlined against the sapphire sky sealed his determination.

Come live with me and be my love.

He had to say those words to her and soon, or he would burst.

"Got to do some riding, fellows. Got to see a lady about a wedding."

He couldn't believe he was saying those words, but they poured from his throat sweet as molasses.

"You do that," Tommy shouted after him as Cole hurried off to mount Arrow. "Tell her I've got a hankering to spoil me a little niece or nephew, so she'd better say yes."

Wade signaled Yancy to get started, and smiled at his brother as the wagon started off toward town.

"I thought for a minute we'd have to lasso him and drag him to Juliana like a bawling calf," he called after the two injured men.

"Naw," Tommy shouted back, "he's just as loco in love as she is—only scared of it. I felt the same way a hundred times."

Why doesn't that reassure me? Wade groaned to himself as he climbed into the seat of the wagon loaded with bodies. But then Rawdon was a very different man from his little brother. Tough, experienced, with enough years of being alone to appreciate the loving adoration of a beautiful woman. He wouldn't take Juliana's love for granted. And when he set his mind to something, Wade suspected, he never once swerved from his course. If he was set on making Juliana happy, Wade sensed he would.

"Giddyap," he ordered the horses as the wagon rolled away from the ranch house. The sooner he finished up in town, the sooner he could get back and find out his little sister's decision. After all these months—years, really—of their worrying about her, Juliana's well-being and happiness would finally be assured.

· 26 ·

Juliana heard Gil's horse on the path long before it came into view, and she ran down to greet him, filled with a desperate need for reassurance that everything had gone as planned.

"Easy as pie," Gil informed her, grinning down from the saddle as she walked beside him on the trail leading up to the cabin. "Right about now, Line McCray will be heading up to Fire Mesa, expecting to find poor Joseph Wells and meeting up instead with Rawdon and your brothers and the rest. Heck, I'd give my right arm to see the look on his face!"

"Oh, Gil," Juliana said as he swung down from the saddle and faced her in the bright sunlight of the yard. "Do you really think this will put an end to it? That all this will be over today?"

"Sure I do, Juliana. Your brothers never had a chance to get close to McCray himself before. He's always in town, surrounded by men from his outfit—and it's risky for them to show themselves in town, especially with that crooked sheriff ready to do whatever McCray tells him.

This way, they'll smoke him out, corner him on their own territory, and make an ending of it."

"You mean kill him, don't you?"

"If need be, yes," Gil replied, his face sober. He sighed. "Sometimes, in these parts, honey, there's just no other way."

Something was different about Gil, Juliana decided. The way he was looking at her. He looked outwardly the same, lanky, freckled, his blue eyes twinkling down at her as affectionately as always. But that special hungering look was gone, the one that told her he wished they could be more than friends. In spite of the fact that they were alone together out here, with her hand on his sleeve, he kept shifting from foot to foot, as if he was impatient to get away.

"I just stopped back to tell you that everything went well in town," Gil explained, flushing a little. "I . . . want to ride over and see how Josie and Kevin are doing. I bought them some presents in town."

"How thoughtful of you, Gil! Maybe I'll go with you." It suddenly appealed to her to get away from the cabin and chores for a while, but the flicker of dismay that immediately crossed his face checked her enthusiasm. At once she realized her gaffe, and suddenly it all became clear. Gil wanted to see Josie—alone.

"On second thought, Skunk does need me to gather up some berries for the tart he's baking tonight—as part of the celebration," she put in quickly. *If there was a celebration.*

A sudden noise from the slab of buttressed red rocks a dozen yards down the trail made her break off, and together she and Gil hurried forward and peered around the bend, scrutinizing the land dipping away in every direction. There was nothing to be seen except a deer far down in the basin, nosing at a silver ribbon of stream. The rocks were silent, the mountains as serene as ever, shimmering amethyst in the rising heat. The only sound came from the cabin, where Skunk, as usual, banged around the pots and pans and hummed as he worked.

"Guess we're getting jumpy." She laughed as they turned and walked together back up the trail.

"You can't ever be too careful." Gil stuffed his hands in his pockets. "That must've been a rock falling from above. I'll stick around a little while just to make sure."

"Oh, don't be silly, Gil. Go to Josie."

Gil gazed into her face. "Juliana—you love Rawdon, don't you?"

"I wouldn't make a very good poker player, would I, Gil?"

"If you set your mind to it. Tommy tells me he taught you a thing or two about playing cards when you were kids—and about cheating at 'em."

"But there's no way to cheat at love, is there?" Juliana hugged her arms about herself, chilled despite the warmth of the day. "One either wins honestly, or the game doesn't count. And it looks like I'm playing a losing hand."

"Can't you recognize a bluff?" He gripped her shoulder. "Come on, Juliana, you're no quitter."

"The deck is stacked against me. Cole has never let himself be tied to anyone—he likes moving around, being on his own. What frightens me the most is how independent he is. He doesn't need me or anyone else."

"Don't let him fool you. Everybody needs someone."

Suddenly she couldn't bear to talk about her own troubles anymore. "And you, Gil," she said, turning the subject before the tears welled up in her eyes, "do you need Josie?"

"I'm not sure yet, Juliana." He stared down for a minute at his boots. "But I'm beginning to believe that I do," he finished slowly.

"Good." She smiled, truly glad for him. She raised up

on tiptoe suddenly and kissed him on the cheek. "What are you waiting for? Go to her. Bring her back for supper tonight. She ought to join in the celebration—if there is one."

"There will be." Feeling a strange sense of release, Gil hoisted himself deftly into the saddle, relieved that he had Juliana's blessing. Part of him, out of habit, had been prepared to stay loyal to her—just in case she changed her mind. Now he found himself relieved that she wouldn't. There was no reason on this earth why he shouldn't turn his attentions to Josie.

"Are you sure you'll be all right here?" He cast a quick, thorough glance around. Everything was quiet. The pines swayed lightly in the breeze.

"Of course, silly. Anyway, Skunk is here. *Go on.*"

The cabin door opened right after Gil rode off and Skunk stomped out, carrying a basket.

"You get your pick, little sister." He grinned. "Gather the berries, or bake that tart. Which'll it be?"

Feeling stifled already by the cabin, she immediately reached for the basket. "My baking can't compete with yours, Skunk."

"You know where to go? Down by that there gully— just beyond the aspen there's some dandy berries. You've never tasted a piece of heaven until you've tasted one of my berry tarts."

"I can hardly wait." She started down the path to the gully for the second time that day, the basket swinging from her arm. "Skunk?" She whirled back to face him suddenly, her lovely face uncertain. "When do you think. . . . they'll be back?"

"Oh, who can say? By dark, for sure. Don't you worry, now, little sister, they'll be fine. Your brothers are two tough hombres, the both of them. The man ain't been born yet who can best 'em. And that Rawdon character

—they don't come no tougher than him. They'll be back, every one of 'em."

Feeling slightly reassured, Juliana set off, but she couldn't shake the uneasy feeling that had come over her. All the while she picked the berries, even when she was licking the sweet berry juice from her fingers, she had an odd sensation of being watched, that prickling sixth sense that often precedes the realization of danger. Yet every time she stood up and scanned the surrounding countryside, there was no one to be seen—just the small creatures of the hills and the tall, brown weedy grasses that sprouted beneath the burning sun.

It was midafternoon when she returned to the cabin. "I'm back, Skunk," she called out, thirsty suddenly for water. But when she paused outside the cabin door, with her hand on the dipper, she suddenly couldn't move. It was as if a cold shadow had passed over her, dark and swift as the wings of an eagle flying low.

She glanced around, and wondered what it was that had alarmed her. Then she realized it was the silence. It was huge, deafening. There was no singing or banging from the cabin. Skunk, who always made a great racket as he worked, was making no noise at all.

Juliana dropped the dipper back into its cradle beside the bucket. She started for the door. "Skunk," she called out again, a trace of fear entering her voice. "Skunk, where are you—"

Her voice broke off as she saw the blood seeping out from beneath the cabin door. A sticky crimson pool leaking out, puddling in the dust.

Suddenly she was ten years old again on a cloudy spring day. Skipping home from school, eager to tell Mama she had won the spelling bee. Breathless, racing ahead of Wade and Tommy in her excitement. Then, seeing the blood beneath the door. Smelling what she only later realized was the stench of death. She had started forward, but Wade and Tommy had grabbed her. Their faces were pale as new snow, but they dragged her back, held her, yelled for help in voices that shook. Other store-keepers had come running and dragged her away while Wade and Tommy burst inside the store. . . .

Juliana blinked. Sweat had broken out along her brow, dripping in crystal droplets along her temples. She was not ten now. No one was here to pull her back. She had to find Skunk . . .

Oh, dear Lord, what had they done to him?

His throat was slit. Blood was everywhere in the cabin, but mostly surrounding Skunk's body. Openmouthed, he sprawled across the floor, the same floor over which she had danced only last night, the same floor where he had tussled playfully with Tommy only yesterday, the same floor she had swept clean and spotless only this morn-ing . . .

Now Skunk's corpse and Skunk's blood bathed the cabin floor. Juliana's knees buckled. She choked on the bile that rose in her throat. As she clutched at the door for support to keep from falling, horror engulfed her, making her head spin dizzily.

Only a little while ago, he had been alive, handing her the basket, sending her on her way . . .

Who had done this? What animal, what crazed animal, had done this?

She whirled about, her heart in her throat, as if expect-ing the killer still to be lurking in a corner or under the table. No one was there. Unless, in the back room. . . .

Danger. She felt it as keenly as a knife blade at her own throat. Fighting off her faintness and her fear, she acted without deliberate thought. She reached down to the gun Skunk wore still in his holster, the gun he'd never even had a chance to draw. She wiped the bloody barrel on the rag folded on the countertop, the one she'd used that morning to dry the dishes. She locked her hands about the pistol, and cocked the trigger.

She started slowly toward the bedroom. Her heart was thumping painfully in her chest. Terror beat through her, but she kept going. She wouldn't run from the person who had done this to Skunk. She wouldn't go after Gil, or try to hide. If that monster was still here, she would kill him herself, because he deserved to die.

But the back room was empty.

Juliana's skin crawled. Knife Jackson's tar-black eyes and pockmarked face crept into her mind. Who else would kill in this manner?

Somehow, Knife had found this cabin. She remembered the noise she and Gil had heard earlier, like a rock dislodged along the trail. Knife must somehow have followed Gil back from Plattsville.

A horrible thought struck her, and her hand shook as she clutched the gun. Josie. Gil could be leading him straight back to Josie. It was Josie whom Line McCray wanted, maybe even more than he wanted the Montgomerys.

She had to warn them, and fast. Already she was out the door, running to the lean-to where the horses were kept. But suddenly she felt a huge weight hit her from behind, an immense body tackling her into the dust.

Juliana went down screaming, the gun clattering from her grasp. She twisted around as her attacker straddled her, but she could not get a look at his face. His bandanna covered all but his eyes, yet there was something vaguely familiar about him. She didn't have time to think about it, she was fighting for her life. She clawed at his neck, drawing blood under her fingernails and kicked out frantically with her legs, but he was too large and overpowered her.

"Damn you, you wildcat," her captor swore as he grabbed her wrists, jerked her upright, and rammed her hands together behind her back. Tears squeezed between her eyelids as he tied her wrists together with a rope that bit so viciously into her flesh, Juliana cried out in pain.

"It'll be much worse than this before it's over," he taunted in a muffled voice that was vaguely familiar.

Shock ripped through her as a voice that was unmistakable to her ears answered him. "Damn right it will, Bart. She might be a damned wildcat, but I'm just the man to tame her."

John Breen suddenly stepped out of the brush, as elegant and unruffled as though he were strolling through the big parlour at Twin Oaks. Juliana blinked, thinking she must be seeing things. But no, the sunlight reflected like hazy molten gold off his burnished hair and tan shirt and pants, and seemed to touch his lean, handsome face with an amber glow as he came slowly, relentlessly toward her.

"You've caused me a lot of trouble, Juliana, and I'm afraid you're going to have to pay for it," he said softly.

Her heart began to hammer in painfully rapid beats.

Breen was smiling widely, his topaz eyes burning through her in a way so strange and intense, it made her cringe.

"But we'll discuss that later, when we get where we're going," he added pleasantly, then nodded, almost to himself. "Where I'm taking you, honey, no one will find you."

He was close enough now for her to smell his hair pomade, and nausea engulfed her. She struggled to suppress her terror. Pale hair hung limply in her face, tangled from her struggle with Bart Mueller. It was Mueller who held her still, one hand gripping her elbow, the other coming up to pull his bandanna away from his face. All the while, John Breen came closer.

When she tried to shrink from Breen's approach, Mueller held her rooted to the spot. All the blood had drained from her face, and she stared at the man closing in on her as if he were some handsome devilish specter in a nightmare, drawing in for the kill.

Breen reached up and touched her hair. Smiled that flashing, patronizing smile she remembered all too well. Then drew back his arm and struck her full force across the face.

Juliana fell to her knees. Red pinpricks of light exploded in her head and jarring pain rattled her teeth. She gave a low, anguished sob as the pain throbbed through her jaw and spread, convulsing throughout her entire body.

"Howdy, honey," Breen said quite pleasantly. "It's time we got back together again. I missed you real bad. And don't you worry. I'm going to see to it that nothing separates the two of us ever again."

· 27 ·

She was being baked alive. Engulfed by dry, scorching flames. Withering into bits of dust. Or so it seemed.

Caked with grit, head thrumming with pain, Juliana slumped in the saddle before John Breen for hours (or was it days?) tormented by the deadly heat of the sun. She lost all track of time and direction. Her face was on fire. Her hair hung like straw in her eyes. She felt as if she'd been riding on this horse through these barren hills and hopeless valleys all her life, and she couldn't remember a time when her throat wasn't packed with grit and when hellfire did not seem to shimmer orange and yellow all around her.

And still John Breen pushed on.

Once, Bart Mueller suggested they stop and rest, but Breen snapped at him to keep moving.

He then spurred his horse to an even faster gallop across the parched valley floor they were crossing at the time, and Juliana felt a momentary relief as the dry, hot air slapped her cheeks. But soon the molten rays of the

sun enveloped her again, and even this small refreshment
lost its effect. She sagged against Breen, no longer able
even to support her own weight in the saddle. She felt as
if life were seeping out of her, crumbling away beneath
the cruel glare of that merciless sun.

When dusk came, the cool air washed over her like
mist from the seas, but by then she was too exhausted
even to notice. *Where are we going?* she wondered for
perhaps the hundredth time, but she hadn't even the energy to ask John Breen, and a cavern of hopelessness
swallowed her.

On they rode, forever it seemed, until at last, when she
felt the last shreds of consciousness slipping away, she
became suddenly aware that the horse beneath her was
slowing, then coming to a stop. John Breen swung from
the saddle and rough arms pulled her down. Her legs
collapsed, and he caught her, laughing. Not a pleasant
sound.

Mueller drank from his canteen long and greedily.
Breen dumped Juliana on the grass, and drank his fill as
well. Only then did he hunker down beside her and hold
the canteen before her dazed eyes.

"Water, honey?"

Cracked lips tried to answer him. It hurt to even move
her mouth.

Breen's grin widened. He looked like a devil in the
murky, fading light. "Well, maybe later. I'd better make
camp first. Got to make my little bride-to-be comfortable,
don't I?"

He left her lying there, parched, too weak even to rise
to her knees, stretched across the grass in a heap of exhaustion.

An hour later he gave her a half-dozen sips of water.

"Not too much. You'll be sick, and we can't have that,
now, can we?"

Juliana couldn't even open her eyes to look at him, but

she had never hated a voice as much as she hated that one. After drinking the water, she closed her eyes and slept, sick and weary beyond words, unable to move.

She dreamed of Cole. Of him holding her, kissing the nape of her neck, stroking her breasts. She dreamed of a bed of flowers, cool, fragrant flowers, with Cole stretched out beside her, tickling the tip of her nose with a daisy. Its petals were perfect, white as ermine.

He loves you. A voice whispered sweetly in her ear.

Then she was reaching out to him, calling his name.

Cole, Cole. But he was gone. And the flowers were all shriveled and dead. As she reached out her arms her hand fell upon something wet and sticky lying amid the decayed petals. It was the carved figure of the horse Cole had been working on that night at his campfire, and it was dripping with blood.

She awoke, sobbing in terror. The dream fell away like a curtain, and it was dawn. She was in John Breen's camp in the middle of nowhere. Mueller was gobbling greasy strips of meat and hardtack, John Breen was sipping a cup of coffee. And watching her.

Juliana passed a trembling hand across her red-rimmed eyes. After a moment she tried to sit up, and groaned.

Breen came to her. He stood for a moment, saying nothing, then knelt down beside her and lifted her to a sitting position. He handed her a plate of meat and a biscuit, and set a steaming cup of coffee down beside her.

"We're leaving pronto, so you'd better eat what you can. Won't be stopping again until nightfall."

And they didn't.

By then, she was almost past caring what happened to her. She couldn't think of anything but the racking pain in every muscle in her body, of unending thirst and gnawing hunger. Even supper huddled alongside Breen and Mueller over a glowing campfire left her feeling empty and sick. The food was keeping her alive, just barely, but she felt as if she were dead already, for these men hated her, and she knew that it was only a matter of time before they reached their destination and her real punishment at the hands of John Breen would begin.

The next few days were a blur. At last, the torturous journey ended. John Breen pulled his lathered horse to a halt and Juliana forced her eyes to focus on the windswept ridge upon which she found herself. It was a barren shelf of land jutting beneath a still higher escarpment that extended out over the desert like a giant crab's claw. Prickly pear, juniper and piñons grew here. She looked out, squinting, and saw mountains in the distance, cloaked in ponderosa pine. Nearer at hand were a series of buttes and flat-topped mesas, dun-colored in the haze of the day. A kangaroo rat squealed, dodging from behind a rock to spook Mueller's horse. Then there was silence. The place seemed to Juliana to shimmer with some blazing evil. Her scalp tightened as Breen dismounted and helped her down. The sun-baked earth was hard, unyielding beneath her feet. A lizard sunned itself in the dirt, and from somewhere far above came the cry of a vulture. Even the sun in the blazing azure sky seemed a living thing, alive with menace.

Now what happens? she wondered as the men made camp and she sank onto the hard ground, her limbs lifeless. *How will Cole or Wade or Tommy ever find me here? It's the end of the world—or so it seems. A place as forlorn, as isolated and full of desolation as the moon.*

Suddenly, the realization reached her that she would never leave this spot alive.

John Breen would do whatever he wanted with her here, for as long as he wanted, and then he would kill her. She knew it as clearly as if she could read his mind.

Glancing over at her suddenly, he grinned, that officious stretching of his mouth across his teeth that she had come to despise.

"How do you like this place, honey?"

Juliana stiffened as he strode toward her, reached down and dragged her to her feet. He began unknotting her bonds.

"Might as well make yourself at home. We're going to be here a while. There's a stream back there, behind the rocks. Maybe we'll have a bath together this afternoon. You sure could use one, and so could I."

"Why are you doing this?" She heard herself asking the question, her own voice sounding half-dead already in her ears. When he didn't answer, she rushed on with an agonized urgency to know.

"Why didn't you go out and find a woman who *did* want you? Just tell me *why.*"

Suddenly, his eyes, more brilliant even than the sun, sharpened on her face with frightening intensity.

"Because I chose you," he said, and hauled her into his arms, close against his chest. "From that first moment, when I saw you in that ballroom, beautiful as a goddess from some ancient Greek myth, I knew that I wanted you. And what John Breen wants, he gets." He kissed the top of her head, ignoring the way she tried to flinch from him. His hand came up to cup her breast, his thumb stroking its crest beneath the bedraggled organdy gown.

"And it all started right here, Juliana—at least, not far from here. With that kid. I killed him and stole the gold for myself and that's how it all began."

What was he saying? Distraught by the way he was touching her, the possessive hold of his hand upon her breast, she could scarcely make sense of his words.

She kicked him then with all her strength and jumped back, and surprisingly he released her. She faced him, breathing hard, biting her lip, for she half expected him to strike her, but instead he was staring almost through her, speaking in a low rushing tone that reminded her of a brook that could not be stopped from spilling over a falls.

"I wanted to bring you here. To this spot. So close to where it all began. Maybe then you'll understand me, and why you could never get away from me. Because I always get what I'm after. You know why? Because I'm smarter than other folks—and I'll do anything, whatever it takes, to get what I want. That's the difference, sweet Juliana, between those of us who win in this life and those poor damned losers like Edward Tobias and Line McCray and that ugly piece of scum back there in that cabin, the man Bart killed on my orders."

Skunk. He was talking about Skunk.

"I wanted you to find him. I wanted you good and scared when I got my hands on you—I remember how much violence upsets you. You see, I've got to teach you a lesson, Juliana, a lesson about you and me. You"—and he leaned down closer to her, letting his eyes rake every inch of her slender form—"are what I want—and I will kill you before I let any other man touch you." An ominous silence followed, in which she could hear the uneven rasp of his breathing. "Did Cole Rawdon touch you, Juliana?"

Watching his eyes, gold-flecked marbles set deep within his tanned face, and seeing the tension creased in his forehead, she didn't have to think about her answer.

"No," she said firmly, staring him down.

With a flash of anger she added, "But he never hurt me or frightened me the way you have."

"You called out to him in your sleep."

Startled, Juliana let this remark hang in the air. She moistened her lips with her tongue, waiting.

"I think I'm going to have to kill Mr. Cole Rawdon," he said quietly, a thoughtful expression forming across his features. "As part of your lesson."

"No!" Juliana sparked to life at this. Blood drummed in her temples, and she felt her fingers curling into fists. "There's no reason for that. He didn't touch me—he was bringing me back to Denver for the reward . . ."

"But he took you out of the Plattsville jail. Killed two men doing it."

"He didn't trust Sheriff Dane," she explained desperately. "He thought Dane would keep the reward for himself."

"You're lying." Breen's lips stretched out, not in a smile this time but in a snarl, reminding her of the bear that had trapped her in the tree. "You wouldn't be trying to protect him so much if he was planning to turn you in. Besides, I know he's somehow mixed up with those brothers of yours."

"No, he isn't," Juliana began, frantic now, her heart seeming to freeze in her chest, but her words were interrupted by Bart Mueller, calling to Breen from the rocks of the escarpment.

"Rider in the distance, boss. Maybe more than one—just a speck, really, but they're kicking up trail dust—can't see how many."

"Indians?" Breen snapped.

Mueller shrugged his beefy shoulders. "Maybe. You'd best have a look."

Cole, Juliana thought with a leap of hope, but immediately, fear gripped her. If it was him, and perhaps Wade and Tommy with him, Breen and Mueller would kill them—they would watch the riders' approach and lead them into a trap. She felt panic rising in her, clogging her throat. If she could get away, sneak away and warn them —or at least distract Breen and Mueller so that they lost the advantage . . .

She had to try. For the moment neither Breen nor Mueller was watching her. Both were perched on top of the escarpment, shielding their eyes with their hands, peering far into the distance.

There was no time to think or to plan. *Move.*

Juliana ran.

She darted across the clearing, toward a tumble of rocks behind the ridge, not knowing what lay beyond them. Her feet flew across the hard-packed dust, making a soft, scraping sound. If she could only reach cover, if she could get behind the rocks before they spotted her missing, she might be able to keep ahead of them, losing them among the broken boulders of the foothills . . .

But she heard a shout even before she reached the first jutting stones.

"Get her, damn it," John Breen yelled, and glancing back, she saw that both men were clambering down from the escarpment, sprinting toward her, their faces harsh with determination.

She ran faster.

Shots rang out. She scrabbled over the shallow jumble of rocks and found herself at the foot of a sloping, chaparral-covered butte that stretched beyond the escarpment, winding its rocky trail all the way to the stream John Breen had mentioned. There was cover ahead, if she could only reach it. Manzanita, piñon, and the yellow-orange flowers of the agave loomed ahead amid the jutting rocks and natural ledges. She stumbled forward, catching her foot in a weed, but she managed to stay upright, pulling it free with a gasp. She kept going, her heartbeat a locomotive, her cheeks puffed out with the exertion of running. She knew full blast the terror an animal must feel when it was being hunted.

She reached the rocks and began a frantic climb, her gaze darting desperately about for a place to hide. Nowhere. They could pick her off on this trail like a fly on a wall.

As terror bubbled within her, she saw the opening, a

tiny, jutting space beneath an overhanging oak, and, stooping, she staggered in, fighting for breath. She found herself in a miniature cave, a natural enclosed shelf, not much bigger than a shed, surrounded on three sides by granite rock. She backed against the wall, feeling its hard burning surface press into her back. Dizzy, she tried to catch her breath, wondering how long it would take them to find her. Were they coming? Had they somehow lost her on the trail?

She didn't dare peek out from her meager shelter to see.

She heard the sound of boots on rock, hard, scuffling. Pebbles clattering aside. The soft rustle of trampled leaves and brush. One of them was coming.

Juliana fought back panic. She had seen the fury on John Breen's face when he saw her running away. She still remembered the sharp whack of his hand across her cheek. He would do more than strike her this time. He might even kill her.

She edged backward, and her foot struck something. A stone. No, a rock. Twice the size of her hand, with sharp, grainy edges. She reached down with trembling fingers and clutched it.

Her palms were slippery; it nearly tumbled from her grasp. But she closed her hand about it tightlyand held it. If she had to . . . she would . . .

She had to think of Cole. And of Wade and Tommy. She had to get to them, warn them away from this place —and if she had to kill whoever was out there, then she would.

She swallowed back the terror and took deep breaths. The cave smelled of rotting leaves. It was damp. Something small and brown scurried past her feet and out into the sunlight. Juliana shifted ever so carefully, positioning herself so that she was standing a little to the side of the opening, so that she could see whoever came in before they saw her. . . .

The scrape of a boot sounded just inches away. She could hear breathing, a man's heavy, irregular breathing.

She heard a raspy intake of breath. Juliana wanted to scream. She bit down on her lip so hard, it started to bleed, and she squeezed the precious rock tighter.

Suddenly, Bart Mueller's dark head and broad shoulders poked through the low opening, and he was staring straight up at her as she stood trapped.

There was no time to think, to hesitate even an instant. She swung her arm downward with all her strength.

What she saw after that made the nausea swirl and rise within her. She closed her eyes and choked it back, clutching the wall for support. The rock clattered from her hands.

Bart Mueller was dead. He had to be. When she could bring herself to open her eyes once more and look down, she knew with sickening certainty that he was as dead as a man could get.

She was shaking all over. Would her feet move? she wondered weakly. She had to get out of here. There were no other sounds from the trail, but she knew John Breen wouldn't be far off. He was no doubt searching another area, but even now he could be moving closer.

She forced herself to reach down and pick up Mueller's gun, which had fallen from his hand when she hit him. She checked the cartridge, her fingers trembling. Empty. The gun was useless. She let it fall.

Then she stepped over Mueller's body, over the stream of blood running from the gash in his scalp, and out into the open once again. No sign of Breen. Maybe, just maybe she could get away. Maybe she could get to Cole in time to warn him . . .

She heard a sound and, spinning, saw John Breen less than twenty feet from her, crouched beside a thicket of manzanita, one hand leaning against the reddish bark, the other drawing his gun.

He was staring straight at her.

"Stop right there, you bitch, or I'll shoot you where you stand," he yelled, his usually smug face for once a fiery red.

Juliana froze for an instant, poised in motionless silhouette on the overgrown trail. She knew Breen was just furious enough to shoot. But she wouldn't stand and be captured like a mouse too frightened to flee the murderous claws of a cat.

She whirled and began to run, zigzagging up the trail, grabbing at branches with her hands, struggling for toeholds as the slope steepened and the rocks tumbled away beneath her feet. Her palms and fingers were bloody and scratched, a branch scraped her cheek, but she stumbled on, her pace only quickening as a shot thundered past her, the bullet slamming into rock only inches from her head.

She ducked sideways, and staggered onto a lip of rock surrounded by a steep limestone wall. It was a little crest, another shelf of stone amid the piñons and juniper.

A dead end.

She was out of breath. She could run no farther. But she had to. She couldn't give up, she had to keep going until she was dead and could fight no more. She struggled to draw a breath, her hands on her tortured chest, and then suddenly, the sound of a gunshot kept her pinned like an insect to the spot.

John Breen scrambled and jumped his way to the ledge, his pearl-handled Colt aimed all the while at her heart. "Now you've asked for it, you bitch," he cried, his voice hoarse, as he cornered her beneath the cloudless blue sky.

His face was flushed a horrid purple.

"Mueller," he shouted, but Juliana, suddenly overcome with rage at this man who had tormented her for so long, shook her head.

"He won't answer you. He's dead."

Incredulity crossed his face. "You killed him?"

"I wish it had been you instead," Juliana whispered.

"You're going to wish like hell it had been, honey."

Juliana's hands were on the huge slab of rock embedded in the slope behind her. The rock was hot, burning her flesh. The sun beat down mercilessly upon her head. She wheezed out a breath, keeping her chin high. So it had come to this. Well, then she would die. Maybe she would suffer first, but then it would be over. She would not beg. She would not give him the satisfaction of watching her plead for her life.

"I would have married you, Juliana, and you'd have been looked on by the world as a queen—the esteemed wife of one of the world's richest men. But no, you had to ruin everything. So now I will take from you what should have been mine long ago. What would have been mine beginning with our honeymoon night. I will savor it to the fullest, and then I will kill you and be rid of you forever."

In his eyes she saw a feverish lust, and she realized with a queasy little skip of the heart what he intended to do.

"Just shoot me," she cried, her voice ringing with fury. "Your touching me would be worse than any death . . ."

"He's not going to shoot you or touch you ever again, Juliana," said Cole Rawdon from a rocky peak almost directly above.

She swung her head at the same moment John Breen did toward that cool, beautifully steady voice.

Cole's tall form stood poised beside a desert willow, his Colt .45 clasped in his hand, pointed at Breen. Juliana thought she was dreaming. The riders Mueller had seen in the distance—they couldn't have reached this spot so quickly.

But he was here. He had come.

"Drop your gun, Breen," Cole ordered, his voice cutting as sharp as a bowie knife through the hot air. "You can't win this one. Drop it now."

Breen squinted upward into the sun, trying to make out the other man's face. His own features were twisted with fury, then slowly they smoothed themselves out as he made a tremendous effort to regain control of the situation.

"Who the hell are you?"

"Rawdon. Drop that gun."

Breen craned his neck yet again, trying to get a better look at the man above him, but the sun was too bright in his eyes. "I'll make a deal with you, Rawdon—" he began, but Cole interrupted him.

"A bullet goes between your eyes on the count of three if that gun isn't down and out of reach by then. I'm counting, Breen."

Reluctantly, the older man let his weapon slide free. Juliana, surprised by her own agility, scooped it up without thinking. Then Cole began making his way down the slope with surefooted grace.

Breen's voice echoed strangely in Cole's mind. The rocks played tricks, and the fact that he had tracked Juliana to this spot so close to where Jess Burrows had tried to kill him must be having an effect on him. Seeing that escarpment where he and Liza had camped that last time had brought back the queerest sensations. Peculiar. Peculiar, too, that Breen had brought Juliana to this damnable place.

He searched her face as he jumped down the last stretch of the slope and landed on the lip of rock where she was rooted, the gun clamped between her trembling hands.

"Are you all right?"

She nodded, her eyes huge, brimming with vivid emotions that seemed too strong for her delicate face; but aside from being disheveled, her clothes torn and hands scratched, she looked whole, and he said a silent prayer of thanksgiving. He'd tracked her like a madman these past days, stopping only when darkness made it impossible to go on, for fear he would somehow lose the trail—thinking of nothing but finding her before whoever had slit Skunk's throat could turn their viciousness on her. He had thought he was chasing another bounty hunter panting after that damned reward, but he couldn't understand why Juliana's captor was traveling southwest instead of toward Denver. He hadn't ever expected John Breen himself, but it was just as well. This would save him the trouble of going all the way to Denver to deal with the bastard. He'd take care of Breen here and now so that he could never hurt Juliana or anyone else again.

He hadn't had a good look at Breen from up above; from there he couldn't see much except his size and the shape of his hat, but as he shifted his gaze from Juliana's face to the enemy who had hounded her for so long, shock tore through him, rocking him to his soul. Stunned, he almost dropped his gun.

Jess Burrows.

Impossible.

His own astonishment was mirrored in John Breen's handsome features. Breen's color turned from fiery sienna to ash.

"K-kid?" he gasped, then gave his golden head an incredulous shake. "No . . . he's dead," he muttered, half to himself.

Juliana stood like a statue, her gaze riveted to Cole's face. Shock glazed his eyes and froze his lips. Oh, God, what was happening?

At something in his expression, a chill colder than any mountain river trickled through her.

"I saw your grave, Burrows," she heard him mutter hoarsely. "Yours and Liza's—in San Francisco. I tracked you there myself."

His words made Juliana gasp and turn to Breen, as if seeing him for the first time. They also seemed to penetrate John Breen's stunned amazement.

He shook himself out of his stupor, a muscle jumping in his neck. "Then I fooled you just like everyone else, Kid," he said slowly. "Not a bad plan, eh?" He gave a short laugh. "Liza's tombstone was real all right. I killed her after we hit Frisco. She talked too much. And she never stopped bawling about what we did to you. There's some poor drifter buried where my grave is supposed to be," he added with a sly half-smile. "I wanted a fresh start, you see, as John Breen. Not Jess Burrows, drifter, gambler, killer," he said slowly, quietly, "but an honest man building a modest fortune. Only that fortune grew and kept growing. That gold I stole from Henley—it gave me my start, but I did all the rest. Whatever it took. Until I could have anything I wanted, anything in this whole damn world that money could buy." His glittering gaze fell on Juliana, her arm resting now on Cole's, her white face peering at the man she'd rejected as though he were an insect or a lizard crawled out from under a rock.

"That is, I've had everything I wanted except for one thing. Her." The way he said the word made Juliana's skin crawl.

"I don't know how the hell you survived, Kid, but I'm glad to see you." He moistened his lips. Juliana could see him thinking, picking his words. "Damn right I am. You were good. Hell, you were the greatest shot I've ever seen. Funny, you never told me your real name—and I never figured afterward you were Cole Rawdon. Hell, I thought you were dead." He cleared his throat. "And after that day, I always regretted that you got so riled about Henley. We could've been partners for a long time —you could've had half of everything I've got now. And you still can." His voice grew stronger, picked up enthusiasm as he went along, all the while studying Cole's cold, set face, a face Juliana scarcely recognized.

She had seen him furious before—icily furious—and she had seen him flash with anger—but never had she seen anything as unnerving as the complete lack of emotion she saw now. Merciless, that was what came to mind. Utterly cold, like stone—no, colder than stone—he looked like a man carved of iron, uncrackable, invincible.

What was going through his mind?

"Give me a day with her, Kid. One day. She's beautiful, isn't she? Well, you can have her—when I'm done. You just keep everyone away and let me have my fill of her—get her out of my blood—you know what I mean? And then I'll turn her over to you and make you a full partner of every business I own. Fifty-fifty, that's what it'll be. You'll have the girl for as long as you want her, and you'll have millions overnight. More money than you ever dreamed of."

Cole gazed at him a long time. "I dreamed about killing you, Jess," he said slowly. "That's what kept me crawling through that desert, that's what kept me from quitting and dying in my own blood under the moon, before Sun Eagle found me after two days and saved my life."

Cole spoke with eerie quiet. Beneath Juliana's fingertips, his muscular arm was rigid. "Then, after I tracked you to San Francisco and found the graves, I thought the dreams would stop. But they didn't. Not for years. And never completely. I still have them occasionally. Now I know why."

Breen's chin quivered, and Juliana saw the flick of his

tongue as he licked a bead of sweat from his upper lip. Cole's voice went on, low and methodical.

"We have unfinished business between us, Jess. Business that's been haunting me for years, keeping me from resting easy at night. Now I know why. There's Henley, and there's what you did to me. And now there's what you've done to Juliana. Hell, that alone would be enough to seal your death warrant. It means you'd best save your breath, because you're about to breathe your last."

"Now, Kid . . ." Breen began, then started at something he saw above Cole's shoulder, at the top of the slope from where the bounty hunter had first appeared. "Mueller, don't shoot the girl . . ." he yelled, and then everything happened at once.

Juliana whirled instinctively in that direction, but it took her only an instant to see that the slope was empty. It was a trick. Breen was going for the hideaway gun in his boot, and he was fast, faster than Juliana could have imagined, but even as she tried to jump in front of Cole, screaming "No!" he shoved her aside and fired with his other hand.

John Breen went down on his knees, but he still managed to shoot. The bullet danced off the rocks above Cole's head even as the bounty hunter, never flinching, fired again, and this time, Breen thudded face first at Juliana's feet.

She couldn't even scream. She stood staring at that golden head dripping with blood, at the arms twisted obscenely beneath him, and felt herself suddenly enveloped in strong arms.

"It's over," Cole said.

Then she was being cradled against him, sheltered from this awful place by his arms, his voice, his lips upon her hair. How many minutes passed before she lifted her face from his chest and looked into his eyes, she never knew. She only knew that all the coldness was gone from his features. He was her warm, handsome Cole, the man who had made love to her on a feather bed in a cabin tiny as nowhere, the man who had put his life on the line for her again and again.

When he gazed down at her, his softened face tugged at her heart. An aching tenderness shone from those fire-blue eyes.

"This might not be the right time to tell you this—or the right place—but all the time I was searching for you after I found Skunk's body, I swore that if I wasn't too late, I'd tell you the truth. What I should have told you long ago. What I know better than anything else in this world."

She waited, scarcely able to believe her ears. If he said what she thought he was going to say . . .

"I love you, Juliana." The fierceness of his words was accentuated by the way his hands tightened possessively around her waist. "Heaven help me, I love you with all my life. I need you, dammit, and if you want to take a chance and hook up for life with a man like me. . . ."

"You mean a man who's wonderful, courageous, handsome, bullheaded, infuriating, stubborn—did I say handsome. . . ."

"I mean a man with a lot of enemies, who's not very good at avoiding trouble, who gets shot at maybe once a day—or so it seems lately, ever since I met a beautiful little easterner who tried to steal my horse. Instead she stole my heart."

"Tried to steal your horse? I did steal your horse," she reminded him as his lips tantalizingly brushed her cheek.

"But I got him back," Cole corrected.

"Oh," Juliana sighed, so blissful with his arms around her this way that she forgot where she was and what was directly behind her, "shut up and kiss me, Rawdon."

"You heard the lady," came a shout from the slope above them, and turning as one, they saw Wade and

Tommy, along with Gil Keedy, waving down at them, grinning like a trio of fools.

"Took 'em long enough," Cole growled as Juliana called a joyful greeting. "I got back to the cabin first and had at least a few hours start on 'em. Reckon Breen saw their trail dust from twenty miles away—I sure did. You'd think they'd have better sense . . ."

"If you had any sense, you'd kiss me to seal that proposal," Juliana murmured, grabbing the front of his shirt. "Unless you're planning to try to wriggle out of it . . ."

"The only wriggling that's going to be done is beneath the blankets," Cole told her, grabbing her firmly and staring down with glinting eyes. "You savvy, Miss Montgomery?"

"I *think* so. . . ."

"Shut up and kiss me then," Cole grinned, and so, accompanied by shouts and cheers from the slope above, she did.

· 28 ·

The wedding took place three weeks later in the big parlour at Fire Mesa. The last of the summer wild-flowers perfumed the air and brightened the house, which had been scrubbed, polished, dusted, and gussied up, as Tommy called it, with new curtains and rugs and bright chintz pillow cushions ordered all the way from Denver. With Josie's help, Juliana had brought a lustrous glow to the old oak floors and paneling, had freshened each of the spacious rooms with feminine, personal touches. Her mother's old music box sat on the mantel, alongside Cole's carved horses. Outside, autumn leapt into the canyons and hillsides with a burst of tingly cool air, but the sun shone like golden honey upon the magnificent hills and the valley stretching away in emerald splendor. Inside, its windows thrown wide, the house sparkled with life and beauty and seemed to catch the joy of its new mistress and to glow with a mellow warmth it hadn't known in many years.

Juliana descended the staircase in the white silk gown her mother had worn when she wed Andrew Montgom-

ery. Wade and Tommy had saved a good many of Sarah
Jane Montgomery's prized possessions after Juliana had
gone off to St. Louis. They had packed them away in a
cedar chest and stored this chest in a bank vault in Independence all these years, always planning to bestow the
contents on their sister one day when they were reunited.
When the box had arrived a week before the wedding,
Juliana hadn't the slightest idea what she would find inside until a beaming Tommy presented her with the key.
When she saw the music box, her mother's favorite china
cat, a crystal perfume bottle that had sat on Sarah Jane's
bureau in the bedroom above the general store, and the
wedding gown, among a dozen other near-forgotten treasures, tears had sprung to her eyes. There was a photograph, too, of Mama and Papa, which Juliana hadn't seen
since she was a child. She held it between trembling fingers, staring at the portrait of her parents, Mama seated,
Papa standing straight and tall, with a hand upon her
shoulder.

As a grown woman, Juliana had studied the dear faces
remembered so blurrily from her childhood. In her father, she saw clearly once more all the sturdy strength
and rugged handsomeness she remembered, and the
sound of his voice and his laughter when he threw her in
the air and caught her seemed to float back to her as well,
causing the tears to stream down her cheeks in bitter-
sweet recollection. In her mother's portrait she saw again
the pale beauty who reigned over her childhood memories, but with a woman's eyes she now observed as well
the sad eyes and careworn set to her mother's thin shoulders that she had never noted as a child. This delicate
woman whom Aunt Katharine had characterized as disreputable because she had once worked in a saloon was
no harpy or tramp, but a fine and gentle lady, who at one
point in her life had faced poverty and desperation, and
had worked at the only employment she could find in

order to survive. Juliana knew now in a way she had never known before that there was no shame in that: hadn't she herself labored to exhaustion as a hotel maid on the Colorado border when her money had been stolen? And hadn't she learned in a way never to be forgotten that the wealthy and powerful could sometimes be lower than a snake, and those whom society might judge harshly could hold the kindness of angels within their hearts.

Like Cole, she thought. Shunned by some, feared by most, Cole had ridden his own lonely, perilous road, keeping his own counsel, burying the need and pain and kindness inside him so deep, he had even convinced himself it was no longer there. Mama would have adored Cole. And Papa would have respected him. He was so strong, so proud and independent, yet like Papa, he needed the love of a family. *He just never realized that until he met me,* she thought rather smugly, and then hugged her parents' photograph to her breast.

Wade and Tommy insisted that she keep it as a wedding gift—the first part of their wedding gift, they added. The second part, they told her the morning of the wedding, was somewhere in the pile set on the mahogany side table in the parlour, among gaily wrapped gifts from Josie and Gil, Gray Feather and Yancy, all of whom attended the wedding dressed in their Sunday best.

But beside Cole, everyone else paled that day in Juliana's eyes. When she floated down that staircase tightly clasping her bouquet of yellow roses, her silk slippers making the barest rustle upon the oaken floor, she saw not the array of smiling faces staring up at her, not the beautiful old house nestled like a dark jewel amid the glorious Arizona scenery, not the Plattsville preacher waiting to perform the marriage ceremony—no, she saw no one, nothing but Cole. With his carefully combed black hair just touching the white collar of his lawn shirt, his dark, handsome face tilted up to watch her approach, he filled her mind and her heart with an outpouring of love so intense, it made her burn inside. Never had she seen him more devastatingly handsome or magnetic as he looked that bright morning in his elegant black suit, white shirt, and knotted silk cravat. Each step she took toward him made her heart pound faster, her blood heat within her veins. When she reached the bottom of the staircase, where he waited for her, her smile could have lit the desert at the moment of blackest midnight.

Cole leaned down and gazed at her through the gauzy curtain of her veil. She saw the fierce love glinting in his eyes, the softened desire in his face. In that moment, from the trees outside the window, came the song of a hummingbird. The heart-stopping beauty of it sweetened the crystalline morning air for a precious moment, then ceased.

Cole gazed intently into the beautiful green eyes of his bride. "Come live with me and be my love," he implored Juliana softly, so no one else could hear.

Her rapt face spoke her reply. This man who had needed no one, and had wanted nothing but the solitude of his own campfire and his own path, needed *her,* wanted *her.* And she needed and wanted him with every fiber of her being, every part of her heart, body and soul.

She placed her hand in his.

The ceremony was simple, charming, and heartfelt. Afterward, there was dancing, feasting, champagne. Wade and Tommy toasted the couple, Juliana danced with all the men and hugged Josie, teasing, "Soon perhaps we'll be dancing at *your* wedding—yours and Gil's," and consoled her brother over the loss of the young woman who had been the latest to consume his thoughts and attentions.

"Please try to be happy for them," she coaxed Tommy when at one point he stalked out the kitchen door to sulk in the vegetable garden. "Josie needs someone steady and reliable to be a father to Kevin, and *you* don't exactly strike me as being ready for that just yet," she pointed out.

To her surprise, Tommy had given her a half-smile of agreement. "Well, actually, Wade and I are planning to settle down, maybe start a horse-ranching business with Cole—if he's agreeable, of course—but as for this husband business—you know, Juliana, I don't reckon I am quite ready for that yet. A little too settled for my taste. And"—his smile widened to a full Tommy Montgomery grin—"I have to confess, when I rode into Plattsville to pick up that cedar trunk from the stage, I ran smack into the new schoolteacher just arrived from Kansas City. Lord, but she's a pretty little thing. Sweet, too. Matter of fact, I'll have to leave the wedding a little early, if you don't mind, because I'm taking her on a picnic. . . ."

She didn't worry any further about Tommy's broken heart.

The guests were gone by sunset. She and Cole were alone at Fire Mesa.

Autumn wind rattled the window panes as Cole swept her into his arms and carried her up the stairs to their bedroom. The last fading rays of the sun burnished her hair to glistening waves of gold as she leaned her head against his chest, listening to the low, rhythmic beating of his heart.

A small black velvet box sat upon the sea-green quilt covering the huge four-poster bed.

"Open it," he told her, placing it in the palm of her hand as he set her down beside the bed. "It's my wedding present to you."

Juliana had never seen him so happy. His blue eyes glowed, his whole body was relaxed, warm with pleasure and anticipation. "Marriage agrees with you," she teased as she slid open the box.

"The honeymoon sure will," he shot back.

She laughed, then let her gaze drop to the gift in her hand. And there, nestled in a bed of velvet, was a heart-shaped gold locket and chain, which Cole lifted out and fastened with sure fingers about her throat.

"It's exquisite," she breathed, and felt she was going to burst with happiness.

Cole cupped her chin. "When I first met you, you stole my heart, Juliana," he said quietly, and she was touched by the quiver of emotion in his voice. "Now I'm giving it to you. All of it. I hope you'll remember that—in case I forget to show it sometimes or to say it. . . ."

"I won't let you forget," she whispered back, standing on tiptoe to kiss him on the lips. Their arms encircled each other, bodies touching, clinging of their own accord. The kiss deepened. His arms came round her, crushing her to him, and the passion flashed between them, a blaze of lightning zigzagging between two loving hearts.

He undressed her, stripping away the silk gown, the chemise and silk stockings, unlocking the thick gold mane of her hair from the pins that had held it in place; she undressed him, her fingers brushing the soft, curly black hair on his chest, stroking him, then kissing him with a yearning need that intensified with each moment.

They loved each other in the waning afternoon, as sunset bloomed in the sky over Fire Mesa, and then twilight came, lavender-gray, soft as down, drifting over the mountains, the mesas and plains, and the fine old house in the midst of horse country.

When morning dawned, bright and serene as a girl on the first day of school, Juliana saw the gift that had been overlooked, a large pink-and-blue-ribboned package set on the oak bureau beside the window.

"It's from Wade and Tommy," she reported back to Cole, as she read the card and plunked the package and her own naked body back onto the bed.

"I saw Wade take it from the pile downstairs and bring it up here yesterday, but I forgot all about it," Cole remarked rather absently, for he was drinking in the sight of his lovely bride as she wore nothing but autumn sunshine.

"What are those boys up to now?" Juliana muttered as she struggled with the ribbon. Cole snapped it in two for her easily, and then lifted open the lid of the box.

Juliana started to giggle.

"Baby clothes," she announced, lifting the dozen various miniature nightgowns, booties, bonnets, and tiny blankets one by one. "Oh, aren't they precious? And aren't those boys ridiculous? We've only been married less than a day. . . ."

"No harm in planning ahead," her husband commented, grinning at the sight of the finely made little clothes. The sight of them gave him a strange warm feeling in the pit of his stomach, a feeling that went along nicely with the tight, hungry sensation Juliana's tousled hair and naked loveliness inspired. "I think they've got the right idea here," Cole said slowly, gathering her into his arms. He breathed in the fresh, flowerlike scent of her hair. "This is a big house, and we've got a lot of rooms to fill up. Can't hurt to get started. When it comes to fulfilling family responsibilities, there's no time like the present, that's what I always say . . ."

"I've never heard you say that before . . ." she murmured.

He pinched her bottom. "I've never been married before."

The kiss they shared was long and intimate. "Now I am," he added, threading his fingers through her hair. "Very married. And we've got all these little baby clothes sitting here, going to waste, with not a single baby to wear them . . ."

Juliana gasped with pleasure at what his mouth and his

hands were doing to her. "We can't have that," she agreed breathlessly, moving her hips tantalizingly against him, and pressing soft kisses against his chest.

Joy, desire, passion, love—all of these flowed through her as she held him close and nibbled at the corners of his lips. "There's only one thing to do," she whispered, closing her eyes as one delicious sensation after another washed over her.

He studied her flushed face, and lifted an eyebrow questioningly.

"Come live with me and be my love," she smiled, echoing the words of the poem he had spoken to her only yesterday, delighting in the luscious flow and meaning of each word, "and our love will fill up all these rooms and those baby clothes too, and our hearts will be full as a stream in springtime. . . ."

"Sounds damn good to me."

And as he held her tight, cherishing her with all his being, and made love to her on that fresh and rosy day, they both knew that it was indeed good—as good as anything on earth could be, as close as mortal man and woman could ever come to heaven.

They made love beneath a shining sun—and touched the stars.